GARY GATLIN

THE STORY OF A
RELUCTANT HERO

CARL F. HAUPT

Carl F. Haupt/CH Press
Printed in the United States of America

This is a work of fiction. Names, characters, places, and incidents are a product of the author's imagination. Locales and public names are sometimes used for atmospheric purposes. Any resemblance to actual people, living or dead, or to businesses, companies, events, institutions, or locales is completely coincidental.

Gary Gatlin/ Carl F. Haupt -- 1st ed.

ISBN 978-1-7328761-1-8 Print Edition

ISBN 978-1-7328761-2-5 Ebook Edition

This book is dedicated to

Ruth Tucker Haupt, my mother, never gave up on me through my rebellious years. She kept food on our table and clean clothes for her husband and eight children through the Great Depression. Often times she went without food so that her family could eat.

Sarah Ann Donahugh Haupt my wife for sixty-seven years has been by my side through some very difficult times with never a complaint. She has always been alert to the needs of others.

Christine Glanz who entered my life as a much-needed computer technician very quickly impressed me with her love and concerns in helping older citizens. On the first day that I met her I had to force her to accept any payment for her work. There is nothing what-so-ever with which she cannot be trusted.

Brenda Ainley, sent to me by Christine, to help with the copy editing of this book accepted this work with total dedication to getting the best possible story on paper.

ACKNOWLEDGEMNTS

I would like to thank Mark Graham and Mario Acevedo for their support and dedication.

PART I

CHAPTER ONE

June 1939

I am plagued with doubt about what I've been asked to do. People believe in me, and I feel I'm here for a greater purpose, but do I have what it takes? The strength? The wisdom? And courage! Do I have the courage? Can I possibly deliver?

For days now, these questions had tumbled through Gary Gatlin's mind. He thought that once he embarked on his journey, knowing there was no turning back, he would be able to accept his decision and move forward. His anxieties would calm, and then surely he could think clearly about the task ahead.

But peace of mind would not come.

Also keeping him unsettled was the constant noise and motion around him. Even on calm waters, the *Star of Jakarta*—a cargo ship with space for a few passengers—was an unceasing din of hatches clanging, winches keening, pipes banging, and the blare of loudspeakers and crewmen shouting. Gary's bunk rose and fell in rhythm with the steady motion of the tramp steamer corkscrewing across the stormy Pacific. Though the ship weighed 6,000 tons, the ocean jostled it about in a rough *up, down,* and *roll-to-the-right* manner that had continued unabated minute after minute, hour after hour. It was as if the troubled sea were a metaphor for his troubled mind.

He sat up, carefully so he wouldn't bump his head against the bottom of the upper bunk, and swung his legs off the mattress. His stockinged feet rested on the floor—or the *deck* as the crew insisted—and through the metal plates he felt the syncopated rumble of the ship's steam pistons. He gripped the bunk's frame to steady himself as the ship listed to one side, then rocked in the other direction.

With bleary eyes, Gary blinked at the glaring light from the gooseneck reading lamp where it jutted from the wall close to his bunk. Turning his wrist to the light, he read his watch, a new Hamilton Meadowbrook, a graduation gift from his parents. The time was 8:42 p.m. Yet another restless night. Beside his pillow lay a dog-eared agricultural journal, which he'd been trying to study.

Gary thumbed the journal's pages, appraising its accumulations of his notes, lists, and sketches about everything a farmer needed to know about growing fruit of all kinds, from planting through cultivation and harvesting. This journal, and the other four like it in his suitcase, represented his mission. What his family had entrusted him to do was visit Formosa and the Japanese farmers living there. His purpose was to learn as much as he could about Japanese farming techniques and bring this knowledge back to their Utah farm. It was a mission he'd been preparing for during the last many months, but considering his experience at his father's side, plus his years learning Japanese from the Mitsuis in Anaheim, it was as if the purpose of his entire life until now had been to prepare for this journey.

He closed the journal and tucked it under his pillow. This unceasing anxiety preying on his mood was something new, almost a depression. When he reviewed his tasks and itinerary, everything should fall into place. He and his parents had crafted this plan in meticulous detail. But now that he was on his own and the burden of completing the plan rested on his shoulders, doubts crept into his mind. Considering that all his family's information about Formosa was second-hand at best, once he got there, how far off might their planning have been?

Something else bothered him. Gary reflected on a failed romance and wondered if breaking it off with Beverly Harris had been wise. A man his age—twenty—should be in a relationship with a woman and making plans for a family. But she was Mormon, he was not, and he likened a union with her as a cautionary tale from Scripture.

Tucked inside the journal was the draft of a letter he had begun to Beverly. It began with a quote from Genesis 4:16-17.

"Then Cain went out from the presence of the Lord, and settled in the land of Nod, east of Eden. Cain had relations with his wife and she conceived..."

The letter went on to say: "Based on what I observed when I attended your church with you, and after a great deal of serious thought, I foresee major problems if we were to marry. Your church could not accept me as a Gentile, nor would you be able to accept my ways. We would reach an impasse that would divide us and be amplified when children came into the family. I hope we could always remain friends, but I think marriage, sadly, is out of the question."

Suddenly, a loud metallic banging coursed through the ship, and the noise broke him from his reverie. A storm was brewing, and he decided to go out onto the deck to see if it was moving toward the ship, or away from it. He bent down to slip into his brogans.

"Is that you rustling down there?" The voice came from the upper bunk and belonged to Arlo Bryant, a printing-press salesman from Indiana and Gary's cabin mate.

Gary stood to look at Arlo eye-to-eye. Arlo was stretched out on the mattress of the upper bunk, blanket bunched beneath him, still in his clothes minus shoes.

"Thought you'd be out." Gary pantomimed puffing on a cigarette. Ship's rules forbade smoking in a cabin, which he appreciated since he himself was not a smoker.

Deep lines creased Arlo's meaty face, framed by thick hair cropped close so it resembled fur. His head belonged on a mastiff, Gary thought, but he was a nice-enough guy. "Later," said Arlo. "I'm meeting the purser and a couple of others for a game of poker while we ride out this crummy weather. You in?"

Arlo always asked and Gary always refused. "Not this time," he politely declined.

"I notice you're not sleeping much," Arlo said.

A sudden wave smashed into the hull and the lights flickered off. The compartment was plunged into terrifying darkness, then an instant later the lights flickered back on.

Gary glanced about nervously. "Still trying to get used to the boat."

Arlo chuckled. "It's more than that. I can tell. It's what they taught us in sales training. How to read people." He pulled a packet of Lucky Strikes from his shirt pocket and shook out a cigarette.

Gary tapped his temple. "Well, there's nothing going on in here that should worry you."

"I'm not saying it's worrying me," Arlo jabbed with the cigarette, "only that it's worrying you. It's about a woman, right?"

"Some. How did you know?"

"Because a man's troubles always boil down to one of two things: women or money. And you're too young to have troubles over money."

Gary smiled wryly. Arlo was always saying pithy things like this.

"It's just that everything is new," Gary admitted. "For me at least. Leaving home. All that." During the long slack hours together, he and Arlo had had plenty of conversations about this trip and their subsequent business abroad.

"Yeah, I get it. Nothing in life is a sure thing. Takes a while to accept that," said Arlo lipping the cigarette. "But at least we're going in the right direction."

"What do you mean?" asked Gary"

Arlo held up a crumpled copy of *The Los Angeles Examiner*. The headlines mentioned the continuing bloodletting in the Spanish Civil War and the buildup of military forces across Europe. "A betting man wouldn't lay down money about peace over there. Let's hope the U.S. has the good sense to sit this one out, unlike the last time."

Arlo sat up, cross-legged. His head almost touched the overhead. "But I'd take odds about the Pacific. Not much happened out here during the Great War. I mean nothing like Belleau Wood. I was there."

"Yes, you've told me. You were with the Marines."

Arlo unbuttoned his shirt cuff. "Did I ever show you my scar?"

"Several times."

"Yeah. Right." Arlo smoothed his shirt cuff. "Anyway, aside from whatever noise the Japs are making in China, it's no big deal. These Orientals are always squabbling among themselves. Do you really think the Japs would provoke a war with America?"

"I hope not."

"Was that part of what was bugging you?"

"Some." This was true.

"Well, forget it. Ain't no one in the Pacific gonna mess with Uncle Sam."

5

A loud grinding echoed through the ship, like a winch straining against a heavy load. The noise added to the compartment's stale, claustrophobic atmosphere. Because of frequent storms they had had to keep the porthole closed, and the ship's ventilation barely circulated fresh air.

In a hasty motion, Gary tucked his shirt into his pants. "I'm heading out." He reached for his coat hanging on a wall hook. The coat had been a bon voyage gift from his mother. He slipped the coat over his shirt, and as he fastened the buttons he appreciated its ample dimensions. It was made of sturdy canvas with a fleece lining that kept the chilly, damp sea air at bay.

Thinking about the coat and the watch he so cherished brought back the memory of his excitement over the prospect of his first voyage aboard an ocean-going ship. *Such an adventure.* The morning the *Star of Jakarta* had departed Wilmington, a suburb of Los Angeles, and as Gary watched his parents and sister on the pier recede in the distance, his anxieties increased. The ship moving away from the shore felt to Gary as though he were passing through a portal, a threshold dividing his life, between that of a naïve youth at home, and an uncertain future. Reflecting on his family, he saw them as staunch Americans, proud of their German heritage but prouder yet of their American life. Gary's father had gone so far as changing the family name from the original Gatling to the more American-sounding Gatlin. This was a common practice among German immigrants who wished to distance themselves and their families from the militant stance of their native land.

He had traded the wide-open country of Utah for this cramped cabin—just the bunk beds and two metal lockers with a shared desk shoehorned between them. As the compartment's sole occupants, Arlo and Gary had more room than most of the other passengers or the crew, save for the officers. Gary had paid extra for this modest luxury to safeguard the cash he'd brought to finance his journey, $5500, which he kept secured in his locker. For his part, Arlo also locked up his secrets, so Gary felt safe with him.

But on this ship, there was no shortage of tools that could pry open anything short of a bank vault. At first he had kept the money on his person, then realized that he could get robbed-- or worse--so he stored it in his locker instead. Some of the crewmen were a rough lot by any measure, knots of scarred gristle covered in tattoos. These ruffians boasted of time behind bars, so Gary was certain they'd pounce on any chance to mug him if he were careless enough to make it worth their trouble. So safeguarding his money remained a worrisome priority.

When Gary was ready to exit the cabin, he clutched the door handle, holding tight for a moment as the ship lurched around him.

"Stay dry," Arlo said.

Gary let himself out. In the corridor, lit by dim electric lights, he proceeded to the stairs—or *ladder* as the crew called it—and climbed up and out to the deck.

A blast of cold, wet air swatted his face and quickly chilled him to the bone. The ship rolled and bucked beneath him, but by seizing a handhold, he remained upright.

The deck was a narrow space along the back of the superstructure facing the midship cargo hold. Rain drummed the canvas awning stretched overhead and sluiced off in icy rivulets that shone silver in the light from the portholes. The elevated height of the deck above the waterline exaggerated the ship's tossing and pitching. The ship heaved upward—Gary felt himself lift off the deck—then as the ship dropped, he remained airborne for just a second before crashing solidly to the deck, where he had to brace his knees to keep from falling. It was like being on a monstrous carnival ride. The first day out he'd gotten seasick, but a diet of club soda and saltines had eased his nausea, and since then he had adapted to the constant shifting movement.

Two men along the railing stood as silhouettes against the gray and black mosaic formed by waves crashing over the main deck, the water foaming as it sloshed around the cranes, the life boats, and the broad hatches over the cargo holds. The lit ends of their cigarettes traced red smears against the inky darkness as they too seesawed up and down. For a moment, Gary pitied smokers who braved the worst of any weather to satisfy their habit, yet here he was himself, braving the same weather regardless.

One of the men, another passenger whose name Gary couldn't remember, turned to acknowledge his presence. Dots of rain glistened on the man's long, horse-like face. Shadow from his hat masked his eyes. He grunted something and turned back around.

Gary inched along the railing close enough to overhear some of the conversation between the men. They managed to communicate by speaking only when the roar of the ocean softened to a growl. Gary hadn't actually intended to eavesdrop, but listening to other people's problems distracted him from his own.

"Of course the rich hate socialism," the man with the hat shouted over the sound of the waves. "It holds them accountable for when they screw up the economy."

"You can stuff socialism in the garbage," his companion replied. "I wanna keep what I earn. Some bum needs money, let him work for it."

The ocean howled and the men interrupted their discourse, then as the waves receded, they continued.

"What about your duty to society?" the man in the hat asked.

"Ha!" the other one countered. "The guy who claims it's for the good of the masses says that as he putting his hand in your pocket."

Gary leaned away so he wouldn't get pulled into their debate. He focused on the outline of the ship as it appeared from this vantage. Dark clouds swallowed the moonlight, but he could see well enough to appreciate the ocean roiling about them. The ship groaned, and he imagined it as a great iron beast wrestling the storm, struggling to stay intact, fighting to stay afloat. He noticed the two men had left the deck and gone back inside.

Gary wasn't truly worried that the steamer would sink. But the ship's abrupt movements reminded him that nothing in life, as Arlo had stated, was a sure thing. Then again, risk nothing, gain nothing.

Gary remained outside, where he noted another man on the deck, approaching him. Despite the man's heavy rain-gear, Gary recognized him as one of the ruffians on the crew, this one the meanest looking. It was obvious, from the man's surly demeanor, that his intent was to rob him. Gary prepared to defend himself, and as the man positioned to strike him, Gary moved in. The man lifted his arm, and Gary, drawing on the jujitsu he had learned from Hajime Mitsui, grabbed the raised arm and threw the startled man to the deck. At that very moment, a large wave smashed over the bow of the ship, and, as Gary clung to the rail, in a moment's time swept the would-be robber under the rail and into the angry sea. Shocked at what had happened before his eyes, Gary dashed to the captain's cabin and breathlessly reported what had taken place. The captain listened to what Gary had to say, but answered wearily, "Unfortunately, son, in these seas, there's nothing we can do."

***

Back in his bunk, Gary thought hard about the man who'd been washed overboard. He couldn't remember much about the man—he'd hardly seen him. Would someone miss him? Did he have a family? What had brought him to a life of crime? And the way he'd disappeared, it was as if he had never existed. Maybe his death had been a message to Gary. *Be careful about the way you live.*

Gary's thoughts again turned to his family and the faith they had placed in him.

Faith. Faith was strong. Stronger even than this ship that could weather such a frightful storm.

Suddenly, as clear as day, Gary acknowledged this faith and embraced it as his own. As he did so, its warmth coursed through him, giving him strength. He determined that he would nurture this faith until the time he was compelled to act, and when that happened, he would do his duty.

The values he had learned from his parents, and all the "life lessons" they had taught him, flooded his mind and his memory. Even as a lad of four, he had begun to observe how his parents lived, how they treated each other, and other people as well, and now he could easily hear their voices in his ears as he moved through life.

Chapter Two

June 1924

Five-year-old Gary Gatlin jogged along behind his father, Hans, who muttered and grumbled in resentment at what he was seeing. They advanced through the northern orchard on their farm, passing through cool pockets of shade beneath the apple trees, then stepping into broad swaths of glaring sunlight. The time was a little past eight and the morning's coolness was already giving way to what promised to be another sweltering day. The cloudless Utah sky was a sharp blue that seemed to go on forever.

To keep up with his father, Gary trotted over the coarse ground, leaves and twigs crunching beneath their shoes. He had looked forward to today, that special day when they'd tap into the river to irrigate their farm. All that water sluicing through their ditches and into their orchards would bring a refreshing break to the usual summer monotony.

But this morning their farm hand, Jeremiah Edson, had knocked on their kitchen door with alarming news. Someone had snuck onto their property and torn up their earthen irrigation ditches. As Gary listened to the exchange between his father and Jeremiah, he understood what a disaster this could be. Today was their only turn in two weeks to tap into the river, and if the damage weren't repaired, the water would spill out of the levees and run where it wasn't needed, wasting both water and money.

"Mormons," Gary's father had muttered through clenched teeth.

Gary was used to hearing his father blame Mormons whenever things went wrong around their place. He didn't understand the difference between himself and them, other than they were Mormons and he was not. At least that's what his parents told him. As far as he was concerned, everybody looked the same, and dressed the same, and worked the same. Then what made them different, and why were the Mormons causing trouble?

Just past the edge of the orchard, Jeremiah was inside the main feeder irrigation ditch, hard at work with a hoe. The brim of his tattered straw hat cast his big head in shadow. When Gary and his father approached, Jeremiah paused to lean on the handle of his hoe. Hans, anxious to assess the damage, rushed to the top of the levee, Gary hard at his heels.

The levee was the highest point on the farm save for their house, which stood on a rise to the southeast. From this vantage point, looking north toward Freetown, Gary could see the shallow river valley as it curved around the green foothills of the Wasatch Mountains to the east. Stands of willow and cottonwood marked the riverbank. To the west, the flat bleakness stretched toward the Great Salt Lake, the horizon swallowed by a gray haze.

As they evaluated the destruction of their ditches, Hans explained to Gary the reason for their concern. One side of the levee looked as though a giant had taken a big bite, then spit the dirt and rocks into a pile at the bottom of the irrigation ditch.

Jeremiah set the hoe next to a shovel and used that to spade dirt back up on the levee. "It's not that bad, now that I'm working it."

"Still," Hans sighed, "it's wasted work that would be better spent elsewhere." From the shadow beneath his hat, his eyes glinted with irritation.

"It's probably the Rockwell boys," Jeremiah said.

"You sure?" Hans asked. "If it's them, I'd like to put a stop to this."

"Haven't heard nothin' specific. I'm just guessing."

Hans grunted. "Yeah. Mormons," he growled bitterly.

Gary watched Jeremiah to see how he reacted. He knew the farm hand was a Mormon, but what people called a "Jack Mormon" on account that he drank coffee and smoked. But Jeremiah pretended not to have heard.

Hans pulled a watch from his trouser pocket, read the time, and then jammed the watch back into his pants. "We've got three and a half hours before the water boss gets here," he said. He jumped into the ditch and grabbed the hoe. When his father stood beside Jeremiah, Gary could see that he was as tall as the farm hand though not as big boned. His hair was sandy colored and fine, unlike the thick, dark mop that curled from under Jeremiah's hat.

His father pointed with the hoe into the gouged side of the levee. "Son, I need you to inspect the rest of the ditches and let me know if someone's done more of this." He bent down and picked up a rock the size of an apricot. "If you see anything in the ditch this big or bigger, jump in there and throw it out."

Gary started to run off when his father added, "One more thing. When you're done, come back here. I need to know where you are before we let the water loose."

"Yes, sir."

"Now get going."

Gary was as familiar with the layout of the farm and its ditches as he was with the inside of their house. He knew north, south, east, and west, just as he knew up from down. From the time he could walk, his father had put him to work. His chores included straightening his room, helping his mother set and bus the dinner table, tending the chickens, and collecting all the farm tools in the shed at the end of the day. His favorite tasks were those after dinner when his mother had him sit at the table, looking through picture books and practicing the alphabet.

Now, he did as his father ordered, walking the levee and scoping out the ditch. Where the main ditch branched off toward the east and west orchards, someone had stomped on the corner, crushing the slope until it settled in a heap at the bottom of the junction. Curious, he studied the shoe prints in the dirt and wondered who had done this and why.

The closest home to theirs was a good distance, a mile he'd remembered his father saying. In any case, getting here involved a good bit of time. Surely, whoever did this had had better things to do.

Gary hopped into the ditch and pitched the scattered rocks onto the levee. A gopher snake slithered out from a nearby rock and raced away from him.

"Better get," he called after the snake, "before the water gets here and you drown."

Climbing out of the ditch, he searched for a stick in case he ran into another snake that wasn't as harmless as this one. He inspected the length of every ditch to the southern orchard, found two more places where the levee had been damaged, and headed back. He met his father who was coming the other way and reported what he'd seen.

"Good job, son."

"Dad, if these boys are doing a bad thing, how come you don't get your gun and shoot them?"

His father's laugh surprised Gary. "Well, as mad as it makes me, nobody's done anything worth getting hurt over. They're just boys causing mischief, that's all."

"Why?"

Hans sighed. "Too much energy and not enough supervision."

"What does that mean?" asked Gary.

Hans didn't answer, but reached for Gary and tousled his hair. "Go back to where Jeremiah is. Wait for me there."

***

When Gary's stomach rumbled he knew it was noon, time for lunch. The sun hovered directly overhead. His father had asked if Gary wanted to head home and eat, but he refused. After all this work, he'd be missing the best part of the day—when the water boss opened the sluice gate and let all that water gush onto the farm.

Hans and Jeremiah waited by the sluice gate, where the farm's ditch connected to the main runoff from the river. Circles of sweat stained their underarms.

Dust appeared from behind a big, black automobile jostling its way toward them along the river road. The car approached and came to a stop by the sluice gate. It was a new car, its windows and shiny black paint filmed with dust and road grime.

The door opened and the county water boss, Mr. Watson, slid out. He planted his cowboy boots in the dirt and grasped the windshield frame to haul his large body out of the car. In spite of the heat, he wore a suit and tie. Sweat matted his shirt collar and darkened the crown of his gray hat. His ruddy face resembled a wilted pumpkin.

"Hans," he said cordially, reaching to shake Gary's father's hand. "Things going okay?"

Gary expected his father to mention the damage caused by the Mormon boys, but he didn't. Maybe that was because Mr. Watson was a Mormon himself.

Watson fished a large key ring from his belt, and, huffing as he did so, knelt by the padlock securing the sluice gate. He opened the padlock and levered his big frame upright, the effort turning his face red. He yanked a pocket watch from a vest pocket.

Gary's father pulled out his watch as well. He signaled to Jeremiah to crouch over the sluice gate.

"I got twelve noon, exactly," Mr. Watson said.

"Same here," Hans replied.

Jeremiah pulled the sluice gate upward and set it on the levee. It was a simple wooden board about the width of a door. As the gate slid upwards, water gushed under it and cascaded down the ditch. Gary watched the water, fascinated as it rolled along in a dirty, foamy torrent.

"I'm going to get lunch," Mr. Watson said. "I'll see you back here at two."

Gary's father waved and proceeded along the levee, poking at the water's edge with a shovel. Jeremiah trailed behind him with the hoe. They headed down each of the farm's ditches to the furrows dug between the trees, to coax the spreading tentacles of water until the surrounding dirt turned shiny and dark.

Gary helped his father by scratching the ground with a small garden hoe to draw the water through the furrows. The sun reflecting off the water made Gary squint and reminded him of how hot the day was.

"Farming sure is hard work, dad."

"Anything worth doing is, son. And you keep going. Whatever you start, it's important to persist until you're successful."

"Persist?" His father often used words Gary didn't understand.

"It means, stick to it."

Gary stabbed the ground with the hoe. "Yes, I will persist."

His father smiled.

The water rose to the top of the ditch banks. At this point, the silt had settled and the water flowed clear as glass. Once in a while, fish would get sucked through the sluice and they'd swim in lost circles through the farm's ditches. Gary would try to snag one, but they darted from him quicker than flies. The only times he'd catch one was when the sluice was closed and the last of the water drained away. The poor minnows would flop helplessly in mud puddles, and he would scoop them up in a tin can and hurry to the runoff canal to fling the tiny fish to freedom. Rescuing the fish made him feel like a hero.

***

Mr. Watson returned at 2:00 to lock the sluice gate, and Gary and his father walked home. His mother had left sandwiches wrapped in a cloth in a clean bucket. Hans carried the bucket to Jeremiah and the three of them sat under a pear tree to enjoy their belated lunch.

Later, they returned to work, minding the water so that it flowed as needed. Gary kept so busy that he noted with a start that the air had gone cool and the sun was dipping low on the western horizon.

"Things look about right, Hans," Jeremiah said.

"Yup, I guess we're done for the day."

Jeremiah touched the brim of his hat and sauntered off in the direction of his battered Model T Ford by the shed. He hunched over the starter crank to work it, the engine fired up, and the car chugged toward the road.

Gary and Hans paused at the well pump by the stoop that led into the kitchen. A large pail sat upside down on a crude table by the pump, next to the towels and soap Gary's mom had laid out. His father removed his hat and unbuttoned his shirt before filling the pail from the pump. Both he and Gary washed up, and as they dried their hands and faces they savored the aroma of homemade bratwurst and sauerkraut spilling through the kitchen screen door. Mary knew how hard they'd worked and was preparing a special German meal she knew they'd enjoy.

***

"You need to forgive and forget," Gary's mom, Mary, said.

Ever since he'd taken his place at the dinner table, Hans had been complaining about the damage done to the farm's ditches. "It's those Mormon boys," he repeated.

"You don't know that," she replied.

"Then who else?"

"Regardless," said Mary, "the Bible says we are to love our enemies." She gazed at him and reached across the table. "I want you to say that during Grace."

Gary's father relented with a chuckle. "As usual, Mary, you're right." He took her hand and Gary's and began the prayer.

***

After dinner, when the dishes were washed and arranged in the drying rack, Gary again took his place at the table next to his father, who sorted through their mail and newspapers. The electric bulb overheard filled the kitchen with a warm yellow glow. His mother was seated in her usual place, close to the stove and the icebox. She examined one of the important family books—what she and Gary's father called a ledger—as she made notes on a scratch pad. With her free arm she cradled Chrissy, Gary's infant sister, who was tucked under her blouse and busy suckling. Mary's brunette hair was gathered in a scarf wrapped around her head. The night was quiet save for the rustling of papers and Chrissy's baby sounds.

When his father said, "Mary," the abrupt sound of his voice made Gary sit up. Hans read from a letter. "Phil Speight in Anaheim says I can get a premium on Utah potatoes. He's got several buyers lined up. All I have to do is deliver an order."

She set her pencil aside. "How much will you make?"

Gary looked at his mother and his father as the conversation bounced back and forth across the table.

"I can negotiate that with Lothar Muller. I'll deliver his spuds and my fee will pay for the trip."

"What about expenses?"

"I'll keep those to a minimum. I'd plan on camping beside the road as much as possible."

"Is that safe?"

"You know I'd be careful."

His mother traced her pencil along a column in the ledger. "What about profit?"

"That'll come from what I bring back." He pointed to the letter. "Grapefruit, lemons, oranges, and strawberries are all in season. If all goes well, our fruit stand will be the only ones north of Ogden selling them."

"How long would you be gone?"

"Well, one way, it's about 900 miles. I figure four days there, four days back." His father narrowed his eyes as if visualizing a map.

"Ten days. Two weeks at most. Jeremiah should be able to handle the work here while I'm gone."

Mary frowned. "He's not going with you?"

Hans smiled. "No. Jeremiah will need to be here to tend the farm. I'll be taking Gary with me."

Gary stared at his father, not sure what any of this meant, but certain he was being brought into something very important.

His father reached across the table and tousled Gary's hair. "You and me driving the truck all the way to California and back. Are you up for the adventure, son?"

CHAPTER THREE

March 1924

Gary sat on a vegetable crate so he could get a better view of the world through the windows of their family's Ford stake-bed truck. At times he imagined himself on the bridge of a ship as they rolled mile after mile through the ever-changing landscape of low green hills, steep cliffs, and open expanses of arid wilderness.

His job was to hold onto the road map and give it to his father when he was asked, and to watch for the distinctive US91 signs reminding them they were on course. The other signs were mysteries to him, and he thought that when he learned to read he'd be of more help to his dad. Gary watched admiringly how his father listened to the truck's engine as though it spoke a secret language of grunts and rattles, and he was able to expertly manipulate the gearshift and pedals to get the machine to do his bidding.

Two thousand pounds of potatoes were loaded in wooden cribs in the truck bed, a tarp lashed tightly on top to protect the load. They continued at a steady clip of 45 mph, which Gary at first thought was amazingly fast. But after an hour he got used to the pace and even thought it slow when roadsters zoomed past them, dust flying. Gary and Hans, in turn, cruised past other cars and trucks parked alongside the highway, often with plumes of steam escaping from overheated engines.

When they drove past the first stalled car, Gary asked, "Why don't we stop and help those people?"

"Because if we did, then we'd never get to California," his father replied. "They have their problems, we have ours. Besides, some of those people might be up to no good."

From then on, Gary stared at people on the road, wondering which of them were good and which were troublemakers. But the risk of danger didn't worry Gary too much, with his dad at his side, and actually added to the thrill of this adventure.

When they stopped for gas, Gary was fascinated watching the gasoline rise into the glass cylinder of the pump and then gurgle into the hose as his father refilled their tank. At the end of their first day of travel, they spent the night in Fillmore, parked in a lot beside other trucks for protection against thieves and hijackers. The drivers gathered around a communal fire in the center of the lot and chatted about the weather, the roads, and the government. When it was time to bed down, Gary curled up inside the cab while his father slept on a makeshift cot on top of their cargo.

The next morning, Gary stirred awake and found his father already at the fire pit cooking eggs and heating water for coffee, washing up and shaving. After breakfast, they shoved off.

The highway followed a downward slope into a Nevada desert that was even more desolate than what they'd crossed in Utah. The road was long and for the most part dusty, and they stopped only for gas or to eat. Gary noted that Hans always kept a couple of filled, spare gas cans that he might need on long stretches between filling stations. They stayed on their planned route until they were just south of Santa Clara, Utah, where they stopped again for the night.

***

The next morning, again after a good breakfast, Hans and Gary were back on the road with their load of potatoes. They stopped for gas on the outskirts of the small town of Las Vegas. From there, the highway climbed again, gradually as it wound through rocky hills where cactus and green brush grew alongside the road. As they passed an oversized colorful sign decorated with a smiling pretty girl holding a crate of oranges, his father read out loud, "Welcome to California."

Gary perked up. After all the talk of California, he prepared himself to see the state in its full glory when they crested the top of the long rise. But when they rolled over the summit and he craned upward in his seat to take in the Pacific Ocean, which he was sure would be spread out before them, all he saw was more plains, flat and dusty as a floor that needed sweeping. It wasn't the California Gary had been expecting. It still looked like Utah or Nevada! He knew there was an ocean in California, and he wondered where it was.

At the end of the third day, they again looked for a place to camp along the road. Finding a suitable-looking spot, they stopped and prepared for the night. The next morning, the journey resumed.

After a time, they began to see farmland, although it looked hotter and dryer than their place back home ever did.

On their fourth day on the road, the highway curved through rugged mountains down to the outskirts of San Bernardino. They passed rolling hills and farmland and several small towns, finally reaching their destination of Anaheim. Hans drove the truck through the town center and ended up at a large shed beside the railroad. The place smelled of rotting produce. Parking the truck, he got down while Gary climbed into the cargo bed to guard the potatoes while his father went into the shed. The California sun beat mercilessly on Gary but he stayed put. Inside the coolness of the shed, men moved crates of produce from shelves to hand carts, smoking cigarettes as they worked.

Hans returned with an older man who wore a tie, puffed on a cigar, and grinned a lot. His hat shaded a pulpy-looking face. The two men stepped close to the truck. His father waved at Gary and introduced the man as Mr. Speight.

The man glanced at Gary before lifting the tarp to inspect the potatoes. "Mighty fine," he said, and heartily shook Hans's hand. When Mr. Speight disappeared around the corner, Hans climbed into the truck to back it into the shed, where the workers clambered on board and began emptying the potato cribs into carts.

Gary and his father followed Mr. Speight through the shed to an attached brick building. Speight ushered them into his private office where they sat around a table. The windows were open and bright sunlight filled the room. An electric fan stirred the air and rattled the papers lying about but didn't ease the heat much. A woman in nice clothes brought lunch: a tureen of stew, hard rolls, and butter. While they ate, Gary listened to his father and Mr. Speight exchange grownup talk about farming and money.

The woman returned to collect the dishes and handed Mr. Speight a slip of paper. Reading it, he spun in his chair toward a desk, where he removed a strongbox from a drawer. He opened the box and counted out a sum of bills, an amount of money so large that Gary eyebrows lift upward in amazement. *They were rich!*

Mr. Speight tucked the bills and the slip into an envelope, which he offered to Gary's father. "Hans, pleasure doing business."

Without any ceremony, Gary's father calmly took the envelope and shook hands with Mr. Speight. Their business concluded, Gary and his father returned to the truck.

Gary said, "That's a lot of money you got, Dad."

His father raised a finger to his lips, then whispered, "Don't talk about the money, son. Someone might hear you and decide to rob us. Best to pretend that we're poor with nothing to steal."

Gary thought about this. Since they'd left home this trip had presented all types of risks. They had to stay away from people who looked like they might need help, were constantly on the alert to protect their cargo, at night gathered with other truckers like farm animals in a corral, and now had to lie low to avoid attracting attention. But he wasn't scared. He knew his presence meant an extra pair of eyes to watch for the bad guys, and his dad was big and strong.

He peered out the cab's back window and saw that the bed had been swept clean, the tarp and ropes neatly bundled. "What now, dad?"

"We need to buy fruit," his father replied. "Now that the truck's empty, we gotta load it back up before we return home."

"Today? We just got here."

His father laughed. "No, not today. We're going to look around, relax a bit."

"How about we see the beach?" Gary asked.

His father tousled his hair. "Of course. I promise."

Driving through the town, they headed west on the main road, a two-lane asphalt strip with wide dirt shoulders bookended by vast orchards. Many fruit stands lined the road. When they approached them, Hans slowed for a better look. Gary also rose in his seat to see.

Some stands were simple wooden frameworks—a slanted roof

over a counter that itself was made of planks set on top of crates. Other stands were more like the shed his family owned. On these, the front and sides could be closed and locked, or opened up. The way the fruit was displayed also varied. It was either piled in loose heaps, or dumped in crates or bins, or sometimes carefully arranged in neat stacks as his father and mother did at home. The signs were likewise different. Gary couldn't read them but he could tell the difference between the crude scrawls and the professionally painted ones

Passing stand after stand, his father finally halted at one, attracted by the many cars already parked there. At this stand, the fruit was piled on tables and in open cribs. An older woman with a sunburned face waved a towel to shoo away flies. The customers were mostly women in city clothes. They loitered around the fruit, picking up samples to squeeze and sniff, to either put back or collect in a basket.

A gangly, fussy man with a thin mustache stood behind the center table. He wore a plaid shirt and overalls, and he was kept busy weighing fruit on a scale or making change from a cash box on the table. His straw hat was surprisingly clean, looking brand new. He squinted suspiciously at Gary's father, looking him up and down as he made his way through the fruit stand. When Hans picked up a grapefruit, the man in the mustache asked, "You buying that?"

He spoke in a loud voice that caused the other customers to turn and look.

When Hans didn't answer, the man said, "Or just squeezing 'cause you got nothing better to do?"

The man's question and tone astonished Gary. From his time in their family's fruit stand, he knew you always spoke pleasantly and politely to customers.

While the man glared at him, Hans put the grapefruit back and cocked his head at Gary, signaling to return to the truck.

As they drove off, Gary said, "That man wasn't very nice."

His father shrugged. "Life is too short to let someone like that get under your skin, son. His loss, too. He keeps his fruit, I keep my money."

They paused at several more stands. Again, his father inspected the fruit but didn't buy any. Gary tried reading his father's expression for a clue about what he thought of the fruit stands, but he remained tight-lipped and stone-faced.

Pressing down the road, late in the afternoon a sandwich sign on the road caught their attention. About twenty-five yards beyond it, the sun glistened off a stand painted a brilliant white. Gary counted six cars parked between the sign and the stand. His father slowed as they circled past to halt next to the cars on the other side

Inside the shed, people were clustered around the tables and cribs of grapefruit, oranges, lemons, and baskets of strawberries. At a back table, a short man in a white shirt and straw hat counted money. Close by there was a boy who appeared to be about Gary's age, the first kid he'd been this close to since they left Utah. The boy jumped around inside the stand, making a game of shooing flies. Gary studied him, who with his dark skin and straight black hair reminded Gary of the Utes back home. Because the man and the boy resembled one another, Gary concluded they were father and son.

A pair of women strolled through the stand, whispering to each other as they examined the fruit. They collected their purchase in a straw hand basket, which they handed to the man.

"A dozen oranges," the man said in English, and then spoke in an unusual language to the boy, who reacted by reaching under the table and withdrawing a paper sack, which he gave to the man.

27

The man bagged the oranges, counting out each one. When he reached twelve, he picked an additional orange from the crate and dropped it in the bag.

Gary noted that his father smiled approvingly as the man did this. His father held up a grapefruit. "How much for one?"

The man shook his head. "For you, no charge."

With a nod, Hans stepped away. He opened his pocketknife and quartered the fruit, juice running over his fingers. He gave one piece to Gary. He had eaten grapefruit before, but this was sweeter and juicier than any he remembered.

"Very tasty." Hans wiped the juice that was dribbling down his chin.

"I'm glad you like it," the man replied.

"I notice you sell fruit at a baker's dozen. I do the same at home."

The man grinned. "As Henry Ford said, 'If you never do more than what you're paid to do, then you'll never be paid for more than you do.'"

Gary's father allowed a toothy smile. "I have the same quote pinned above my dinner table."

The man glanced at their truck. "You are a farmer?"

"From Utah." Gary's father extended his hand. He towered over the man. "Hans Gatlin."

The man gave a curt nod and shook hands. "Hajime Mitsui. It is my pleasure."

Gary's father beckoned. "This is my eldest, Gary."

Hajime uttered several words in his language and the boy hustled to his side. "This is my son, Ichiro."

The boy bowed his head. "*Hai.*"

Gary answered. "Hi."

Hajime asked, "What brings you to Anaheim, Mr. Gatlin?"

"Hans, please. I'm here to buy fruit and take it back home to sell in my stand."

"You have a supplier?"

"Not yet." Gary's father panned the crates of fruit. "I like your setup and would like to discuss business if you have the time."

"Of course," Hajime said. "Did you bring anything from Utah?"

"A load of potatoes that I've already delivered."

"Is that what you grow?"

"No. But that is what's in season. I grow apples, pears, and apricots."

Hajime smiled. "I also grow apples. Perhaps you'd like to see my orchard. I would appreciate comments from a fellow apple farmer."

"The pleasure would be mine," Gary's father replied.

Ichiro took small side steps from his father and smiled at Gary. With each step, his smile grew wider. Gary noticed that Ichiro was slyly distancing himself from Hajime, who was focused on what Hans was saying. When Ichiro reached the end of the table, he made a face at Gary and took off running.

Gary took off after Ichiro, the two boys sprinting in circles over the dirt like a couple of wild ponies. Ichiro would stop short, and just as Gary was about to tag him he'd dash in another direction.

After several frenetic minutes, Ichiro halted, his shoes sliding through the dirt. When Gary caught up with him, Ichiro was doubled forward, laughing.

Gary had to catch his breath before he said, "You run fast."

Ichiro replied in Japanese.

Hajime called to them, saying in Japanese and then in English, "Ichiro, come here. I need you to help some customers."

Ichiro trotted back to the shed, Gary beside him. They helped an older lady carry sacks of lemons to her car.

Gary's father was behind the center table, also helping Hajime with customers. As they worked they chatted about themselves, and Gary listened, fascinated.

"Hajime, you were born here?"

"No, in 1912 I emigrated from Fukushima. But it was here that I met and married my wife and we have three children. Ichiro is my eldest."

The setting sun painted the shed in orange tones, then dipped below the trees. The landscape darkened as if God had closed a curtain. The air immediately cooled. The last of the customers climbed into their cars and drove away.

Hajime and Ichiro began consolidating fruit into crates and stacking the empties. Gary and his father helped, and all four of them loaded the crates into Hajime's Dodge truck.

When they closed the sides of the shed and locked it up, Gary's father said, "We had better move along for now. We have to find a place to spend the night."

"Where?" Hajime asked.

"We'll find something. Along the road from Utah we camped out."

Hajime grimaced with concern. "I would not recommend that here. We have many drifters and hobos. Most are harmless but there are a few who can cause serious trouble."

"I can go back to town and ask my German contacts about a place."

"Why don't you stay at my farm?" Hajime asked. "You can park your truck there. I have a big dog that keeps the bums away. My home is small but we can make room. My wife will enjoy the company."

Gary liked this idea. He'd rather hang out with Ichiro than spend yet more time around grownups.

Gary's father removed his hat and wiped his brow. "I should decline, but I won't, as I do appreciate your hospitality. If you don't have room inside, that's no bother as we were planning to sleep outside anyway."

"Then it is settled. You will stay with us."

Ichiro asked a question in Japanese and Hajime replied. Ichiro smiled at Gary.

Gary smiled back.

CHAPTER FOUR

When they left the Mitsui's fruit stand, Hans drove his Ford truck close behind Hajime's Dodge. As they motored up the highway, Ichiro leaned out the passenger window of the Dodge's cab. He waved excitedly at Gary, who poked out from his window to wave back.

"Son," Gary's father admonished, "what have I told you about sticking your arms out the window while we're moving?"

Duly chastised, Gary reeled himself back in and settled into his seat. Over in the Dodge, Ichiro also retreated into the cab, evidently similarly rebuked by Hajime.

As twilight darkened the landscape, Hans switched on the truck's headlamps. They proceeded directly toward Anaheim, then Hajime veered onto a dirt road that cut through dense orchards obscured in gloom. The Ford's headlamps shone against the dust cloud that rose from the Dodge's tires.

Gary studied the landscape but couldn't see much in the darkness aside from an occasional light of a farmhouse shining through the walls of trees. Several minutes passed and then the two trucks turned onto another road. Their headlights flashed across a wooden sign.

"Dad, what did the sign say?"

"Mitsui Farm," his father answered. "Beware of dog."

Remembering Hajime's comment about a big dog, Gary lifted up in his seat to spot the beast. He spied a farmhouse up ahead, its exterior lit by a single bulb above the porch door. The Dodge continued past the house to a shed and slowed. Gary's father halted his Ford truck.

A large, short-haired dog lunged from the darkness and paced menacingly in front of the Ford, ears folded back, growling and barking. Its fangs glistened in the glare of the headlamps.

"No kidding, that's a big dog!" exclaimed Hans.

The Dodge backed into the shed, and its headlamps dimmed. Hajime climbed out and approached the Ford, stepping into the twin ovals of light from the headlamps. He snapped his fingers and shouted in Japanese to the dog, which had stopped barking when he saw Hajime and then circled Hajime's legs, tail wagging. Hajime said to Gary's father. "Hans, you can park right there."

Gary's father doused the Ford's headlamps and the scene coalesced into figures illuminated by the porch light. When he cracked his door open, the dog started to bark again, and Hajime restrained it by the collar.

"I'm not certain your dog welcomes us," Gary's father said.

"Call him by his name, Sanda," Hajime explained. "It means thunder."

"An apt name." Hans called out in a calm voice. "Sanda. Sanda." Sliding warily out of the truck, he took a knee and extended his hand. "Sanda. Sanda."

The dog's tail swished back and forth. Hajime relaxed his hold and, head down, Sanda advanced toward Hans. He let the dog sniff his fingers and then he scratched it between the ears. Gary got out of the truck and sank to his knees beside Sanda to pat its muscular shoulders. The dog's hair was stiff and bristly.

"Well," Hans said, "he's certainly fierce enough to scare off any bums."

Hajime laughed. "Sanda earns his keep."

A shadow moved across them. Gary turned to see a woman silhouetted in the farmhouse door. She hailed Hajime in Japanese.

He replied in kind then explained in English. "My wife, Anzo."

Gary's father stood and removed his hat. "It's a pleasure, ma'am."

Gary also stood and nodded, not certain what to do except repeat what his father just said.

Anzo bowed. "*Hai. Hai.*"

Hajime said something else, and Anzo snapped a reply.

"Is there something wrong?" Hans asked.

"My wife was not expecting two extra people for dinner."

"We mean no bother. Gary and I can find room and board in Anaheim."

"No. Please," Hajime insisted. "We will make do." He said something to Anzo, again in Japanese, and she smiled and stepped back into the house.

Ichiro and Gary followed their fathers inside. They entered the kitchen, which was small and well ordered, and, like Gary's home, lit by a single bulb hanging from the middle of the ceiling. Gary's stomach rumbled at the aroma of a cooked meal. The enticing smell came from a pair of steaming pots on the burners of a small stove. Sanda halted at the threshold and remained outside as the screen door closed.

"If you don't mind," Hajime requested, pointing to their shoes. He and Ichiro untied their shoes and put on cloth slippers furnished by Anzo. Gary and his father leaned against the wall and removed their boots, which they lined along the wall.

Anzo handed them a moistened towel to wipe their hands. Her

large dark eyes regarded Gary and his father now with warm hospitality. A loose yellow dress and a white apron draped her short, slender frame and she moved with nervous energy. Wisps of shiny back hair spilled from under a red scarf tied over her head. An infant gazed at Gary from a harness slung across Anzo's chest.

A small girl with pigtails watched the proceedings from the kitchen table.

Anzo pointed to her and said, "My eldest daughter, Junko." She stroked the infant's head. "My other daughter, Hisa."

Anzo's introduction surprised Gary as he was surprised that she spoke English.

Hajime arranged bowls on the table as well as forks and spoons for their guests. For the family, he provided chopsticks. He indicated where Gary and his father were to sit. Anzo set the pots on the table. One was filled with white rice, the other with chicken mixed with vegetables. She said something to Junko and Ichiro, who stepped from the table, bowls in hand and waiting politely. Anzo spooned rice and the chicken-vegetables into their bowls and they retreated to the next room.

Gary didn't want to be at the grownups' table so he asked, "Dad, is it okay if I eat with Ichiro?"

"Certainly, assuming there's no offense."

"Of course not," Anzo replied.

"Before you go," Hans said. He reached for Gary's hand. "Hajime, if you don't mind, I'd like to ask for the Lord's Blessing."

"I am honored." Hajime smiled. "We are Methodists."

Gary closed his eyes and listened to the prayer. Afterwards, everyone said, "Amen."

Ichiro led Gary to the next room, where he tugged at a string hanging from the ceiling. An overheard bulb lit up a room that was furnished with bookshelves, a chest of drawers, a work desk stacked with papers and ledgers, and two cots pushed against the wall.

Junko and Ichiro sat cross-legged on a straw mat. Gary joined them and admired how easily they picked up their food with chopsticks without spilling so much as one grain of rice.

He asked, "Can I try?"

Ichiro grinned and handed over his chopsticks. Gary fumbled to hold them and studied how Junko manipulated hers. He tried to mimic her technique but to no avail, as he couldn't even pick up one of the larger pieces of chicken.

Ichiro laughed at him. Gary also laughed, noting how clumsy he must appear to his new friends. Giving up, he gave the chopsticks back to Ichiro and dug into his bowl with a fork.

***

Gary and his father bunked for the night in their truck, as they had during the trip from Utah. Hajime bid them goodnight and turned off the porch light. Gary gazed at the starry sky, amazed by this adventure. Tired from their long day and the interesting evening with the Mitsuis, he dozed off. He was awakened in the darkness when Sanda jumped into the truck bed and slumped against him. He scratched the dog's scruffy neck and fell back asleep.

A warm light caressed Gary's face and he awoke.

"Good morning," his father said. Hans stood beside the truck, in his pants and undershirt and with a towel slung around his neck. He splashed his face with water from a bucket perched on the fender of the truck. His hairbrush, razor, and soap lay on a nearby towel, and he checked his reflection in the small mirror he carried with him.

Gary stretched his arms and blinked away the sleepiness. He looked for Sanda and saw that he was in the shed, following Hajime.

Now that it was daylight, Gary scoped out the Mitsui farm. The leafy trees of the surrounding orchards glowed a golden yellow in the morning light. The air was fragrant with lemon.

Anzo prepared scrambled eggs and fried the sausage that Gary's father shared. By the way Ichiro and Junko devoured the sausage, Gary could tell it was a treat for them.

After breakfast, Hajime asked, "Hans, would you like to tour the orchards?"

Gary's father replied, "Of course."

Gary was eager to tag along; however, Anzo came out of the house and had some instructions for Ichiro. He hung his head, proceeded to the shed, and came out with a rake. Gary realized that Ichiro had been assigned his chores. While he'd rather go with his father, Gary decided to stay with Ichiro. He found another rake in the shed, and the two of them gathered twigs and leaves from around the house and shed. Sanda lay in the shade of the house and watched.

Ichiro made one pile and Gary another. When Gary turned around, Ichiro abruptly bolted toward him and leapt into Gary's pile, scattering leaves and twigs. Laughing and waving the rake, Ichiro ran in a circle, taunting Gary.

He had no choice but to kick Ichiro's pile and chase after him with the rake. Ichiro stopped and the boys sparred, banging their rakes like spears. Sanda joined the mayhem, barking playfully.

Anzo charged out the back door of the farmhouse, Hisa harnessed to her chest, and scolded Ichiro, who looked down and shuffled his feet. Sanda slinked away, tail between his legs. Anzo regarded Gary but said nothing. He knew why she was displeased, though. She returned to the house, and Ichiro began raking up the mess they'd made. Feeling guilty for getting his friend in trouble, Gary helped. Ichiro then smiled at Gary and they both laughed.

***

After an hour, Hajime and Hans returned to the house. Gary and Ichiro were still raking.

His father said, "Gary, get in the truck. You and I are going into town."

Gary looked at Ichiro. "Can Ichiro come along?"

"Another time, perhaps."

Gary took his rake back into the shed, then waved goodbye to his friend and climbed into the truck. Once in Anaheim, his father parked outside a grocery market. He said, "While I'm shopping I need you to watch the truck. Can you do that?"

"Yes, dad," Gary said and waited in the cab. The minutes passed and boredom set in. Deciding he could better guard the truck from the bed, he climbed out of the cab and into the back. From this commanding vantage he could better observe the street and watch for any trouble.

A group of boys his age strolled along the sidewalk and continued to a vacant lot catty-corner from Gary's location, where they tossed a ball in a game of catch.

Gary wondered what was keeping his father. He looked back at the boys and was envious at how much fun they were having while he remained in the truck, bored.

Then he had an idea. He could just as easily watch the truck from the lot. So he jumped off the truck and hustled over to the where the boys were playing. The largest of the bunch, a chubby kid with freckles and sandy hair, said to Gary, "I've never seen you before. Where are you from?"

"Utah," Gary answered. Though he told him his name, the other boys kept calling him Utah as they threw the ball back and forth.

Out the corner of his eye, Gary saw his father walking to the truck, his arms weighed down by a crate full of food. Forgetting about the other boys, Gary ran to his father, only to be met with a disapproving glare.

"I thought I told you to watch the truck."

"I was." Gary pointed to the lot. "From over there."

His father lifted a section of the siderails and was shoving the crate onto the bed when he noted, "My rope is missing."

Uh oh. Gary knew he was in trouble. He scrambled for an excuse and said, "It was an old rope, wasn't it?"

"That doesn't matter." His father pushed the siderails back into place. "I'll have to replace that rope with a new one, which costs money. But that's not what's most important. I told you to watch the truck and you told me that you would. You gave me your word, and I trusted you."

Gary felt the sting of shame. "Dad, I'm really sorry."

"Remember that you have to keep your word, regardless of the circumstances. Always."

Gary cast his gaze to the ground. "I understand, Dad. It won't happen again."

His father tousled his hair. "All right then. If the loss of some frayed rope was all this lesson took, then I guess we're doing okay. I trust you'll remember the lesson."

***

At the second wake-up on the Mitsui farm, as he ate breakfast Gary was greeted with a happy surprise.

"We're going to the beach," his father announced.

From that moment, the morning was a series of dizzy activity as Gary helped his father get ready. In midmorning, everyone piled into the Ford. Hans drove while Hajime, Anzo, and the infant Hisa squeezed into the cab. Gary, Ichiro, and Junko settled in the bed. Sanda was left behind to guard the house, although his head drooped dejectedly and he looked sad that he wasn't being taken along.

For miles they drove along a highway where all kinds of cars and trucks zipped past. Gary and Ichiro stood and clung to the stake posts to enjoy the passing landscape. The orchards gave way to low hills overgrown with gnarled oaks and thick scrub. When the air turned cool and hazy, Gary knew they must be close to the ocean.

He stood on tiptoes to see around the cab. Up ahead, the rocky hills became sandy dunes carpeted with reeds and swaths of a bright green plant.

The highway passed through a cluster of shops and shacks, and when the truck turned left, all at once the Pacific Ocean burst into view. It was an endless pan of sparkling blue water that filled the horizon, north to south. Closer in, the water turned a beautiful shade of green before it was churned into white foam that tumbled onto the beach.

Gary wanted the truck to stop so he could jump out, but they kept rolling forward, dunes to the left, surf to the right. He glanced at Ichiro, who appeared just as excited.

The truck drove past a ragged row of cars parked side-to-side. People busily arranged blankets and picnic baskets on the sand. The truck steered to face the dunes. No sooner did they stop when

Gary and Ichiro peeled off their shoes and socks and catapulted from the bed. While Junko waited for her mother, the boys ran pell-mell down the beach, the sand hot beneath their bare feet. Ichiro sprinted full speed toward the water with Gary racing behind.

They reached the cool, wet sand, then splashed head-long into the surf. The cold water was a shock at first, but then felt refreshing as it washed over them. Gary's legs pumped as he walked further out in the deepening surf and into an incoming wave. He braced himself for its impact.

The surge of water was more powerful than he'd expected and it tossed him backwards. The wave roared over him, sweeping him up onto the beach. The water retreated with a hiss and he was left sitting on the sand, surrounded by tiny white creatures flopping in the foam.

Gary spit out a mouthful of seawater. It tasted of salt and minerals. Laughing and soaked head to toe, he staggered to his feet. Ichiro was beside him, just as wet and laughing just as hard.

Wiping his face, Gary looked back to the Ford truck. His father and Hajime were setting up a table. He waved his arms and hollered to get their attention, but the rumble of the crashing surf swallowed his voice. Realizing that his father might need him, he started back to the truck. Deciding to make a game of it, he slapped Ichiro on the arm and took off running. He sensed Ichiro was hard on his heels but didn't risk looking back for fear of losing his lead.

They reached the truck, Gary just one step ahead of Ichiro. They halted, both out of breath. Gary's wet clothes clung to his body in a chilly embrace.

Hajime reproached them gently, knowing they were having a great time. "When you boys play on the beach, don't get into the water unless one of us is with you. The undertow can get you."

"What's undertow?" Gary asked.

"It's a current along the bottom that can pull you into deep wa-ter," Gary's father explained. "Before you know it, you could be in the middle of the ocean."

Ichiro said something in Japanese that made Hajime grunt in approval before he translated, "And there's another danger out there as well. Sharks."

The word made Gary shiver with alarm. He imagined those ferocious sea beasts prowling unseen beneath the ocean's surface, ready to eat him.

"Okay," he said. "I won't go into the water alone." Ichiro nodded assent as well.

***

When they tired of running through the surf, Gary and Ichiro made sand castles that were devoured by the rising tide as it lapped up the beach. He watched his father and Hajime take off their shirts and roll up their trouser legs. Both of them braved the surf and, like Gary, were tossed head over heels by the oncoming waves. With Junko next to her and the infant in her arms, Anzo only stepped where the foam washed around her ankles, and if a large wave threatened, she and Junko scrambled out of reach onto dry sand.

For lunch, they ate noodles and chicken with vegetables served in small containers Hajime called *bento boxes*. Hans cut slices of salami, tomato, pickle, and onion that he served with mustard on hard rolls.

Although Gary grew bone-tired, he didn't want the day to end. Late in the afternoon, as the sun touched the horizon, a trail of glittering light played across the water towards the beach. Then, as the sun set, the trail faded and the sky and ocean began turning a dark blue. Directly overheard, stars began to poke through the darkness. Night here unfolded just as it did in Utah, only it seemed more magical.

His father lit a fire with driftwood they gathered, and Gary scooted close to enjoy its warmth.

He studied the circle of faces arranged around the fire. His father, Hajime, Anzo, Hisa, Junko, and then Ichiro. He had known the Mitsuis for only three days, and even though he couldn't speak their language, they felt like family.

Although they were sad to leave the beach where they'd had so much fun, it was time to go, and the seven climbed back into the Ford and left for Anaheim and the Mitsui farm.

The next day, Hans said to Gary, "It's time for you and me to be heading home. I'm buying a load of fruit from Hajime to sell at our stand."

Gary's heart grew heavy. He wasn't ready to leave.

"But there's more, son. Hajime and I have been talking about you and Ichiro, and I spoke to Mom on the phone last night. We think it would be a great opportunity for you to learn Ichiro's language and a lot about how the fruit is grown if you were to stay here until I come back for you in August. You could probably even learn to eat with chopsticks!"

Gary thought about what this meant. "You're leaving me behind?"

"Only for a short time, son. I'll be back in late August, to bring a load of our fruit and pick up a new load of Hajime's, and you'd go home with me. And then, if all goes well, next summer, Ichiro can spend the summer with us in Utah."

Gary didn't know what to say. Understanding that he might not see his mother for two months made him realize how much he would miss her and their family.

"Dad, I don't know. What about Mom? Our farm?"

"Don't worry, son," his father reassured him with a warm chuckle. "Your mom and I will manage until you get back."

Chapter Five

"*Ichi. Ni. San. Shi. Go.*" Gary counted each stroke of his rake across the ground.

Beside him, Ichiro recited in kind. "One. Two. Three. Four. Five."

In the ten days since he'd been on the Mitsui farm, Gary was surprised at how much Japanese he'd learned. In the morning, when he would first meet Anzo, he'd bow and say, "*Ohayōgozaimasu. Watashi wa mō ha o migaite kao mo aratta. Shigoto no junbi ga dekimashita.*" Good morning. I have already washed up and brushed my teeth. I am ready to begin my chores.

Anzo would bow in return and say, "*Shigoto wa asagohan no ato in shinasai.*" Your chores can wait until after breakfast.

Besides the language, Gary had to get used to something else in the Mitsui household: the different diet. They didn't eat many potatoes nor much meat and bread, but ate lots more rice, cooked vegetables, chicken, and fish than he did at home. He found he was enjoying Anzo's cooking, and he never left the table hungry.

The Mitsui home was about the size of his home in Utah. It had four rooms: the kitchen with the dining table; the bedroom for Anzo and Hajime with a crib for Hisa; the other room with Hajime's work desk, the book cases, and the cots for the boys and Junko; and the bathroom with a large storage cabinet that contained the water heater. Also, unlike his home, the Mitsuis had indoor plumbing and hot and cold running water. By the back door there was also a large basin with a tap.

His days were much like those on the family farm in Utah. Breakfast, then work. After the morning meal with Ichiro, Anzo would send the two boys outside to look for Hajime. Usually he was in the shed preparing crates of fruit for the stand. Other times they'd find him somewhere in the orchard, inspecting the trees and the irrigation ditches.

This morning, as Anzo gathered the dishes after breakfast and the boys were putting on their shoes, Sanda began to bark ferociously. Anzo peeked out the kitchen door and then called to Ichiro in an urgent voice, "Go find your father. See what is bothering Sanda. Hurry!"

The two boys raced outside, glad that the day began with some excitement. While Ichiro searched for his father, Gary headed straight to Sanda, who was barking and growling at something, or someone, in the shed. Gary crept close and saw that the dog had cornered a raccoon. The masked critter paced on top of a stack of fruit crates, hissing and baring its teeth.

Because of his experience with raccoons at home, Gary knew better than to spook this one. From its vantage point on top of the crates it could jump onto his head to bite and scratch him. He would need a long switch to chase the critter away. He ran back to the pile of litter he and Ichiro had raked the previous day and grabbed a long, skinny tree branch.

Returning to the shed, he advanced on the raccoon, edging between the dog and Hajime's Dodge. He jabbed and poked at the raccoon. Sanda continued to jump up and growl and bark. At first the fight was fun and exciting, but the raccoon wasn't giving up. It fact, it was getting meaner by the minute. The animal bit viciously at the stick and held on. Gary wasn't sure what the raccoon would do, and was afraid if he let go of the stick, the animal might attack him.

Ichiro hollered behind him. *"Araiguma! Araiguma!"* Raccoon. Raccoon.

Hajime grabbed Gary's shoulder and pulled him backwards, then lunged forward with a bucket of water and doused the raccoon. The creature sputtered, now a wet ball of fur.

The raccoon shook its pointed head, snarled once, and sprung off the crates. It landed by the Dodge truck and scrambled underneath. Sanda followed the raccoon's retreat with a series of barks. The raccoon emerged from under the front of the truck and sprinted toward the trees, Sanda snapping at its tail. Climbing up into an apple tree, the raccoon clung to a high branch, looking soggy and defeated.

Hajime recognized that the raccoon was a threat to the fruit on his trees and would have to be either trapped and moved, or destroyed. He would deal with it later.

He set the bucket on a shelf. "Playtime is over, boys. We have work to do."

Gary reflected that his father used to say the same thing after something fun and out of the ordinary would happen on their farm.

Hajime unstacked the crates. "Boys, get your wagons and take this fruit to the basin and wash it. If you see any fruit that looks like the raccoon touched it, throw it out."

Fortunately, only two lemons bore what looked like claw marks. When the boys were done, they repacked the fruit in the crates. As they worked, Hajime stacked other full crates in the truck bed.

Once the truck was loaded, Gary and Ichiro climbed into the cab for the drive to the fruit stand. During the trip, as Gary regarded the lush orchards, he scoped out the far-off hills. They reminded him of the Rocky Mountains surrounding his home. The memory made him think about his mother and father and try to imagine what they were doing at this same moment. That thought made them seem close, as if they were just on the other side of those hills, even though he knew they were far away.

Time at the Mitsui's stand was much like the hours he typically spent at his family's. First, clean up by collecting whatever trash might have accumulated overnight, then sweep the hard-packed dirt floor and wipe the tables. Hajime would unload the truck, the crates being too heavy for the young boys. Gary and Ichiro raced to see which of them would get to drag the sandwich sign onto the shoulder of the highway.

When the stand was ready, the fruit neatly stacked and the crates arranged just so, Hajime would sit behind the center counter in a wooden chair and read a newspaper. Gary's father often did the same. To pass the time, Gary and Ichiro challenged each other to see who could count to one hundred first, first in Japanese, and then in English. Most of the Mitusi family's conversation was in Japanese, and Gary was learning quickly, now able to understand most of what was being said.

With the arrival of the first customer, Hajime would fold his newspaper and tuck it with the cash box under the counter.

The car would ease close to the stand and stop. Sometimes the customer was a man, sometimes a woman. Often though, women arrived in pairs. But whoever the customer was, Ichiro and Gary would watch, smile, and be polite, but they never stared, as Hajime had instructed them.

Their tasks included fetching paper sacks, picking up loose fruit that fell to the ground, wiping it down before restacking it, shooing away flies, and most important, keeping an eye on the cash box. If

Hajime was busy with a customer, he'd ask one of the boys to stand behind the counter.

This day, in the afternoon, although many cars drove past, none stopped. The air clouded over and turned humid. Hajime, who had gone to the shed for something, stepped out and studied the sky.

"Mr. Mitsui," Gary asked in Japanese, "what is the matter?"

Hajime fluffed his shirt as if to cool himself. "Nothing. It looks like rain and I hope it will, but people don't like stopping when it does." He smiled. "Well, if we don't have any customers, I can at least show you boys some jujitsu." He led the boys to a patch of soft grass to the right of the shed. "Ichiro," he ordered, "pretend you are Sanda and want to attack me."

Ichiro growled and ran straight at his father. Hajime grabbed one of his arms and flipped him onto his back. Ichiro lay in the grass, blinking.

"Are you okay?" Hajime asked.

Ichiro sprang to his feet. "What did you do? I want to learn how you did that."

"It is called jujitsu, a Japanese style of fighting without weapons."

"You mean like rassling?" Gary asked, using "rassling" since he didn't know the word in Japanese.

Hajime laughed. "No, it is not rassling. Here, your turn. Come at me."

Gary charged him, and before he knew it, he was flat on his back in the grass as well. He hopped up and stood beside Ichiro. "Please, Mr. Mitsui, teach us jujitsu."

"Stand there," Hajime pointed to a spot in the grass, "like this." He planted his feet shoulder-width apart and let his arms hang loosely to his front. From this position, he taught them basic stances and moves. "The trick is to use your opponent's weight against himself."

The boys practiced a couple of takedown moves, but nothing as dramatic as the flip Hajime had demonstrated.

The clouds parted and bright sun lit up the road once more. As if on cue, a sedan pulled up beside the stand and a woman in a fancy dress with matching gloves, shoes, and hat, stepped out.

"Back to work, boys," Hajime said.

Ichiro slung one arm around Gary's neck. "We want to learn more."

"Perhaps this weekend we'll visit the Japanese club and watch a demonstration," Hajime said.

***

Some days, on the way to the stand, Hajime would detour to Anaheim, where he'd stop outside a house and honk the truck's horn. A teenage boy would run out and climb into the cab. His name was Kenzo Nagatomo. He was a standby temporary helper hired to watch the stand so Hajime could attend other errands.

Kenzo was about as tall as Gary's mom, and, like the other Japanese, had hair that was shiny black and perfectly straight. He kept to himself, and when he wasn't attending to customers, he read whatever book or magazine he brought along. Gary and Ichiro asked Kenzo if he knew jujitsu, but he didn't seem to know much about it and his moves were mostly shoving the boys down, an easy feat because he was much bigger than either of them.

This day, Hajime left Kenzo alone at the stand and took the boys with him to a hardware store in Anaheim. Gary noticed the gum and candy by the cash register and hoped that Hajime would buy some, but he didn't. Instead, he bought several bronze pipe fittings for his irrigation system. When he placed them on the counter, he said, "I'm putting in a new irrigation ditch." Gary could tell he said that to make small talk with the cashier.

The cashier was a heavy man with a red face and thick jowls that reminded Gary of the water boss back in Utah. But whereas the water boss was friendly enough, this cashier acted like he'd just sucked on an especially sour lemon. He sat on a wooden stool, and when he moved to take care of Hajime he wheezed like a tire going flat. As he tallied the pipe fittings, he wrote on a receipt pad.

Without prompting, Hajime said. "I have another two acres that I'm planning to improve."

"*Hmmph,*" the cashier replied. "You know, it wasn't too long ago there weren't many of *you* types around here. Now there are more and more Japs and less and less of us."

When the cashier said *Japs,* Gary noticed that Hajime winced uncomfortably. He recognized the meanness in the cashier's tone. People in Utah used the same tone when they addressed his mom and dad. Gary stepped against Hajime and leaned into his hip. The cashier glared at him, and Gary responded by glaring back.

The cashier dropped the fittings into a paper sack and pushed it across the counter. "That will be three fifty-four."

Hajime stared at the cashier, looking stunned and hurt. After a moment, from his trousers he withdrew his wallet and a leather coin purse and counted out what the man said he owed. Cradling the bag, he nodded. "Thank you."

The cashier curled his lip as though he still had a bad taste in mouth, then sat back on his stool.

On the way back to the truck, Ichiro asked, "What is going on?"

Gary said, "I'm sorry for what that man said to you, Mr. Mitsui."

Hajime shrugged and said gently, "It is nothing. Flies are a bigger bother."

53

"Back home," Gary continued, "people say mean things to us, meaning my family and me, when we go out."

Puzzled, Hajime looked at Gary. "Why is that?"

"Because we're not Mormons. Most of the people where we live are. And we're German. People call us krauts and the Hun behind our backs."

"We must learn to forgive others for their ignorance," Mr. Mitsui commented.

"Sometimes that's not easy, Mr. Mitsui."

"Indeed. But just because a task is difficult doesn't mean we shouldn't do it."

"You sound like my dad."

Hajime chuckled. "Your father is a wise man. Listen to him."

***

Every week, Gary received a letter from his mother, which Anzo read to him after dinner. The first letter to arrive in August said:

> Dearest Gary,
>
> I trust that the Lord is keeping you safe. We are excited to hear what you're learning in California.
>
> The harvest of our peaches is beginning. Presently your father is contracting for Mexican fruit pickers to help with the harvest. You remember how it is. After weeks and weeks of patiently waiting for the fruit, it seems that we must gather everything at once.
>
> When the fruit has been picked and crated, your father will deliver a load to Mr. Mitsui. He's planning to be there August

18th, or thereabouts depending on the truck. Be ready to re-
turn home then.

I miss you. Please behave and be a good boy.
Remember your prayers.
Love,
Mother

***

To note the day of Hans's arrival, Anzo circled August 18 on the calendar hanging above Hajime's desk. Every morning she handed Gary a red grease pencil for him to mark that particular day. He counted the days until he would see his father again. When he was down to five days remaining, Gary would step out to the porch and stare up the road, hoping that his father might arrive early.

Nights, Gary lay awake. He could feel the minutes creep by and was sure August 18th would never arrive.

One morning he was shaken awake by Anzo. "Time to work."

Gary sat up and took a moment to realize what day it was. He jumped to his feet, suddenly alert. "It's August 18th! Today my dad will be here!" He ran to the desk and scrawled a big red X over the date on the calendar.

When he and Ichiro were helping Hajime get the truck ready, Gary asked, "Mr. Mitsui, is it okay if I stay here today? I want to see my father as soon as he shows up."

"That is no problem. I've arranged for Kenzo to take your place."

After the truck left, Anzo put Gary to work sweeping the house while she washed clothes. In the late morning, Sanda barked a warning.

Father! Gary thought excitedly.

He dropped the broom and ran out to the porch in his bare feet. Up the road, rumbling over the dusty road, approached the Ford truck.

Gary hopped and danced. "My dad is here! My dad is here!"

Anzo stepped onto the porch and watched. Junko appeared beside her.

The Ford rolled closer. Gary sprinted to the truck, whooping in delight, Sanda following, barking. When Gary gazed upward into the cab, his father at the steering wheel, he looked just as Gary remembered him—heroic and commanding.

The truck rattled to a stop. A tarp was cinched tight over the load that filled the bed to the top of the stakes. The driver's door opened, and Hans swiveled his long legs out to rest his boots on the running board.

Gary ran to his dad. Hans slid out of the truck and in one strong motion hoisted Gary to his chest. "How ya doing, son?"

Gary hugged his neck. "I've missed you, dad."

Hans held him in one arm and turned to greet Anzo.

She bowed. "Hajime is at the stand. He will be returning this afternoon as he's expecting you."

"Good. I want him to have first choice on what I've brought. The peaches are mine. The potatoes are from a friend near Provo."

Hans set Gary down. "Well, son, what have you learned since you've been here?"

Gary bowed and said, "*Ohayōgozaimasu, otōsan.*"

Hans bowed as well.

"It means, good morning, father."

"What else have you learned?"

"Ichiro and I helped Mr. Mitsui in his orchards. I learned how to do everything in Japanese."

Hans smiled. "Very good. Anything else?"

Gary assumed the jujitsu ready stance. "I've learned jujitsu. It is fighting without weapons."

Hans tousled his hair. "We must always be prepared to fight. And to do so without weapons is a Godly thing."

Chapter Six

July 1930

Gary and Ichiro, now eleven years old, watched Hans guide the John Deere Model GP tractor along the string indicating where the new irrigation ditch would go. Its big, cleated tires—the wheels painted bright yellow—bit into the ground as the plow behind the tractor cleaved the hard, crusted earth.

Gary walked backwards in front of the tractor, giving hand signals to his father, who constantly shifted his gaze from Gary to the right rear wheel that rolled just along the string. Ichiro and the farm-hand, Jeremiah, followed the tractor with shovels and spaded the loose dirt off to the side.

When Hans reached the end of the string where it was tied to a surveyor's stake, he halted the tractor to raise the plow, then steered to the right and parked. He left the engine idling and walked back to Gary.

They considered their morning's work. Fresh furrows marked where the new ditches would connect to the existing main irrigation canal. On the north side of the farm, the side closest to the river, stood the apple and pear orchards. To the south grew the rows of sproutlings planted two years ago and which needed another three years before they bore fruit. Tending orchards was an exercise in patience.

Hans removed his hat and wiped the sweat off his brow with a handkerchief. "Rather impressive, no? It would've taken us the better part of two days to dig what the tractor did this one morning."

Gary agreed. However, although the tractor had saved them hours of hard work, they still had to finish each ditch by hand.

The tractor had been a significant expense, but already his father was making money with it by hiring it out to other farms. These last few weeks, the emerald-green tractor had become a familiar sight rumbling along the county's dirt roads.

"Any chance I can drive it?" Gary asked, hopefully.

"Maybe next year," his father replied, eyes twinkling. "The tractor's quite a handful to operate, and you're not quite big enough." He put his hand on Gary's shoulder. "See all that work we've done, the way we've laid out the ditches? What does that tell you?"

Gary didn't follow. "I don't know."

"It shows that you have two things to sell." Hans extended a finger. "One, your physical labor. The digging of the ditches." He extended a second finger. "And two, your knowledge, which you gain through education and experience. In this case, the layout of the ditches and all the planning and understanding of water hydraulics that goes with it. We're not just digging ruts in the ground but creating an irrigation system. And a good one. That's the value we're adding to the farm."

"I got it, dad."

"Good." Hans patted Gary's shoulder. "Back to work, son. That ditch isn't going to dig itself."

***

Gary and Ichiro worked side by side as they expanded the furrow into a ditch. It was to be two feet wide and three feet deep. Hans had provided a board cut to the dimensions to use as a template to make sure the ditch was the proper size. The boys would fit the board into ditch and either deepen the bottom or square out the sides as needed.

Gary swung the pickax hard and planted it in the furrow so the handle jutted straight up. Sweat stung his eyes, and he removed his hat to wipe his face. Because of the heat, both he and Ichiro had left their shirts hanging in a nearby apple tree. Despite this precaution to remain cool, their undershirts were matted with perspiration. "Let's take a break," he said.

Ichiro leaned on the handle of his shovel. He too was breathing hard. "Sure."

They walked to the tree where their shirts hung. A galvanized steel water jug stood in the shade, with a cup fashioned out of a tin can resting upside down on the lid. After filling the cup, Gary gulped a swallow and handed the cup to Ichiro. They passed the cup back and forth, filling and emptying it several times.

For the last seven years, Gary and Ichiro had alternated where they stayed each summer. Because Ichiro now attended public school, his English was reaching a point that it was almost natural for him. To help Gary keep up with his new language skills, Hajime sent him bundles of newspapers and magazines in Japanese. Sometimes he included a 78-rpm record of Japanese music, poetry, or a school lesson.

A delightful breeze stirred through the orchard, and the cool, moisture-laden air that it brought broke the heat.

Rain, Gary thought, *thank God.*

He stepped from under the tree to take in the vista. A big

difference between here and California was that the orchards around Anaheim grew on land that was more or less flat. You couldn't see far through the rows of trees.

But here, the orchards sprawled across rolling, undulating land that sloped down the Malad River valley. Looking north, Gary studied the clouds scrolling along the Wasatch Mountains. The clouds were the color of gray smoke and dragged beneath them a misty haze of rain.

Ichiro approached, the shovel perched on his shoulder. "What do you figure?" he asked. "A half hour before the rain hits us?"

Gary stared up at the advancing bank of clouds. "Something like that."

Ichiro started back to the ditch. "So that's a half hour of work before the rain gets here."

***

"This is Lester Gonzales," Hans said, introducing the stranger to Gary and Ichiro.

Gonzales had arrived in an immaculate Chevy AC, the shiny car painted chrome yellow with crimson wire wheels. He wore a mouse-gray suit, a colorful tie, a fedora the color of chocolate, and white-and-brown spectator shoes. On his left wrist he wore a gold watchband, on his right a gold bracelet, and gold rings with gems decorated three of his fingers. A pencil mustache lined the upper lip of a chiseled face slick with perspiration.

"It is my pleasure. Such fine-looking boys," Gonzales said as he shook Gary's and Ichiro's hands in turn. For a man who made a show about having more than plenty, his grip was calloused and surprisingly hard. His English carried a Texas-Mexican accent.

Hans explained, "Mr. Gonzales is the broker for the Mexican laborers we'll need to pick the harvest."

Gonzales removed his suit coat, folded it, and laid it inside the Chevy. Suspenders held up his trousers. He fished a pack of cigarettes from his shirt pocket. "Mind if I smoke?"

Gary knew that his father didn't care for smokers, but since they were outside, he gave the go-ahead.

Gonzales flicked open a gold lighter and lit a cigarette. His gaze panned the house, the sheds, the tractor, the surrounding orchards, and the new irrigation ditches. "I see you're expanding. Congratulations. Most farmers I know are cutting back."

"I personally," Hans began, "was not directly affected by the stock-market crash. I don't own any stocks, and whatever I've bought—" he motioned to the tractor— "I paid for in cash. Same for the new land. What's helped me is the steady rise in the price of apples while the price of most other produce keeps dropping."

"You should be getting a dollar seventy-five per bushel," Gonzales commented.

"Hopefully a penny or two more," Hans added. He pointed to the sproutlings at the far side of the orchard. "Besides, I'm thinking long-term. If you own an orchard, you have to. Meanwhile, people have to eat."

Gonzales pivoted in a small circle, dust collecting on his fancy shoes. He nodded as if impressed by what he saw. After a moment, he pulled a small note pad from a hip pocket in his pants. "What's your yield?" He uncapped a fountain pen.

"Apples, eighteen hundred bushels. Pears, six hundred."

Gonzales jotted in his note pad. "I'll collect the crews in El Paso and Mesilla, and they'll travel by train to Perry. From there I'll bus them to Freetown. If you want to save yourself some money, you can pick them up and truck them here. Or, for a fee, I can bring them."

"I'll get them," Hans said.

"Mind you, it'll be harvest season so every hour counts. The clock starts as soon as you get the pickers, regardless if you're ready for them or not. If the men are just sitting around, you and I are both losing money."

"I'll be ready," Hans replied, his tone a little gruff as he resented being reminded of how to tend his business. He withdrew a note pad of his own and consulted it. "I figure two dozen pickers. I want experienced men, too. No deadbeats."

"Don't you worry, Mr. Gatlin. My crews are professionals, working the fields and orchards from Sacramento to Mineral Wells. Whatever you grow, they can pick." Having finished his cigarette, Gonzales dropped the butt and ground it under the toe of his shoe.

Hans said, "I'm not paying for any damaged fruit that was carelessly picked."

"Understood. The men are only paid for the bushels you accept."

Gary thought about this. Besides all the year-round expenses of maintaining the orchard, when harvest time rolled around the farm had expended a considerable amount of money even before they sold one piece of fruit. But he knew from sitting at his mother's side when she did the books, that every year their profit grew much like their sproutlings: little by little. He appreciated that his parents were always planning ahead, so even when they faced a financial setback—such as when the truck needed replacement of a left rear axle—his father took it in stride and soon had the truck up and running.

Gonzales put away his note pad. "We've got a deal." He and Hans shook hands. "I'll mail you a contract." Gonzales returned to the

Chevy. As he got into the car, he put on his sunglasses and lit another cigarette, then waved goodbye.

Hans, Gary, and Ichiro watched him drive off.

"Remember what I explained about having two things to sell?" Hans remarked. "The pickers make their money because of their physical labor. Gonzales, because of what he knows. Guess who puts the most in his pocket?"

***

Gary and Ichiro sat in the family Ford Model "A" Tudor Sedan. Gary's mother, Mary, was at the wheel. The aroma of fresh baked apple pies wafted from the straw basket in the back seat next to Ichiro.

They headed to Freetown, where Mary planned to first drop off the pies at a diner that paid a dollar for each. Then she'd donate a load of used clothes and canned goods at the County Food Bank. She made it a point of mentioning to Gary that it was their Christian duty to help out the less fortunate.

Freetown wasn't much of a town, more of a collection of shops at the intersection of the state highway and the county road. Mary parked outside Ruth's Diner in the dirt lot beside a Plymouth coupe and a truck. A sign in the diner's window said: *Today's Lunch Special. Bowl of Chicken Soup. Half sandwich. Slice of pie. 15¢*

She hauled out the basket with the pies. "This won't take long. You boys mind the car until I return."

Gary followed his mother, however, and opened the door for her to enter. He wondered how long this was going to take, because along with delivering the pies and collecting her money, she liked to take in the local news and gossip.

Ichiro got out of the car. He and Gary leaned against a fender.

"We should've brought a ball and played catch," Ichiro said.

"Yeah, maybe next time."

Ichiro jolted forward and grabbed the back of his head. "Ow!" A small rock landed beside their feet.

Gary looked to the other side of the car. Two boys ambled close, both of them smirking cruelly. One boy was almost a head taller than the other, but there was an obvious resemblance, and Gary figured them for brothers.

"Hey, redskin," the bigger one shouted.

Ichiro rubbed the back of his head and checked his fingers for blood. He glanced sideways at the boy.

The two strangers circled around the Ford, alert, menacing, like a couple of stray dogs spoiling for a fight. Gary and Ichiro took a couple of steps from the car.

The older boy looked thirteen, his brother ten, maybe nine. Because of their sunburnt complexions and patchwork clothing, Gary could tell they were local farm boys like himself.

"What do you guys want?" he asked.

The older boy's eyes drilled hatefully into Ichiro. He and his brother breathed heavily, their nostrils flaring. Gary hoped these boys would say their piece and move on. But the way they clenched and unclenched their fists, he knew they were here to cause trouble.

"We don't like Indians," the older boy said.

Ichiro remained quiet.

Gary wanted to see his friend's reaction but dared not take his eyes off these boys. As the air became brittle with tension, his muscles hardened into tense knots.

"What's-a matter?" the older boy continued. "You don't say nothin' cuz all you know is Injun talk. *Booga booga booga.*"

"Leave us alone," Gary said.

"What are you, an Indian lover?" the smaller brother taunted.

"Dirty Indian," the bigger boy said. Suddenly, he jumped forward and swiped at Ichiro. Luckily, Ichiro was ready. Ducking the blow, he danced to the side.

Frustrated, the older boy cursed. "You too chicken to fight?" He readied his fists.

Gary noticed that the younger brother was inching toward Ichiro, positioning himself for a double-team attack. At the instant the brother launched himself at Ichiro, Gary swung his foot out, tripping the boy. He landed face down in the dirt.

Seeing his brother take a fall enraged the older boy. He leapt at Ichiro with a flurry of wild haymakers. Applying the jujitsu he had learned, Ichiro parried the attack and slipped away.

The smaller boy started to get up.

Gary warned him, "Stay down unless you want to get hurt."

The older brother whirled toward Gary. "You don't say nuthin' to him." He charged at Gary, who sidestepped, grabbed one of his arms, and yanked him forward off balance. Gary neatly levered the boy over his hip, flipping him to the ground. The boy landed on his butt, sitting in a clumsy heap, and blinked in confusion.

Gary and Ichiro kept light on their feet and stood shoulder to shoulder.

The two brothers staggered upright, their faces smoldering with rage. "This is not over," the older boy growled.

"Okay, hold it," a man's stern voice commanded.

During the commotion, a sheriff's car had pulled up, and a uniformed deputy climbed out. Gary recognized him as David Packer from the times he'd visited the family fruit stand. At the diner, curious faces pressed against the window.

"James Ballard," the deputy said to the older boy, "what's the problem?"

"It was that Indian," the boy pointed at Ichiro. "He started it. Me and Thomas were walking by minding our own business when he started mouthing off to us."

"That's not true," Gary replied.

"Liar," James and Thomas replied in unison as they dusted the front of their pants.

Mary burst out the diner door, carrying the empty basket. "What's going on?"

"Mrs. Gatlin, that's what I'm trying to find out," Packer answered.

Everyone stood in a circle and stared at each other in silence. Gary knew Ichiro wasn't going to say anything because he felt the deputy wouldn't believe him. Ichiro rubbed the heel of his hand against his eyes to blot tears. He looked terribly upset. Gary felt ashamed for his friend and for himself that this had happened.

Packer finally spoke. "Since no one is talking, how about you all go your separate ways?"

"That's what we were doing," James said. "Until that guy made trouble." He mumbled a parting shot, "Dirty redskin," then pulled his brother's shirt. "C'mon, Thomas."

"Gary and Ichiro," Mary ordered, "get in the car." She opened the driver's door and tossed the basket into the back seat. "Deputy Packer, we'll be on our way."

Hooking his thumbs into his pistol belt, Packer squared his shoulders. The sun glinted off his deputy's star. He cleared his throat. "Mrs. Gatlin, these things don't happen among people of the faith. We Mormons are not troublemakers. Perhaps if your family was to visit the temple this Sunday—"

Mary's cheeks flamed. "Deputy Packer, having lived in this

county as long as we have, I am very much aware of who the actual troublemakers are." Without waiting for his reply, she slipped behind the steering wheel and started the car. "Now, if you don't mind. I'm on my way to the food bank."

***

Mary told Hans what had happened to Ichiro. For his part, Ichiro said that he'd forgotten what was said. But he remained quiet, and from his brooding the Gatlins could tell he remained insulted and hurt.

After a couple of days, Mary and Hans announced that they were all going to take a picnic up to Bear Lake. They loaded the Model A and drove up the highway through the mountains to Logan, then continued to Pickleville, a small resort at the edge of the lake.

Ichiro perked up. "I can smell the water. It's different from the ocean but I can still smell it."

A line of dense pine obscured the lake, but Gary could see blue water peek through gaps in the branches. Hans parked alongside the road next to the trees. When Ichiro climbed out of the car, he wasted no time pushing through the undergrowth until he reached the gray sands of the lakeshore. Gary hustled after him.

The water stretched to the north and south like a great sheet of sapphire-blue glass. Grassy hills stippled with brush surrounded the lake, and though it was the middle of summer, snow remained in the craggy recesses of the distant mountains.

"What do you think?" Gary asked.

"It's beautiful," Ichiro replied without taking his eyes off the lake. Then he said, "I know why you brought me here."

"What do you mean?"

"I know I've been acting strange. Keeping quiet and all that. I didn't mean to be rude."

"Don't worry about it."

"It's just that I don't understand why people say bad things about me. What have I done?"

"Forget those jerks from the other day."

"It's not just that. People in California say the same things."

Gary didn't know how to respond. He kicked at rocks in the sand and looked back across the lake. Finally, he bent over to pick up a rock and cocked his arm. "I bet I can skip a rock farther than you."

He launched the rock and it skipped once, twice, three times before it sank in a ring of ripples.

"Ha!" Ichiro chuckled. "Let me show you how it's done." He chose a smooth, flat rock and flung it.

Gary counted the skips. "One. Two. Three. Four." He got another rock. "Watch this."

The two boys laughed, and as they continued the contest, the world's problems disappeared like the ripples they made on the water.

CHAPTER SEVEN

July 1934

Every Fourth of July, the local Issei Association sponsored a field day and picnic at Huntington Beach. *Issei* means first-born, and it was applied to the first generation of Japanese immigrants to the United States. The festivities were held on Independence Day to show that although these Japanese families were new to this country, they were loyal Americans.

Many of the activities included athletic contests such as volleyball games and foot races. One race involved teenage boys, and Gary and Ichiro were eager for the challenge. They took up positions for the 100-yard sprint, which they would run barefoot. Bystanders lined up along the impromptu track that ran down the beach, parallel to the water. A ribbon of paper tape demarcated the finish line.

Mr. Azagawa stood to one side of the runners. "Get ready," he called.

The dozen runners lowered into position, eyes fixed on the finish line. The distance was a hundred yards—a football-field length—away, and Gary was well aware of the effort he would need to win. He dug his toes into the sand for purchase.

"Get set."

The runners lifted into the starting pose and braced themselves.

"Go!"

The runners catapulted down the track. Cheers exploded from the bystanders.

Lightning fast, Ichiro burst into an early lead. Gary raced close behind him in the pack, which dwindled with every step as other runners fell away. At fifty yards, Gary, with his longer legs and greater stamina, was able to break out of the pack and stay close to Ichiro's heels.

Gary kept focus on the finish line; everything else in his vision was a blur. Breath burned his throat. His heart pounded, his pulse hammered against his temples. His body begged him to let up, but instead he pressed harder. He kept his eyes locked on the finish line, but he could sense Ichiro right beside him, not giving up an inch. Gary did not dare turn his head because that would've cost him a precious second. They flew at the front of the pack. His gaze shrank to tunnel vision and he was aware of little besides the burn in his throat, his pounding heart, and the finish line.

At twenty yards from the tape, he tapped into his last reserves. He was bigger and stronger than Ichiro, and sure he would out-power him to the end.

Gary's lungs screamed.

Ten yards.

He began to see red.

Five yards.

I won! he thought, feeling the victory.

At the last second though, incredibly, Ichiro lunged forward and broke the tape, mere inches in front of Gary.

Thundering across the finish line, they slowed to a stop, chests heaving. The rest of the runners flashed by, but Gary barely noticed.

Ichiro was bent over, hands propped on knees. He tilted his head back and glanced at Gary with an expression of admiration and triumph. They had pushed each other to the edge of exhaustion, to the limits of pain. These races were not just contests of speed and athletic ability, but also agonizing tests of their manliness and pride.

Gary gathered his breath and strength to wave at Ichiro, to acknowledge that he had won…this time. "Nice going, my friend," he gasped, gulping air. "Good race!"

***

Later that day came the final round of the jujitsu exhibition. This event, as part of the July Fourth celebration of the Japanese people in their new country, took place in the section of the park they had reserved for their festivities. Sweat trickled into Gary's eyes and down his torso beneath his shirt as he prepared to compete. He squared off against Daniel Kawasaki, an advanced student of jujitsu, like himself.

Gary wiped the sweat from his eyes and considered his opponent. Daniel was large for a Japanese, for he was taller than Gary and big-boned as well. Furthermore, Daniel claimed to have descended from a family of champion Sumo wrestlers. The match was two out of three, and they were each one-for-one. Daniel was as quick as he was over-sized, and Gary couldn't leave anything to chance.

The referee, Mr. Osuma, was a small, no-nonsense man whose face looked as though it were made of leather. He grunted a command. "Bow to your opponent."

Gary and Daniel bowed to one another.

"Get ready."

Both boys tensed into the ready stance, nerves so tight that their knees and fingers quivered.

Osuma made a chopping motion with his hand as he barked, "Fight."

Gary lunged for the lapels of Daniel's shirt. Daniel grabbed Gary's wrists and leaned backward as he brought his right leg between them to begin a hip throw.

Anticipating this, Gary held tight to the shirt and rolled over Daniel's hip as he twisted at the waist and planted his feet. The momentum yanked Daniel off balance. He tumbled to the grass out of control just as Gary let go and regained his footing. Gary stumbled backward two steps and then caught himself while Daniel landed on his butt and toppled to one side.

Osuma pointed to Gary. "*Shōsha.*"

Gary had won the match.

Daniel scrambled to his feet. He and Gary bowed to one another and ran back to where their families were watching. Panting for breath, Gary dropped down cross-legged beside Ichiro.

Ichiro elbowed him and whispered, "That was very good, the way you faked him out."

Gary kept his expression plain, but inside, his heart was flush with victory. He was proud that he had beaten Daniel. The contest had been quick, over and done with in mere seconds, years of training compressed into action that manifested itself in the snap of a finger. Blink, and you lost.

They watched the remaining bouts, and after the last match, Atsushi Saito, the judge of the jujitsu events, marched to the center of the field. For a distinguished jujitsu champion he looked a bit portly to Gary. Then again, Gary realized he would never dare take him on. Everyone stood to acknowledge the judge. Saito addressed the assembly in his booming voice. "The skill displayed today was most impressive. Every one of you has demonstrated your dedication and willingness to apply yourself and learn. You all fought well and brought honor to the sport of jujitsu. You have given full measure to your heritage, and you have made me proud. *Domo arigato.*" He bowed.

All bowed in return.

With this, the exhibition was over.

Judge Osuma approached the team. Gary wondered how he and Ichiro would be rewarded for winning their bouts.

Osuma set his hands on his hips and sucked at his teeth as he looked over the space where they'd had their competition. "You did a fine job, boys."

Feeling somewhat abashed for the kudos he had expected, Gary quietly accepted the praise as an adequate reward.

***

Now that Gary and Ichiro were fifteen years old, Hajime left them to tend the fruit stand while he went about his errands or returned to the orchards.

One afternoon, a Dodge coupe convertible roared up the highway, sunlight gleaming off its royal-blue body and chrome headlamps and bumpers. It zoomed past, then halted with a screech of tires and backed up to the stand. Three young men, college students maybe, were crammed into the only seat. The Dodge pulled up short with a spray of gravel from beneath its tires. The men spilled out of the convertible in a flurry of laughs. The driver was tall and dark-haired. The other tall fellow was blond with a lantern jaw. The third passenger had the compact build of a wrestler. They were well dressed and loud and acted as if the world owed them a good time. Gary figured they might have been a little drunk.

They huddled before a side table and cracked inside jokes with one another. The wrestler snatched a lemon off the table and pitched it to his blond buddy. Gary didn't appreciate their playing catch with the produce. They could do whatever they wanted with the fruit ... after they'd bought it.

He and Ichiro exchanged annoyed looks, and were about to say something when an older Model A truck rattled to a stop beside the Dodge. A middle-aged Mexican woman eased out the driver's door while a pretty younger woman exited from the passenger's side. They wore nearly identical plain dresses and battered shoes, and because they resembled one another, Gary presumed them to be mother and daughter.

Stepping up to the stand, the two women spoke quietly to one another in Spanish as they inspected the lemons and grapefruit, which they collected in a basket. Gary took his place behind the center table next to the cash box.

The wrestler crept behind the women, getting closer with every step. The younger woman noticed and drew away. "What do you want?"

"So, you speak English?" he asked, taunting her.

"Of course I do."

"Then why are you gabbing in Spanish?"

The older woman shot him a puzzled look and commented to her daughter in Spanish.

"Speak English," the wrestler said, talking slowly and louder, as if he were addressing the hard of hearing. "You wanna speak that wetback gibberish, go back to Mexico."

Both women recoiled from him. The mother put her basket on

the center table, evidently changing her mind about buying the fruit.

Where did these guys learn how to behave? Gary thought. *Who dares to talk to women this way?*

Ichiro had been watching too, and he was the first to make a move. He raised his voice. "You and your friends need to leave."

The wrestler-type pointed to himself, acting astonished. "Me?" Smirking, he sized up Ichiro.

Gary advanced from around the table. The two tall guys stepped in his way. Dark-haired guy said, "This is between them."

"It's our fruit stand," Gary answered.

"I said," the blond man insisted, "that it's between them."

Suddenly Gary felt that he and Ichiro were stranded. He didn't want trouble, but he didn't know what these fellows were up to. Maybe they were out on a lark at others' expense, or maybe they were hooligans who got their kicks badgering people.

He looked up the empty highway toward Anaheim and wondered where was Hajime? If he were here, how would he handle this?

"We don't want trouble," Ichiro said.

"Then keep your yap shut," the wrestler replied, stepping close to Ichiro.

But Ichiro didn't back down, even though the wrestler outweighed him by at least forty pounds. "You need to go."

"We'll go when we're good and ready."

"Now," Ichiro insisted.

"I'm tired of your lip." The wrestler bent his knees and brought his arms up as he sprang forward.

Ichiro blocked one arm and grasped the other in a hammerlock. He levered against the arm and sank to one knee, putting his weight into the hold. The wrestler's face exploded with surprise and then bunched with pain. He followed Ichiro to the ground as he yelped with agony.

"You let him go," the dark-haired guy said. He started for Ichiro when Gary snagged him by the collar and swept his ankles. The man fell face first into the hard-packed earth.

Gary let him go and immediately faced the tall blond man.

He lunged at Gary, who easily batted aside his hands and grabbed his shirt collar. With a simple twist of his pelvis, Gary levered the man over one hip and flipped him. On his way down, the man's heel caught one of the tables, jarring it hard, upsetting the stacks of fruit. When he hit the ground, lemons rained upon his head.

The wrestler staggered to his feet. First massaging his arm, he then straightened his shirt and smoothed his hair back into place. "You guys are lucky I got things to do today. Otherwise I'd stay here and tear you and this place apart."

"Just go," Ichiro said. "And don't come back."

The three men climbed back into the Dodge. The wrestler lit a cigarette and sneered at Ichiro. Dark-hair gunned the engine and they sped away, shouting obscenities over their shoulders.

Gary let go a long sigh. Things could've gone badly if those men had had weapons, and he was glad nothing worse had happened. He became aware of the two Mexican women watching him, their large dark eyes filled with both gratitude and apprehension. Gary picked up their basket and handed it to the mother. "Ladies, I hope you're not done shopping."

***

At the end of each day, after washing up, eating dinner, and attending to the last of their chores, Gary joined the Mitsuis as they gathered at the kitchen table. Gary and Ichiro read. Anzo sat with little Hisa on her lap and either sewed or finished a crossword puzzle in English. Junko usually drew or colored in a notebook. And like Gary's father, Hajime finished the day at his desk in the next room, making entries in the farm journal.

Gary opened a thick book lent to him by Kenzo Nagatomo, who was now in college. The book's cover was made of coarse woven material, threadbare and worn from years of use. Gary read to himself the title, Kanji script-embossed into the cover. *Heike Monogatari.* The Tale of the Heike—the Tiara family.

Kenzo had said that if Gary wanted to really know the Japanese language, their history and culture, then he should study this cherished epic poem. He said this more as a challenge, thinking Gary would never follow through.

But Kenzo had underestimated Gary. Something about the Japanese language clicked in his head. It was hard learning, but that didn't frustrate him. To the contrary. With every bit of understanding, he felt his head was being filled with wisdom of those ancient peoples. In working the fields and practicing jujitsu, his muscles grew; in learning Japanese, so did his mind. He admired the frontispiece with its illustration of men and women in traditional Japanese garb, rendered in delicate ink washes.

He flipped to the first page of the poem and hesitated, intimidated by the dense text and that he was about to embark on a prolonged journey. He read to himself the first two lines and tried to absorb their meaning. The prose was not just in Japanese, but in classical Japanese, stiff and yet highly nuanced. He took a deep breath and then recited aloud, taking care to properly enunciate each word in poetic rhythm:

"Gionshōja no kane no koe, shogyōmujō no hibiki ari.
Sarasōju no hana no iro, jōshahissui no kotowari wo arawasu."

The bells of the Gion Temple ring with the fleeting nature of all things.
The white flowers on the twinned trees imply that to prosper is to eventually fail.

Hajime rushed into the kitchen from his office study. "Who just spoke that?"

Gary was alarmed by Hajime's response. "It was me," he replied sheepishly. He raised the book.

"That was you? Astonishing! I thought it was one of my boyhood master poets reciting that piece." Hajime glanced at the book. "*Heike Monogatari.* That is a difficult work. Gary, how can you do this?"

He shrugged, embarrassed by the attention. "I don't know. I just do it."

Hajime beamed. "Gary, you are destined for many wonderful things."

Chapter Eight

Gary watched his father and the water boss, Mr. Watson, as they studied the water sluicing from the Malad River diversion canal into the Gatlins' irrigation system. Although it was almost 11 a.m., the weather remained cool enough for Hans and Mr. Watson to keep their jackets on. This week the first brisk morning had arrived to announce that autumn was around the corner.

From his last trip to Anaheim, Gary had brought back a sheaf of notes that Hajime had helped him prepare, details about how to better irrigate the orchards. Gary opened a notebook in which he was keeping all the information on a new irrigation system for his family's farm. He entered what he had learned from Hajime about the Mitsuis' farm and their methods.

He tracked the water as it flowed down the new network of ditches and compared the water's progress to his drawing.

The farmhand, Jeremiah Edson, hard at work nearby, poked at a ditch with his shovel and then stepped away. For a moment he let his gaze drift toward the horizon. Farming was hard work, but the labor gave one a sense of feeling closer to the earth, and more appreciative of Nature's beauty.

Gary said, "Jeremiah, thanks for sharing your concerns about my new system."

Edson, daydreaming just a bit, barely shifted his gaze from the lovely landscape and answered with a distracted, "Don't mention it."

The gratitude that Gary owed Edson was from the farmhand's pointing out a significant difference between farming in Anaheim and farming here in Utah. Gary's original plan to improve the irrigation system was a network of pipes like Hajime used. With such pipes the Gatlin farm wouldn't lose as much water through evaporation and could more efficiently direct the water to where it was best needed. This method promised the same harvest yield for half the water usage. Everything about Gary's plan was an improvement, although it did have one significant flaw, one that Edson had noted.

"Mischief," he had said. "I'll bet no one in California is messing with your Japanese friend's irrigation system."

Which was true, Gary remembered.

"You lay those pipes and those Mormon boys will clog 'em and wreck the fixtures. Making repairs will take a lot of coin."

When the Mormons, or whoever it was, vandalized the Gatlin's irrigation system, it usually required only a few hours of spadework to make repairs. Replacing valves and unclogging pipes would be significantly more costly in terms of both time and money.

So Gary had had to amend his original plan by using open concrete ditches instead of pipes, which could then be controlled according to the overall design. This, he figured, would reduce the likelihood of vandalism as well as decreasing the amount of water loss from soaking into the ground. By Gary's calculation, it would also be an economic plus, as it would be less costly than a network of pipes.

After inspecting that the water flowed as predicted, Gary returned to the numbers in his notebook. Most people thought of farming only in terms of the hard labor involved in tending the soil, not realizing the amount of planning and record-keeping that successful agriculture required. He recognized that the earliest form of writing had nothing to do with literature, but rather with record-keeping, documenting crop yields. While poets were passing their stories orally from generation to generation, it was the supposedly dumb dirt farmers who developed the art of writing and mathematics. Because just as it is today, Gary thought, the ancient farmers had to contend with the same issues of water hydraulics, crop yield, loss, and, hopefully, profit.

Hans and Mr. Watson left the diversion canal and walked through the orchards that had already been picked during the first harvest. Random apples littered the ground. The two men continued on to a bare knob of hard dirt that overlooked the new orchards. Hans gestured to some sproutlings and then called out, "Gary, come here."

Gary closed his notebook and hustled over to them.

"I want to show you this," Hans said to the water boss. "It's not just new ways to irrigate that we're learning from the Japanese, but also their grafting techniques. Gary, show him your notebook."

Gary opened his notebook to a tab. The section had his sketches and notes about apple grafting techniques. He had learned a great deal from Hajime and the Japanese way of growing fruit. He had also read much of the writings of Luther Burbank, a horticulturist of the time who had authored many works about growing and grafting in different ways.

"You have to pay a lot of attention to what you're doing," Hans explained. "But the effort is worth it. For example, he pointed to a short, young tree— "you can graft sproutlings onto an existing trunk in order to utilize its root system. If we had to nurture the sproutlings we'd planted in the ground until they bore fruit, we'd have to wait eight to twelve years. This way we can harvest a new crop in three to five, which will also allow us to determine the size of the fruit and increase our yield."

"What do you figure your yield?"

Hans looked at Gary. "Son?"

As Gary flipped to another tab in his notebook, he could see that Mr. Watson looking at him rather skeptically. He pointed to list of tabulated figures. "Here's what we're expecting from all the apple trees." Then pointed to another list. "Here I've broken it down by variety."

He flipped the page. "Here is where I've listed the costs per acre, and from that, the costs per bushel."

Mr. Watson took the notebook and studied the numbers. He flipped from page to page and then returned the notebook. "You figured all this on your own?"

Gary nodded. The question made him think he might have done something wrong. "Did you see a mistake?"

"Nope," Mr. Watson said. "It's just that most of the other farm kids rarely have the gumption to pick up a hoe for weeding, and here you're doing all these fancy calculations about your trees. It's nice to know that at least one of you young people appreciates the science of farming."

***

The high point of Gary's week was the letters he received from Ichiro. The letters didn't relay a lot of important news, mostly anecdotes about school and the Mitsui farm. What most interested Gary, though, was what Ichiro shared about his jujitsu lessons. When Gary read his friend's descriptions of new techniques, he couldn't help but feel envious. Of course he was happy for Ichiro and wished him all the best, but he was discouraged that here in Utah he had no one to mentor him in any of the Japanese martial arts. In order to keep up the skills he had learned, Gary practiced his techniques in the barn when no one was around. Not only did he practice alone, which didn't give him the opportunity to spar against an opponent, he had to hide his training sessions; otherwise, people would gossip that he was experiencing fits of lunacy.

Today he practiced barefoot on the hard-packed floor he had swept clean. A dummy fashioned from gunnysacks dangled from a rafter. On the front of the dummy he'd sewn strips of canvas to act as lapels he could grasp. The dummy swung from a rope, which allowed him to practice both grasping and counterbalance routines. While this helped some, with no one to critique his moves he worried that he might be picking up bad habits.

Every summer when he and Ichiro reunited, the first chance they had time to themselves, Ichiro would share what he'd learned and Gary would spend hours catching up.

***

"C'mon, Gary," Chrissy yelled from outside the kitchen. "You're wasting daylight."

"I'm on my way," Gary replied, peeved at the way his younger sister gave orders, especially on her days at the fruit stand. For a thirteen-year-old, she sure enjoyed acting like the boss. He nudged open the kitchen screen door as he slipped into a denim jacket. The cool morning was still gray with twilight.

Chrissy was dressed for work, a checkered blouse gathered into her jeans, the jeans rolled up at the cuffs, a straw hat on her head.

Her blond hair was woven into braids. She had just let the chickens out of the coop. A dozen hens wandered into the weeds and grass for insects while the rooster strutted to a fence post, flew to the top, and began to crow.

Gary climbed into the old Ford truck and cranked it over. He wondered when his father would get around to buying a new one, but he knew his dad was pretty close with a dime. Hans was known to pinch pennies so tightly it was a wonder they weren't stamped with his fingerprints.

He backed the truck into the shed, where Chrissy waited by crates of produce for the fruit stand. No sooner had he stopped when she began heaving crates onto the truck's bed. After they'd loaded the crates, she ran back into the house and returned with the cash box, a large Thermos of water, a jar of tomato juice, and a lunch pail their mother had packed. Chrissy stowed their provisions in the cab and jumped into her seat. "Let's go."

The dirt road leading from the farm crested a rise where the road connected with the highway. By now, the dawn's light haloed the Wasatch Mountains, and the valley was gathering its brilliant colors.

As the truck rattled onto the highway, Chrissy prompted Gary the same way she did every time they were alone on the road. "When can I drive?"

"When you get your license," he answered.

"Why not let me practice now?" she argued. "You've seen me on the farm. I can handle the truck, the car, and the tractor same as you." Chrissy claimed she could do anything as well as Gary could. Whether or not she had experience in the task was another matter.

Gary fell back to his standard response. "That's on the farm. Right now we're on a public road."

"So what? This truck is still the same truck."

"If dad wants you to drive the truck, you'll drive the truck. Take it up with him."

***

The fruit stand was just a short distance from where the farm road met the highway. Gary checked his wristwatch. They had to be open by 8 a.m., and they had plenty of time.

But when they rounded the bend where their fruit stand appeared seventy yards distant, Gary and Chrissy both cried out in shock. Their proud stand resembled a pile of wood scraps.

"What happened?" Chrissy asked.

What indeed? Gary thought, his insides churning. The stand was well constructed, and during the winter could withstand the worst of blizzards. Just yesterday he and his mother had been at the stand, so whatever happened had occurred overnight.

Gary reduced their speed so that they crept up to the ruins. The closer they approached, the more apparent the damage. The front doors had been smashed into kindling, allowing the stand to collapse on itself.

Gary stopped the truck, and he and Chrissy bolted out to inspect the damage. His father had meticulously sunk two stout posts on either side of the stand just to keep someone from accidentally crashing into it, and Gary's anger rose as he saw that neither post was so much as scratched. Obviously whoever had run into the stand had deliberately aimed between the posts. Parallel tires marks leading to and away from the stand gave mute confirmation to his suspicion.

The nefarious vehicle had rammed through the tables inside the stand and the impact had ripped the side doors off their hinges. The front supporting posts had been sheared at the bottoms, causing the roof to lean forward precariously.

Chrissy studied a scuffed dent in one of the front doors. "See how this looks rounded? And it's so low? That means a car probably did this. A truck bumper would have left a higher mark."

She was probably correct, but that didn't change their situation.

"Who would do this?" she asked, her cheeks flaming with anger.

The damage was obviously intentional. "Maybe some guys joyriding."

"Or maybe the same bunch of Mormon delinquents who tear up our ditches," Chrissy noted angrily.

"Yeah, it could be them," he answered.

"Somebody wants to shut down our stand." Chrissy began pulling the smashed pieces apart. "So the best thing we can do to show them they can't stop us is to get back to selling fruit."

"A lot of the posts and boards are broken," Gary noted. "We'll have to replace them."

"We can salvage enough for now to set up a table or two." Chrissy looked up to the sky. "The weather is good so we can stay out here all day."

Typical Chrissy. She was as stubborn as a Jennie mule, but she always did what she set her mind to.

They improvised a couple of tables. In doing so, they obliterated much of the tire mark evidence. Surprisingly, the roadside sandwich sign remained in good shape and Gary dragged it to the highway.

As he and his sister unloaded the crates and arranged the apples and pears, cars and several buses drove past. Many slowed, perhaps out of curiosity.

A boxy Chevy AE station wagon pulled up and stopped. The front passenger window scrolled downward and a woman wearing a scarf and eyeglasses poked her head out. "Is this the Gatlin fruit stand?"

"It is, ma'am," Chrissy answered proudly.

"You have the best fruit." The woman took in the damage. "But I see you have problems."

Chrissy picked up an apple. "Yes, ma'am, a little. But there's nothing wrong with our fruit. You won't be disappointed."

The woman looked at Gary, who grinned. "She's right."

"Okay," the woman replied. She turned to her driver, exchanged a few words, then climbed out. "It's a sale."

She spent a $1.25, buying a crate of pears and mixed apples before motoring off. Chrissy counted the money into the cash box she'd hidden behind a stack of crates.

"Now that the stand is open for business," she said, "why don't you drive back to the farm and tell dad about this? Maybe if you two bring tools and lumber we might fix the stand before dark."

"I don't think it's wise to leave you alone."

Chrissy frowned. "What am I now, a baby? How many times have I watched over the farm all by myself?"

"That's different. That's the farm, private property. This is next to the highway." Sometimes Gary thought that his sister was too headstrong for her own good.

He was about to say something more when he noticed a Ford sedan veer off the highway toward them. As the car rolled to a halt, he recognized the lettering on its driver door: Box Elder County Sheriff.

Deputy Packer climbed out. Like always, Packer liked to march around with his thumbs in his gun belt, which made his chest puff out.

He nudged the broken wreckage with his shoe. "Seems like you Gatlins have run into another string of bad luck."

"Not bad luck," Chrissy replied fiercely, "just bad neighbors."

"This doesn't happen to any of the Mormon stands. Might want to consider that." Packer scanned what was left of the tire marks leading to and from the stand. "Any idea who would do this?"

"I thought solving crimes was your job," she snapped.

"Chrissy, hush," Gary said. "Actually, Deputy, there is something you can do. I need to drive back to the farm and tell my dad about this. I'd be obliged if you could watch over my sister while I'm gone."

Packer snorted. "I have the feeling that my company is not particularly welcome."

"Welcome or not, it would be appreciated."

Packer grudgingly agreed. "It might be wise if I stay."

Now it was Chrissy's turn to snort. She crossed her arms and sat on an upturned crate. "Go on then," she said to Gary. "Get going."

He retrieved the lunch pail, water, and the Thermos from the truck and set them beside his sister.

She said, "I hope you're not going to be gone that long."

"In case you get hungry."

"I'm hungry," Packer said. He knew Mary's cooking to be the best.

Chrissy handed him the lunch pail. "Be my guest." She had been taught to be thoughtful of others, and although she didn't much like Packer, she remembered her manners.

Packer lifted the cloth napkin arranged over the food. He reached into the pail and pulled out a packet wrapped in wax paper. His eyes widened when he opened the packet. "Mmmm, a slice of your mom's apple pie."

"Enjoy it," Chrissy said, "because it's better than anything you'll get from a Mormon."

***

In the late afternoon, as Gary and his father worked on the fruit stand, a Dodge Custom Sedan approached and parked beside them. Gary recognized the car as belonging to Lehi Smith, an elder and bishop of the local Mormon church.

Hans had been sawing a post that Gary steadied on a sawhorse. Both straightened, and Hans rested the crosscut saw on the post. Gary watched his father and noticed that his face darkened with suspicion.

The Dodge's driver door swung open and out stepped Smith. He was a tall, severe-looking man, and his black suit added to his lugubrious appearance. A black fedora shaded his gaunt face.

Hans stiffened, and Gary worried that his father's antipathy toward Mormons and his anger over the vandalism of the fruit stand would make him take a swing at Smith.

The Mormon elder halted and panned the wrecked fruit stand and the materials Gary and his father had brought to repair the damage. Smith worked his thin lips, which deepened the furrows in his creased face. He and Hans glared at one another for a long moment. Finally, Smith said, "Brother Packard told me what happened."

Hans replied, his tone even but heavy, "Since you're here, that means you know who did it."

"The church will address the delinquents." Smith reached into his suit coat and pulled out a leather wallet. He plucked two crisp five-dollar bills and offered them to Hans.

Gary's father regarded the money, then stared at Smith. "I'm not interested in charity."

Smith took a small step forward. "It's not charity, Mr. Gatlin. Please consider it as recompense for damages suffered. If nothing else, as a favor to me."

Hans nodded at Gary. "You take it."

Hesitantly, Gary took the money from Smith's hand. Smith's eyes never left Hans's. He stepped back.

Tucking the wallet back into his coat, Smith said evenly, "One more thing, Mr. Gatlin. *Hans.* My apologies."

Hans tipped his head. "Accepted, sir."

Smith returned to his sedan and drove off.

CHAPTER NINE

August 1936

Gary and Ichiro raked piles of loose branches, fallen apples, and other debris that littered the Gatlin farm from the late July harvest. Gary retrieved the Ford truck and drove it while Ichiro walked alongside and pitched the material into the truck bed. The work wasn't as hard as it was monotonous. Ichiro climbed onto the running board next to Gary and clung to the mirror as they proceeded to another orchard on the farm.

The fragrance of ripe apples filled the air. Dirt and leaves crunched beneath the truck's tires as they rumbled along. The sounds and the orchard smells gave Gary some wistful moments. Next year would probably be the last time that he and Ichiro would spend time like this.

"What are your plans after high school?" Gary asked. While Ichiro was here, Gary made it a point to converse in Japanese to keep his language skills fresh.

"When I go to college I'm thinking about joining the R.O.T.C."

"You're going into the army?" Gary replied, astonished. "I didn't think you were the type."

"They pay a monthly stipend. It isn't much, but it will help."

"But then you have to serve."

"That's a big part of my decision. I'll serve as an officer and that will let me demonstrate my gratitude to this country." The truck rattled over a bump, and Ichiro held tight to keep from being tossed free.

"Sounds corny, I know," he continued. "But growing up and hearing the way people talk about us Japanese, hopefully my going into the military will show that we're just as ready as anybody else to fight for this country. Maybe show that we Japanese can be more than farmers and gardeners."

"You really think there will be another war?" Gary asked.

"I sure don't want to think so," Ichiro answered. "I pray for peace."

Gary remembered his father obsessing over the recently started Spanish Civil War. *Let's keep out of this one. What do we owe those crazy Europeans anyway? We already sent a million of our boys once and thousands didn't come back. And today, even we loyal German-Americans are still getting our noses rubbed into the dirt because of the war. Another conflict serves no one but the devil. I don't want it to happen again.* He had been looking at Gary when he said this.

"But what are you going to study?" Gary asked Ichiro. "You have to get a degree."

"I'm not sure. I like mathematics, but I don't want to teach."

They reached another pile to be picked up. Gary halted and hopped out of the truck to help Ichiro.

As they heaved the branches into the truck bed, Gary asked, "Mathematics? Why not engineering?"

"That's a possibility. What about you?"

"Farming," Gary replied.

"Farming?" Ichiro repeated.

"What's wrong with farming?"

"Nothing," Ichiro said, "but I want to do something else with my

94

life. I dunno, maybe after the army I'll be a lawyer, and from there become a politician."

"You?" Gary chuckled. "A senator? A governor? President?"

"Why not? I was born in this country, same as you."

True. But Gary couldn't entertain the thought of being anything but a farmer. A successful farmer but a farmer nonetheless. He knew plenty of local farmers who called the political shots over how the county and state was run, so being a farmer meant more than tending a patch of dirt. Maybe he needed to follow Ichiro's example and set his sights high.

***

Though summer kept its grip on Box Elder County, everyone waited for the first blast of cool weather to remind them that fall and the end of the harvest season was closing in. Soon the rhythm of the community would change. Students would return to school and the last of the migrant fruit pickers would surge through the area like an autumn storm.

To celebrate the end of the summer, the county farmers association sponsored a festival in Brigham City where families could forget their farm routines for a day.

Contests featuring tests of strength and athletic abilities were the crowd favorites. Gary competed on the track-and-field team from Freetown. On this day, it didn't matter if you were a Mormon or not, the only thing that mattered was your ability to beat the teams from the other towns. Perry was their main rival.

Gary and Ichiro jogged across the high school track toward the bleachers. Gary was still collecting his breath from having taken first place in the 880-yard run. Like the other competitors, he was dressed in an athletic top and shorts. They hurried off the track so that girls could begin the 440 relay.

The two boys were about to take seats on the bleachers when Mr. Williams approached. He owned the Freetown Tack and Seed Store and Gary had known him most of his life. In the last year, Gary had experienced a growth spurt and now stood appreciably taller than Mr. Williams. He was still getting used to looking down on people he had spent his youth looking up at.

Mr. Williams extended his hand. "Gary, congratulations on the win."

They shook hands and Gary replied, "Thanks."

"Now we need you to enter the mile," Mr. Williams added. "Nathaniel Brewster turned his ankle in the broad jump and can't run."

"I'm not a miler."

"Kid, you're a horse. If you win the mile then we'll tie Perry for awards."

Gary figured there was probably a bet among the civic leaders at stake. He looked across the bleachers to the other competitors. Among them were Arnold Evans and Fred Smith, both champions at their schools.

"I don't know, Mr. Williams."

Ichiro nudged Gary. "Go on. You can beat those guys."

Gary knew Ichiro wanted to race himself, but to keep out ringers, the rules allowed only local competitors to participate.

"I've already won my two races," Gary said. "I don't think it's fair that I race in everything."

"Nonsense," Mr. Williams replied. "What's not fair about it? Quit being so humble."

Loud cheers marked the end of the girls' 440 relay. An official blew his whistle for the runners to gather for the mile.

"It's now or never," Mr. Williams noted.

"That's all right." Gary sat on the bleacher bench.

The race official shouted for the runners to take their places. Then he said, "Get ready."

For a moment, Gary pictured himself getting into a runner's crouch.

The starting gun went off, the crowd roared, and the runners bolted down the oval track. Gary watched them take off like antelope, their long, bare legs flashing in the sun. They completed the first lap, then the second, the third, and the entire time Gary stewed with guilt that he had disappointed Freetown by not competing.

Though Fred Smith crossed the finish line with a wide lead, Gary thought, *I could've beaten him. I know I could've.*

With the completion of the mile race, the festival was all but over. Gary huddled with the Freetown team and was handed his two blue ribbons. Thankfully, Mr. Williams had not mentioned to anyone that he had asked Gary to run the mile so no one pestered him about it.

Gary and Ichiro made their way across the field to the dirt parking lot where families were loading the cars and trucks. He found his family gathered at their Ford sedan.

Chrissy was leaning against the car. She had her head down and was busy admiring the four blue ribbons pinned to her running shift. When she noticed Gary, she beamed. "First place, the 100-yard dash, the 220 hurdles, the 220-yard run, and the running broad jump. Maybe I'll be in the Olympics. What about you?

"The 440 and the 880." Having not run the mile, he was in no mood to brag.

Hans fit a picnic basket into the trunk of the sedan. He clapped a hand on Gary's shoulder and led him from the others. Once out of earshot, he said, "Son, I heard that Nathaniel Brewster dropped out of the mile and that Zeke Williams asked you to run. Why didn't you?"

So Mr. Williams had told someone else. "I didn't think it would've been sportsman-like."

"What do you mean?"

"I'm sure I could've won, but me winning all my races? That didn't seem fair."

"Where did you get that idea?"

"From you."

Hans smiled. "I think you misunderstood me. When you show up to compete, then compete fairly. Don't hold back on account of others not being good enough. May the best man win, right? If you're the best man, then race and win."

The words chafed Gary. Sometimes it hurt being the nice guy.

"Son, remember the Bible story in the Book of Matthew? About the servant who buried his talent?"

"Yeah."

"Then don't bury your talent. It does no one any good. Be it your money, your physical abilities, or your knowledge, put your talents to work."

His father's comments made Gary feel more sheepish, and he blushed.

Playfully, Hans tousled his hair. "Son, you now stand taller than me, but you'll never be too tall for me not to mess with your hair."

Gary laughed and pulled away.

Hans said, "Lesson learned, okay? When we get home make sure you and Ichiro get the truck and its load squared away. He and I are leaving first thing in the morning."

The reminder saddened Gary. Until this time, he had always

accompanied his father and Ichiro for the long drive to Anaheim. Now he was to remain behind and help his mother supervise the last harvest.

Hans said, "Son, you're practically a grown man. I need you to watch over your mom and Chrissy. It's time for us to move on with our responsibilities."

***

To get the most out of their crop, Gary's mother canned apples using her famed apple pie filling recipe. It was an industrial process that took over most of Gatlin house while Hans was off to California. The effort began with Mary hand-selecting apples. Gary and Chrissy would take turns washing the apples and turning the hand crank on the apple peeler-corer. As they worked, they collected the peels and cores in a slop bucket for the hogs. Afterwards they sliced the peeled apples, several baskets worth.

Mary picked one of the slices at random and bit into it. She offered the slice to Chrissy. "Taste it. See how sweet it is. That helps you judge how much sugar you'll need. What do you think?"

Chrissy chewed the slice and thought a moment. "About four and a half cups of sugar for each cup of corn starch?"

"That's seems about right," Mary answered.

Gary stoked the cast-iron stove while his mother and sister set out the many pots they needed. He boiled water in a large pot to sterilize the quart-sized glass jars and their lids. Using a set of wooden tongs, he plucked the jars and lids from the water to let them air out on a clean grate.

Chrissy stirred cinnamon, nutmeg, lemon juice, and pinches of salt into the syrup mix boiling in the pot. They all sweated from the heat radiating from the stove and the pots of steaming water, but their discomfort was offset by the enticing aroma of the canning syrup.

When the syrup was ready, they filled the jars in assembly-line fashion, first packing the apple slices into the jars, ladling in the syrup, using a knife to get rid of the bubbles, screwing on the lids, and finally arranging the filled glass jars on a rack in a boiling water bath. After taking the jars out of the bath and allowing them to cool, Gary crated and carried them to the cellar. At the end of the day they were all exhausted but immensely satisfied that the job was done. Mary rewarded Gary and Chrissy with the special apple turnovers she baked using leftover filling.

"Mom, these are delicious," Gary said appreciatively.

After a couple of days had passed, Mary inspected each jar to make sure the lids were flat, meaning that the apple filling had not spoiled. None had. She and Gary applied gummed labels—handwritten with *Mary Gatlin's Superior Apple Filling*—to each jar.

Mary sorted through her list of clients. In a county where women vied to make the best apple filling, hers was acknowledged as the favorite, and so she had many orders to deliver.

She wrote out an invoice and handed it to Gary. "Our first batch goes to the Good Eats Diner."

Gary read the invoice. He was to deliver twenty-four jars, enough to make a dozen or so large pies. He packed two cases, hefted them into the Ford sedan, and then drove to his destination on the highway near Freetown.

Along the way, he wondered if he'd run into Beverly Harris, whose family owned the diner. He knew she was sweet on him, and she was really pretty, and fun to be around. She took care of herself and in some ways reminded him of his sister, Chrissy, mostly in their stubbornness about getting things done. While he liked Beverly, what kept him from getting close to her was that she was a Mormon. Dating her would be like dating the Freetown tabernacle. There would be no end to gossip and speculation as to when he would convert. On the other hand, this being Utah, there was no possibility that she would leave the LDS church.

Gary hadn't considered himself religious, but now their differences in religion were becoming a moat that seemed to grow wider and deeper every time they met. He was hoping that she wouldn't be in the diner today because seeing her brought all kinds of mixed feelings about the two of them.

The Good-Eats Diner faced Highway 89 at the eastern edge of Freetown. The building was a simple clapboard structure with large, curtained windows. Gary stopped on the gravel highway shoulder that served as the parking lot.

He picked up one of the heavy cases and headed into the diner. With his arms full, he nudged the front door open. The first thing he noticed was the smell of fresh coffee. Though the diner was a Mormon establishment, Beverly's dad was a smart businessman and was eager to sell the forbidden java brew to the gentiles.

"Let me help you with that," Beverly said as she rushed from behind the cashier's counter. Her rosy cheeks dimpled with a smile. She wore a plain white apron over a loose yellow dress, neither of which could disguise her attractive form. A ponytail of auburn hair swept the back of her collar. "Set the crates right here." She patted the end of the counter. "I'll take them to the kitchen."

When Gary was close to her like this, the differences between them somehow didn't matter. All he wanted was to be this close, and even closer.

"What do we owe you?" she asked.

"It's right here." He pulled the invoice from his back pocket and flattened it on the counter. "There's one more case in my car. I'll be right back."

As he walked out, he wondered what to do next. His mother wasn't expecting him back right away so he could hang around the diner for a while. Talk with Beverly. Let her flirt with him.

Gary's thoughts immediately braked to a full stop. Outside, James Ballard stood beside the Gatlin sedan. This was the first time Gary had seen him since the Ballard family had returned to the area some time ago. Whatever hopes Gary had that there wasn't going to be trouble vanished when James sneered and taunted, "What brings you out here, kraut head?"

Gary raised his hands. "I've got no beef with you."

"But maybe I got a problem with you." James's lips curled into a menacing snarl. The sleeves of his work shirt were rolled to his elbows, showing off thick forearms. James enjoyed bullying others. He still bore a grudge from the time Gary had humiliated him years back.

"I've got to get something from my car and then I'll be on my way," Gary said.

James blocked his path. "But you'll still be here, at least till I'm through with you.

A dozen insults sluiced through Gary's mind, any of which would've have ignited this short-fused idiot, so it surprised him when James asked, "When are you guys gonna stop being sinners?"

That was rich--James Ballard of all people, the heartless oaf, wondering about other people's sin.

"You Gatlins are nothing but a bunch of apostates."

"That's a big word," Gary said, noting James's use of religion to justify picking a fight.

"What are you talkin' about?" James arched an eyebrow.

"Apostates. I'm surprised you know what it means."

"I know plenty of what it means. Non-believers. People like you."

"I'm not going to argue."

James bumped into him.

Gary backed away. "Don't do this." He knew that unless someone intervened, he and James were going to tangle. Gary wanted to glance back at the diner and hoped someone was watching, maybe even Beverly, and that they would come out and put a stop to the brawl before it started. But he did not dare look away from James. He knew how he fought. James like to initiate a battle with a one-two punch to the face, followed by an upper cut to the jaw. Few opponents could withstand the three hammer-like blows.

"Do what, you dirty gentile?" James growled, his arms tensing. "Dirty kraut."

"Just let me finish my work here and I'll go. Tell everyone that you beat me up, if that's what you need." He tried to circle around to the sedan.

James pushed Gary's shoulder and clenched his fists.

Gary brought his hands up, knowing a fight was inevitable. James led the attack with a left jab. Gary then launched a jujitsu counterattack, parrying the jab. As expected, James followed with his right. Gary grabbed James's wrist and pivoted under his arm. He hip-checked James and rolled him forward and over. James somersaulted and slammed onto his back.

Gary let go and retreated a couple of steps.

James lay stunned. Gasping, he blinked at the sky, and slowly peeled himself off the ground, bits of gravel clinging to his arms.

"Wow!" a man exclaimed.

Gary turned to see several diners crowding the entrance.

"I don't know what you did," the man said, "but you laid that guy out like a dead fish."

The other bystanders laughed.

James staggered to his feet. His eyes simmered with humiliation and hatred. He brushed dirt and gravel from his clothes and limped from the diner.

Gary retrieved the second case of jars, and knew this wouldn't be the end of things, that he'd run into James again.

CHAPTER TEN

March 1937

Gary drove his family's Ford sedan north on the highway. Beverly Harris sat in the front passenger's seat, a blanket wrapped over her winter coat for warmth

The Ford's headlamps lit up the road, now swallowed in darkness. Moonlight and the stars illuminated the surrounding landscape and highlighted patches of lingering snow. Gary was thankful for the good weather, as a spring blizzard wasn't uncommon at this time of year.

They were on the way home from a dance at the Box Elder High School in Brigham City. Beverly hummed contentedly, "Pennies from Heaven."

But Gary was far from content. In fact, his thoughts whirled like leaves in a tornado. He enjoyed Beverly's company and it excited him in pleasant ways when he was with her, especially when they were alone.

The source of his anxiety was what she'd said during the dance. He had brought refreshments from the canteen, a lemonade for her, and a Coca-Cola for himself.

Beverly regarded his drink, then said, smiling, "You had better enjoy those while you can."

He didn't need her to elaborate on what she meant, which was,

Once we're married, then you'll have to give up drinking Cokes and your other sinful, gentile ways.

Logically, Beverly and Gary dating—assuming it worked out—would lead to an engagement and then marriage. Why else continue courting?

He was dating her because he liked her, liked being with her, and spending time together was the best way to know one another. But what he was learning about her didn't sit well.

First, it was her presumption that they would get married. He turned this notion over in his mind, examining it every which way, and decided that he was fifty-fifty about the idea. In terms of her personality and appearance, she was a catch. There was no doubt she would make a wonderful companion.

However, it was the other thing, the religious thing, that doused his enthusiasm like ice water.

She assumed that a condition of any nuptials would be his conversion to the LDS faith. But Gary had grown up around these Mormons, and for him to join their church would be to renounce his own beliefs and heritage--in essence, proclaim that most everything about his past, including what his family had taught him, was wrong.

Gary gripped the steering wheel so hard that his hands cramped. He flexed his left hand, then repeated the gesture with his right.

"What's the matter?" Beverly asked.

Gary hesitated as he thought of an answer. "My hands are a little sore. From using a post-hole digger."

"Oh," she replied, and went back to humming the song.

Guilt stung him like a wasp. He had just lied, a white lie, but still a lie. That's what this relationship was forcing upon him. Lies.

What was so hard about telling Beverly the truth?

He glanced at her.

She beamed back at him. "What?"

"Did you have a good time tonight?" he asked, and was immediately exasperated with himself for being chicken, unable to say what was really on his mind.

She adjusted the blanket wrap. "Didn't you?"

He put his eyes back on the road. "Yeah, sure. Why not? It was fun."

She reached from under the blanket and clasped his forearm. Her touch made his heart leap with unexpected warmth.

She asked, "Are you going to see your Japanese friend this summer?"

"I'm hoping so but it depends on him. Graduating from high school brings a lot of changes."

One idea Gary had been kicking around was to visit Ichiro for an extended stay, and maybe during that time, when he was away from Beverly, hope that her interest in him might wane.

The highway passed through Freetown. They drove by the Good-Eats Diner, now dark and shuttered for the night. At the next street he turned off the road. Her home was up a ways, the front yard illuminated by a porch lamp.

Beverly sat up as they rolled to a halt by her mailbox. The curtains in the front window moved slightly. She smiled. "We're being watched." Light from the porch lamp silhouetted her profile. "You're awfully quiet."

"I guess I've got a lot on my mind."

"About what?"

About us, he wanted to say but couldn't admit it.

"I'm thinking about tomorrow," he said, stalling, lying. "About what I have to do to help my dad."

"Well, I had a great time tonight." She cracked the door open. He kept the motor running.

"Are you walking me to the door?"

"I need to get going."

"Okay," she said, her frustration noticeable. She pecked him on the cheek. "I hope your work tomorrow won't be too hard. See you Monday at school."

"Yeah. Of course."

Beverly climbed out of the car. She folded the blanket and dropped it on the passenger's seat. "G'night, Gary."

He watched her approach the front door of her home. It opened and he glimpsed Beverly's mother just inside. Beverly paused at the threshold. She turned and waved, then stepped inside, the door closing.

He breathed a sigh of relief. *Thank God tonight is over.* He did a U-turn and returned to the highway. Within a half hour he should be home and in bed.

A few minutes after leaving Freetown, something glittered in his rearview mirror. He let up on the gas and studied whatever it was.

Headlamps burst behind him, the lights bright as explosions. Blinded momentarily, he looked away and kept the Ford under control.

The car behind him swerved around to his left and cut him off. A beat-up Chevrolet Confederate coupe zoomed into the cone of light projected by his headlamps. The Chevy braked as abruptly as it had appeared. In a panic, Gary jammed on his brake to avoid a collision.

Tires shrieking, he skidded to a stop mere inches from the rear of the Chevy. The Ford rocked on its springs and the engine stalled. Gary gasped for breath, and he was certain that his heart had quit beating.

The driver's door of the Chevy opened, and into the bright light from the Ford's headlamps stepped Thomas Ballard. He looked bigger than what Gary remembered, a huge, menacing pack of muscle. From Thomas's expression—hard-set, thin-lipped—Gary knew there was going to be trouble. Any chance for a peaceful way out of this vanished when Thomas reached back into the Chevy and pulled out an ax handle. On the other side of the Chevy someone else slid out. No doubt it was James, Thomas's younger brother.

Gary depressed the clutch pedal and grabbed the gear-shift lever. He would throw the Ford in reverse and get away from these two. Then he remembered that the engine had died. By the time he got it restarted the Ballards would be on him.

He pushed his door open and jumped out, moving away from the Ford and the Ballards. Menacingly, ax handle at the ready, Thomas advanced while James circled behind the Ford.

Gary backed away, keeping his head pivoting from side to side so he could track both brothers. The temperature had dropped appreciably, and vapor from their breaths clouded the air.

The Ballards intended serious harm, of this Gary was certain.

"I want no trouble from you."

Thomas cradled the ax handle under one arm. With his free hand he fished a cigarette from inside his coat. Then he produced a match that he ignited with a snap of his thumbnail. In the flare of light from the match, his face appeared large, spectral, and his eyes were like twin red embers. He dropped the match, and when he stepped on it he staggered a bit as if drunk.

Thinking that Thomas was trying to distract him, Gary whirled around to make sure James kept his distance.

"Let's not do anything we'll regret," Gary said.

"I already regret that we didn't do this sooner," Thomas replied, slurring his words, the cigarette in his mouth, the end bouncing with every word. "So it's time we teach a lesson to a kraut gentile like you."

"Yeah, teach you a lesson," James repeated, finally speaking. "Too bad we can't do this in front of a crowd."

Dozens of jujitsu moves flashed through Gary's mind. One against two was tricky, especially when one opponent had a weapon. The question was, who to take out first? Thomas, because he had the ax handle? Or James, the easier target?

Gary had another ploy. Keep the Ballards talking. Let whatever rage that heated their blood cool down until they lost their enthusiasm. Or hope another car drove by and interrupted the confrontation. Looking to the left and right, he wanted to see the telltale glow of approaching headlights.

Nothing but darkness.

When Thomas puffed on his cigarette, the light from the ember brought his face out of the gloom. He slapped the thick end of the ax handle against his palm. "You know, Kaiser-lover boy, it's a good thing you're graduating soon. That way you won't have to show your face around here after we beat you good."

"Beat you good," James parroted.

Gary thought of another option. He could dash into the woods behind him and get lost in the darkness. But all he'd be doing is delaying this matter to another day. And it could mean that these two idiot brothers might take out their frustration by wrecking his car. No, better that he stand his ground.

Ballard tossed his cigarette and it bounced on the asphalt, spraying sparks. "Gatlin, I figured you were smarter than this. If I was facing a couple of tough guys like me and James, I'd be shaking in my boots. And here you are, like a bunny rabbit sitting on the railroad tracks, too stupid to see the train coming."

The brothers inched closer, like snakes.

"What do you want from me?" Gary asked, feeling the trap pinch tighter. "An apology? If that's what it takes, then I'm sorry."

Thomas shook his head. "That isn't gonna cut it. You wanna apologize, then get on your knees and beg."

"No!" Gary surprised himself with his defiance.

"Your choice," Thomas said. Grasping the ax handle in both hands, he cocked it over one shoulder like a bat and rushed forward.

Gary stepped to his left, out of Thomas's way as he swung the ax handle. But Thomas's footing was off and he teetered to one side.

Gary caught Thomas's wrists and the ax handle flailed in empty air. The move twisted Thomas's wrists and the ax handle flew from his grip. Gary kept stepping through, feeling Thomas lose his balance. Gary pivoted further. Thomas tipped over and his feet left the ground. He spun in midair, legs splaying, and his back slammed against the asphalt. Gary kept a firm grip on his arm.

He had to give Thomas credit. The oaf was as tough as a boar hog. No sooner had he hit the ground when he shouted, "Damn you, Gary, I'm gonna kill you."

The threat tripped a lever inside Gary. Thomas was not going to give up unless Gary took drastic measures. He straightened the arm and kicked Thomas in the armpit. *Hard.*

The move was not jujitsu and would've been condemned by any of his instructors. Still, Gary felt a grim satisfaction that no matter the circumstances, he would always best these two bullies.

But when Thomas howled in agony, Gary's triumph evaporated, and he immediately knew he'd gone too far.

"My arm!" Thomas shrieked, "I can't move my arm." His face withered in pain. Hugging his injured arm, he rolled onto his belly.

"What did you do?" James demanded.

For a second, Gary thought James was going for the ax handle, until he stepped over it and reached for his fallen brother.

Thomas rose to his knees. Eyes clenched tight, he remained curled in pain. When James tried to help him up, Thomas protested with tortured grunts.

Gary stepped away and tried not to give in to the shame of what he'd done. It was their fault, he assured himself. But a smaller voice debated, *You didn't have to kick him like that.*

James hoisted Thomas to his feet, and they shambled to their car. James helped his brother into the passenger's side, then climbed into the driver's seat. With a sharp rasp, the engine sputtered to life, and the Chevy rumbled off down the highway.

Fifteen minutes ago, Gary's biggest worry had been Beverly Harris. Now those concerns shrank to nothing. He had wanted this business between him and the Ballards to have ended once and for all.

Instead it had gotten much worse.

***

Gary drove home, his thoughts spinning in miserable confusion. He didn't know what to do, or what to disclose to his parents. Wordlessly, he entered the kitchen. His parents and sister were at the table, acting as if they always stayed up this late when it was obvious they were up because Gary had been out.

"After a date with Beverly I thought you'd be on cloud nine," his mother said. "But by the look on your face, it looks like you ran over a dog."

"It's not that," Gary muttered.

She lifted a hand towel from a plate, revealing a scrumptious-looking pie. "Hungry?"

Usually this late, he would've devoured every slice. But eating pie was the furthest thing from his mind.

His sister watched, a smile of curiosity tweaking her lips.

"Chrissy," their mother said, "go to bed."

Disappointed at missing whatever drama threatened to unfold, Chrissy whined, "But mom."

"Go to bed," Mary insisted.

Huffing in frustration, Chrissy pushed away from the table and disappeared to her room.

Hans offered a chair. "Have a seat, son. Tell us what's troubling you."

"Let me hang up my coat first." Once in his room, Gary closed the door. Though he was wide awake, he wanted to crawl into bed and pretend tonight had never happened.

Headlamps from an approaching car splashed across his window. This wasn't good news. The car halted and the doors squeaked open, first one, then another. Two sets of footfalls proceeded to the kitchen porch.

The knot in his throat hardened when a knock sounded at the door. He heard muffled voices, then his father called him.

Returning to the kitchen, Gary felt like he was walking to the gallows. Deputy Packard and another man stood between the table and the door. The deputy kept his hat on. The stranger had removed his, and with thick, gnarled fingers worried the brim. The man appeared about his dad's age. Gary recognized the stranger's ridged brow, the dark hooded eyes, the angular jaw, the thick shoulders, the heavy stance. He could only be Mr. Ballard, Thomas's father.

Gary swallowed to tamp down the queasiness.

Mary got up from the table and took her place beside Hans, who said, "Gary, this is Dexter Ballard."

Gary remained rooted in place, paralyzed with anguish and guilt.

He expected Ballard's eyes to be brooding with vengeance— Mormons could be a mean, unforgiving lot—but his expression remained humble and contrite.

"My son Thomas came home hurt bad," Ballard said, his voice low and unsettled. "So bad I was obliged to call the sheriff's office. Thomas said you and him got into a tussle, and when he was down, you dislocated his shoulder. I want to hear your side of the story."

Hans's jaw clenched as he stared at Gary.

After sighing to clear his mind, Gary related the fight as best he could remember.

Ballard interrupted, "Were they drinking?"

"Thomas acted tipsy, but I didn't see either one of them drink."

"I found beer bottles in their car," Packard said.

"And I found cigarettes in Thomas's coat," Ballard added. His face crumpled a bit, and his eyes grew moist. "I didn't raise my boys to be Jack Mormons, but kids today . . . It seems like the world's moving so fast that young people get swept up by the changes and forget what you've tried to teach them."

Gary wanted to say that he hadn't intended to hurt Thomas, but that wasn't true. At that instant in the fight he'd wanted Thomas to pay dearly for every insult he'd uttered against him and his family. But he had been wrong to hurt Thomas the way that he had.

"We'll help pay your medical bills," Mary said.

Ballard shook his head. "I'm touched by the offer, Mary, but we can manage. Maybe what happened was a blessing, at least that's one way to look at it. Maybe it was the Lord telling my boys that the world was done putting up with their nonsense."

"That also applies to you, Gary," Hans said, chastising his son.

Gary lowered his head and muttered, "Yes, sir."

"I guess I've taken enough of your time." Ballard replaced his hat. "Mary. Hans. I bid you good night."

Packard saluted by touching the brim of his hat and followed Ballard out the door.

No one in the kitchen moved as they listened to the deputy and Ballard get into their car and drive off. As the car motored into the distance, Gary felt the burden on his heart ease.

But the stern looks from his parents reminded him that he was still in hot water. Deep hot water.

"Honestly, Gary," his mother began, her voice sharp with re-crimination. "Brawling on the highway with a couple of drunks?"

"I didn't want to," he replied, head hanging, "but you heard what I told Mr. Ballard. Thomas and James forced me into it, gave me no choice."

Hans took in a deep breath and let it out. "All right, son. Consider it a lesson learned all the way around."

"Am I excused?" Gary asked, hopeful. He wanted time alone to brood.

"Take a chair. Your mother and I have something to discuss with you."

Hesitantly, Gary took a seat at the table. Apparently, the chiding wasn't over.

His mother left the kitchen for Hans's study and returned with several journals and a stack of letters in envelopes. Hans selected one of the journals, opened it, and showed the pages to Gary. They were sketches of apple grafts with accompanying captions.

"Can you translate these to Japanese?" Hans asked.

Gary perused the notes and flipped to other pages, all filled with similar annotations. "It will take time, but sure."

Hans spread the letters across the table. The envelopes bore American and foreign postmarks. Many of the inscriptions were in Japanese. "I asked Hajime if he could provide more advanced grafting techniques, and he referred me to these apple growers in Formosa."

Gary let his gaze wander from the journal, to the envelopes, and to his father. *What was this about?*

Hans pulled a letter from one of the envelopes and handed it to Gary. The top half of the text was in Kanji script, the bottom its English translation. The letter was from the Agricultural Commission in the Taihoku Prefecture, and it extended an invitation to Hans.

"You're going to Formosa?" Gary asked, incredulously.

"No, you are," Mary replied. "At least if you want to."

Gary's mind whirled. Only moments ago he felt as if his life was collapsing, and now his parents were expanding his world to encompass fantastic opportunities.

"W—What about college?"

"You can still enroll, but—" Hans tapped the letter— "what you'll learn in Formosa is more advanced than anything you could learn here in America."

In disbelief, Gary slumped against his chair.

"You won't be leaving for a while yet," Mary said. "The trip will cost money, and we have to save up."

All Gary's uncertainties about the future vanished, replaced by a great clarity that shone before him like a beacon. It was as if everything that he'd been doing, learning about farming, growing apples, the Japanese culture, and becoming not just conversant in Japanese but fluent, was now opening a road, an incredible opportunity, before him.

Gary looked at his parents, his eyes shining. "Oh my gosh, Mom, Dad! Yes! I'll do it."

PART II

CHAPTER ELEVEN

June 1939

Gary stood along the deck railing of the merchant steamer *Star of Jakarta* as it plowed into the harbor of Keelung. He gazed in awe at the rugged hills lush with green vegetation framed the harbor town. A gray haze drifted across the highest peaks that rose beyond the town. Dozens of small boats dotted the bay. On them, bare-chested men tossed fishing nets into the sapphire-blue water. Powered craft of all sizes and in all manner of repair chugged past, smoke from their exhaust stacks curling into the tranquil air.

Soon after he had boarded the steamer in Wilmington, Gary's initial sense of adventure had given way to stabbing self-doubt. Then, at their first stop in Oahu, his spirits lifted by the panorama before him. He became enchanted with the exotic splendor of the Pacific and was overcome by an awareness that a grand adventure awaited him. With every day heading west through the majestic ocean, his spirit fairly tingled with growing excitement at the opportunities in store for him.

One important fact he learned about Formosa was that it had been ceded to Japan after its victory in the Sino-Japanese War of 1894.

"And it's a good thing," his cabin mate, Arlo Bryant, had explained during one of their chats, "because the Japanese brought order and the rule of law to the island. That makes Formosa a safe place to do business. It's not quite modern but it's on its way."

Since Arlo's destination was Manila, he had disembarked there with the promise they'd keep in touch. No one else had taken his place, so Gary had the cabin all to himself. He appreciated the extra space and privacy but missed the long talks he'd had with the loquacious businessman.

The steamer slowed as it cruised past an island sheltering the entrance into the Keelung harbor. Gary lingered at the railing and tried to take in all that he saw, a kaleidoscope of color and activity. The ship turned toward a concrete wharf where other steamers were berthed. The docks were brimming with activity, busy as anthills with crews loading and unloading freight. Stacks of cargo crowded the wharf.

The *Star of Jakarta* eased into an empty slip, and Gary marveled how a ship of such size was able to so precisely and delicately nudge against the pier. Hawsers snaked from the ship's main deck, and scores of men on the dock engaged in a choreographed routine to secure the steamer into place.

Gary returned to his cabin and retrieved his luggage. He traveled as lightly as possible. He slung his leather portfolio over one shoulder and in each hand he hefted a suitcase.

Inside his coat he carried his unfinished letter to Beverly Harris. He had promised himself that he'd finish and mail the letter once he arrived in Formosa, but on the way here, he had had things to occupy his mind other than a woman he might never see again.

To safeguard his money, he stashed it in a money belt and in hidden pockets inside his jacket. Even so, he remained wary. A crewman had related his story of being stripped naked during a mugging and losing everything. But a contributing detail was that the crewman had gotten drunk in a bawdy house. Gary figured that if he stayed away from such rough places, he should be fine.

He queued in the line to disembark. A uniformed Japanese customs officer checked that departing passengers all carried passports. Gary really wanted to try his Japanese with a native speaker, but when it was his turn, the officer only glanced at his passport and waved him along.

Exiting the confines of the ship and emerging onto the gangplank, the broad expanse of open air became a dramatic metaphor of leaving one world for another. He took a deep breath of sea air and repositioned his fedora. Descending onto the wharf, he followed his fellow passengers toward a row of buildings.

He waited in another line leading to the customs office. A sign over the door announced in several languages, Japanese and English among them: *Welcome to the Protectorate of Formosa. Please have all necessary documents ready for inspection.*

The queue moved with assembly-line regularity toward a row of desks. Again, as on the ship, the customs officer didn't engage in chitchat. He took Gary's passport, pantomimed for Gary to remove his hat, compared him with the passport photo, then made an entry into a ledger. He stamped Gary's passport, returned it, and whisked him along.

Gary proceeded into an adjacent room filled with tables where passengers opened their luggage for inspection. His suitcases and portfolio were given cursory glances, and then he was waved on, inspection apparently satisfactory. After that, he was ushered outside onto a street choked with all manner of conveyances: trucks, bicycles, cars, men and women with handcarts, oxen-drawn wagons. Electric wires crisscrossed from pole to pole. The humid air became clammy and he feared what the weather would be like in the middle of summer. He caught snippets of conversation, in Japanese and Chinese, and other dialects he didn't recognize.

So much color and movement threatened to overwhelm him, except that thankfully he could read the many signs written in Kanji. His final destination was Taihoku, a brief train ride away. In short order he oriented himself and saw that the rail station was a mere three blocks away.

He hadn't gone ten feet when a barefoot teenage boy, mop-headed and wearing tattered clothes, emerged from the bustling crowd. Bright-eyed and brimming with energy, he gestured to Gary's suitcases and repeated in rapid-fire Japanese. *"Anata no sūtsukēsu o hakobu?"* Carry your bags?

Gary handed over one of the suitcases, but the boy insisted on carrying them both. Gary admired his hustle and gave the go-ahead. On the way to the station, the street became part urban thoroughfare and part menagerie. Chickens were constantly underfoot and wandered in and out of the busy traffic. Stray dogs idled in the shade, under carts and at the thresholds of open doors. Cats studied their domain from window perches. Fish swished in crowded buckets. Ducks quacked from inside wooden pens. A boy even younger than the one toting Gary's luggage herded a goat by smacking its hindquarters with a leafy branch.

The street had its own smell--rather, smells. A brown sludge that streamed along the gutters stank of raw sewage. Older women squatted next to braziers, grilling duck or fish and sending plumes of smoke into the air. Other times, he'd walk through clouds of perfumes wafting from sidewalk vendors. And everywhere it seemed, people were smoking tobacco.

As curious as he was about his surroundings and the amalgam of people, they were equally curious about him. He was the only blond, and taller by a head than anyone else around him, so he was as out of place as a pine tree in a flower garden. Apparently, *don't stare* was not a familiar admonition in this culture.

By the time they arrived at the train station, the teenager was having trouble hauling the luggage, and Gary took one of the suitcases from him. He studied the ticket windows and noticed that one also exchanged money. After converting ten dollars into yen, he bought a second-class ticket for the next train to Taihoku, which was leaving in a few minutes. Not sure how much to tip his young porter, Gary decided to pay him half of what the ticket had cost. The boy took the coins, grinning and bowing enthusiastically before turning around and disappearing out of the station.

A conductor shouted in Japanese and Chinese for people to board the train. Gary settled into a smoke-filled car, across the aisle from where two local businessmen in rumpled suits were holding court. They welcomed Gary with circumspect nods and went back to chatting in Chinese and puffing on their cigarettes.

For as crowded as Keelung was, there wasn't much to the port town. A few minutes after pulling away from the station, the train entered a wooded landscape strewn across steep, rocky slopes. They plunged into a tunnel, and on the other side the hills fell away and the vista stretched out over terraced slopes and wide swampy fields.

The ocean came back into view and the train ran parallel to an extensive concrete wall that hemmed a broad river basin clustered with small boats. The train rattled and jolted, then the engineer blew its whistle as it clattered through a neighborhood of makeshift dwellings piled on top of one another. The scene blurred past. Laundry hung in haphazard streamers. Chickens and cats prowled the uneven rooftops. He traded fleeting glances with down-and-out folks watching the train.

The train chugged into a covered station. Moments later he was out on the walkway. If Keelung had seemed immersive and exotic, Taihoku was that, times ten. Gary gazed about in bewilderment at the contrast between the old and the new.

Not surprisingly, another teenage boy appeared, also eager to carry luggage. Gary said in Japanese, "I'll let you help, provided you can tell me where to find my hotel, the Ivory Paradise."

The boy was startled by Gary's fluent use of the language. Then he answered, "It is not far," waving his hand.

Gary pointed to one of his suitcases. "You take that one. Let's go."

After walking a short distance, he spotted the Ivory Paradise just where the boy said it would be. The hotel was easy enough to identify—four stories tall, painted off-white, and with its name carved in English on the façade above the entrance. The walkway was wide enough to allow taxis to veer off the street and park under the front awning.

Gary spied something else that commanded his attention. At the corner of the street stood a small wooden shed. The sides were propped up to allow shade, and inside an older woman tended to baskets of apples stacked on shelves. A sandwich sign in front of the shed said *Fresh Fruit* in Japanese and Chinese and was decorated with crude paintings of apples, pears, and peaches.

A fruit stand in the middle of the city! Gary couldn't help but turn away from the hotel to investigate. He pulled a coin from his pocket, paid the boy, and dismissed him.

A couple of soldiers in military uniforms strolled by the stand. They each casually plucked an apple from a basket and continued on their way, munching the fruit.

The woman in the stand shouted, "Hey! Those are not free! You take, you pay!"

One of the soldiers looked back at her and smirked.

Their reaction infuriated Gary. Perhaps he should've held his tongue—after all, he hadn't been in this country a day—but he couldn't help himself. Everything he'd been taught in his home, and in the Mitsui's, told him that the soldiers were taking advantage of this poor woman.

"Excuse me," he announced in a sharp voice.

The soldiers halted abruptly and stared at him, astonished by his height and foreign appearance. Moreover, who was this strange giant speaking their language?

"You took that woman's property without paying," he explained. "What gives you that right?"

Both soldiers gaped at him, half-chewed apple in their open mouths.

"You bring dishonor to your uniform."

The comment was like a slap to their cheeks. The men blushed and gulped down what they had chewed.

"Pay what you owe and save some face."

The soldiers bowed stiffly. "*Hai. Hai.*"

They returned to the stand, handed the woman some coins, then departed, walking briskly past Gary, not looking at him.

Gary said to the woman, "My apologies."

Her hair was gathered in a red scarf and her sturdy limbs protruded from a baggy shift. Like everyone else here, she was dark-complexioned, and short, maybe all of five feet tall. But there was nothing small about her attitude. She gave him the onceover as if she couldn't believe what her eyes were telling her. "Who are you, tall stranger?"

Gary tipped his hat. "Gary Gatlin, from Freetown, Utah."

"Uuu-tah?" she replied.

"The United States of America."

"Ah." Her head tipped in recognition. "You are American." She eyed him. "Your Japanese is very good."

"I had a good teacher."

"What brings you to Formosa?"

He picked up an apple. "This. At home my family has an apple orchard. I'm here to learn from your farmers."

"Then you're in luck," she said. "Taste it. It is the best you'll find anywhere."

Gary bit into the apple. It was crisp and succulent and delicious. "So it is." He wiped juice dribbling down his chin. "And could I have the pleasure of your name?"

She bowed. "Nori Chan."

He bowed in return. "Chan? You are Chinese?"

"Yes and no. I'm descended from the original peoples of Formosa, but when China took over the island many generations ago, we adopted their names. Our new masters, the Japanese, consider us Chinese, so Chinese is what I am."

Gary offered a coin for the apple.

She refused with a shake of her head. "It is my gift." She considered his luggage. "You just arrived."

"I have." He pointed over her shoulder to the hotel. "For now, I'm staying there."

"Well," she snorted, "the Ivory Palace appears nice enough, but you won't get much sleep with all the racket from the whores."

Taken aback, Gary replied, "I didn't realize it was that kind of a place."

"No worse than any other along this street that caters to foreign tourists. How long do you intend to stay in Formosa?"

"I'm not sure. A few months at least."

"Then I recommend the Silver Crane Hostel in the Daitatei Bund. It's the Chinese quarter of the city. Not only are the rates cheaper, but the place is as clean and safe as anywhere else in Taihoku."

"The Silver Crane it is." Gary picked up his bags. "Before I go, can you tell me how to get to the Agricultural Commission?"

Nori furrowed her brow. "Why do you want to go there?"

"I want to ask about farming here on Formosa."

She laughed. "They're a bunch of bureaucrats. Experts at taking tea breaks, but farming? Not so much."

"Then what do you suggest?" he asked.

"Depends on what you want to know. I could introduce you to my wholesalers, and from them get an introduction to an orchard grower."

"That would be great! How about tomorrow? I'd make it worth your while."

"I'll have to get someone to watch my stand, but it can be done." Nori smiled warmly. "Tomorrow then, first thing in the morning? Seven?"

"Seven it is."

***

Gary hired a taxi to the Silver Crane Hostel. The Daitatei Bund was a distinctly Chinese enclave and proudly so. Most of the signs were in Chinese, with Kanji script added seemingly as an afterthought. Many people wore traditional Chinese costume, as if to flaunt their reluctance to assimilate into Japanese ways.

The Silver Crane was a three-story building with its back to the seawall. He rented a room on the third floor, having been told that the higher up your room is, the less likely that a thief will sneak in.

129

He tried out the small bed, thankful it was long enough for him to lie down without his head or feet hanging off one end. There was also a writing desk by the window, an armoire with a lock, a chest of drawers, a washstand with mirror, and electricity—one overheard bulb and a lamp beside the bed. A set of narrow louvered doors opened to a tiny balcony. The community bathroom was down the hall. His room looked well kept, and when he ran a finger along the windowsill he was pleasantly surprised that he didn't pick up a trace of dust.

Gary was unpacking when someone knocked on his door. Since he had just arrived he had no idea who had come to call.

He opened the door. The visitor was almost as tall as he, and with his pale gray eyes and ruddy features, was almost surely another Westerner. Silver tinted his wavy auburn hair. A few wrinkles lined the edges of his square features, and from this Gary guessed the stranger was maybe in his early forties. The wide shoulders on his muscular frame indicated he was a man in good condition.

The man extended his hand. "Percival Corbett."

"Gary Gatlin."

"It's a pleasure." Percival's grip was callused and firm. "Just wanted to say welcome to the neighborhood. I'm down the hall in room three-twelve." His accent was distinctly British, but he might have been Australian.

Gary waved him in and shut the door.

Percival slipped a packet of cigarettes from his shirt pocket. He shook out a couple in offering.

Gary said, "No thanks, I don't smoke."

Percival took one for himself and pocketed the rest.

Gary pointed to the balcony doors. "If you'd like to smoke, why don't we chat out there?"

On his way across the room, Percival scoped out the space, which Gary found curious. "What brings you to Formosa?" Percival asked in Japanese, as if testing Gary.

Gary answered similarly, "Business."

"What kind of business?"

Surprised at the stranger's intrusion, he said cautiously, "You're kind of nosy, aren't you?"

Percival pursed his lips, then said in English, "Right you are. Where are my manners? I hail from Portsmouth, England. A proud subject of the Crown." Percival saluted with the cigarette. "I broker light machinery. Drill presses. Saws for lumber mills. That sort of thing."

Reaching the balcony doors, he unlocked them and stepped outside. He struck a match on the doorjamb and lit his cigarette. "Your turn. What brings you to Formosa, Yank?"

"I'm here to learn what I can about Japanese farming techniques." Gary explained the task his family had given him.

"Ah." Percival let out a jet of smoke. "If you're carrying money, and I assume you are, let me recommend a couple of banks where you should open an account to safeguard your funds. The Japanese government bends over backward to ensure a stable banking system, otherwise who would invest?"

"I appreciate the advice."

"One more thing," Percival said, "considering our common heritage."

"I'm all ears."

"This isn't America. Nor is it Europe. It is the Orient. Both compelling and strange. Alluring and dangerous. Keep that in mind."

CHAPTER TWELVE

June 1939

At seven in the morning, Gary arrived at Nori Chan's fruit stand. She was waiting for him, and they exchanged good mornings.

"I brought you something." She pulled a small book from the cloth bag hanging at her side and handed the book to Gary. He flipped through its pages. It was a primer to teach children Chinese and Japanese. "While business is done in Japanese," she said, "most people speak Chinese."

"Thank you. I appreciate the thought." He tucked the book into his portfolio slung over one shoulder.

Nori introduced her cousin Jhai Chan, who would watch the fruit stand while they were gone. Within a few minutes they were at the train station, which at this time of the morning was crowded with commuters and vendors. Gary bought tickets and they settled into a car already occupied with other travelers, many of whom seemed startled by Gary's appearance. He was still getting used to being gawked at because of his blond hair and conspicuous height. The air on the train was hazy with cigarette smoke, and Gary observed that most of the men he had seen were smokers.

Nori and Gary sat next to each other. As the train proceeded from the station, she quizzed him about his business in Formosa and how he came to be so fluent in Japanese.

"When I was five," Gary began, "my father took me with him to Anaheim."

Nori shrugged, indicating she had no idea what place he was talking about.

"In California," he explained.

"Ah, yes. Hollywood."

He chuckled. "Close enough." He told her about how he had met the Mitsuis, then became good friends with Ichiro, and at his father's insistence, learned Japanese.

"Which you've done well," Nori replied. "I'm impressed by your perseverance. When you learn what you can about farming here, what then?"

"I'll return home and apply the lessons on my family's farm. After that, I'm sure I'll enroll in a university to get my academic credentials."

"How old are you, Gary?"

"I'm twenty."

"You're very dedicated. Most men I know your age barely have an idea what they want to do in life."

"I can only speak for myself."

Nori narrowed her eyes at him.

"What are you thinking?" he asked.

"You're not married, are you?"

He splayed the fingers of his left hand to show that he didn't wear a wedding ring. "No."

"Are you betrothed?"

"No, I'm not engaged. There was a woman I was interested in, but things didn't work out."

"What did your parents say?"

"There wasn't much for them to say. It was my decision."

"But your families," she asked, "didn't they object?"

Gary considered her question. "I think I understand your confusion. In my country, marriages are not arranged. It's up to the couple to decide on their own if they want to marry."

Nori arched an eyebrow. "That seems unwise. Young people should let their elders guide them in such matters."

Gary gave her a disarming smile. "Different peoples, different customs."

She smiled back. "Maybe fortune has plans of its own. You may yet meet a woman here in Formosa. The island is full of girls who are both smart and beautiful."

He wagged his finger at her. "Don't you get any ideas about matchmaking. I'm strictly here on business."

***

Arriving in Keelung, they left the train and Nori escorted Gary to the wharf. They passed row after row of warehouses, the area teeming with trucks and carts loaded with bananas, pineapples, peaches, and plums. The aroma from so much fruit brought back memories of harvest season back in Utah.

At one warehouse the bay doors were open, and inside, teenage girls sat around a large tray piled with leaves. Nori explained that they were sorting tea leaves for packing, and that much of the tea from Formosa was shipped to America.

Several warehouses over, Nori led Gary through a door marked, *Majestic Fruit Wholesalers and Exporters.* She said, "There is where I buy my fruit."

A clerk wearing glasses was at a desk, thumbing through stacks of papers. He looked up, and when he saw who had entered, grinned and bowed. "Nori Chan, what brings you here?"

She introduced Gary and added, "I brought him here hoping to meet Akito Saito."

"He just left," the clerk replied, and glanced at a wall clock. "But he should return within an hour."

"That would give us time to tour the rest of the wharf," Gary said.

"Please, ask Akito to wait for us," Nori said to the clerk.

She and Gary proceeded to the docks where stevedores stacked crates onto cargo nets. They worked against a backdrop of huge freighters that seemed as imposing as mountains. Other stevedores climbed up gangplanks, burdened with crates on their backs like hod carriers.

They strolled along the wharf, watching with fascination. It wasn't only fruit that was loaded onto the ships. Gary noticed stacks of pipe and reels of wire and cable. At another ship, its crane unloaded a net full of scrap metal that it dumped into an awaiting truck.

I see how it works, he thought, admiringly. The Japanese imported scrap metal they converted into finished goods. Not only were they inventive farmers, they were also keen industrialists.

Midway down the docks, he and Nori reached a wire fence where armed sailors guarded a gate.

"This is as far as we can go," Nori cautioned.

Gary studied what lay on the other side of the fence. Army trucks towed cannon mounted on wheels, which men unhitched and lined up. Another group of men attached the guns to slings, then hooked them to a crane that swung them onto a freighter. Gary counted twenty-five cannon, and trucks brought still more.

The guns looked brand new, and he surmised that civilian industrial products were not the only output of Japanese factories on the island.

Soldiers in formation marched toward him. Someone barked commands. The formation halted, then turned. More orders were barked, and the formation dissolved into a line of men ascending a gangplank onto a second freighter.

Behind that freighter, a warship bristling with guns floated where it was tied to the dock. He didn't know much about naval vessels but guessed, by its size, that the ship was a cruiser.

Nori tugged at Gary's sleeve. "Let's not linger much longer."

"This is quite the busy military port."

"It's best to pretend that you don't notice," said Nori. "The Japanese can be lenient on many things to accommodate our customs, but what they can't abide is curiosity about their military affairs."

Gary checked his watch. "I think your friend Akito Saito should be back at the warehouse."

When they returned to the warehouse a wiry man was sitting at the office table, and he jumped to his feet when they entered. He hurried to Nori and Gary. "You are the American," he took Gary's hand, "the clerk told me about you."

Gary said, "You must be Akito Saito."

"I am honored, sir." Akito appeared about Gary's father age, with the same wrinkles and leathered complexion brought on by years of toiling outside.

"Please," Gary replied, "Not sir. I'd rather you called me Gary, especially given that you are my elder."

Akito's grip was callused and strong, his fingers scarred much like those of Gary's father. Despite these old injuries, Akito's dark eyes sparkled with energy and mirth as if he were always looking for the positive in life. He gave Gary's shoulder a friendly shake. "So strong, too. Nori, where did you find him?"

She explained how they met, and embellished the recollection with the way he had reprimanded the soldiers who had stolen her apples.

He sized up Gary again. "You're like one of those heroic cowboys in your movies."

Gary shook his head, embarrassed by the compliment. "I only did what I thought was right."

"We need more like you in this world," Akito replied. He gestured that Nori and Gary accompany him to an adjoining bay. Two men unloaded crates from a truck backed against a long table. While Akito wore a simple plaid shirt and khaki trousers, these men toiled bare-chested and wore something that resembled a cross between a loincloth and shorts.

Akito plucked a cluster of small yellow fruit from one of the crates. "This is fruit from my farm. Are you familiar with these?" he asked. "Here we call them Japanese plums."

"Back home we call them loquats," Gary answered. "They're grown as ornamental plants."

"Really?" Akito winced in surprise. "You've never eaten them?"

"I can't say that I have."

Akito unfolded the blade of a pocketknife and sliced into one of the loquats. He parted the fruit to reveal yellow flesh and a pit like that of an apricot. "Try it."

Gary took the loquat and bit into it. He expected a bitter tanginess but the flavor was a blend of apricot, cherry, and plum. He savored the taste and ate the entire fruit. "Wow! I'm surprised we don't grow these. I'll bet they make great preserves and pie filling."

"What is pie?" Nori asked.

Gary realized that since arriving on Formosa he hadn't seen any bakers or a mention of wheat. "It's a pastry with a fruit filling."

"Hmm...sounds interesting," she commented, hesitantly. "Perhaps one day I'll try a pie."

"Akito," Gary said, "Nori sells your apples, which I found delicious. If possible, I'd like to visit your orchards."

Akito sucked his teeth and looked about as he mulled Gary's proposal. "My farm is outside the town of Douliu, in the prefecture south of Taihoku. It's a half day by train."

"I have plenty of time."

Akito pulled a small writing pad from his shirt pocket. "I have much work today." He scribbled into the pad and tore off the page. "However, the day after tomorrow, I'll be at my farm and can show you around." He handed the page to Gary. "Here are the directions to my place."

"I might have to spend the night," Gary said. "Are there accommodations? And I'll need a way to get around."

"There is a boarding house across the street from the train station in Douliu. When you get there, ask around. I'm sure you'll find a car for hire. Somebody is always looking to make extra money." Akito bowed. "Now, if you will excuse me, I must return to work."

***

Colonel Eiji Kagawa stepped from his staff car and climbed the steps of a palatial five-story building. He strode toward the Office of the Governor-General, Admiral Izawa Yoshida, who commander of the administrative district of Taihoku. The guards in dress uniform on either side of the entrance snapped to attention and saluted with their rifles. Inside, Kagawa halted by the desk where the duty officer—a navy lieutenant—checked his name against the roster of scheduled guests.

"I don't see your name, Colonel Kagawa," the duty officer said.

Kagawa withdrew a note from inside his uniform coat and handed it over.

The duty officer inspected the note, and immediately recognized its letterhead as that of the governor-general. He picked up the receiver of his desk phone and placed a call. When someone on the other end answered, the duty officer conversed in guarded whispers. He returned the receiver to its cradle and stood. "My apologies, Colonel. I did not realize the urgency of your visit." Bowing, he handed the note back to Kagawa. "The governor-general is expecting you."

Accepting the note with a curt nod, Kagawa folded and returned it to his coat pocket. He proceeded through the foyer and turned left at the main corridor. The interior was decorated with prints and photographs commemorating the Meiji Period, the time of Japan's modernization and the emperor's return to the throne. Interspersed among those artifacts were framed examples of headdresses and textiles from local indigenous craftsmen. To Kagawa, the interior looked more like a museum than a formal office building, but the governor-general had to represent all the peoples of the Formosa colony.

At the end of the corridor, a navy commander in dress whites waited in front of the double doors. "Colonel Kagawa, the governor-general will see you now."

Kagawa kept his resolute pace. The commander opened the doors with a dramatic flourish and announced Kagawa's arrival.

When Kagawa stepped past, the officer bowed and backed over the threshold, closing the doors as he did so.

The governor-general, Admiral Yoshida, watched Kagawa from behind an enormous, imposing fortress of a desk. Yoshida's eyes were set in thin slits within a wide, fleshy face, crowned by a pate cropped to a buzz cut. To Kagawa, the admiral reminded him of a bulldog. He looked as stiff as the collar of his uniform, plainly decorated with a plethora of ribbons and his badge as Governor-General. The windows were open and electric fans circulated the air.

Kagawa marched over the carpet runner that led across the polished floor. He stopped short of the desk with a snap of his boot heels. "Colonel Kagawa reporting as ordered."

Yoshida waited a moment before responding. His gaze dropped to a folder on his desk, which he opened. He picked up the memorandum Kagawa had submitted to him, marked *Urgent*.

As the deputy head of the Protectorate's Bureau of Army Counterintelligence, it was Kagawa's job to detect and contain espionage. He had been in Yoshida's presence before, but this was the first time he had been granted a private audience. Obviously, the admiral understood the seriousness of the matter Kagawa had brought to his attention.

Yoshida opened an alabaster box on his desk and withdrew a cigarette. He nodded to the box, *take one*, which Kagawa did. The colonel pulled a brass trench lighter from his pocket and thumbed the flint. The wick caught and he leaned across the desk to light Yoshida's cigarette, then lit his own. The admiral pointed to a leather armchair and Kagawa sat.

Yoshida waved the memo. "This is most intriguing, Colonel Kagawa." He exhaled a plume of smoke. "I'd like you to elaborate in more detail."

Kagawa rested his cigarette in the ashtray built into one arm of his chair. Truthfully, he considered smoking a filthy habit, but he indulged to placate his military superiors. "Yesterday I was at the Ivory Paradise Hotel, concluding a meeting with the German military attaché." He paused to let the admiral ask about the attaché, but when he didn't, Kagawa continued. "When I was on my way out the hotel I witnessed the incident mentioned in the memorandum."

Yoshida drew another puff.

"Two of our soldiers had taken apples from a corner fruit stand, and they had done so without paying. The woman who owned the fruit stand berated them, but they ignored her protests. Then a tall Westerner approached the soldiers and admonished them for stealing the fruit."

Yoshida set his elbows on the desk and riveted his gaze on Kagawa. "In Japanese?"

"In very good Japanese. And most disturbing, the manner in which he castigated the soldiers showed that he was quite familiar with our culture."

Yoshida tapped his cigarette into a desk ashtray. "And the soldiers?"

"They were most ashamed, naturally, for the foreigner was correct. They paid what they owed and then proceeded from the location."

"Did you get their names?"

"The soldiers?"

"Yes." Kagawa reached for the memo pad tucked inside his coat.

"I don't need to know their names," Yoshida said. "However, send letters of reprimand to their precinct captain. But nothing too harsh. It was their foolishness that brought this foreigner to your attention, no?"

"Yes, Admiral, that is correct."

"What else can you tell me about this foreigner?"

"Only that he was tall, as Westerners are. Blond. A young man in his early twenties. Athletic."

"His name? Where is he from? What is his business on Formosa? Where is he staying?"

"That's what I need to find out, Admiral."

"What about the owner of the fruit stand?"

"Her name is Nori Chan, a local Chinese woman who's run that stand for years. From what the city police know, there's nothing suspicious about her."

Yoshida turned his gaze back to Kagawa's memorandum. "Colonel, let's jump to the next step. You obviously didn't bring this to my attention unless you have serious concerns."

"That is correct, Admiral. What I recommend is that you allow me to open a special dossier on this mysterious stranger."

"In your position in counterintelligence, you don't need my permission to do so."

"True, but a special dossier authorized by your office would give me extralegal powers to act with greater dispatch. The sooner we find out as much as we can about this Westerner and his business here, the better for all of us."

"Consider it done, Colonel." Yoshida stubbed the butt of his cigarette into the ashtray and cleared his throat. He folded his hands on the desk, indicating that the meeting was adjourned. "Remember that he remains a foreign national. We must tread carefully to avoid an international incident."

"Which is why I asked for extralegal powers, Admiral." Kagawa rose to his feet and stood at attention. "If I have to act with extreme measures, I will do so efficiently and quietly."

CHAPTER THIRTEEN

June 1939

That afternoon, shortly after meeting with Akito Saito, Gary returned to Taihoku. Nori Chan stayed in Keelung, since her cousin was minding the fruit stand and this gave her a day off.

Back in the Daitatei Bund, Gary bought a street map and familiarized himself with his surroundings. His first order of business was to find a bank to deposit his money for safekeeping. Among other places of note, the map indicated the location of the American Consulate, a mile due east of the Silver Crane Hostel. Surprised that he hadn't thought of it sooner, he decided to visit the consulate. The walk took him through the densely packed center of the city, past a large market, a traffic circle swirling with conveyances old and new, and a couple of schools set within well-tended grounds.

The consulate was a nondescript square building that stood alongside the tree-lined main thoroughfare running north-south. A guard at the entrance, a US Marine in a khaki uniform with corporal's stripes, sat behind a receptionist's desk. The marine reacted with a double-take when he saw Gary.

"Hello there," Gary announced, amused that even a fellow American was startled by his tall, blond appearance. "I'm new in town." He set his passport on the desk. "Gary Gatlin, Freetown, Utah."

The marine flipped through Gary's passport and logged the visit in a ledger. Returning the passport, he asked, "What do you need?"

"I'm just stopping by to say hello."

"In that case, hold on." The marine picked up the desk phone and asked for Miss Fletcher.

A moment later, a door at the back of the foyer opened and a primly dressed woman in her middle thirties stepped out. She headed straight to the desk. "Miss Blanche Fletcher. I'm the secretary to Mr. Maurice Sinclair, the senior consulate to Formosa."

"How do you do, Miss Fletcher," Gary replied. "Gary Gatlin."

Gary explained his business. Miss Fletcher replied by speaking a phrase in Chinese. Gary shook his head to indicate he didn't understand.

She switched to Japanese. "I hope you know at least enough Japanese to get by."

He answered in kind: "Perhaps more than enough."

Miss Fletcher blinked in astonishment. She replied in Japanese, "Quite good. You should do fine."

Switching back to English, Gary said, "My priority at the moment is to find a trustworthy bank."

Miss Fletcher gestured for his map. She took it and flattened it on the desk, and after uncapping a fountain pen circled several places. "I recommend any of these banks. Since your business is farming, I also could have you speak with Mr. Donald Anderson, our agricultural affairs representative. Unfortunately, he and Mr. Sinclair are out today."

"That's quite all right. I've already made arrangements to visit a farm."

"Have you contacted your family?" Miss Fletcher asked. "Told them you're here safe?"

When Gary said that he hadn't, she asked the Marine guard to give him a telegram transmittal form. "As a courtesy to you, Mr. Gatlin. We can also handle your mail correspondence if you like. Corporal Jensen will give you the routing number to the consulate. I can't guarantee that letters will get here any faster but at least they won't get lost along the way."

"Whatever you suggest," Gary said appreciatively.

"One more thing," she continued. "That you show no interest in Japanese military activity while you're here, which may be difficult because there's quite a bit of it."

"So I've seen."

"The governor-general of Formosa has been exceptionally hospitable to foreigners. However, back in Japan, pretty much all foreigners, even missionaries, have been expelled from the home islands. So watch your step. If you get into trouble, don't hesitate to contact us, but in any case do not provoke our Japanese hosts."

"I'm here to learn how to grow fruit, that's all."

"Good." She capped her pen. "I'm happy to have met you, Mr. Gatlin. Now if you will excuse me, I have other duties."

She left Gary to complete the telegram. He addressed it to his family farm in Freetown:

Arrived in Formosa. Safe. All is well. STOP
People are gracious. Touring apple orchard. STOP
Send letters to American Consulate - Formosa.
Routing number 89-167243 STOP
Gary

***

Afterwards, Gary opened an account in the Yamatochō Industrial Bank, which was conveniently close to the main railroad terminal. The manager, Mr. Shitaba seemed honored that Gary had sought him out.

Mindful that he'd been cautioned by both Nori Chan and Miss Fletcher to take no notice of the Japanese military, it proved a challenging task. The center of town was packed with administrative buildings staffed and guarded by soldiers and sailors in a variety of uniforms, and every other block seemed to be occupied by military barracks or a motor pool.

The next morning, Gary caught the train heading south from Taihoku. He stowed his briefcase and traveling bag under a bench. Among his fellow travelers were two portly Chinese men in business suits, one in gray, the other in blue. The train rumbled out of the city across levees built over a series of rice paddies.

A shadow flashed across the car's windows and Gary looked outside. A large two-engine airplane roared low overhead, its red circle insignia blazoned conspicuously under the wing tips and along the fuselage. The airplane banked slightly and three more of a similar type soared into view. In the distance, the sun glinted across a formation of smaller aircraft, fighter planes he guessed. The airplanes appeared to be circling a large airfield about a mile and a half away. So much for ignoring the Japanese military presence.

The tracks ran parallel to the Tamsui River, which unraveled into shallow streams that meandered along the muddy river basin. The basin widened and narrowed as it wound through the rugged mountains that dominated the valley.

The train slowed as it entered a town. Smoke plumed from factory stacks. Another train rolled beside Gary's, railcar after railcar piled with freshly mined coal.

The trip fell into a pattern. In the wide, flat areas, rice paddies adjoined the rail tracks, and farther out, orchards covered the rolling hills. Beyond them, terraced farms layered the lower elevations of the mountains. Other times, the train passed beside marshaling yards where military trucks and artillery had been lashed to flatcars.

As they moved along, Gary was lost in a daydream when the train suddenly lurched, decelerating abruptly, whistle shrieking. Everyone in his car reached for the closest handhold to avoid being pitched to the floor. From the nearby cars he heard items crashing and people cursing in protest.

As the train screeched to a stop, Gary and his two companions regained their balance. The one in the blue suit asked, "Why are we stopping?" He pulled a window fully open and stuck his head out.

Curious like everyone else, Gary peered out another window. He expected that a wreck or a stalled truck might have obstructed the track ahead. Soldiers flanked the train. The men wore field uniforms and carried rifles at the ready, bayonets fixed.

Blue Suit yelled to the soldiers, "What's going on?"

A soldier hollered back, "Brigands."

"They attack the train?"

"Never you mind," a gruff voice answered. "Get your head back inside the train before we use your fat face for target practice."

The Chinese men pulled in quickly from the windows and returned to their benches.

"Brigands?" Gray Suit asked worriedly. "Bandits are in the area?"

"They raid the villages and steal what they can," Blue Suit explained. "Sometimes they ambush the roads and the trains."

Bandits? Though they were surrounded by soldiers and guns, Gary didn't sense any danger; in fact, he felt a thrill as though he were in the middle of a stagecoach holdup in the Wild West.

The soldiers closed upon the train. He heard a man barking orders and boots tramping into his railcar. A stern-faced soldier, obviously an officer because of his tall boots and Sam Browne belt with holstered pistol, marched from the vestibule. "Your identity papers." He glared at Gary.

Everyone offered their identification cards, which the officer only glanced at. However, he snatched Gary's passport and studied it for a moment, before thrusting it back at Gary. The officer continued down the aisle.

The two Chinese men lit cigarettes and puffed nervously. Commotion outside piqued Gary's attention. When he moved closer to the window, Blue Suit tugged at his sleeve and shook his head, cautioning Gary not to show any interest.

From this angle, Gary could see toward the back end of the train. Men and women in peasant clothes, most of them obviously poor, were being herded from the train at bayonet point. Soldiers dumped their baskets and bags on the ground, scattering the contents. Gary watched, perplexed at this harsh treatment.

The locomotive whistle blew, and the train began to crawl forward. The last scene Gary observed was of the peasant men grouped together and forced to their knees, hands behind their heads. Were these bandits, he wondered, or simply locals being rounded up? Whatever it was, he found it all very disturbing and foreign to him.

As the train gained speed, the mood in the car relaxed somewhat. Blue Suit and Gray Suit cracked jokes and chain-smoked as they chugged along. Gary looked at his watch and wondered about the train's progress.

Gazing out the window, he hoped that this would be his one and only episode involving brigands and soldiers. The click-clack of the train ultimately lulled him to sleep and he dozed off until the conductor awakened him: "Next stop, Dailou,"

Eager to get off the train, Gary gathered his briefcase and traveling bag and waited in the vestibule of his railcar.

***

Compared to the packed confines of Taihoku and Keelung, Dailou wasn't much more than a rural whistle stop, a forlorn collection of warehouses and mercantiles packed around the train station.

When Gary stepped onto the street, a local man immediately latched onto him. "You sir, may I be of assistance?"

Gary looked the man over. The stranger was neatly dressed in western clothes, save for his bare feet in sandals. Like everyone who hustled around the train stations, the man was all eager smiles.

"I need a place to stay," Gary replied.

"You are a tourist?" the man asked.

"Actually, I'm here to visit the farm of Akito Saito and—"

"You are in luck, my friend. My next errand will take me right by Akito's place." Beaming, the man pointed to a dusty Ford Model T stake-bed truck. "I am Hsu Ming-Han. It will be my honor to give you a ride."

Minutes later, they were chugging along the rutted dirt road leading north out of Dailou. The bed of the truck was packed with crates of ducks, and a boy of about seven was perched on the rear bumper to keep them from falling out.

"You like my truck?" Hsu asked. "It's so very modern. Yes?"

Gary agreed, but didn't share with Hsu that back in Utah, Model T's had long since been replaced and were regarded as jalopies.

"It was made in Yokohama," Hsu proudly declared. "In the most modern of factories. Yes?"

"If you say so," Gary replied with a smile.

Hsu pointed out the electrical poles set in the thicket along the road. "We have electricity. Everything is becoming so modern. You have electricity in America? Yes?"

"Yes, thankfully."

Hsu loved to talk, about everything. His truck. The weather. The growing seasons. An article he had read in yesterday's newspaper. Only when the truck dropped into a wide pothole did he pause long enough to double-clutch the transmission and power their way out. A half-mile down the road, they passed a large cart pulled by a dun-colored ox. The simple wooden wheels of the cart were taller than the Model T and squeaked loud enough to be heard above the truck's chattering engine. An elderly driver sat hunched on the cart in front of his load of wicker baskets filled with loquats. He tossed a cigarette butt that bounced off the Model T's windshield.

"Not everybody appreciates the modern," Hsu said.

At the next bend, the thicket gave way to rows of apple trees. Gary sat up, attentive. The road continued over a curve and then toward a pond on the right. Beyond the pond sat a wooden house with a thatched roof. At first glance, he regarded the building as a primitive structure until he noticed its glass windows and a wire connection to it from a nearby electrical pole.

Hsu veered onto a well-worn path that circled between the pond and the house. Dogs raced from the porch, barking. Hsu tooted the horn, and the noise scattered ducks from in front of the truck. The homey details reminded Gary of farm life back in America.

No sooner had the Model T stopped than Akito Saito burst out the front door of the house. "Welcome Gary. I hope Hsu didn't talk your ear off."

Gary climbed out of the Model T. He paid Hsu his fee and said, "See you this afternoon for my ride back to Dailou?"

"You got it, boss. Yes?" Hsu replied with a salute and drove off.

"Bring your things here," Akito said, opening the front door.

The interior of the house was uncluttered and simple to the point of being austere. The floor was bare planks with a few rice straw mats, the furniture either wicker or heavy wood. Gary set his bags alongside shoes and sandals arranged by the front door. A pair of smaller pink slippers alerted him of a woman's presence. Gary removed his own shoes and placed them next to the others.

Akito pulled a chain attached to a ceiling bulb, and light brightened the room.

Gary spied a framed photo on a cupboard. The photo was of a younger Akito sitting beside an attractive Japanese woman, just as young.

"Is this your wife?" Gary asked.

"Was my wife," Akito replied. "She died during the Spanish flu epidemic."

"My condolences." Gary said, as he thought, *Who owns the pink slippers?*

The front room opened to an office, complete with a roll-top desk nearly identical to the one owned by Gary's father. The desk and an adjoining table were covered with neat stacks of folders and journals. Charts and a calendar tacked to a nearby wall added to the reminder of his father's home office.

Akito led Gary outside and got right into the business of running his farm. The back of the house faced a shed containing wheelbarrows, farm tools, and a battered Velocette motorcycle. He showed

Gary a map of his plots of peaches, strawberries, apples, apricots, lychee, longan, and loquat.

"It's hard work keeping track of so many different plants, each with different cultivation requirements," Akito said. "However, such a variety of plants reduces loss to any one disease or pest."

At a ditch he explained how he diverted water from the Hasshō-kei River.

"How do you irrigate those orchards?" Gary motioned to trees uphill from them.

"Let me show you." Akito brought Gary to where two ditches ran parallel, one three feet higher than the other. Pitched between the ditches was a wooden contraption, a conveyor-belt-like device of linked buckets. A long pole with what resembled bicycle pedals at either end lay atop the bank of the uppermost ditch, and this pole served as an axle for a wheel driving the conveyor belt.

Akito hopped onto the pole and held to a second, smaller pole for balance. He placed his feet on one set of the pedals and began walking, his feet shifting from pedal to pedal as they swung around, rotating the larger pole and its attached wheel. The conveyor belt's buckets scooped water from the lower ditch and lifted it to the upper, splashing about a half-gallon in each scoop.

"Rather remarkable," Gary noted admiringly.

They were on the way back to the house when a woman interrupted. "Father."

The sound of a female voice surprised Gary, and he turned to see a young woman walking toward them. Her pace was brisk, as if she had important news. The shade from a broad-brimmed straw hat obscured her face. A loose, colorful shift was draped over her torso. Her baggy pants were gathered at the knees, above shapely calves. Wooden sandals slapped the bottoms of her feet.

Akito's daughter, the owner of the pink slippers, Gary thought.

As the young woman approached, her features materialized from the hat's shadow. Her face was slender, with high cheekbones and plump lips defining a small mouth. Dark eyebrows drew attention to her large, inquisitive eyes.

"My daughter, Kasumi," Akito said. He introduced Gary and described his business on the farm.

Gary bowed in greeting. She bowed back. As Akito was about Gary's father's age, he guessed Kasumi was close to his own age, if not a bit younger.

Kasumi asked in an admonishing tone, "Father, what are you doing here? Don't you have an appointment with the tax bureau?"

Akito yanked a pocket watch from his trousers. "Oh my, I've lost track of time. Forgive me, Gary; I must rush off."

Looking distraught, he scrambled back to his house, emerging with a messenger bag strapped to his back. Then he disappeared into the shed and rolled out the Velocette motorcycle. "I'm so sorry, Gary. I had completely forgotten this appointment. I will be back as soon as I can. Kasumi, please keep our guest company until I return."

He hurriedly donned leather gloves, a cloth helmet, and sunglasses. Grasping the motorcycle by the handles he pushed it along, gathering momentum until he hopped on the saddle. The engine coughed and whined to life. Oily blue smoke shot out the exhaust. He acted with such speed that it was obvious he didn't need any help. Gary stood back and watched Akito get the bike going.

As the motorcycle puttered to the road, Akito hollered over his shoulder, "I'll be back when I'm back."

Gary knew enough of Oriental culture that it wasn't proper for a young woman to be left alone in the company of a man who wasn't an immediate relative. An intense awkwardness settled over both young people. He couldn't leave, and didn't feel he should stay, even though Mr. Saito had asked his daughter to see to him in her father's absence. Then what to do?

"Well," she said, sighing. "Since you're here, I guess it's up to me to show you around."

Gary relaxed then, letting Kasumi take the lead.

They spent the afternoon touring the orchards. A breeze rustled the leaves. Birds sang and fluttered above them. Although Kasumi spoke with learned interest about the farm, Gary really wanted to talk with her about other things. What was her life like? What did she like to do? Basically the kind of get-to-know-you chitchat you engage in when you're interested in a woman.

Interested in a woman? This woman? Kasumi? How did this happen?

As they walked along, more of a casual stroll, she also seemed to be taking her time with him, as if she too were trying to give herself permission to speak about what was on her mind. At least that's what Gary surmised in his sideways glances at her.

"What do you consider yourself?" Gary asked. "Japanese? Chinese?"

Kasumi knit her brow. "That's an interesting question. I am full-bloodied Japanese. My grandparents arrived from Japan, but both my mother and father were born here, as was I also. Since Formosa is a protectorate of Japan, everyone who calls Formosa home is by law Japanese."

"Then you are Japanese?" Gary pressed.

"Whenever I meet someone from Japan, they always ask where I'm from. I tell them, Formosa. So I guess I'm Formosan to them. But to others on Formosa I am Japanese. And I live among the

Chinese. So it depends." She smiled at Gary. "But in all cases, I am always Kasumi Saito."

Their walk brought them back to the house. The rumble of an approaching engine, followed by the toot of a horn, told Gary that his driver, Hsu, had returned.

"My bags are inside," he noted. Kasumi fetched them.

"I'm sorry I have to leave before your father returns. Thank you for your hospitality," he said. "I plan to come back tomorrow, if that's okay?"

"I'll tell my father to expect you."

Hsu tooted his horn again. The hogs now in the back of his truck grunted in chorus. Gary climbed into the passenger seat and waved to Kasumi.

When the Model T reached the road, Hsu said, "You need to hide your feelings better."

"What do you mean?"

Hsu pointed to Gary's eyes. "I caught that. Yes? The looks between you and Kasumi Saito. You might be from the other side of the world, my friend, but man, woman, sparks, fire. Yes?"

Gary felt himself blush. "I don't know what you're talking about."

Hsu laughed. "Kasumi's a very pretty woman. And smart." He tapped his temple. "But headstrong. Like her father, yes?"

"Okay, I grant you that Kasumi is nice to be around. But romance is not why I'm here in Formosa or why I visited their farm. Forget that idea."

"It's not me who should be the one forgetting, my friend." Hsu paused. "Yes?"

Gary ruminated about Hsu's comment. "Hmmm . . . Yes." Every conversation he tried after that tailed off with indifference. All he could think about was Kasumi.

Hsu turned a sharp corner and slammed on the brakes, stopping inches from a large branch that blocked the road. In the back of the truck, the hogs toppled and squealed in protest. Dust filtered through the truck's open windows. Hsu gulped nervously and swallowed. "That was close, my friend."

The branch spanned the width of the road, making it impassible.

Looking over the situation, Gary said, C'mon, Hsu. "The two of us can pull this thing out of the way."

As they climbed out, Gary picked up on something odd. The branch was long enough to block the road but he couldn't see the tree it had fallen from. None of the trees around them were any taller than the electrical poles. "This is strange," he said. "It's almost as if someone has deliberately placed this branch in the road." .

Gary expected Hsu to reply; when he didn't, Gary turned to him.

Hsu was staring over Gary's shoulder, ashen-faced. Disconcerted, Gary pivoted to look.

Two rough-looking men in tattered clothing pointed rifles at him.

One of them growled, "Hands up, foreign devil."

Chapter Fourteen

June 1939

Gary, stunned and terrified, stared at the two men, his hands held high, the hair on the back of his arms and neck tingling. His pulse thumped hard against his temple. Time slowed, and his vision shrank to a narrow tunnel focused on the two brigands menacing him with their rifles.

They were both lean with taut musculature, like well-fed predators. One man was unusually tall for an Asian, and the shorter of the two bore a ragged scar on his face that pulled one corner of his mouth into a cruel sneer. They were barefoot and clad in ragged shorts and military shirts, the sleeves cut off. Both wore leather cartridge belts with long curved knives in sheaths, and each man had a large cloth pouch slung from one shoulder.

Their dark eyes studied Gary, pushing against him with chilling intensity. With their inky black straight hair—cut to a length just below their ears—terra-cotta complexions, high cheekbones, and almond-shaped eyes, Gary, even in his terror, was surprised at how much these brigands resembled some American Indian tribesmen.

Scarface wore a collar of animal claws. He whispered to his companion and they advanced warily toward Gary. The man barked a command in Chinese, and Gary shook his head to show that he didn't understand. However, through the corner of his eye, Gary saw Hsu prostrating himself in the dirt.

Gary decided to remain standing. Perhaps there would be an opportunity to overpower these men by employing jujitsu. But if that didn't work, he risked not only getting himself shot, but Hsu as well. Better that he play it cool for now.

Scarface stepped close, and looking up, locked eyes with Gary and repeated his command. Again Gary shook his head.

The taller bandit circled behind Gary, out of view. Suddenly, he kicked Gary in the back of one leg. Gary's legs crumpled and he sank to his knees. The muzzle of the taller brigand's rifle hovered close to Gary's left temple. His mouth went dry as dust. Scarface grabbed Gary's wrist. He snatched the watch and dropped it into his pouch. He patted down Gary's shirt and trouser pockets, emptying them, collecting his wallet, passport, coins, pencil and note pad, hotel key, and pocketknife.

Scarface leaned close to Gary and grinned a mouthful of yellow teeth. He asked, "Maybe you understand the Japanese?"

"I understand."

"Good. Where are you from, yellow-haired giant?"

"America."

Scarface huffed, unimpressed. The taller brigand unwound a rope from his waist. He grasped Gary's hands and brought them together. He coiled the rope around Gary's wrists and cinched it tight.

Gary listened desperately for the approach of a vehicle, hopefully one packed with soldiers that would rescue him. But the road remained quiet, empty.

The taller brigand stepped away. He snarled at Hsu and then ransacked the truck.

Scarface grabbed a handful of Gary's shirt. Hoisting Gary to his feet, he pointed him toward the thicket. With the butt of his rifle, he shoved Gary, signaling him to get going. Hsu was left behind, lying in the dirt but unhurt. The taller brigand hustled ahead, and the three of them broke through the underbrush. Gary looked back over his shoulder at Hsu, who hadn't moved. He felt as though the earth were opening up, that he was being swallowed and lost forever.

***

They trudged for hours, climbing and climbing what seemed to be endless hills that grew ever higher and steeper the longer they continued. Gary's mind floated in and out of his predicament. At times he hallucinated that he was back at his family's kitchen table eating apple pie or running carefree along the California beach with Ichiro.

Then a branch would smack his face and Gary would be slapped back to the present. He'd never perspired so much in his life. All of his clothes were soaked through, and his mouth was parched.

At last they halted within a dense copse of leafy trees and crouched in the shade. Gary was so exhausted that he fell to his knees and took deep breaths. The brigands remained alert and kept their rifles handy. They didn't speak much, and when they did, it was only in guarded whispers.

Scarface reached into his pouch and brought out green leaves fashioned into balls about the size of a radish. He unwrapped one; it was a wad of brown rice. His partner reached into his pouch and they each gobbled four of the rice balls. Until he had seen the brigands eat, Gary hadn't realized how hungry he was.

Scarface uncorked a gourd, and both brigands chugged from it.

Scarface offered Gary a drink. Though the water tasted as though it had been steeped in some kind of tea, nothing had ever tasted so refreshing. After Gary had swallowed several mouthfuls, Scarface poured the rest over his head, cooling him.

The brigands stood, and remaining quiet as statues for several minutes, cocking their heads in one direction, then the other. Satisfied that nothing seemed out of the ordinary, Scarface motioned Gary to his feet, and they resumed the long, miserable trek.

***

Late in the afternoon, they veered onto a narrow rocky trail that cut across the side of a mountain so overgrown with vines and thicket that it seemed not even a rabbit could wiggle through.

The trail curved down a draw cleaved into the ridge. Another brigand materialized from the brush. He gestured to Gary's captors, then stepped aside to let them continue. They bent forward to pass beneath overhanging branches that wove together to form a leafy tunnel, gloomy and impossibly humid.

Yet another brigand appeared ahead. He lifted a cloth tarp and Gary was ushered into a cave-like enclosure, a hideout made of leafy branches thatched together. Gary's head raked the ceiling, making him stoop to enter. A tiny, smokeless campfire flicked in the center of the floor, its wavering light illuminating a circle of fierce-looking men.

Scarface herded Gary to a spot opposite one brigand who sat on a crate while everyone else sat cross-legged in the dirt. The eyes fixed upon him reflected the campfire like glowing coals. Comments in a strange language murmured around him. The scene reminded Gary of a passage from *The Last of the Mohicans*.

Scarface pushed Gary to his knees and untied the restraining cord. Gary massaged his wrists where they'd been rubbed raw.

The brigand resting on the crate looked older than the others. He was a compact knot of gristle, appearing as if the worst of circumstances had tried to eat him, only to spit him out as too tough to chew. The campfire picked out the silver in his hair. His round face was scarred like the business end of a battering ram.

Scarface and the taller brigand dumped the loot from their pouches onto a straw mat, which was passed along the circle to the elder. Besides Gary's belongings, they'd stolen Hsu's watch, his money, and small tools from the truck. The elder picked through the loot, nodding agreeably at Gary's watch before fastening it on his wrist. He examined Gary's passport and compared the photo to his prisoner. After whisking the money into a clay bowl, he handed Hsu's watch and Gary's key and pocketknife back to Scarface.

The elder stared at Gary and spoke in an accented Japanese, his voice surprisingly deep, "I am Wu Jen-feng, chieftain of the Mountain Leopard Tribe of the Paiwan people. And who are you, yellow-haired stranger?"

Gary's throat was so dry that his reply came out as a croak. "My name is Gary Gatlin. I am an American."

"You speak the Japanese well for a foreigner."

"Yes. I had a good teacher."

"In America?"

"Yes."

"How long have you been in Formosa?"

"Four days."

One of the other brigands interrupted Wu and pointed at Gary. Wu then said, "America is a big country, so we've heard. Where in America are you from?"

"Utah."

Wu replied, "Uuh-tah," then added a comment in his native language, which the circle of men repeated, chuckling. He shifted his position on the crate. "Gary from Uuh-tah, how much do you know about us?" Wu panned his men with an outstretched finger.

"Very little."

Wu set his elbows on his knees and leaned toward Gary. Light from the campfire gave the elder's face a menacing, spectral aspect. "We are called brigands. Bandits. *Savages*. Simply for wanting to protect what is ours. Our land. Our ways. Our language."

Gary, his anxiety abated somewhat, said, "It's a familiar-sounding story."

"How so?"

"In America, we have Indians who lived much like you, and they fought against the theft of their land."

"So you know? We live like animals hunted within our own home."

"On the way to Dailou," Gary said, "our train was stopped, and soldiers dragged people off the train. Were they your people?"

Wu sat up straight. "You noticed? Foreigners pretend not to see what happens to us. And yes, those you saw were either Paiwan or Taiyal, but there are many of us aboriginal tribes, and the authorities—Chinese and Japanese—like to keep us in our place." Wu stamped his sandaled foot into the ground.

"What do you want from me?" Gary's stomach grumbled. He was so famished that he'd grown queasy.

"That is a question I'll answer later. But as I am your host, what do you want from me?"

"Honestly? I'm very thirsty and hungry."

Wu snapped his fingers. "Of course, first things first." He grunted an order. A moment later, a brigand entered the hideout with a board serving as a tray. On it were crude wooden bowls filled with rice and vegetables. A larger bowl contained parts of some kind of bird. The bowls were passed around and Wu made sure Gary had his portion. All the food had been thoroughly cooked but was served cold.

Gary ate with his fingers and cleaned his bowl. Though he could finish another bowl, he didn't ask for more. He drank his fill of the tea-water from a gourd.

On Wu's order, the bowls and gourds were collected. He asked Gary, "How do you feel now?"

"Better. Thank you."

"Good." Wu slapped his knees. "You came from far away. Your family paid for your passage?"

"Yes."

"And they provided money for you to live and study in Formosa?"

"That is correct."

"Then you must be rich."

The statement made Gary want to laugh. "Not hardly. We're farmers, that's all."

"On your farm, how many horses do you own?"

"No horses. We have a tractor and a truck."

Wu rocked back as if startled. "And a car, I suppose?"

"Yes, we have a car."

Wu mulled his thoughts. "So, your family owns a tractor, and a truck, and a car, and they have the means to send you a long way from home. Don't tell me you are not rich."

Though impressed by Wu's logic, Gary didn't give in. "We are not rich."

"All right," Wu replied. "I'll give you that, since you lived in

America. You are not rich but you have money. More than any of us."

What was Wu getting at?

The elder brigand patted his stomach. "Did our food agree with you?"

"So far, it has."

"Good. We need to keep you healthy. Considering the distance between here and Uuh-tah, the negotiations may take time."

"What negotiations?"

"For your ransom, visitor from America."

***

Since they'd first captured him, it seemed that at every turn, Gary's situation kept getting worse. But at least they'd given him something to eat--even though it was to keep him alive enough to exchange him for money. How would his family react? Only yesterday he'd sent them a telegram that all was well in Formosa, and here he was now, a kidnapped prisoner somewhere in the mountainous wilderness.

Wu and a few of the other brigands left the hideout. What meager light filtered from outside turned dark, though the enclosure remained stifling. Gary lay in the dirt and closed his eyes. While still suspicious of his captors, he was so worn out that he fell asleep.

Agitated chatter woke him. Blinking himself awake, by the light of the campfire he saw that it was only Scarface and himself in the hideout. Outside, the brigands scrambled for their gear and whispered warnings. Someone threw aside the door tarp and hissed a command to Scarface, who leapt to his feet. He kicked dirt on the fire and then lunged at Gary, hauling him out the door and to the trail.

What's going on? Gary's thoughts raced confusedly, his mind as uncertain as his feet stumbling in the darkness. He could barely see the back of Scarface's head, and he reached out to clutch his shoulder so as not to lose him.

Gunshots rang out, the loud, staccato reports punching through the stillness and hammering Gary's nerves. Bullets clipped the leaves around them. His mind catapulted from confused to terrified.

Scarface grunted, wounded, and fell to the ground next to Gary. Gary dropped to the ground beside him. In the distance and approaching swiftly, men shouted in Japanese and crashed through the brush like so many mad bulls.

"Second squad, this way."

"Bring the machine gun forward and rake the trail."

"Hold your fire! The first squad is on the trail."

Gary laid his hand on Scarface's side, felt his ribcage, felt him tremble. Where were the other brigands? They'd scattered like lizards.

This was his chance to escape. He would surrender. What did he owe these brigands anyway? He shouted in his best Japanese, "Don't shoot! I give up."

"No prisoners!" someone down the trail shouted back. "Kill these criminals like the vermin they are."

A volley of rifle shots hacked the branches over Gary's head. If the Japanese found him, he was as good as dead.

Scarface wheezed, his breath was labored. Gary recalled Wu's statement that his people lived like hunted animals. He thought about the people herded off the train and forced to their knees. He remembered the Indians from back home. How the old timers would gaze mournfully across the land and remember how it had been taken from them by lies and by force. This was as true for the Paiwans as it had been for the Utes.

Though this fight between the brigands and the Japanese wasn't his, an instinct to do the right thing made Gary roll Scarface onto his back and drag him off the trail.

Stealthily, Gary crawled backwards on his hands and knees through the bramble, struggling to pull the heavy brigand with him. Thorns caught at his clothing and raked his skin. Though Scarface was gravely wounded, like a true warrior he clung to his rifle. Gary wrestled the brigand a couple more feet, then stopped and listened for the soldiers. They were still down the trail, but closing in.

Gary continued until he reached a depression within the thicket, perhaps where animals had bedded down. He dragged Scarface into the hollow and pulled branches down to obscure their path.

A large, dark stain on Scarface's shirt caught his attention. It was wet and warm. *Blood.* Carefully, Gary unbuttoned the shirt. Blood pumped dark and shiny as oil from a hole in Scarface's chest. Gary would have to try to stop the bleeding as best he could. He positioned Scarface with his head and shoulders on a slight rise and then ripped loose the pocket of his shirt to stuff into the wound.

Soldiers appeared moving up the trail, the rickrack of branches breaking up their silhouettes so they moved like spiders across a web. Their bayonets caught the moonlight. They prodded the hideout and looked inside.

One whispered, "Someone turn on a hand torch so I can see."

"Don't be a fool," another rejoined. "You use a hand torch and the brigands will put a bullet through your head for your troubles."

A soldier crouched where Scarface had fallen.

Gary reached for Scarface's rifle and pulled it close. The gun was an antique bolt-action relic, the barrel cut down and the stock repaired with wraps of wire and leather. Carefully, Gary worked the bolt, and a brass cartridge glittered faintly in the chamber. He was so nervous that he had to tell himself to breathe. Locking the bolt, he brought the rifle to his shoulder and aimed it at the soldier through the trees.

CHAPTER FIFTEEN

June 1939

The darkness reduced the Japanese soldier to a simple black silhouette moving against a jumbled mosaic of grays and black. The low ambient light reflected faintly in the soldier's eyes, and Gary was sure he was staring right at him. His finger tensed on the rifle's trigger, and he struggled against the desire to squeeze. Deafening heartbeats hammered the inside of his chest, and it astonished him that the soldier couldn't hear the sound.

Scarface stirred, and in a panic Gary pressed a hand on the wounded brigand's chest to keep him still.

The soldier's bayonet pushed aside the branches. He was perhaps twenty feet away. At this distance, Gary was sure he couldn't miss.

But if he fired, then what? Even if he killed the soldier, his comrades would descend on Gary and Scarface like wolves. He might be able to escape by retreating deeper into the thicket—but what about Scarface?

A gunshot echoed in the distance. Gary twitched. Then another gunshot echoed.

"It's the brigands!" a voice down the trail shouted in Japanese. Gary, with his fluent knowledge of the language, , understood exactly what was being said.

The soldier pulled back from the thicket and crouched on the trail. "What do we do?" Gary could hear him clearly.

More gunshots reverberated in the darkness.

"First squad. Second squad," an authoritative voice commanded. "Assemble on me. The brigands are making a stand up the hillside. This is our chance to wipe them out."

The soldier on the trail joined several of his comrades as they disappeared into the gloom. Gary remained tense and kept his rifle trained at the fading sound of the soldiers scrambling across the mountainside.

Another gunshot rang out, followed by yet another. Then a volley of rifle shots. The shots continued in a ragged cadence as they seemed to retreat into the distance.

Then silence. And more silence. Gary lay in stillness so profound that he could hear the breath rumble softly in Scarface's throat.

At last the danger had passed and Gary felt he could take a deep breath. He and Scarface were alone. Setting the rifle aside, he examined the pocket-bandage on Scarface's chest wound. The bandage was soaked through, so Gary, utilizing what was at hand, tore a scrap from his own shirt and used it to replace the saturated bandage.

He pressed his hand against Scarface's forehead and discovered it was dry and alarmingly hot. Twisted alongside the brigand was his provisions pouch. Gary groped inside and retrieved a small gourd, which he uncorked and sniffed. Tea-water. Cradling Scarface's head, Gary gave him sips. Scarface swallowed painfully. He brought his hand up, touched Gary's face, and mumbled something.

Gary cupped water in his hand and used it to blot Scarface's feverish brow. "Don't die on me, friend," he whispered in Japanese. What to do? Gary could sneak away, but where would he go? He couldn't risk blundering around in the darkness. He decided to wait until morning. Besides, he was exhausted. His nerves had been stretched to the limit and held tight for what seemed an eternity. He was ready to go limp and try to forget where he was, what was happening to him.

***

He didn't know when he'd fallen asleep. It was the snap of a twig that jolted him awake, and the bright light of morning filled his eyes. Blinking in confusion, for an instant he had no idea where he was. When he tried to move, a thick growth of bramble pressed upon him. He was lying beside a wounded man dressed in rags. He himself was filthy, his clothes ripped and soiled.

As the details coalesced in his mind, he realized where he was and what had happened.

He heard voices in the aboriginal language. The brigands had returned. He wasn't sure what to expect, but at least now he wasn't alone.

Two of them were on the trail right next to Gary's hiding place. They studied the ground and followed the path of disturbed leaves and grass where Gary had dragged Scarface. They easily spotted Gary and Scarface and one of them called out; a moment later the brigand chieftain, Wu Jen-feng, joined them. Guns at the ready, Wu beckoned for Gary to come out.

He didn't know what kind of reception he would get. Wu's cold expression gave away nothing. With rifles pointed at him, Gary crawled out of the thicket. Glancing around, he counted ten brigands. His pulse pounded.

He relaxed somewhat when Wu ordered his men to drag Scarface to the trail. Tenderly, they lay him in the dirt and examined his wound and bandage. Wu asked Gary, "You treated him?"

"I wish I could've done more."

"You saved his life. Why didn't you run away?"

"I was sure the Japanese would shoot me. And I couldn't abandon your man."

Wu looked at Gary, his face touched with empathy. "It was a brave thing that you did." Without another word, he unfastened Gary's watch from his wrist and handed it to him. "This belongs to you, and you should have it back."

"Thank you," Gary said gratefully, as he put the watch back on his wrist. "What happened last night? I heard a lot of shooting. Did you lose many men?"

Wu pointed at Scarface. "He was our only casualty. We're used to fighting the Japanese. We lure them deeper into the mountains, which we all know as well as we know our mother's names. The Japanese get strung out and we pick off their stragglers." Wu gestured for one of his men to step forward. The brigand showed off his recently acquired Japanese rifle and cartridge belt, complete with a load of fresh ammunition. Wu said, "These forays against us are a major source of resupply." Gary smiled at the irony.

He looked at Scarface. The brigand's face was pale, and it glistened with sweat. But the man's expression remained stoic. "Will he survive?" Gary asked.

"Not if we stay here." Wu instructed his men build a stretcher from a tarp, rope, and a pair of stout branches. He gave Gary a pouch with a gourd-canteen and a dozen of the rice balls, half of which he devoured right away. After carefully rolling Scarface onto the improvised stretcher, two of the brigands hoisted it onto their shoulders. On Wu's command, they proceeded in single file along the trail. When they reached the bottom of a long downward climb, Gary took his turn carrying one end of the stretcher.

The trail took another turn upward. Then, after reaching the summit, Wu told his men to rest and asked Gary to follow him down a trail spur. They emerged onto a primitive road that ended in a clearing littered with the stumps of what had been huge trees. Some of the stumps were more than ten feet in diameter. As they drew close, Gary sniffed a familiar odor.

"You know the smell?" Wu asked.

"Camphor."

The chieftain motioned toward the stumps. "Formosa is one of the world's suppliers of camphor. The government supports several monopolies that harvest the material. However, to harvest camphor you have to fell the tree, killing it."

Until now, Gary had never given any thought to where camphor came from. He noticed that the road followed a trail of camphor stumps. "Looks like the Japanese have been busy."

"They are exporting as much of the camphor as possible."

Gary noted, "It's used for medicine and to make celluloid and gun powder."

"Our people recognize it as a most beneficial herb," Wu replied. "The problem is that the Japanese search for the largest trees and harvest them. But it takes twenty years for a camphor tree to be of useful size. At this rate, the Japanese are going to wipe them out."

Wu led Gary to the rusted wreck of a truck now overgrown with vines and grass. "They build roads that encroach deeper and deeper into our land. So we endeavor to make the harvesting of the camphor as dangerous as possible. If it weren't for us, the Japanese would've harvested the last tree years ago."

They returned to the trail. Wu's men had rested up and they

resumed carrying the stretcher. After another hour of hiking, they reached a fork in the trail where Wu brought his men together for a short powwow. Gary watched from the shade. After dismissing his men, Wu returned to Gary and knelt beside him.

"I need to show you something else," Wu said. "I've directed that Chiang Zhu-Mei—"

"Who?" Gary asked.

"The man on the stretcher."

Ahh, Gary thought, *Scarface*.

Wu continued, "He'll be taken to our home village for treatment."

The litter bearers lifted Scarface's stretcher, and along with four other men disappeared up the trail. Three brigands remained, the most heavily armed of the group. They carried newer examples of rifles, cartridge belts bristling with ammunition, and long machete-like knives.

"Are we expecting trouble?" Gary asked.

"When you're a Paiwan," Wu replied, "you are born into trouble, like it or not."

On Wu's order, they headed down the slope and spread out, one man on point, then another brigand, then Wu, Gary, and the remaining brigand as rear guard. They traversed several ridges and valleys, crowded together like wrinkles in a blanket. By keeping track of the sun when it appeared above the dense canopy of leaves, Gary could tell they advanced east.

The man on point raised one hand and crouched on the trail, on the edge of where the trail crossed an open clearing. Wu tapped Gary's shoulder and indicated for him to follow to the edge of the clearing. Once there, Wu pointed up and to the right through a gap in the trees.

Gary craned his neck to see. Beyond the rim of trees circling the clearing appeared the spine of a ridge, and on the ridge a guard tower stood about five hundred yards away. The tower was an open-sided shed mounted on tall poles. At this distance Gary couldn't tell if the tower was manned, but considering Wu's cautious manner he assumed that it was.

"Japanese army," Wu explained in a whisper. He thumped the shoulder of the man on point, who rose to his feet and crept along the edge of the clearing, bypassing the trail. They proceeded single file behind him, and once on the other side of the clearing got back on the trail where it tunneled through the brush.

After a half hour, the man on point raised his arm and everyone stopped. As before, Wu brought Gary cautiously forward.

From this vantage they looked upon a long clearing that had been hacked through the forest. The clearing reminded Gary of a logging road from back in Utah. The clearing was about twenty feet wide, and in the center stood a wire fence strung along a series of stout wooden posts.

Gary puzzled over the utility of the fence, as the wire strands didn't look robust enough to deter anyone crawling through them. That was until he noticed the glass insulators connecting the wires.

"The fence is electrified?" Gary whispered.

Wu nodded. "The fence runs from here all the way to the coast near Toran. It's meant to limit our movements." He pointed to several humps of dead creatures rotting along the fence. "But mostly the fence kills wild animals and stray cattle. Sometimes the careless peasant or child."

"But the fence was built for you," Gary pointed to Wu and his men.

The chieftain chuckled softly. "That fence only shows how stupid the Japanese think we are. When they started clearing the forest, I sent several men posing as laborers to see what the Japanese were up to. So even before the first strand of wire was installed, we Paiwans were well aware of the fence's purpose."

From working on electric fences back in Utah, Gary had experience with them. "I imagine keeping that fence operational in this humid climate must be a challenge."

"More than a challenge, it's a waste of money. The circuits keep corroding. Sometimes a cow will blunder into it, be electrocuted, and as it falls dead will rip out the wires. The Japanese are constantly sending out repair parties."

Wu grinned. "The fence has proven to be more of a hazard to them than it is to us. When they get too complacent we sabotage the lines and wait in ambush. And when we have to cross the fence, we simply cut the wires or burrow underneath them."

"Why do the Japanese bother?" Gary asked.

"You have to think like them." Wu tapped his temple. "If they decide to abandon the fence, then all those associated with its construction will lose face. Plus, someone is making good money selling all that wire and electrical equipment to the army."

Wu took a sip from a gourd and passed it to Gary. "But don't underestimate the Japanese. To them, Formosa is a field they intend to farm until it becomes barren. They have no interest in maintaining a balance with nature, or respecting us as a people."

Gary returned the gourd. "I appreciate what you're trying to do."

"It's a matter of survival," Wu said. "The Japanese are bringing modern ways, but they don't ask if we want them or not. Our people are forced to relocate from our ancestral homes in the mountains to live in the lowlands and eke out an existence as impoverished farmers. The Japanese do provide schools, but to attend, our children are forbidden to dress in our traditional clothes, or speak our language. Young women are forced to remove their beautification tattoos. In the name of 'safety,' our guns are taken away and we can only access them during authorized hunts."

Gary thought guiltily *What the Japanese are doing to the Formosan aboriginals is a mirror of what was done to the American Indians.* And his family's farm was on land that had originally belonged to the Utes. But before them, the Shoshone. And before them, the Navajo. Going back to prehistoric times, he was certain there were other tribes who had claims to the land. Still, the Utes had been swept aside at gunpoint, and Gary had listened to old timers who were there when it happened.

Wu squared his shoulders. "But enough of this complaining. We must always move forward." He snapped his fingers and one of his men trotted close. Wu reached into the brigand's pouch and returned the rest of Gary's belongings. "Please excuse what we had to do. My man will escort you back to the road where we first took you prisoner."

"There I'll be set free?"

"You're free now, my friend. But I don't think you can get back on your own."

"Point taken." Gary offered his hand.

Wu looked at it and knit his brow.

"In my home," Gary explained, "shaking hands is a sign of understanding and trust."

Wu shrugged. "Among the Paiwan, we just say, 'May God keep you until next time.'"

***

Gary and his escort hurried along the trail. Wu's man moved as quietly and swiftly as a cat. Gary struggled to keep up, and he surmised that the brigand was testing him. But he wasn't about to give in, and he continued along the trail with his escort.

Late in the afternoon, when the sun dipped below the tops of the trees, they crept through thick underbrush. Then, just like that, Gary was on the dirt road at what appeared to be the spot where he'd been captured. He turned to thank the brigand, but the man had vanished.

Gary remained on the shoulder of the road, taking stock of his situation. He imagined this is how a bird felt when released from its cage. His body seemed to have no weight, and nothing would stop him from running in any direction that he pleased. And after spending so much time on the narrow mountain trails, the dirt road seemed extravagantly wide in comparison. He regarded his clothing. He usually took pride in how he presented himself, and at the moment, in his torn and dirty clothes—he rubbed a hand across the stubble of a beard—and his disheveled appearance, he most likely resembled a bum in a hobo camp.

His stomach rumbled, reminding him to get going. He walked to where Hsu's truck had been but saw no evidence of it. The dusty road was nothing but a confusion of tire marks and hoof prints.

Which way now?

The closest sanctuary would be Akito's farm. To the left. Gary started walking.

***

As Gary continued along the road and twilight sank around him, nothing looked familiar, and he was worried that perhaps the brigand had left him at the wrong place. Then he heard dogs barking off to his right. A moment later, a rectangle of light revealed a small pond. A cow stirred where it was tethered beside the pond. This had to be Akito's home.

The closer Gary approached the house, the fiercer the dogs became, snarling and flattening their ears. To keep them at bay, he picked up a stick to use as a switch.

The front door opened, and Akito appeared, shouting in Japanese.

Gary shouted back, "Akito, it's me, Gary Gatlin!"

Akito ran to him, ordering the dogs to get back. He slapped Gary's shoulder. "Are you all right? What happened to you? Hsu said you'd been taken by the brigands."

Gary clapped his hand on Akito's to keep it on his shoulder. After his ordeal with the brigands and the soldiers, being on safe ground like this, and with a trusted friend, his eyes watered with gratitude and relief.

"Come inside. We'll get you cleaned up." Akito guided him through the front door. "I'll bet you're hungry."

Kasumi waited inside. She clutched the collar of her robe.

"I'm sorry to disturb you," Gary said apologetically.

"What do you mean?" Kasumi replied. "You need help." She beckoned him to a chair.

Akito brought Gary his briefcase and travel bag. "Hsu returned these."

Gary set the bags on his lap and noticed that while their contents had been rifled by the brigands, nothing was missing. "At least I have a change of clothes."

"I'll heat water for a bath," Kasumi said, and turned about for the kitchen.

Akito pulled up another chair and sat opposite Gary. "We'll get you fed and cleaned up. I have plenty of sleeping mats so your spending the night is no problem." He gave Gary's knee an avuncular squeeze. "And then what, my friend?"

Gary had trouble reining in his thoughts. All that was on his mind now was a meal, a bath, and some sleep. "My nerves are frazzled and I'm exhausted. I guess the next thing, after some rest, is to get back to Dailou and catch the train to Taihoku. Do what I can to put this behind me and not let it happen again. It's been a nightmare!"

Chapter Sixteen

October 1939

Colonel Eiji Kagawa and his assistant, Sergeant-Major Kosuke Murakami, were escorted by a navy lieutenant through the palatial corridors of the office of the governor-general for their meeting with Admiral Yoshida. They climbed stairs to the third floor where the lieutenant led them to the governor-general's executive conference room.

Kagawa read his watch. 11 a.m. on the dot. He had urgent business on his mind and he entered without invitation. Besides, his meeting with Admiral Yoshida was scheduled for 11, and Kagawa considered punctuality a cornerstone of military efficiency.

Inside the room, a group of businessmen and military officers were collecting their paperwork. They bowed to the admiral before heading out the door.

Yoshida remained seated at the head of the long table and acknowledged Kagawa with a nod. The colonel and Murakami marched to the table, clicked their heels as they snapped to attention, and bowed smartly.

Yoshida gave a nod, and the two men straightened. "Colonel Kagawa, who is your assistant?"

"Sir, he is Sergeant-Major Kosuke Murakami, of the *Kenpeitai.*

He is a distinguished veteran in our campaigns in China and Manchukuo with a specialty in rooting out spies and saboteurs."

As Kagawa introduced him, Murakami offered an abbreviated bow. Combat service ribbons decorated the front of his olive-green dress tunic. His nickname among the troops was *Badger*, both for his compact, muscular body and his fierce manner when provoked. And like his namesake, it didn't take much to provoke Murakami. But in the presence of his superiors, he was as restrained as a well-trained guard dog. "To serve you, Governor-General, is to honor the emperor."

"Are you also *Tokkō*, Sergeant-Major?" Yoshida asked, meaning, are you also in the secret police?

Murakami answered curtly, "*Hai.*"

"Will such services be necessary, Colonel?"

"I feel they are, Admiral."

On the table, a stack of documents sat in front of Yoshida and he laid a hand on top of them. "I'm looking forward to your briefing. I spent the morning haggling with my agricultural and economic development officers about how we're to deal with the new quotas of produce that we're to deliver to our army in China. Those bureaucrats in Tokyo think that increasing the output of our farms is as simple as pulling a lever."

Kagawa nodded sympathetically as Yoshida complained. An ambitious man, Kagawa was envious of Yoshida's status as an admiral and governor-general. What he did not envy was Yoshida's political machinations. Kagawa couldn't imagine having to balance all the competing duties, especially with civilians. Farmers were always whining about being squeezed for money. *Squeeze them at bayonet point,* thought Kagawa, *and then see how compliant they'd become.*

Yoshida pushed the reports aside. He sighed as if relieved of the burden, at least temporarily. "Well Colonel, what do you have?"

Kagawa gestured to the adjacent wall. Murakami snapped open his leather map case and slid out a rolled-up map, which he pinned to cork panels on the wall. The map was of Formosa. What distinguished this map from similar maps of the island were the red lines that spread south from Taihoku like a growth of roots.

Murakami stepped aside as Kagawa stood close to the map. The colonel began, "The red marks show the paths of the American Gary Gatlin. As you can see, Admiral, he's been using the railroads to facilitate his visits about the island. Lately he's been traveling quite a bit on the Jūkando Main Line." Kagawa traced the route with his finger. "Most recently he's shown a particular interest in Tainan and Kōyrū." Kagawa tapped both cities.

Yoshida folded his hands. "We've just begun construction of a new ammunition factory in Tainan."

"And there's the Edo airfield," Kagawa added, "which just received the deployment of Mitsubishi G3M medium bombers."

Yoshida's gaze ranged across the map. "What is Gary Gatlin's business that requires so much travel on his part, especially on the Jūkando Main Line where it goes past so many depots and marshaling yards?"

"Ostensibly, research on our farming techniques."

"Oh?" Yoshida arched an eyebrow.

"That's what he declared on his customs forms when he entered the country. And in his travels, his destinations have always been related to some farming activity. He's visited markets, wholesalers, agricultural supply stores, and several farms."

"What do you know about this Gary Gatlin?"

"According to the birthdate on his passport, he is twenty-one years old and comes from Utah."

"Uu-tah?"

"It's a prefecture within the United States," Kagawa answered. "It's a mountainous region known mostly for agriculture and is the home of a polygamous religious sect called Mormons."

"Is Gatlin a Mormon?"

"No sir, he is a Lutheran. That is a denomination of the Protestant Christian—"

Yoshida raised his hand to interrupt. "Is his religious background germane to his activities?"

"I don't think so, Admiral."

"Then let's move on to more relevant information."

Kagawa pointed to Murakami, who explained in a deep, authoritative voice, "One of my men posed as a civilian and shared a train compartment with Gatlin as he traveled from Taihoku to Tainan. My agent struck up a lengthy conversation, and the American was quite forthcoming. He shared that he had come to Formosa specifically to study the grafting of fruit trees and agricultural practices, of which he said the Japanese had the most advanced techniques in the world. He also showed a journal with notes and drawings that he's collected."

"I understand that his Japanese is quite good," Yoshida said.

"More than good, Admiral, his fluency is remarkable. My agent reported that Gatlin is very well educated not only in the language but in our literature and history as well."

"How did he learn Japanese?"

"Gatlin said he befriended a family of *nisei* farmers in California." The sergeant read from a note pad. "Hajime Mitsui."

"Have you researched them?"

"I've submitted an inquiry to the Military Central Intelligence Bureau in Tokyo. They answered that they have no information on either Hajime Mitsui or this Gary Gatlin. Then again, our intelligence resources in America are not very substantial."

Kagawa said, "In the meantime, we've kept Gatlin under surveillance."

"And you have assigned men to follow him?"

"Sergeant-Major Murakami is in charge of the surveillance team."

"How many men, sergeant?"

"Five agents, Admiral. That allows us to keep a constant watch on his apartment," Murakami explained. "It's in the Silver Crane Hostel in the Daitatei Bund. When the American leaves the hostel, we continue to keep him under our eye."

Kagawa gestured again to the sergeant, who tacked a second map to the wall, which like the first map was marked extensively with red lines.

"Here are his movements in Taihoku," Murakami said. "He has an account in the Yamatochō Industrial Bank where he deposited fifty-four hundred American dollars, cash. Twice, he's had additional funds wired to him from the First National Bank in Los Angeles, California."

"Who sent him the money?"

"That, I don't know. Gatlin claims that his family is funding his stay here."

"He hasn't done anything to confirm that he is a spy," Kagawa said. "As he travels about the city, he can't help but pass by the military facilities along the major corridors."

"Have you seen him take photos?" Yoshida asked.

"As far as we can tell, he doesn't have a camera."

"Has he had any business with the American Consulate?"

"He's made several visits," Kagawa replied, "and his stays are brief."

"Who does he see?"

"Mostly whoever is on duty. The purpose of his visits seems to be to pick up his mail."

"Isn't that odd?"

"Unfortunately, no, Admiral. Several of the European consulates offer the same service as a courtesy to their fellow countrymen. The mail service here is unreliable. Letters and packages are frequently opened and the contents pilfered. But his routing of the mail this way prevents us from looking through it as we could normally do."

"Have you investigated his room?"

"Not yet, sir. As I had mentioned, he is staying in the Daitatei Bund, and the Chinese residents would quickly spot one of my men. Only housemaids are allowed entry into the rooms."

"Perhaps you can bribe one of these maids?"

"We undoubtedly can. But these Chinese can't keep their mouths shut about anything. While we might learn something about Gatlin, he will in turn learn that we have him under surveillance. We don't want to tip our hand prematurely."

"So he has no idea he's being watched?"

"I'm positive."

Yoshida steepled his fingers and pursed his lips. He stared at the map and after a moment asked, "So you have nothing more than coincidence in explaining why this American is seen close to activities of strategic importance."

"There is more, Admiral, which you will find quite suspicious."

Murakami ran his hand across the central part of the island on the map as he said, "He has visited the villages of Tusuat-sha,

Purat-sha, and Tabuya-sha, all of which reside squarely within the aboriginal zones."

Yoshida scowled. "Why is he visiting the brigands?"

"He brings them sundry supplies. Items for cooking, carpentry and gardening tools, some medical items such as tinctures and bandages."

Yoshida allowed a troubled whisper. "Brigands." He riveted a hard gaze on Kagawa. "Colonel, what is his interest in these dangerous savages?"

Kagawa replied with a cruel, scheming smile. "That is what we intend to find out, Admiral."

***

As laborers harvested apples and pears on Akito Saito's farm, he and Gary inspected fruit brought in wheelbarrows to the crating shed. Inside, another crew unloaded the wheelbarrows into crates and tossed bruised or blemished fruit into the discard barrel to be fed to the hogs and cattle.

Gary was particularly interested in the apples, especially those grown from grafted trees. Over the summer, he'd kept track of their growth and jotted his impressions of their size and appearance in his journal.

"What do you think, Gary?" Akito asked

Gary selected an apple and swiped it on his sleeve before studying its color, shape, and size. He bit into the fruit, his teeth crunching through the taut skin before plunging through the crispy flesh. The apple's moist and succulent flavor burst into his mouth and he couldn't keep the rich juice from dribbling to his chin. He wanted to smile and swallow at the same time and wound up choking.

Akito slapped his back.

Gary wiped his lips. "It's excellent. Sure to fetch you a premium." He tossed the remainder of the apple into the discard barrel. As delicious as the apple was, if he finished every piece of fruit that he'd tasted today, he would've been full hours ago.

Abruptly, Akito asked, "Have you heard from the Paiwans?"

"Yesterday," Gary answered, "when I arrived in Dailou, Chiang Zhu-Mei was waiting for me." Gary had explained to both Akito and Kasumi about what had transpired when he'd been kidnapped by the brigands.

"How is he doing?"

"Much better. The Paiwan are a hardy people."

"What did he want?"

"Only to relay a message from Wu Jen-feng that his tribe appreciated my gift of pots and pans and some medical tinctures."

Akito's eyes crinkled with concern. "You need to be careful, Gary. The Japanese don't like the Paiwan. They consider them too independent and a threat to the island's security."

"Trust me, Akito, I'm not sticking my nose in anything dangerous. I'm simply here to learn how to grow fruit as good as yours." Gary picked up an apple from a crate to make his point and then replaced it. "But if the Paiwan need humanitarian help, then it's my Christian duty to do what I can."

"Have you been approached by anyone from the police or the army?"

Gary chuckled. "Not at all. I'm sure they have more important things to do than waste time keeping tabs on an apple picker from Utah."

Akito laughed with him, then walked away to join a group of laborers enjoying a smoke break. Gary surveyed the activity around him, the methodical work of the pickers on the ladders, the way they dumped their baskets into the wheelbarrows, the wheelbarrows pushed in relays to the crating shed, the laborers in the shed filling and stacking crates. Everything was done by hand, so there was only the shuffle of feet and crates, the occasional exchange of conversation, and the rustle of leaves whenever a breeze pushed through the orchards.

The autumn tranquility put Gary at a peaceful ease and he began thinking about how much longer he'd remain in Formosa. Perhaps until next April—that would make it about a year since he'd arrived. This thought made him cognizant of the calendar and that a date for his departure floated somewhere in his future.

He looked forward to returning to America, to Utah, to home. He imagined long discussions over what he'd experienced. What he hadn't yet shared with his family was his capture by the brigands. He was safe now. He would save that tale for another time. It would make for a good war story at the dinner table, one that he would certainly relate again and again.

But the notion of leaving Formosa turned bittersweet. He hadn't intended to become enchanted with the island and its people. He would have to say goodbye to all the wonderful folks he'd met here, people who had eagerly extended the hand of friendship—Nori Chan, Akito, Kasumi, and even Wu and his tribesmen.

Gary found his musings circling back to Kasumi. In keeping with Asian custom, they hadn't spent much time alone and every conversation they'd had concerned itself with farming. He didn't know much about Kasumi other than that she didn't hesitate to speak her mind. But she was more than pleasant to look at, was clever, empathetic, industrious, and the sparkle in her laugh and in her eyes were details that lingered in his mind for days after he'd left her presence.

The buzz of an approaching motorcycle engine broke the quiet.

In the direction of the road, a dust cloud rose from behind the trees. The motorcycle engine grew louder, and the farm dogs barked to herald its arrival. A moment later, Akito's Velocette appeared, slowed, and drove past the house, blue smoke jetting from the exhaust pipe. Kasumi was at the controls, her braided hair hanging out the back of the cloth helmet, the dark sunglasses looking unusually large on her small face. A waist sash kept her baggy blouse from billowing around her, and her short work pants revealed her shapely calves. Approaching the storage shed, Kasumi killed the engine and the Velocette coasted to a halt. She extended a leg to brace the motorcycle and keep it upright. Upon removing the sunglasses she beamed at her father.

Akito shook his head and muttered, "My daughter, she has no shame."

Gary didn't comment but he understood. In Formosa, as in most of Asia, women—and especially daughters—were supposed to be demure, retiring creatures. And Kasumi was anything but. She was the only child and the only other family member in the household, and Akito depended on her to keep the farm running. And that meant he had to disregard society's expectations of his daughter's conduct. For her part, Kasumi reveled in her independence and celebrated her freedom by buzzing around on the motorcycle whenever she could.

She pushed the motorcycle into the shed and emerged, having removed the cloth helmet, and was tying a red scarf over her head.

"Daughter of mine," Akito groused, "why must you flaunt yourself this way?"

Kasumi's smile remained bright. "So you don't take me for granted, father dear." A courier bag hung at her side. She pulled it to her front and opened the flap. "I brought you the mail. This and that from the market. Matches. A bag of salt. And a newspaper." She handed the newspaper to Akito, who, without glancing at it, passed it to Gary.

It was the *Formosa Nippō*. Usually the headline was about something that happened in Japan. This time the headline read: ***War in Europe!***

It had been weeks since Gary had concerned himself with international news. But these words in bold Kanji type unsettled him. He read on. The article mentioned Polish provocations that had prompted a German invasion this last September. France and England vowed to resist further German encroachment. The narrative had a pro-German slant, which didn't surprise Gary.

During his time in Formosa, Gary had learned that the Japanese were sympathetic to the Germans even though the two had fought as adversaries during the war twenty years earlier. Today, the Japanese were chafing against European colonial constraints just as the Germans were pushing back against the impositions of the Treaty of Versailles. As a result, they had common rivals, the Dutch, the French, and the British.

Akito studied him. "You're looking very glum, my friend."

"What the world doesn't need is another war."

Akito shrugged. "Are you worried it will reach us?"

Gary thought about this. The enormous Pacific Ocean and half the world lay between them and these troubles. The serenity of the orchards calmed him. He folded the newspaper to finish reading it later. "No, not at all," he said. "I think Formosa is a safe place to be."

CHAPTER SEVENTEEN

March 1940

Gary let his English neighbor, Percival Corbett, into his apartment. Percival entered with a canvas backpack slung over one arm. The two enjoyed meeting when they could; conversing in English was a comforting reminder of home for them both. As Percival liked to smoke, they settled at the small outdoor table on Gary's narrow balcony. A late morning breeze brought the muddy smell of the Tanui-Kan River from below.

Percival rested the backpack on his lap and pulled out a stack of dog-eared newspapers and magazines that the hostel's residents had passed around. Even those expatriates who claimed not to be bothered with the news were as obsessed as anyone else about the troubles on the other side of the world. A few months ago, few bothered with politics; now everybody speculated about the war in Europe and what it might mean for Formosa.

Gary thumbed through the stack. The most recent issues in English were of *The Times* and the *Malay Mail*, which he'd already read thoroughly.

Percival set a small tin can on the table and pulled a packet of Players from his shirt pocket. He lit one of the cigarettes and dropped the smoldering match into the tin can. "Do you have cups? Spoons?"

Gary thought the request odd, but retrieved a pair of ceramic cups with spoons from where they rested beside his washbasin. When he returned to the table, Percival was sliding a vacuum bottle from the backpack. "I prefer to accompany my smoke with a drink, but since you don't like a proper beverage, I brought us a suitable alternative."

He uncorked a vacuum bottle and filled one cup, then the other. The steaming brew brought a heady aroma.

"Coffee!" Gary exclaimed. He'd had nothing but tea since he'd been on the island. "How did you manage this?"

Percival answered with his typical enigmatic smile. "This is the Orient. With the right connections, anything is possible." He set two glass jars with screw tops next to the vacuum bottle. One jar contained sugar, the other, clotted cream.

Gary spooned sugar and cream into his coffee. "Your being English, I should think you'd be a tea man, through and through."

"During the war, I served alongside your boys in the 16th Infantry Regiment and learned to appreciate a good cup of joe." Percival smiled and raised his cup. "Cheers, mate."

Like many veterans, Percival was at first tight-lipped about his earlier wartime experiences, but in the ensuing months he'd loosened up a bit. Now Gary knew about Percival's service with the Royal Naval Division. It seemed that when the war had started, the British navy had more men than billets on ships, and the extras were sent to fight in the trenches. Percival served as an engineer and pioneer officer, performing engineering and construction tasks.

Gary enjoyed listening to the stories. He was well aware of the hardships suffered by the men who fought, but the tales of adventure and derring-do entertained and inspired him. For his part, Gary shared his story of being held captive by the brigands. Percival was most interested in how the Japanese soldiers reacted and in details about the electric fences.

But in looking at Percival now, seated comfortably at the table, cup of coffee and cigarette in hand, against the backdrop of boats floating lazily on the river, Gary couldn't imagine his guest as a hard-bitten war hero.

Percival tapped ash into the tin can. "What do you think?"

"About what?" Gary replied.

Percival motioned toward a copy of *The Times*. "The Phoney War. It's been six months since Hitler invaded Poland, and all that's happened is the British and French armies sitting behind the Maginot Line and staring at the Nazis."

"If that's all that's going happen, that's okay by me." Gary sipped his coffee.

"Quite," Percival replied.

The truth was, this new world war was already boiling over. German U-boats had sunk the aircraft carrier *Courageous*, the battleship *Royal Oak* at Scapa Flow, as well as countless smaller ships and cargo steamers. For their part, the Royal Navy had hunted down the German pocket battleship *Admiral Graf Spee*, where her captain scuttled her off the coast of Uruguay.

"Your president Roosevelt isn't helping matters," Percival said. "He's stepped up the embargo against Japan, restricting their imports of oil and iron. And he's established a neutrality zone to contain the ambitions of the German navy. Too bad the American people don't see it that way."

He pointed to an article in *The Times* describing the activities of the America First campaign that resisted any encroachment by the United States into the war in Europe.

"Everybody's got war jitters," Gary said.

"Even our hosts, the Japanese," Percival noted.

Within the last few weeks, more policemen were patrolling the streets and army checkpoints appeared with greater frequency. The Japanese had also given up the pretense of an enlightened governorship, as they treated the locals with suspicion as if they were all brigands.

"What about your farmer friend?" Percival took a pull from his cigarette.

"Akito Saito?"

Percival nodded.

"He's definitely not happy," Gary explained. "He told me the Agricultural Commission has upped his quota to the government, which he is forced to sell at a discount. To make up the difference, he's had to raise the price of what he sells to the public wholesalers. My friend Nori Chan has to then up the price of what she's selling in her fruit stand."

"Costs go up but not wages."

"Exactly. The price of produce has risen so much that people are buying fruit that used to be fed to the hogs."

"Who is receiving all the extra produce?" Percival asked.

"Seems obvious, the military."

"But why now?"

"Maybe they're stepping up their campaign in China," Gary replied. "Lately I've noticed an acceleration in the construction of military depots, like the ammo and supply dumps at Tainan, Rokko, and Kōyrū. And more and more of the railroad cars are reserved for the transportation of military equipment and soldiers. They've also been stockpiling coal and—"

An airplane suddenly roared overhead and interrupted Gary. They tracked the two-engine Mitsubishi until it disappeared from view.

Percival said, "And so many airplanes."

"That's so true," Gary remarked. "When I accompany Nori Chan to the wholesale markets in Keelung, I've seen the big Kawanishi flying patrol boats at the harbor. And the airfields are thick with newly arrived airplanes. All this activity doesn't bode well."

"You're rather observant." Percival stubbed out his cigarette butt in the tin can. "Are you sure you're not a spy?"

Gary laughed. "Far from it. But you'd have to be blind not to see what's happening.

***

Percival smoked another cigarette, and they talked more about the news. Afterwards, Percival gathered his belongings. Gary thanked him for the coffee. Since he had the rest of the afternoon free, he decided to visit Nori Chan, both to buy fresh fruit and to glean more gossip.

He left the hostel and was about to cross the busy street that demarcated the boundary of the Daitatei Bund. At the curb ahead, a man tied honey buckets to the ends of his carry pole.

Gary hadn't yet grown accustomed to the stench of the raw human sewage—referred to as night soil—the locals collected as fertilizer. Like the other Westerners, what he appreciated about the Silver Crane Hostel was that it provided flush toilets. But to the locals, using them was akin to pouring money down the drain. Middlemen paid for franchises of night soil, which they collected in "honey buckets" and sold to farmers. Considering the fastidious nature of the Japanese, Gary found the practice contradictory. But the honey buckets were secured with tight lids and the outsides were wiped clean, keeping down the smell and the flies.

There was another facet to this business that Gary tried not to think about. It turned out that many of the catfish served in local restaurants had been raised in nursery pens on a diet of night soil. Such was the cycle of life for the catfish, and it was a dish Gary never ordered.

The instant he crossed the street, two men in plain clothes approached from behind. Two more in police uniform stepped from the shadows of a market stall. And then two more advanced toward him, only they wore the olive-drab uniforms of the military. Plus, they looked older, around forty. One was stout, the other taller with shiny cavalry boots and officer's rank. Both carried holsters.

The officer growled, "Gary Gatlin, you're to accompany us."

The two police officers grasped Gary's arms. His face registered alarm, and his instinct was to resist, but even if it were possible for him to overcome some or all of these men using jujitsu, where could he go to hide? "What's this about?"

None of the men answered. The sergeant raised an arm, and from the chaos of traffic a boxy, black car bolted toward them. It halted abruptly, tires chirping. The soldier opened one of the rear doors and Gary was pushed inside. The soldier followed him into the back while the officer climbed into the front seat.

"I demand to see the American Consulate," Gary said.

"Mr. Gatlin," the officer replied, "you are in no position to make demands."

***

Gary was escorted to the office of the governor-general, and in short order found himself facing Admiral Izawa Yoshida. Gary thought that while Yoshida was not a physically imposing man, there was no mistaking his authority and gravitas. And though Gary had not been introduced to either the officer or the soldier who had brought him here, he learned by eavesdropping on their conversations that their names were Colonel Eiji Kagawa and Sergeant-Major Kosuke Murakami.

Yoshida asked Gary to produce his passport, studied it, and then stared at Gary for an uncomfortable time. He pointed to the arm-chair in front of his desk. "Please, sit."

"I'd rather remain standing, if you don't mind."

Kagawa and Murakami each placed a hand on Gary's shoulders and pressed him into the chair. He wanted to punch them both but remained compliant as he sat, stiff with resentment and wariness.

"I'd like to know what this is about."

Murakami swatted the back of his head. "You will address the governor-general with the respect he is due."

Gary fought back with all his resolve to not launch himself at the sergeant-major and knock him down. Instead he said, "Admiral, sir."

Yoshida nodded and allowed a smirk. "This is simply a courtesy meeting."

"Am I the only American offered such hospitality?"

In his peripheral vision he saw Murakami wind up to swat him again, but a tiny shake of Yoshida's head made the sergeant-major hold back.

"I've met officials from your consulate, so the answer is no."

"Am I under arrest?"

"Of course not. Why would you think so?"

Gary braced himself against the arms of the chair with a slightly forward movement. "Then I'm free to go?"

Kagawa and Murikami again pressed down on his shoulders.

"We have questions," Yoshida said.

Realizing he was not going anywhere soon, Gary relaxed his posture, although seething inwardly. He crossed his legs. "Very well, ask away."

Yoshida said, "Colonel Kagawa."

The colonel stood beside a map on the wall. "You've been seen in Tainan and Kōyrū, among other places, and have shown particular interest in our military facilities."

How long had they been watching him? Gary replied, "Your trains pass right by. How can I not see them?"

"What is your business in Formosa?"

"If you've been following me all this time, you very well know my business."

Kagawa's jaw clenched. He glared at Gary, then looked away to compose himself.

Yoshida asked, "Have you met the brigand criminal Wu Jen-feng?"

"I've had the pleasure."

"Explain the circumstances."

"His men ambushed the car I was in."

Kagawa stabbed his finger on the map. "Here? Near Dailou?"

"That's correct."

"Then what happened?"

"They kidnapped me."

Kagawa moved his finger in a circle. "And took you where?"

"I couldn't tell. We wandered up and down the mountains. I was lost the entire time."

Murikami leaned over Gary and barked, "How many brigands? What were they doing? Why did they let you go?"

Gary looked at Yoshida. "Admiral, I thought you said this was a courtesy meeting. Appears more like an interrogation to me."

"Sergeant-Major," Yoshida said in a low voice.

Murikami cleared his throat and stood straight.

"Thank you," Gary said. "There were about a dozen men. They seemed like a hard-luck bunch just scraping by. I guess they let me go because I was an extra mouth to feed."

"When did this occur?"

"Several months ago. Soon after I arrived on your beautiful island."

Kagawa brought his face to Gary's and glowered. "Do not patronize us, Mr. Gatlin. Understood?"

Gary nodded. "Understood, Colonel."

"Why did you not report the incident?" Yoshida asked.

"I didn't feel I had to. The brigands took me, stole my money, then let me go."

"You are here to study our farming techniques. Why?"

"Not all your farming techniques, Admiral, primarily the grafting of apples and anything else that can help us improve production back home. Why? Because your farmers have the most advanced techniques in the world."

Yoshida's mask of hostility shifted a little and a smile of pride slipped out. He picked up Gary's passport, flipped through its pages once more, then offered it to Kagawa. The colonel handed it back to Gary.

"Is our business concluded, Admiral?" Gary pocketed the passport.

"For now."

When Kagawa and Murikami reached for Gary's arms, he shrugged them off. Standing, he faced the admiral and bowed stiffly. He gave his most formal farewell. "You honor me with your hospitality, Governor-General. I look forward to the day when I can repay in kind."

Yoshida tipped his head.

Kagawa opened the door and summoned an orderly. "Escort this man outside."

***

Kagawa shut the door behind Gary Gatlin and returned to the admiral's desk.

"What do you think, Colonel?" Yoshida asked.

Although he didn't like their recent guest, there was much about the American that Kagawa admired. He was tall and carried himself with an athletic demeanor. His Japanese was faultless. And he exhibited a genuine manner, which meant he was either extraordinarily honest about his intentions, or was a superb spy because of the masterly way he hid them.

"The truth is, Admiral, I don't know enough about him to give an accurate assessment."

Yoshida looked to Murikami. "And you, Sergeant-Major?"

Murikami couldn't contain himself. "He is big, yes, as are most of these arrogant white devils. But also soft and lacking respect and discipline."

Kagawa interjected, "No one masters Japanese without discipline, Sergeant-Major."

"I do not hold him in the same regard as you, Colonel."

"I'm not asking that you do. But what we cannot do is underestimate an enemy."

"Potential enemy," Yoshida corrected.

"A potential enemy is best regarded as an enemy," Murikami replied.

"I'll grant you that, Sergeant-Major," Yoshida said. "Here's my question for the two of you to answer. Is Gary Gatlin a spy or not?"

"And if he is, Admiral?" Kagawa asked.

"Then sit tight on that information, Colonel. When the time is right, we will act with the appropriate measures."

Kagawa knew exactly what measures the admiral meant, which is why he'd detailed a thorough, pitiless man like Murikami to this task.

Yoshida placed his hands on the table. "Colonel, you and the sergeant-major will continue with your surveillance of Gary Gatlin."

Kagawa and Murikami bowed. "*Hai. Hai.*"

CHAPTER EIGHTEEN

August 1940

Gary and Akito made their way through the apple orchards. A morning rain had left the ground slick and muddy, and a heavy, humid, earthy smell rolled across the fields.

They were inspecting the apple budlings Gary had grafted onto the trees earlier in the spring. All summer he had tended to them, and with the autumn harvest just around the corner he was both curious and happy with the budlings' progress. The apples still needed another month to reach maturity, but he was certain that his grafts would produce choice fruit. To jot his observations, he crouched and balanced a notebook on his knee.

Gray clouds tumbled above, growing darker by the minute and threatening yet more rain. He noticed that Akito's chickens were nowhere to be found, so evidently they—as dumb as poultry were reputed to be—were smart enough to seek shelter.

With that thought came rain pattering through the trees. Fat drops splashed against the pages of his notebook, which he shut to keep his pencil marks and ink from smearing. Akito however, continued, seemingly oblivious to the shower.

Gary decided to store his notebook in the house before the rain turned his pages into mush. As he trotted to Akito's house the rain let loose, and he managed to reach the protection of the eaves just as the deluge came in roaring sheets. Water swiftly overflowed the irrigation ditches and snaked in rivulets across the orchard. Through the torrential blur he could barely see Akito.

After wiping moisture from the covers of his journal, Gary assessed how wet he'd gotten. His hair and shirt were damp but not soaked.

The window shutters were open, and he heard Kasumi in the kitchen. Entering through the back door, he found her lighting the kerosene stove and setting a kettle on the burner.

"It got chilly," she said. "I'm going to brew tea. Where's my father?"

"Still outside. He's apt to drown in this downpour," Gary said jokingly.

"He does this," she looked out the window, "standing out there in the rain."

Gary slipped out of his shoes and left them by the door. "I'll bet he asks why no one looks at you funny when you stand in the sunshine."

"How do you know that?" she asked.

"My dad used to do the same thing. A big difference is that it gets pretty cold in Utah, and getting wet at the wrong time could bring on pneumonia. My mother would yell at him, but my dad said he was used to it. Getting drenched. Getting covered in snow. Said it was all part and parcel of being a farmer."

The water boiled, and Kasumi filled a teapot. "I've got work to finish in the office," she said. "You're more than welcome to join me."

Gary followed her to the room next door, where she set the teapot and cups on the table. The table was stacked with ledgers and bundles of receipts. Wordlessly, she sat at the middle of the table where the documents were arrayed in front of her. She leafed through a ledger she had bookmarked previously.

He sat in the chair at the head of the table, and as he sat there he became aware of the near proximity between the two of them. He enjoyed being this close, but made it a point to act uninterested, since the closer he was to Kasumi, the more his thoughts weren't about apples or farming. While he didn't want to disturb her, he saw this as an opportunity to draw her into a conversation. He liked talking to her, but the only topic he could think of now was, "How are the government quotas affecting you?"

"They're a mixed blessing," she replied, surprising him with the quick answer, almost as if she were waiting for him to ask. "True, we're obligated to sell them a larger share of our crop at a discount, but in turn, we've convinced the agricultural commission to pay for the farm hands. That puts otherwise idle people to work. And we keep the best produce for our wholesalers. There are ways to game the system."

Gary hadn't expected such an astute explanation and couldn't think of anything else to say. So he fell silent as Kasumi resumed her work. He thumbed through his notebook as he sat there, and thought about the future. He'd been in Formosa over a year now, and when his budlings reached maturity, this would be the second harvest he'd documented since arriving. How much more could he learn about grafting techniques? Maybe it was time he began to make definite plans for his return home to share what he'd learned.

The tea had had enough time to brew. He poured a cup for Kasumi and one for himself. She thanked him with a quick nod and sipped.

He drank his tea and appreciated the comforting warmth that it brought him. Periodically he glanced at Kasumi though was careful not to stare. Her long, black hair hung past her shoulders. As she read, she would absently hook a strand behind her left ear, then the right. The gesture revealed her face in full profile to Gary.

Growing up, he'd never thought about Asian women. The women he'd been raised around were good-looking enough, and for the most part, smart and fun to be around.

Kasumi was, he had to admit, exceptionally pretty. Gary knew she'd had a few suitors, but devoted as she was to her father, she'd promised to never leave his side. Gary hadn't broached the topic, but Akito still mourned the loss of his wife, and Kasumi felt it was her duty to lessen his burden.

"You're looking at me," Kasumi said without taking her eyes from the ledger.

Gary blushed. "Sorry."

Kasumi put her pen aside. "I guess we need to talk about some things."

Gary sat up, alert, ready to be chastised for crossing a line. "If I did something…"

She looked uncertainly away from him, then back toward the kitchen, then down at her paperwork. "I don't know where to start."

"If I've done something wrong, then start at the beginning."

"What?" she gazed at him, her eyebrows arched in surprise. "Why would you think you've done something wrong?"

"It's that, well—" Why were the words he wanted to say becoming so elusive?

"Gary, I think about you."

Her announcement stunned him.

"You make me think of many things, Gary," she continued softly.

"I've been thinking about you as well."

They stared at one another.

After a moment, she said, "This is awkward, isn't it?"

"More than it should be."

"So what happens now?" she asked. "You and I are old enough to make important decisions."

The awkwardness Gary felt took an abrupt turn. "What kind of decisions?"

She said, "I don't want to make a fool of myself and waste my time wondering if you feel about me as I feel about you."

Gary felt his pulse race. "I don't know how to answer. The truth is that I try not to think about you, because if I did, I'm not sure where things between us would lead." It seemed that he and Kasumi were careening right toward each other, and in the aftermath of the collision his life would never be the same.

Her breath became shallow, as if she were expecting him to make the next move. Hesitantly, he slid his hand across the table and laid it over hers. She turned her hand over and their fingers interlocked. Hers were warm and firm and inviting. The air was electric with anticipation and trepidation.

"There is one thing on my mind," Kasumi said. "Something that I must know."

"Go ahead."

"Before we proceed, I have to know your plans for leaving Formosa." She gestured to his journal. "All your work has been for your farm back in America. You're going to leave soon."

Gary felt her fingers tighten as if she were holding onto him. He thought about all the times in all these months that he'd been around her. He had made it a point to keep occupied with his work so he wouldn't be distracted by her. Clearly, Kasumi had been doing the same.

"Before I go, there's a lot I have to sort out," he said.

"About your work?"

"That, and about us."

***

Gary stepped off the train the moment it halted in the Shinsha station. Without hesitation he walked outside and down the block, where he passed markets and barbershops, their front doors open wide.

At the corner he looked to his left and saw a Ford Model T truck rolling toward him. Nori Chan waved at him from inside the cab. The driver of the truck slowed enough for Gary to catch the passenger door as it was flung open. He clambered onto the running board. The truck accelerated and Gary swung through the door. Nori scooted over to make room on the seat and squeezed herself between Gary and the driver.

"You're a big guy," the driver remarked, an older man with the dark complexion of an aboriginal.

The truck turned onto a side street, then turned again at the next. Both the driver and Gary studied the rear-view mirrors to make sure they weren't followed, which they weren't.

Normally, Gary didn't care if the Japanese wasted their time tailing him during his travels from Taihoku to Dailou and Chen's farm. But today he planned to deliver a load of provisions to Wu Fenjeng's tribe. The delivery didn't include weapons, but the Japanese considered any help to the brigands as aiding and abetting an enemy.

"I got everything on your list," Nori stuck a thumb back toward the truck bed.

Earlier, Gary had given her money and a list of supplies—sugar, cooking oil, matches, assorted hand tools. "Good. Thank you."

If he had personally bought the provisions, that would have aroused suspicions by the police and the army. Ever since his meeting with the governor-general, Gary felt as though he were under a microscope. If Nori bought the supplies and hired the driver, she was just another local making her way through her day.

Something else that Nori had done for him. Considering these uncertain and perilous times, she had convinced him that it would be wise if he carried "runaway money." What she meant was a stash of gold coins sewn into a money belt. The coins could buy emergency supplies, or just as importantly, persuade an official to look the other way. Together they visited a gold merchant in Keelung where Gary bought twelve US $10 gold Eagles. He had sewn the coins into a custom-made belt that he made it a point to always wear. Presently, the heavy belt sagged against his hips, but the weight comforted him.

The truck continued over a series of levees passing through fields of sugar cane, then over the bridge crossing the Taikō-kei River, then through more cane fields. They proceeded past hamlets crowding the road and then up hills terraced with tea farms. The road curved up and around a steep hill. Mile by mile, the road grew rockier and more twisted and plunged deeper through the forest. The road became a trail, then a pair of faint ruts through the grass, and finally ended in a small clearing on a rocky bluff. The driver braked.

Gary climbed out and scrutinized the surroundings. The far side of the clearing dropped into a wooded valley, and the other sides were walled in by dense underbrush.

The air was still and oppressively hot and humid. Gary wiped sweat from his face. He drank from a canteen in the truck cab and poured water into his hat to soak the crown and keep him cool.

Nori Chan climbed into the back of the truck and pushed the two crates of provisions toward the rear of the bed. Gary and the driver carried them to the edge of the clearing.

Gary felt a presence behind him. Nori Chan's eyes cut over his shoulder. When he turned, he saw three brigands behind him, one of them Wu Jen-feng, another was Chiang Zhu-Mei...Scarface. They all cradled new Japanese rifles.

Wu Jen-feng waved his arm. Another armed brigand rose from a hiding spot by the road. Then from the brush, four tribal women carrying bamboo litter poles emerged through the wall of leaves. The women were barefoot and tiny, not even five feet tall, but looked as though hewn from sturdy wood. Their faces bore dark chevrons tattooed across their cheeks, and they wore modern blouses over traditional baggy shorts. Nori Chan greeted them with a bow, and they exchanged pleasantries in a tribal language.

Then, astonishingly, from behind Wu Jen-feng, Gary's neighbor Percival Corbett strode into the open, a leather camera case hanging from a strap around his neck. He was drenched in perspiration, and his ruddy face was bright red from exertion.

"What are you doing here?" Gary, obviously surprised, asked in English.

Percival shrugged out of his backpack and rested it by his boots. "Adding to my memoirs," he answered in Japanese.

"What does that mean?"

"I'm taking a sight-seeing jaunt. Wu Jen-feng—" he pointed to the chieftain— "is providing guides."

"To go where?"

Percival tapped the camera case and pointed east. "The mountains between here and the coast are among the most spectacular in this part of Asia. I'm hoping to get pictures of them published."

Gary thought this somewhat odd, but then, the British were known to be eccentric.

"I could use the company," Percival added.

Gary's plan had been to deliver the provisions, then continue to Dailou. But the invitation intrigued him. He knew that soon he'd have to return home to America, so why not accompany Percival for the adventure? Who knew what he'd learn? "How long will I be gone? The day?"

Percival laughed. "We might reach the base of the mountain range by nightfall. Plan for three days."

"All right." Gary returned to the truck, and from his travel bag picked what he thought he'd need. He stuffed the items and a canteen into a large cloth tote bag, then told Nori Chan, "Please deliver my travel bag to Akito. Tell him I'll see him later in the week."

In the meantime, the women had lashed the crates to the litter poles. On Wu Jen-feng's order, they shouldered the load. He said, "Percival, Gary, from here we part ways. Chiang Zhu-Mei and my other man will escort you."

Scarface grinned at Gary in recognition, then tipped his head toward a path in the weeds leading north. Percival, Gary, and the other tribesman followed him. Wu Jen-feng and his party disappeared into the brush, the women with the litter moving with quiet, athletic ease. Waving goodbye, Nori Chan climbed back into the truck and it chugged back to the road.

Gary waded through weeds that grew from knee height to the waist, and then merged into a continuous tangle of tall brush before they stepped out onto another, clearer trail and continued on. The sound of the truck had long since faded, and the only noises were branches scraping against his clothes and his labored breathing. The going was tough, and he distracted himself by thinking about Kasumi and how it was that Percival and Wu Jen-feng had connected.

They marched for hours, resting only in the shade to drink water.

The evening brought a welcome coolness but they continued, halting finally in a copse of dense brush along one side of a steep ravine. They camped for the night, Scarface heating water for tea over a tiny fire he'd dug in the bottom of the ravine. Though hidden by miles of rugged wilderness, the brigands weren't taking any chances at giving themselves away. After a dinner of cold balls of rice mixed with pieces of some kind of meat, an exhausted Gary unrolled his sleep-mat, then lay beside the path and fell asleep.

Before daybreak, he was awakened by the other men rustling. As the morning brightened, they drank fresh tea, chowed down on more rice balls, then started the day's march. Through gaps in the forest, Gary spied a nearby mountain. The view from its summit would be spectacular. Percival snapped a couple of photos with his Leica camera. But instead of climbing toward the mountain, Gary noted that they were circling past it to remain in the cover of the woods. During a break, Percival was hunched over a map that he oriented with a military pocket compass.

Gary, beginning to be puzzled about this trek, asked, "Why do we keep going east, instead of closer to the mountain?"

"In due time," Percival replied. From this point, as they marched, he kept the map handy, as if to be precisely aware of their location.

In the late afternoon, he halted the group and whispered instructions to Scarface, who crept ahead. While they waited in the shade, Gary surmised that perhaps Percival wasn't interested in the mountains at all. If this trip was not about sightseeing, then what?

The other brigand remained alert, like a guard dog with its ears pricked forward. Gary noted the time on his watch. After ten minutes, Scarface returned. The expression on his otherwise taciturn face appeared pleased, as if he'd found whatever it was he was looking for.

They proceeded at a slow, deliberate pace, Scarface on point, then Percival, Gary, and the other brigand watching their backs. Scarface stopped abruptly and held still, and Percival and Gary joined him to gradually and cautiously step to the edge of the wood-line.

They were along the top of a steep cliff. The vista overlooked a shallow coastal plain that curled around a bay. Beyond that, the ocean expanded to the horizon. The coastal plain was a bright green panorama of rice fields, segmented into a grid by levees and roads. A train—tiny in the distance—crawled toward a small town, obscured by haze.

Airplanes appeared as silver dots circling a faraway airfield. A flotilla of ships surrounded a larger warship in the middle of the bay.

Percival spread the map on the dirt. Gary stared over his shoulder. The map read *Karenko*. Besides the airfield, railroad depot, and port facilities, the map listed an aluminum processing plant.

Careful to remain under cover, Percival studied the town through a pair of binoculars that he'd retrieved from his backpack. He handed the binoculars to Gary, said "Hold onto these, mate," then made notes in pencil on the map.

Gary at last understood what was going on. He inhaled sharply and said to Percival, "You're a spy."

***

Yoshida stood on the admiral's bridge aboard the heavy cruiser *Myōkō*. Through his binoculars he studied the coastline around the port of Karenko. He was on the third day of his tour of Formosa, hosting a delegation from the Imperial Navy Headquarters staff. The trip was a welcome break from his duties as governor-general and allowed him to return to his roots as an officer at sea. One minor disappointment was that the delegation was comprised of staff assistants, with no one of higher rank than captain. Yoshida had wanted to impress his fellow admirals with his keen assessment of the military situation in the Pacific.

He swept an upturned hand toward the coast. "We cannot underestimate the strategic value of Formosa. Not only is the island a vital source of food, coal, and material, but because of its strategic location, we must consider Formosa as a gigantic and unsinkable aircraft carrier. From any airfield on the island, we can unleash an armada of bombers to strike any enemy within a thousand kilometers."

He smiled at his guests, certain that they would relay his insights to the high brass in Tokyo. "Formosa is the springboard from which we can launch devastating blows against Java, the Philippines, Australia, and possibly even the western coast of America."

"It's no secret, Admiral," noted a staff officer with the rank of commander, "that with the British and French having their hands full fighting the Germans in the north Atlantic and the Mediterranean, our biggest threat will be the American navy."

Yoshida grinned. "Should the Emperor direct such an offensive, then I look forward to crushing the Yankees in battle."

Chapter Nineteen

April 1941

Colonel Eiji Kagawa stepped into the personal office of Governor-General Yoshida, arriving at the admiral's personal invitation. He marched to Yoshida's desk and snapped to attention.

"Relax, please," Yoshida said, standing. "This won't take long as I have a busy schedule, but I want to express my thanks to you for your service. It is because of men like yourself that makes leaving Formosa a bittersweet experience."

Kagawa bowed. "I serve you, Admiral, as I serve the Emperor."

On the desk, next to a clock and other knickknacks, lay a small, flat box wrapped in gilded paper. Yoshida removed the wrapping and opened the lid, and offered the box to Kagawa. It was a gift box of yōkan candy pressed into the shape of chrysanthemums. "I'd offer you a cigarette but I know you don't care to smoke. Here, take one. It was a present from my family when they heard of my appointment to the fleet."

"Thank you, sir." Kagawa took one of the morsels of sweetened bean curd. Its delicious taste brought back many fond memories of his childhood and family. "And congratulations on your appointment to head the Third Expeditionary Fleet."

"Thank you, Colonel. While I considered it a distinct honor to serve as governor-general, as a navy man, fate calls me to the sea, to serve onboard a ship."

Kagawa wondered about Yoshida's casual demeanor. In the Japanese military, the differences between ranks were clearly delineated, and the higher the rank, the greater the distinction, especially between admiral and colonel. Such informal displays were reserved for off-duty gatherings between officers of like rank or when with close family. But Yoshida was an admiral and it was his prerogative to act as he pleased without Kagawa's approval.

Yoshida stepped to the large map of China pinned to one wall and passed his hand over the continent's coast, Formosa, and the South China and Philippine Seas. "This is my new area of responsibility. Presently, it's one of support to the army and to protect the southern flank of our forces in Manchuko."

The admiral stepped to the next map, one of the North Atlantic and Europe. "But it's the events here that ordain our future. In signing the Tripartite Pact, the Emperor has thrown our lot in with Hitler and Mussolini. What do you think, colonel?"

"Admiral, I would be grossly out of line to second-guess the Emperor."

Yoshida tipped his head. *Good point.* "However, there are factions within the Navy, and Admiral Yamamoto is one of them, who argue that if our aims are economic hegemony of the Asian Pacific, then we should negotiate with the British, French, and Dutch for control of their colonies. They're in no position to resist militarily. Hitler has crushed the armies of France and Britain. The Dutch have been completely subjugated. To sweeten any negotiations, some within Navy Headquarters even proposed that we send warships to aid the British cause, as we did in the First World War."

Kagawa said nothing, and Yoshida looked at him pointedly.

"Feel free to speak, Colonel. As the head of Formosa's intelligence service, I hope you have opinions."

Kagawa stiffened, not sure how the admiral would react. He spoke slowly and with restraint. "Destiny has presented us with a fantastic opportunity. Our rivals in Asia are flat on their backs and vulnerable." As Kagawa continued to speak, his words became more impassioned. "Our interests in Asia are not only about economic control but also about respect and prestige. The Westerners hold us Japanese in little regard. As a nation we can do better than supplicate for crumbs. We are, in every regard, the equals of any of these powers." Kagawa jabbed a finger at the map of Europe. "If we need to spill blood to prove that, then so be it." Falling silent, he saw that Yoshida was staring at him.

The stare suddenly curved into a smile. He slapped Kagawa on the back. "Well said, Colonel." Yoshida moved his finger to the heel of the Italian boot. "Although the German air force has been pounding the British Isles for months now, the British still have plenty of fight in them. Lately our navy headquarters has shown much interest in the Royal Navy's attack on the Italian fleet in Taranto, Italy, that took place last November. The British launched torpedo bombers from their aircraft carriers to cripple the Italian warships berthed in the harbor."

He clasped his hands behind his back and rocked on his heels. "Our navy has been studying the use of torpedo bombers to attack in this manner, but the challenge is launching torpedoes from airplanes and not having them burrow into the shallow bottom of a harbor. Apparently, the British have figured this out."

Yoshida turned away from the map for his desk. "What's more is that the British executed their attack using biplanes. We have much more modern aircraft and torpedoes coming into service."

These were interesting details, Kagawa noted. He surveyed the Pacific map and his eyes drifted to the east. "And the Americans? They have a significant presence in the Philippines."

Yoshida coughed. "When we do come to terms with them, they will be given a hard lesson in respect. But as a prelude to that, one directive from general headquarters in Tokyo has ordered us to reassess our vulnerability to foreign espionage."

From a desk drawer, he retrieved a manila folder marked CONFIDENTIAL. "Colonel, this is your dossier on the American Gary Gatlin. I've briefed my successor, General Arima, about him and your efforts."

"I appreciate that, Admiral."

Yoshida settled into his chair. "Soon you'll have your hands free to deal with this worrisome Gatlin as you see fit. My last order as governor-general prior to relinquishing my command is this." He retrieved another folder. "I've ordered the detention of foreign nationals."

"Arrest?"

"No, detention. It will be for the security of the state and for their own safety."

"Won't the consulates object?"

"Of course they will. I'm sure that most of those detained will be released, but I'd be surprised if your efforts did not bear fruit."

Kagawa grinned.

"What's so amusing, colonel?"

"It's that this Gatlin came to Formosa to study fruit, and little did he guess that the fruit to be harvested would be him."

**

At the governor-general's change-of-command ceremony, Kagawa stood with the army military counterintelligence contingent in the bleachers beside the reviewing stand. The bleachers faced Taihoku Park, located in the middle of the city's government complex, where battalions of soldiers and sailors had assembled. While Kagawa embraced the spit-and-polish formality of military service, he viewed parades and standing in formation as a waste of time. It didn't take much to train a man to dress appropriately and have him march in circles.

Representatives from the foreign consulates crowded the bleachers. Kagawa had detailed his men to secretly tally and photograph them.

Presently, Admiral Yoshida and his replacement, General Arima, rode in a staff car to inspect the troops, the sun gleaming off the hundreds of bayonets on rifles held at present arms. The car returned to the reviewing stand, where the admiral and the general dismounted and assumed positions behind a battery of microphones.

Yoshida gave his farewell comments. His words were repeated through large trumpet-shaped loudspeakers arrayed to face the bleachers, but his voice echoed against the surrounding buildings so it was impossible to understand what he was saying. Kagawa didn't realize the admiral was finished until a wave of polite applause rippled through the audience.

Next, General Arima gave his comments, and again they were lost in the confusing echoes.

The battalions then ordered their men to cheer in unison; the men raised their arms and shouted, *"Long live The Emperor!"*

The regimental adjutant called the battalions to attention. He saluted Arima—the new governor-general—and presented the troops. For a long moment, everyone remained frozen, the prolonged silence awkward.

Then airplanes roared overheard, waves of them, flying in precise V's. The passing formations blotted out the sun, *shadow, flash, shadow, flash,* to the syncopated growl of their engines. Kagawa recognized the big twin-engine Mitsubishi and Kawasaki bombers, and the sleek Nakajima fighter planes and torpedo bombers. These were the latest in the Japanese air service and equal to any others in the world. Kagawa had made it a special point to learn this as he was privy to classified intelligence. He mused which of these aircraft would be the first to strike the Americans.

***

Nori Chan considered herself a modern woman. She knew that progress would come about only by accepting the future. As she would tell others, *If you spend too much time looking at what's behind, you'll fall into the hole in front of you.*

But Nori was also superstitious, especially when it came to the fortune as revealed by tea leaves. And lately, those tea leaves were not revealing good news. The last two times she read her fortune, she had seen a serpent—bad news in the offing.

Worried that she had not read the tea leaves correctly, early this morning she visited another fortune teller, who read a fresh cup and said, "A big serpent. It bodes darkness. And it straddles a gate."

Serpent? Gate? What did this mean?

A disquieted Nori started her day, walking carefully as if misfortune waited around the next corner.

Her plan was to visit the wholesalers market and put in a new order. The government's recent quotas on produce were squeezing her, but she didn't perceive this as the serpent of bad news. It was something else, something more ominous.

She proceeded out through the entrance of the Daitatei Bund and waited for a break in traffic at the cross streets. Glancing about, she noticed policemen in plain clothes. They were easy to spot because they looked like Japanese interpretations of American policemen in plain clothes from the movies. The men stood with their backs to the walls of the shops, fedoras pulled low across their eyes.

As if on cue, they reached into their coat pockets and pulled out white ribbons that they cinched around their upper sleeves.

From three directions, police cars rushed toward the Daitatei Bund. Uniformed officers clung to the sides of the cars. Their comrades in plain clothes rushed into the street and directed traffic away to clear the path for the approaching cars. They screeched to a stop, the policemen on the running boards hopping to the street. More policemen sprang from inside the cars.

Nori counted at least thirty policemen.

Then a dozen military trucks rumbled through the street and pulled up short beside the cars, soldiers clambering out the backs to line up on the street.

Nori tucked herself into an open market stall, trying her best to hide among the pedestrians cringing against the crates of herbs and vegetables.

The policemen and soldiers queued up outside the gate, their stern expressions showing they were ready to smash heads. Another group of soldiers shepherded a large military car to the front of the line. The soldiers on the running boards leapt to the ground and formed a cordon around the car. When it stopped, two men climbed out, both Japanese, one a tall colonel, the other a senior sergeant who snarled at the proceedings. The colonel consulted with a group of military officers clustered around a map spread on the hood of another police car.

Nori was too far away to hear what they discussed over the commotion of the soldiers and police hustling into position. The colonel said something to the senior sergeant, who climbed on top of the car's front bumper. He shouted a command and officers sped to the front of the column of soldiers and police. Those officers blew shrill shrieks on their whistles. The men in the column readied their rifles and truncheons. Then another volley of whistle shrieks and the column charged through the gate into the Daitatei Bund, shouting, one giant serpent of men in olive green and police blue.

A serpent!

Nori recoiled at the realization. This column was the serpent her fortune had warned about.

***

Colonel Kagawa, Senior-Sergeant Murikami, and their raiding party rushed to the Silver Crane Hostel. The soldiers in the lead burst through the lobby doors and braced the clerks. Though their orders were to corral all the foreign nationals, the Englishman Percival Corbett and the American Gary Gatlin were Kagawa's priorities.

Murikami slapped the search warrant on a front counter. "Bring the master keys."

The soldiers prodded the head clerk up the stairs to the third floor. A ring of keys jangled in his hand. Reaching Room 310, fingers trembling, he struggled to insert the correct key.

"Better hurry up, Chinese mongrel," Murikami threatened, "or we'll bash your head in like we will the door."

The door lock clicked open, and the clerk shuffled out of the way. The soldiers filed in first, Murikami and Kagawa following.

The room was airy and serene despite the ruckus below. Fresh air billowed from the double doors opening to a small balcony.

Percival waited along the balcony railing, watching, puffing on a cigarette. Black smoke curled from a large bowl on the balcony table. Kagawa took brisk steps to the table and studied the contents of the bowl. From the large pile of smoldering ashes it was obvious that the Englishman had just burned some papers. Kagawa locked eyes with Percival, who remained as cool as ice.

The soldiers overturned the bed and mattress, rifled the drawers, and dumped every loose item onto the floor. Triumphantly, one of them displayed a camera in a leather case and a stack of maps.

Murikami thumbed through the stack and selected a map labeled *Karenko*. He handed this one to Kagawa, who noted that a section had been torn from the margin.

One soldier grasped Corbett by the shirt collar and dragged him stumbling toward Kagawa. The colonel nodded at Murikami who then punched Corbett hard in the gut.

He doubled over. Murikami kicked the legs out from under the Englishman, and he crashed facedown to the floor. Murikami dropped with a knee to the center of Corbett's back and wrenched his hands together to cuff them, then hoisted the Englishman to his feet.

Corbett's face was a fiery red. His hair drooped across his face, his eyes teary with pain and apprehension. Gasping, he managed to say in English, "I demand to see the British Consul."

Kagawa answered in Japanese. "I know perfectly well that you understand me, Percival Corbett." He slapped the map across Corbett's face. "Your consul will be notified. But first you will be brought up on charges of being a spy."

A corporal dashed into the room. "Colonel, we just searched the room of the American Gary Gatlin. He's not here."

Kagawa rushed to Gatlin's room. His soldiers were in the process of ransacking the drawers, armoire, and bed. Even as the men piled the American's belongings on the floor, Kagawa knew the exercise was futile. His man was gone.

He opened the door to the balcony and stepped outside. He panned the commotion outside, the soldiers and police hauling prisoners—actually suspects—to awaiting trucks for interrogation.

They had snagged the Englishman, but it was the cocky American that Kagawa wanted trapped and strung up like game. Gatlin was the new prize. The hunt continued.

***

When Gary entered the Yamatochō Bank, the bank president, Mr. Shitaba, rushed from his office to welcome him. Gary thought this odd since Shitaba had never acted interested in him before.

"I've received this from home." Gary presented a telegram. "My family has wired a thousand dollars."

With a handkerchief, Shitaba nervously blotted sweat from his brow and avoided eye contact.

"Is there something the matter, Mr. Shitaba?"

"No, not all." Shitaba wiped his temple. "It's just so warm."

Which wasn't true, Gary noted. The weather was typical for this time of year. Pleasant, if on the cool side during the morning.

"Permit me, please." Shitaba gestured for the telegram. Gary gave it to him, and Shitaba started back to his office.

Why was he so anxious? And why was he handling the matter

personally? His clerks were perfectly competent. Gary said, "Perhaps if I accompany you in case there's a problem?"

"No. No. This is only a brief matter." Shitaba hurried to his office and closed the door. Through the window in the office door Gary saw him snatch a telephone from his desk and make a call. For some strange reason, as Shitaba talked on the phone, he used his free hand, as though to shield his eyes from Gary.

Why was Shitaba acting so peculiarly? Gary settled into a chair in the lobby.

A commotion at the entrance disrupted the calm. The bank guard was pushing against a short, older woman trying to get past. She was Nori Chan.

She saw Gary and cried out, "Get out! The army is looking for you!"

Gary's mind whirled. *The army was after him?*

Nori struggled with the guard. "Gary, you can't waste time."

Gary glanced at Shitaba, who stood frozen with the telephone in hand, his face pale with distress. Shitaba must have called the police to tell them he was here.

Why? Gary would have to answer that question later.

He bolted from his chair and, with a swift jujitsu move, knocked the guard away from Nori. They ran outside, where they heard the echoing scream of an approaching siren. Nori grabbed Gary by the lapel and yanked him to the alley where they crouched behind stacks of broken crates.

A sedan raced by, police officers hanging to its side. Breathless and confused, Gary peered from behind cover to see them rush past and then screech to a halt outside the bank. Lunging en masse from the sedan, the policemen charged into the bank.

The confusion cleared instantly. Gary knew exactly what this meant. He was now a wanted man.

Chapter Twenty

April 1941

Nori Chan hauled Gary by the lapel and led him down the alley, away from the Yamatochō Bank.

Gary imagined the jaws of a trap closing around him. With the government after him, he could think of only one sanctuary.

"We need to get to the American Consulate," he whispered to Nori. Even as he said this, he pictured the route they'd have to take. The consulate was two miles northeast of here. A direct route would have them skirt the northern edge of the main government complex, cross a major east-west thoroughfare, proceed right through the central railroad depot, pass between the ice plant and the tobacco factory, then past a public school. The path was rife with exposure.

To avoid the center of town, they had two options:

Circle south, which would take them through the military barracks and across at least two more busy thoroughfares.

Or, circle north, which involved crossing the east-west thoroughfare, passing through the railroad terminal, but after that they could proceed through the Kenseichō neighborhood and its warren of tenements, shops, and twisting alleys.

To communicate his plan, all Gary had to say was, "Kenseichō."

Nori nodded. She took brisk steps to get ahead of him. Where the alley emptied into the street, she halted and signaled for him to stop as well. Traffic and pedestrians jammed the street. Looking discreetly to the left and right, she made sure the way was clear and gestured for him to hurry.

Emerging onto the street, he followed her to another alley, then through side streets, weaving around and through sidewalk stalls, open-air shops, and stacks of crates and honey pots. All the while, Gary felt as conspicuous as a pine tree in a flower garden.

And so they continued. Sneaking block by block, Gary tried his best to blend in. Despite the cool weather, sweat beaded his forehead, and he worked his tongue to moisten his parched lips.

When they paused in the clutter of people strung along the main thoroughfare, Gary scoped out the traffic. The few cops and soldiers within sight seemed preoccupied with routine duties. He and Nori threaded their way between the trucks and carts slogging over the crowded pavement. They hustled across the railroad tracks, through another stream of traffic, and on to the western edge of the railroad yards.

Here, sentries paced along a line of boxcars, paying little attention to locals taking the shortcut over a worn path along the edge of the rail yard. Nori and Gary did their best to lose themselves in the procession of vendors and vagabonds. But the path was in the open, several hundred yards from any cover. Gary was well aware of his vulnerability, and true panic set in. The distance to any type of concealment seemed enormous, and he was gripped by thoughts of what might lie ahead if he were caught.

Fear sent his mind spinning and his heart racing. He imagined policemen shrieking their whistles and shouting at him, and when he tried to run away his feet remaining immobile as if mired in concrete. He imagined Japanese soldiers springing from the earth and seizing him. He imagined being bound in chains and dragged into a dank jail cell.

Step by step, the jumbled mass of the Kenseichō neighborhood loomed closer. His heartbeat slammed like a bass drum.

Then they dashed across the street and plunged into a chaotic mix of people, shops, and ox-driven carts packed within the jumble of ramshackle buildings.

In his previous travels through Taihoku, Gary had never ventured through this neighborhood, and now didn't get his bearings until they reached the railroad tracks on the far side, the rail line leading north from the Taishōgai market. The American Consulate was two blocks away. Gary, breathing a little easier, could see the proverbial light at the end of the tunnel.

He waited in an alley while Nori scouted ahead.

She rushed back. "Gary, the army has set up roadblocks around the consulate."

He had to see for himself. Hunching over to disguise his height, he ducked behind a table in the first stall by the alley.

Just as Nori reported, soldiers watched from behind wooden barricades set across the street. A car had been stopped and its occupants stood outside as the soldiers searched the interior. More soldiers patrolled the consulate's perimeter. Unless Gary grew wings, he'd never reach this sanctuary.

Scared, defeated, dejected, he shrank back into the alley. What could he do? He couldn't return to the hostel. Plus, the government had certainly seized his money, so now he was penniless.

Why did this happen? All that he wanted in coming to Formosa was to learn how to grow better fruit. But it seemed that the world had folded in on itself, and in doing so, piled on top of him.

"Come this way," Nori said.

"Where are we going?"

"Away from here."

***

December 1941

For eight months now Gary had been on the run, Nori Chan scuttling him from hidey-hole to hidey-hole like a hunted rat. Working in their favor was the fact that the locals accepted Japanese authority only as long as things ran smoothly and fairly. But with the onset of food quotas, forced austerity, and martial law, old resentments returned and so everyday people engaged in passive resistance and dragged their feet about everything. A common refrain was, "The Japanese think we are stupid, and so we'll act accordingly."

For the last few days, thanks to friends of Nori, Gary had found sanctuary and was lying low in a fourth-story room of a tenement building. Over the decades, its apartments had been divided and subdivided until each floor was a maze of tiny, squalid enclosures. Voices and assorted noises filtered through the mildewed walls nonstop, day and night. He was fortunate to at least have a room with an outside window.

He stretched across a stained cot—the only piece of furniture in the place—and let the sunlight streaming through the window warm his legs. Even when he tried to relax his nerves remained taut, and it was this constant tension that wore him down.

His circumstances had been whittled to simple survival. His only possessions were what he wore or carried in his pockets. His coat and trousers were patched. To keep his pants up, he had had to punch new holes in his ever-tightening belt, and he dreamed of steak dinners and bowls of ice cream. He'd given Nori one of his $10 eagle coins, but given the shortages and suspicions that swirled around them, there were things not even gold could buy.

What buoyed him was that Nori said she'd collected his journals from his apartment in the Silver Crane and delivered them to Akito Saito for safekeeping. That meant his years of diligent note taking had not gone to waste.

Approaching footfalls provoked the all-too-familiar surge of panic. He sat up and grabbed his coat, draping it over his lap. Should he have to flee, he'd have to exit through the window to the fire escape.

Steps shuffled to the door. It opened and Nori Chan entered. Closing the door, she offered a small tin bucket, which brought the aroma of fresh food.

Gary squatted on the floor, set the bucket between his feet, and yanked away a cloth napkin covering the food. A steamed fish was curled over a pile of rice and vegetables, and smelled heavenly. He hadn't eaten meat in days and couldn't wait to dig in.

Nori squatted beside him on the floor. "I learned something. It concerns your friend the Englishman."

Gary, now adept at using chopsticks, scooped the sticky rice and fish into his mouth. "Percival Corbett?"

She gave a solemn nod.

"What happened?"

"He was taken to the Fukuzumicho prison. He was interrogated and tortured."

Gary set the chopsticks down, his heart sinking. "Terrible, just terrible," he said despondently. At any other time, learning this dreadful news would have killed his appetite, but he was so hungry he picked up the chopsticks again and continued to eat. "Didn't this bring a protest from the British Consulate?"

"They weren't told about his arrest until recently. I learned that after many months of horrific treatment and neglect, he died. Yesterday."

"Are you sure? How do you know this?"

"The burial detail was Chinese. You know how we like to talk."

Nori unfolded a tattered roadmap of the island. "We need to get you out of Taihoku. You must go south and stay with Akito Saito."

"What about the army?"

"There aren't many roadblocks. The soldiers have either returned to garrisons or have shipped out."

"Is something happening?"

Nori leaned close and whispered, "For several weeks, many troop ships have boarded soldiers and equipment. Everything. Trucks. Artillery. Construction equipment. Piles of food and supplies. The cargo steamers have put out to sea along with a fleet of warships."

"Where are they going? China?"

"The rumors are that it's not China, but I haven't heard where else."

Again Gary asked, "How do you know this?"

"People talk. Though the rank-and-file Japanese soldiers have been good at keeping secrets, mostly because they don't know anything, it's the officers who spill the rice. They say too much during pillow talk with the bordello girls or in front of waiters."

"Interesting, no doubt," Gary replied. "But I need to get in touch with the American Consulate."

"I've tried, but the Japanese keep them under close watch. Any time someone from the consulate leaves their building, at least one police minder is close by. I don't dare get too close, because if I do *I* might get picked up."

Gary thought what a disaster that would be. With Nori gone, he'd be doomed in short order.

"Regardless," Nori said, "the Japanese military preparations have eased travel restrictions. They don't have enough manpower, and when they rely on the Chinese there isn't much enthusiasm. You might as well try to catch rain with a fishing net."

"So, what's your plan?"

"After nightfall, we'll head to the railroad yards."

"Aren't those heavily patrolled?"

"Trust me, Gary," Nori replied. "I'll take care of you."

* * *

"This way," Nori Chan whispered. She was but a voice in the jumbled dark shapes of the railroad yard. From the left, the beam of a locomotive headlamp pierced the night.

Gary shrank back into the shadows. Workers shouted commands, and railcars banged into each other.

"*Psst*," Nori hissed. "Now."

Gary scrambled in her direction, the noise of the train masking his footfalls over the gravel. She whispered to him again, and he picked out her location from a line of empty gondola cars. Closing in, he saw that she crouched against the wheels of one of the cars.

She whispered, "You're to stow away in this car."

He considered that the gondola was open, with nowhere to hide. "Won't the guards spot me?"

"The guards are Chinese, and they collect extra money to not see anything. Remember that gold coin you gave me?" Nori clasped his sleeve. "I put it to good use. Hurry. Get in."

The scheme seemed outlandish, but Nori had insisted this was the best way for Gary to get out of Taihoku and reach Dailou. Gary put his hand on her shoulder. "Thank you, Nori," he whispered gratefully. "I don't know what I'd do without your help."

"The best thanks is that you don't get caught," she replied. "I sent a message to Akito Saito. He's to meet you in Dailou."

Gary clasped a handrail and climbed upward, keeping a low profile, and slid into the gondola. Once over the top, he tumbled over two men huddled in the corner.

One of them cursed. "Who the hell are you?"

"Idiot," the other chimed in, "keep your voice down."

The interior of the gondola smelled like rotted produce. Bathed as they all were in darkness, it took Gary a moment to see, by their disheveled and ragged appearance, that the men were vagrants and not the type to sound an alarm.

Gary whispered in broken Chinese, "Sorry. Let me make it up to you." He'd brought cigarettes, knowing that in Formosa offering a smoke to a stranger was a sure way to make friends. He handed a cigarette to each of the vagrants.

They spread a tarp over themselves. "Friend, join us," the scruffiest of the vagrants said as he gestured for Gary to take a spot under the tarp. "It's not much shelter but better than nothing."

Gary folded his legs so he could fit.

"You are a big one," the scruffy vagrant noted.

"Are you Dutch?" the other asked.

Nori had warned Gary to be careful about what personal information he shared. The less strangers knew about him, the less likely they would be to rat him out for a reward. Or be suspicious that he hid a stash of gold coins on his person. So he replied simply, "No."

"We had a couple of Frenchmen in our car last week," the second vagrant said. "They were headed to Takao. You?"

"Not Takao," Gary said. "Where are you going?"

"Wherever we can find work," he replied.

Gary didn't think these two worked much at anything.

"So tall foreigner," Scruffy asked, "where are you going?"

Gary was thinking of what to respond when the shriek of a train whistle interrupted. Then the locomotive bellowed. *Chug. Chug. Chug.* The engine was steaming up, Gary thought.

The gondola car jolted hard and clanged against its couplers. Gary and the vagrants jostled against each other.

The car jolted again, then began to glide forward. The train picked up speed. The *click-clack* of the wheels quickened.

"Here we go," Scruffy said.

∗∗∗

Rain pattered over the tarp.

The second vagrant grumbled. "As if this ride isn't miserable enough."

"It'll keep the guards under cover," Scruffy said. "They don't like getting wet any more than we do."

Water seeped under the tarp, and Gary shifted to keep his pants dry.

"So, stranger," the second vagrant asked, "you never did tell us where you're from and where you are going."

Gary, still seeking to distract their questions, had one other item to offer, but he had hoped to keep it for a later time. From inside his coat pocket he pulled out a small flask and uncorked it. He passed the flask to the vagrants.

Scruffy sipped and gasped. "Oh my, whiskey!" He passed the flask to his buddy.

"To keep you warm," Gary said.

"Keep us warm and keep us quiet," the second vagrant replied, "which you've done."

***

With so much to worry about, Gary was surprised to find himself dozing. The rocking motion of the train and its rhythmic *click-clack* lulled him to a deep state of drowsiness. But mostly it was his letting go of his fears. He and Nori Chan had done everything possible to keep him safe, meaning that from this moment on, his fate was in the hands of God.

He awoke when the train stopped. He pulled the tarp from over his head. Although it was night, mist blurred the stars, and a bright haze from electric lights surrounded the train. Carefully, he stood and peeked over the sides of the gondola. The train had paused in the railroad yard of an unknown city. He wasn't sure where they were, but they hadn't traveled far enough yet to reach Dailou.

The whistle shrieked and the train started moving again.

He dropped back down and hid under the tarp. In a few minutes he was again fast asleep.

***

It was well into the morning when the train slowed once more. When Gary lifted his head to see, he noticed other men popping up from the gondola cars ahead and the ones behind him. The train was full of stowaways.

He recognized the way the track curved toward a trestle bridge. *We're close to Dailou.*

Past the bridge, the train slowed to a crawl. Gary sank back to the corner. His stomach growled. He couldn't remember ever being so hungry. The vagrants seemed to take their trials in stride, lounging against the back of the gondola car and passing a lit cigarette back and forth.

Suddenly, two men hopped into the car and landed with a thud against the metal floor. Gary shrank back in fear, and all he saw when he looked up at the men was their rifles and bandoliers. His heart clutched in terror.

Then on second look, he saw, to his immense relief, that one of them was Scarface!

"Brigands," the vagrants whispered in fear.

"Wu Jen-feng sent me," Scarface said. "We're here to take you away."

"How did you know I was on this train?"

"Does it matter? We're here."

While Scarface crouched to face Gary, his partner kept a lookout.

"It's not safe for you in Dailou," Scarface explained. "The place is crawling with Japanese soldiers." He stood and clambered up the side of the car. "Come on."

Gary waved a quick goodbye to the startled vagrants, and followed Scarface and his comrade out of the gondola to balance treacherously on the couplers. Tree branches scraped against the train as it inched along. The two brigands hopped off and vanished into the jungle. Gary pushed against a handhold and leapt after them.

***

Gary trailed after Scarface and the other brigand as they trekked into the jungle, then up into the wooded foothills and down a rocky path.

After about an hour of walking, Gary smelled meat cooking. Abruptly, they entered a small clearing where two Paiwan women tended to a campfire with a large rodent roasting on a spit and a pot of rice cooking. At the other end of the clearing, Wu Jen-feng sat on a stump. Around him, half a dozen brigands cleaned and oiled their rifles.

Wu Jen-feng greeted Gary, and the two men hugged.

"You look famished," the chieftain said. "We'll eat shortly." He pointed to the ground. "Sit, I have news to share."

"Good news, I hope," Gary replied.

When Wu didn't answer, Gary knew that the news would not be good. He asked. "What's happened?"

"Have you heard of a place called *Peel Hober*?"

Gary didn't understand. "What place?"

Wu repeated, more deliberately. " Peerl Habor."

"Pearl Harbor. Yes, I have. It's a naval base in the Hawaiian Islands. Why?"

"Last week, the Japanese attacked it. They sank many of your ships. So America and Japan are now at war. You were a simple fugitive, now you're an enemy."

Gary couldn't believe this. It was as if the entire world pivoted on him. He felt the weight of history rolling over him.

What would happen to him? What did this mean for his family? While his life was in tatters, so far he had survived. But what about his family? Nori Chan? Would the war reach them? And Akito Saito? Kasumi?

Gary asked in dismay, "How do I get to Dailou?"

"You won't," Wu answered.

"I'm supposed to meet Akito Saito."

"Plans have changed, my friend," the chieftain replied. "Much has changed."

CHAPTER TWENTY-ONE

December 1941

One of the Paiwan women brought Gary a wooden bowl filled with rice, cooked vegetables, and pieces of meat. Although famished, he ate slowly, scooping the food into his mouth and chewing mechanically, because for him nothing had taste.

As desperate as his situation had seemed before, now it was as if he stood on the precipice of an abyss with no bottom. In his mind's eye, as he peered anxiously into the gloomy depths, all he perceived was limitless tragedy and sorrow. How much longer could he remain on the run? Wasn't he being selfish in expecting Nori Chan and Wu Jen-feng and his tribe to protect him?

When he finished his meal, he stared at the empty bowl and considered it a metaphor for his present circumstances. His clothes were threadbare and tattered, his shoes crudely repaired. Lost in thought about the uncertainty of his fate, he was jolted to the present when one of Wu's men rushed into the clearing.

The brigand whispered breathlessly, "Japanese patrol coming up the trail."

The Paiwan leapt into action. The women wrapped the remaining food into cloth parcels and collected all the bowls and cups. Two men doused the campfire by urinating on the flames. The other brigands shrugged into their cartridge belts and readied their guns. Gary helped the women tie the cloth parcels to their carry poles. In less than three minutes, the group was ready to go.

Wu pointed at the women and one of the men, then to Gary, "You go with that group."

"Where are they going?" Gary asked.

"To the hunting camp. The rest of us will lead the Japanese up the mountain."

"I'm going with you."

"This isn't your fight," Wu replied.

"The hell it's not." Gary balled his fists. After all the months of running and hiding, he was ready to take the offensive. He was ready for action.

Wu gave him the once-over. "Very well." Wu bowed to the women. "I'll see you soon."

The women shouldered their carry poles and slipped expertly into the brush, disappearing as effortlessly as a pebble dropping into water.

Wu started up the trail. But unlike other times Gary had been with them, the brigands didn't try to hide their passing. They were leaving obvious tracks to draw the Japanese away from the women.

The trail snaked up a steep, rocky hill. When they reached a bluff, Wu halted. From where they stood, they could see where the trail wound in and out of the forest below. Wu pulled a telescope from his bag and scanned the trail, then offered the telescope to Gary, who peered into the distance. Like a line of ants, Japanese soldiers marched up the trail. It was odd to see them and realize they were the enemy. For some reason his memory flipped back to Ichiro. What did the war mean to him? Ichiro had said he wanted to join the army as an officer in the ROTC. Would he soon be fighting his former countrymen?

"They won't catch us," Wu boasted. "But we have to give them something to follow."

He directed his men to build a small fire on the bluff and cover it with fresh leaves, which soon raised a column of white smoke.

The brigands continued up the mountain, climbing like goats. They set another smoky fire and continued along the trail, but stopped short of the summit to double back and then slip into the forest.

In the late afternoon they reached the hunting camp. A slaughtered hog roasted on a spit. Now that they were within recognized Paiwan tribal territory, the brigands stashed their weapons and relaxed among their fellow tribesmen. If the Japanese visited, Wu could claim that he and his people were minding their own business, and that they knew nothing of any troubles with outlaws.

Wu gathered several of his men to hold court under a lean-to made of thatched grass. Gary kept to himself and pondered his situation. Nori Chan had sent word through the resistance network that Akito Saito and Kasumi would be waiting for him at the Dailou train station. But the Japanese were there. Might not that mean that his good friends were in trouble because of him? And meanwhile he hid up here. Though remaining here made the most sense, he felt like a coward. If Akito and Kasumi were in trouble, he had to rescue them.

But how?

He didn't know, but if he remained here, he was doing nothing.

Gary approached one of the Paiwan women. She was sorting a pile of berries.

He tried to say "Are we close to Dailou?" in a mangle of Paiwan and Chinese.

"I speak Japanese," the woman said. "What do you need?"

Gary repeated the question, and she answered, "Not far. About five hours."

Gary checked his watch. Five hours would place him in town around midnight. "Which way?"

The woman gestured to the south. "Go downhill. You'll run into a trail alongside a creek. Follow that downstream and you'll come across a road leading to Dailou."

Her directions seemed simple enough. The prudent thing for Gary would be to tell Wu of his plans. But Gary was far past prudent thinking. He had to hurry.

***

Colonel Eiji Kagawa had spent the day traveling from Taihoku on the train and inspecting his detachments along the way to Dailou. The work wasn't especially hard, but the day had been long and trying. He arrived with Sergeant-Major Murakami at the police station for a final status report, and then he'd turn in for the night at a nearby boarding house.

On the day the governor-general's order for detention of foreigners was implemented, Gary Gatlin had vanished. As one extra measure during the roundup, Kagawa had sealed the ports. His execution of the detention plan had been coordinated to the last detail. And yet, despite these precautions, Gary Gatlin was still missing.

Kagawa removed his pistol belt and hung it over the back of a chair at the table in the center of the room. Murakami spread a newspaper on the table, a special edition with a large map of the Pacific. A Rising Sun battle flag decorated the top left corner of the map; bold arrows illustrated the thrusts of recent military victories. The two men sat next to each other.

Murakami tapped a thick index finger on the map. "Colonel, one's heart cannot help but swell with pride. Our Imperial Fleet has smashed the Americans at Pearl Harbor, and within a week we have invaded the Philippines, Guam, Singapore." The sergeant stabbed at each location as he spoke. "Hong Kong, Borneo, and the Dutch East Indies are next. Our ships and aircraft are equal to those of any other nation. But what seals our victory is Japanese discipline and dedication." Murakami clenched his fist. "Japanese spirit is like katana steel compared to the flabby, entitled attitudes of the Westerners."

"Let's not boast too loudly, sergeant-major," Kagawa replied. "It is folly to underestimate our enemies. Our interrogation of the Englishman Percival Corbett showed that he was extraordinarily tough and never gave in."

Murakami grunted. The beatings had been numerous and fierce, but Corbett never wavered from his insistence that he was no spy. Even when Murakami's men seized Corbett's hands and yanked out his fingernails with pliers, the Englishman had given up nothing.

The sergeant-major flexed his thick shoulders and tugged at his tunic to smooth the wrinkles. The glint in his eyes revealed what he was thinking. His doubts stemmed from the fact that the American Gary Gatlin, a fugitive, had slipped through the colonel's dragnet. There was the possibility that Gatlin had escaped the island, but Kagawa couldn't think how that was possible.

The entrance door burst open and two of Murakami's men hauled in a young woman. They shoved her into the middle of the room where she stumbled against the processing counter. The policemen behind the counter jumped to their feet. Murakami and Kagawa rose and pushed away from the table.

One of Murakami's men, a corporal, turned the woman toward Kagawa. "She is Kasumi Saito. Daughter to the farmer Akito Saito."

Kagawa immediately made the connection. It was with Kasumi and Akito Saito that Gary had spent most of his time before he had disappeared.

The corporal slammed Kasumi against the counter. "We caught her waiting at the train station."

"Waiting for whom?" Kagawa asked. The young woman was very attractive and most definitely a fine companion for any man hiding from the law. Kagawa smiled, because after all this time, he knew that the American was going to show up.

***

Gary scrambled down the mountain trail, running hard, running fast. He sensed with absolute certainty that Kasumi was in trouble. She had risked herself for him and was now paying the consequences.

It was well into the night when he reached the farm road that headed east out of Dailou. He paused to read the luminescent dial of his watch: 11:04. To catch his breath, he hunched forward to rest his hands on his knees.

A pair of headlights approached. At least this vehicle was going in the right direction. Gary waited in the brush to see if the truck belonged to the military.

The truck rolled past, and in the moon's dim illumination he recognized the truck as the type belonging to a farmer. Gary sprinted after it, hollering in Japanese, "Stop! Stop!"

When the truck squealed to a halt, he ran into the beams of the headlights so the driver could see him. Hands lifted to show that he meant no harm, Gary approached the truck.

The driver shared the cab with a woman who was probably his wife and a brood of at least four small children. The driver warily appraised Gary, noting the stranger's unusual height, blond hair, and foreign manner. Then he said, "Jump in the back. But if we get stopped by the police or the army, you're on your own."

Gary made himself a spot in the truck's bed among crates of live ducks and a pair of young hogs. As the truck rumbled toward town, he thought about the desperate straits his life was in. He could take nothing for granted, not even his next minute of freedom.

Despite these dark broodings, thoughts of Kasumi lifted his spirits. His world was brighter and more welcoming because of this lovely young woman.

So if he found her, then what? Was this a fool's errand?

Perhaps, he countered, but what else could he do? To do something was better than doing nothing.

They passed a familiar corner market, now shuttered for the night, and he knew they were close to Dailou. When the truck reached the edge of town, he slapped the back window of the cab. The driver slowed enough for Gary to hop out. He waved his thanks, and as the truck rattled away, he proceeded in the direction of the train station.

He flipped up the collar of his coat to disguise himself, although there was no hiding his height and light-colored hair. He walked fast, eyes open wide, his nerves on edge for the slightest danger.

When he was two blocks from the train station, and as he passed a dimly-lit noodle shop, someone whispered, "Gary. Psst."

Startled, Gary instantly knew the voice. It was Nori Chan, now a blurred outline in the shop's darkened interior. He ducked into the shop. "What—how--?"

"Never mind that. Kasumi has been captured," Nori Chan blurted, her voice brittle. "The army picked her up."

Gary closed his eyes to absorb the bad news. "Where is she?"

"The police station."

Gary didn't hesitate to decide what to do next. He took resolute steps out the door.

***

Halting across the street from the police station, Gary remained tucked against shadows. He examined the area carefully. A police officer leaned against the wall by the entrance. He lit a cigarette, and the flare of his match illuminated his well-fed face. The ember of his burning cigarette glowed as he languidly puffed away.

The angle gave Gary a good view into the station through its front window. In the brightly lit interior he saw Kasumi struggling with a couple of soldiers. She tried to wrench free, but the men were rough brutes. One of them slapped her, and Gary took in a sharp breath, feeling the harsh sting, though he kept his reactions in check.

He studied the layout of the street. The station was set against a row of shops, all closed for the night. Maybe there was another entrance in a back alley.

Then, through the window, Gary saw that ape Sergeant-Major Murakami stride into view. Murakami reached for Kasumi and shook her like a ragdoll.

Gary's nerves crackled with rage. He had to save Kasumi now, and the only possible way would be to barge through the front door.

The policeman tossed the butt of his cigarette into the street, then stepped back inside.

Willing himself to remain calm, Gary waited a moment, then walked straight to the police station, up onto the sidewalk, and kicked the door open.

For a moment it was as if time stood still. The soldiers holding Kasumi froze. She gaped at Gary, as did the policemen behind the counter. Murakami and Colonel Kagawa gawked in amazement.

Murakami was the first to shake off his surprise. He bellowed, "Take him!"

The two soldiers let go of Kasumi and charged toward Gary. In a flash, his jujitsu skills rushed back to him. When the first soldier reached him, Gary grabbed his arm and flung him into the path of his comrade. Both men sprawled to the ground in a tangle of arms and legs.

Murakami launched himself at Gary, moving with surprising speed and fury. But Gary was ready. When the sergeant-major grabbed his lapels, Gary absorbed the momentum and rolled backwards. Murakami flipped over him and crashed hard into the wall. In the impact, his revolver fell out of his holster.

Gary grabbed the gun and sprang to his feet. Kasumi was to his left, Kagawa to his right. He panned the two policemen with the gun and ordered them to raise their hands. The two soldiers he had knocked over stood, hands also raised, looking shaken. Murakami lay by the wall, unconscious. Gary gestured with the revolver for the soldiers to join the policemen where he could better cover them.

He met Kagawa's stare. "I understand you've been looking for me."

Kagawa's gaze cut to the gun belt on the chair and Gary realized that the colonel was unarmed.

Kagawa showed no fear; if anything, he appeared annoyed that Gary had gotten the drop on him. He scowled and said, "You won't live to see tomorrow."

"You may not, either." Gary beckoned to Kasumi to pass behind him and make her way out the door. As he backtracked after her, he dared not take his eyes off Kagawa.

"If you want to spare the girl," Kagawa said, calmly, self-possessed, "then give yourself up."

Kasumi held the door open behind Gary. He knew Kagawa wouldn't let him escape without a fight.

Kagawa lunged for his holster. Gary squeezed the revolver's trigger, and the gun discharged with a flash and a boom. The colonel recoiled from the impact of the bullet. His eyes widened and his face hardened with shock, as if unable to comprehend what had happened to him. He sank against the chair, and both he and the chair toppled to the floor. Rolling onto his back, his arms fell open to reveal a dark blotch spreading across his tunic.

Gary went numb with the fact that he'd shot another human being, no matter how deserving. There was no sense of satisfaction or revenge in killing Kagawa, only the grim realization that he'd only done what he'd had to do.

Kasumi pulled him by the collar and yanked him outside. They stumbled onto the sidewalk, into the rectangle of yellow light shining out the door. Kasumi grabbed his hand and tugged him into the pitch-black darkness.

Gary ran beside her, feeling hollow with despair. At any second he expected police and soldiers to charge out of the police station, blowing on whistles and shouting the alarm, but the streets remained eerily quiet.

They sprinted headlong down an alley and then another street.

A truck turned the corner and closed upon them. Gary and Kasumi dashed away from the truck, looking for another alley or a side street. The truck raced after them, the beams of its headlamps throwing their shadows down the narrowing street. Escape seemed futile so Gary decided on his only course of action: to sacrifice himself to save Kasumi.

"Keep going," he shouted to her, then whirled around to face the truck, ready to riddle its windshield with bullets.

The truck screeched to a halt, and a man yelled from the passenger's side. "Gary, don't shoot! It's us!" It was Wu.

Gary lowered the revolver, and the relief washing over him practically drove him to his knees. Kasumi returned to his side.

"Hurry," Wu said. "Get in."

Gary and Kasumi rushed to the truck where Wu pushed them into the cab. Kasumi's father, Akito Saito, was driving.

"How did you find me?" Gary asked.

Wu crammed himself into the cab. "Where else would you go?" He chuckled and grabbed Gary's knee. "Next time, my impetuous young American friend, tell me what you're up to."

Akito ground the gears, and the truck chugged down the road. "If all goes well, Gary, tonight will be your last night in Formosa."

Gary kept the revolver in his lap; he might still need it. "What do you mean, my last night in Formosa?"

"We're on our way to Takao," Wu replied. "By this time tomorrow you should be on a ship, sailing free."

CHAPTER TWENTY-TWO

December 1941

Akito Saito's truck raced south along the main highway from Dailou, the truck jostling as it transitioned from smooth pavement to dirt road, back to pavement, back to dirt road, then finally steady pavement. He stared intently through the windshield, his headlights boring holes into the early morning darkness.

Kasumi sat against her father, Gary next to her, Wu Jen-feng against the passenger door, the four of them crammed tightly into the cab.

Gary was so overcome with fatigue that he barely noticed the bumpy, uneven ride. The intense anxiety of having shot Colonel Kagawa was finally, slowly easing. Although horrified at having taken a life, Gary justified it as an act of war. If the Japanese regarded him as an enemy, so be it. They should expect the enemy to fight back.

The truck's clattering engine faded into a soothing murmur. He drifted in and out of sleep, opening his eyes to see the bright eyes of animals alongside the road reflecting the truck's headlamps. Other times he'd see oncoming traffic, then he'd doze off again.

He was startled awake by someone clasping his hand; it was Kasumi. Her soft touch comforted him, and he sighed with relief, doing his best to hold onto this moment, because there were no assurances of what tomorrow would bring.

When he fell back to sleep, his mind floated from memory to memory, the images appearing in hazy swatches. His father hard at work under the Utah sun. His mother tending their roadside stand. His sister, Chrissy, winning her race in the county fair track meet. He and Ichiro sparring against one another in jujitsu. Nori Chan guiding him through the wholesale market in Keelung.

An abrupt change in the engine's noise roused him from slumber. The truck's tires hummed, and Gary cracked his eyelids open. They were crossing a bridge, and the river beneath them shone like a broad ribbon of pewter.

"Where are we?" he mumbled.

"The Tansui-Kei River," Akito answered. "We're almost at Takao."

Gary read his watch: 6:02. He stretched as best he could, and Kasumi rested her head on his shoulder. A sign beside the road said, *Hōzan, Checkpoint Ahead.*

Akito doused the lights and eased the truck up to the checkpoint, the area lit by smudge pots. Soldiers milled on both sides of the road. They wore khaki instead of olive-drab uniforms, which told Gary they were Chinese and not Japanese.

Akito removed his straw hat and slapped it on Gary's head. "Try not to look so tall."

Gary pulled the hat low over his brow and scrunched as low as he could.

Akito leaned out the cab's window. "What's going on?"

"The usual," groused a soldier. "Now that there are fewer Japanese soldiers on the island, the Japanese make us stand here at odd hours, telling us how important it is. Duty to the Emperor and all that. Meanwhile they're sleeping off their hangovers. What's your business this morning?"

"We're picking up a load of rice in Takao."

The soldier rapped the side of the cab. "Well, if you see any brigands or enemy spies, let us know."

"Will do." Akito meshed the gears, and the truck trundled forward. Gary returned Akito's hat.

The sky brightened from black to dark blue to a lighter blue. One by one, the stars faded as daylight approached. The retreating twilight revealed a large, shallow plain ringed by mountains. The land on either side of the highway was a tapestry of marsh, rice field, and plots of flat land dotted with buildings and trees. With every mile, more and more electrical lines appeared, strung from poles and crisscrossing the road. Farmhouses gave way to industrial buildings. Tall stacks fed the layer of thin smoke that hung over the landscape.

A heavy chemical smell tainted the air. Akito explained, "They smelt iron and process magnesium and aluminum here."

The highway scrolled past houses, warehouses, office buildings, all packed ever closer together until it was one continuous sprawl of urban congestion—the city of Takao, whose harbor breached an opening between the mountains.

They passed a power plant, then the rail yard. A half hour ago it seemed they were the only ones on the road; now trucks of every sort crowded the busy highway.

Once they were in the city proper, the road curved left. They again crossed the Takao-Kei River to enter a residential district. Old women swept the sidewalks. Shopkeepers raised awnings and dragged sidewalk signs to the curb. Laundry hung from balconies. Stacks of honey buckets waited for pickup.

Akito drove through the maze of narrow streets between tall apartment buildings. He halted outside a garage with a wooden door. Wu hopped out and hustled into an adjacent shop. Around its entrance, sketchy-looking men in denim work clothes loitered, smoking cigarettes, eating breakfast rice from bowls, and gossiping.

A moment later, the garage door opened, Wu pushing it from the inside. Akito drove into the garage and shut off the engine. Wu closed the door and locked it.

Gary slid out of the truck, followed by Kasumi. The garage was packed with junk: dented buckets, rusted tools, coils of frayed rope, chains, and rolls of canvas.

"What is this place?" Kasumi asked.

"It's my headquarters," a compact man answered. He stood in an interior doorway.

"This is my brother, Hau," Wu said. "He contracts workers for the docks. Stevedores mostly."

So Wu had a brother? He and Hau did indeed resemble one another. Wu's hair was shoulder-length while Hau's was cut short, western-style. And while Wu wore a mix of aboriginal and peasant clothing, Hau wore a plaid shirt and khaki pants. One trait they shared was a hard, uncompromising demeanor, which was needed to ride herd on a tribe of brigands or a gang of dockworkers.

Hau looked Gary up and down but shared nothing of what he thought. "Come inside."

Gary looked back at Akito and Kasumi. "Is this goodbye?"

"Not yet," Hau assured him. He led Gary past a tiny kitchen where women fussed over a kerosene stove with pots boiling on top. An older woman spooned rice and fish parts into small bowls that she passed through an open window to the men queued outside.

Hau stopped at a closet and handed Gary a stack of denim

clothing and a towel. They continued through a back door to a small porch inside a miniscule yard enclosed by a tall wooden fence. Chickens prowled the damp ground around a row of honey buckets. Tin basins sat on a crude wooden table. Three men stood naked against the table as they washed their faces and bodies with scrub cloths. Gary surmised that Hau ran some kind of boarding house for itinerant workers.

A girl brought a bucket of steaming hot water, set it on the table, and returned inside. She seemed singularly blasé by the men attending to their ablutions.

"I'll let you tend to business," Hau said and left.

Gary saw no reason for modesty. He stripped out of his clothes and poured the hot water into a basin. Using a communal bar of soap and a clean rag, he washed himself all over, toweled off, and lathered his face. A straight razor, strop, and mirror hung from a nail on the wall. Soon he was freshly shaven and slipping into the fresh, clean clothes Hau had provided—dungarees, matching work coat, military-style web belt, and chambray shirt. They fit, though loose, not surprising considering his loss of weight. He took the money belt from his old trousers, and collected his remaining possessions: watch, pocketknife, passport, and shoes. He tossed his old clothes into a pile of other discards, to be ripped into rags, no doubt.

Returning to the kitchen, he helped himself to a large bowl of rice, steamed fish, and cups of tea. When he had finished, he took a moment to luxuriate in how good he felt. He was clean, freshly shaven, and well fed. If he didn't think about his outlying circumstances, life seemed okay.

Hau approached. "Come with me. I get Japanese officials

dropping in at random times to check my work roster, and I don't want them to see you."

They climbed a narrow, creaky staircase to a tiny room on the third floor. Inside, a couple of Chinese workers rested on dingy bunks. One smoked a cigarette and read a magazine. Both men regarded Gary with mild curiosity, then ignored him.

A breeze batted the window curtains. Hau invited him to take a look. "We're in the *Horiechō* neighborhood," he explained. "There's the inner harbor. To the right, you'll see the concrete jetties of the outer harbor."

From this vista, Gary observed a long, narrow spit of land extending from the south to form the inner harbor. Cargo steamers and warships bristling with guns were either moored at the many wharves or cruising slowing through the harbor. In the outer harbor, ships waited at anchor. And everywhere, small boats floated through the waters in the harbors and along the coastline.

Hau pointed to the wharf. "See that ship. The light gray one?"

Gary nodded.

"That's your ship," Hau said. "A Dutch freighter, the *Mooie Zwerver*. Means something like 'beautiful wanderer.'" The *Mooie* looked like a typical cargo steamer, about 300 feet long. "She's sailing for the Dutch East Indies, leaving at nightfall. Since Holland has surrendered, technically the ship answers to the Germans, Japan's new ally, so its passage should be safe."

He pointed to the large, pyramid-shaped mountain at the far right. "That's Mount Tu-Zan. There's a fishing camp on the other side. That's where a boat will pick you up and rendezvous with the *Mooie* later tonight."

Gary was ready to pay Hau at least two of his gold coins. "I appreciate your doing this," he said, "though I have to ask why."

Hau dug into his trouser pocket and pulled out a roll of US twenty-dollar bills. "The American Consulate pays a bounty for any of you that I smuggle out. You're each worth five hundred dollars."

A compelling motive, Gary thought. "How does the consulate verify what you're doing?"

Hau replied, "Show me your passport."

Gary complied, and Hau copied Gary's passport number and personal information onto a memo pad. "This is proof that I at least ran into you." Hau returned the passport.

"If you want more proof that you ran into me," Gary said, "tell Blanche Fletcher hello for me. She's the consulate's secretary."

Hau slapped Gary on the shoulder. "Get some rest. You might be in for a long night." He barked an order to one of the Chinese men. The man grunted, put on his slippers, gathered his cigarettes, and shuffled out the door. After Hau left, Gary lay on the bunk. Outwardly, he appeared calm, but inside he roiled with worry: what had happened, where he had been, what was to come. However, despite the odds, he had made it this far.

Then someone prodded his side. He had fallen asleep and was jolted awake.

It was Hau. He said, "Time to get going."

Gary sat up and rubbed his face, remaining slightly disoriented for a moment. Checking his watch, he read the time: 4:17 in the afternoon.

***

A half-hour later, he and Kasumi were in the back of Akito's truck, hidden from view by a canvas canopy stretched over the bed. The truck motored through the busy city, a riot of sounds and

263

smells. Gary peeked out through a gap in the canvas. They passed over a bridge, a river underneath. Then they started up a road, past a Buddhist shrine, then wound farther up the incline.

After another ten minutes, the truck halted. Gary heard Akito and Wu dismount. Akito opened the rear of the canopy. "This is as far as I can take you before I have to turn back. I can't be driving here after dark without permission from the police. Wu will take you to the fishing camp."

Gary and Kasumi climbed out. She had brought a provisions bag. They were on a wide stretch of road, on the southern side of Mount Tu-Zan, where they overlooked the harbor and, closer in, a military hospital and the beach.

"Then I guess this is goodbye." Gary extended his hand to Akito.

Akito drew Gary close for a tight hug. "Take care, my friend."

"I'll be back for my notes and journals."

"I look forward to the visit. And your journals will be returned."

Akito bowed, then said, "Kasumi, time to go."

Kasumi held onto Gary's hand. "I'm going with him to the beach."

Akito's brow wrinkled with surprise and displeasure. His eyes drilled into Kasumi, then he relented and smiled. "I know better than to argue with you."

Wu gestured for them to follow him. He slipped into the dense brush; Gary and Kasumi followed. They stepped lightly through the weeds and bushes until reaching a faint animal trail, which they took uphill. Gary was amazed that Wu had such intimate knowledge of the land no matter where they went. They climbed the steep mountainside, crossed a pronounced ridgeline, and continued down the other side. At intervals, when the trees parted, Gary could see the broad expanse of the ocean that beckoned his departure.

On a bluff, Wu halted. The ocean stretched before him. Below, a narrow strip of sandy beach hugged the base of the mountain. The beach curved into a tiny cove, where there was a small wooden shack. *The pickup point*, Gary noted to himself.

They hiked the trail down to the cove. The surf beat its cadence against the beach. A local man sat hunched by a small campfire dug into the sand. He was brewing tea and acknowledged Wu with a nod. Inside the hut, two men waited on blankets spread across the sandy floor. They and Gary made their introductions.

The rangy fellow with thinning curly red hair was a Dutchman named Piet Drees. The tall and swarthy man was a Brazilian named Oswald Andrade. As had happened to Gary, the start of the war had stranded them on Formosa as refugees, and they were eager to leave.

Although Gary appreciated their plight, he wanted to spend time with Kasumi. The two of them left the hut and found a shaded spot on the slope where they could sit and keep an eye on the cove. Wu stayed with the man by the fire.

When they were alone, Gary let his thoughts about Kasumi uncoil. "What I want to say is that I'll be back, but I'm afraid that everything I tell you can't be more than empty promises."

Kasumi met his gaze. "All we can do is be sincere with one another and not think too much about things we can't control." She moved closer and rested her head on his shoulder.

"I don't suppose you could leave with me?" he asked timorously.

"I had thought of it."

"It would be dangerous."

"There is danger even if I remain," she replied. "But--I can't leave my father. I am the only family he has left."

"The Japanese authorities will come after you. After all, you were with me when I shot Kagawa."

"I've thought about that as well," Kasumi sighed. "I might hide with the Paiwan. Or I could claim that you'd coerced me and that I had nothing to do with your attacking the train station."

"I doubt the authorities will be very generous with their judgment of you."

She answered pragmatically. "These are trying times for everyone, Gary." She reached into her bag and pulled out a cardboard bento box and a corked bottle of tea. "As we wait for the world to end, let's at least have something to eat." She opened the box and shared the rice balls wrapped in leaves.

The sun crept lower on the horizon. As they ate, they exchanged memories of the time they'd spent together, and favorite jokes. From their vantage point on the slope, Gary doubted that anyone in the world had a better view of this sunset. The sun's rays spread outward, pierced the distant layers of clouds, turning them orange, then red, and finally gray. When the sun dipped below the horizon, the sea breeze changed direction and ruffled the campfire, now a bright flare in the deepening night.

The buzz of a boat engine rose above the rhythmic crash of waves, heralding the motorized skiff cruising toward them. A man at the stern operated the tiller. The skiff rode the incoming surf and beached itself in the cove. The men in the hut joined Wu and the man at the fire, and they ran to greet the boat.

Time for the inevitable farewell. Gary reached into his coat for the money belt cinched around his middle. He popped open the stitched pockets and offered Kasumi three of the gold coins. Although she protested, he insisted. "It's a trifle compared to what I owe you."

Kasumi wrapped the coins in a kerchief and dropped them into her bag. "Thank you, Gary," she said. "You are very kind."

They hustled down the trail. By the time they reached the beach, the Dutchman and the Brazilian were wading toward the skiff while the man who had been tending the fire held its bowline. The tiller-man kept the engine at a loud idle. Wu waved for Gary to hurry.

The drama of the moment settled on him. The sadness of saying goodbye gave way to a biting urgency.

When he reached Wu, he unclasped his wristwatch and pressed it into the chieftain's grasp. Knowing that Wu would refuse, Gary said, "Don't consider this a gift. I'm lending it to you for safekeeping. When I return, I expect it back."

"All right then," Wu replied, smiling as he clasped the watch to his wrist.

Kasumi was right behind Wu. She said, "I'll see you again when you come back for the watch." Her eyes glistened with tears.

Gary nodded and turned away so that Kasumi would not see his own tears. He knew it was time to leave. He squeezed her hand, and she squeezed his. He looked from Wu to Kasumi and said, "May God keep you until next time."

Waves tossed the boat, and the Dutchman and the Brazilian had to wrestle themselves over its side. Gary waded out to the skiff and rolled awkwardly over the gunnel. The man with the bowline scrambled on board. Wu and Kasumi splashed through the water and, grabbing the front of the boat, shoved it backwards into deeper water. The tillerman turned the boat from the beach and gunned the engine. The rolling surf smashed into the skiff, dousing everyone with cascades of water.

Gary and the two other refugees lay low in the skiff as they bounced against the waves. When the skiff settled into a steady pitching motion as it plowed through the swells and troughs, Gary felt safe enough to raise his head.

Stars glittered above. The sky was as black as he'd ever seen it. As he stood peering over the stern, he could barely see the campfire, now just a tiny light. Kasumi and Wu were lost in the distance, but he waved to them anyway. To the south, the lights of Takao outlined one side of Mount Tu-Zan.

The man at the bow stood as lookout and leaned backwards against the bowline for balance. He shouted, "I see the *Mooie!*"

Ahead, maybe a half-mile away, a dark hulk appeared like an abstract hole punched into the darkness. The tillerman aimed straight toward it.

The lookout pulled a flashlight from his pocket. He aimed it at the ship. Gary expected a bright beam, but a piece of cardboard over the lens reduced the light to a tiny dot.

On the ship, a small light flashed. *On. Off. On. Off.* The light went dark, then flashed the same sequence again.

"It's the *Mooie,*" the lookout confirmed.

The tillerman advanced the throttle.

Minute by minute, the skiff sailed closer to the *Mooie,* the steamer growing steadily in size. Gary felt his chest tighten with apprehension. He was so close to escaping Formosa, yet many misfortunes could still befall him. He glanced over both shoulders, nervous that a patrol boat could spoil everything.

At last they reached the *Mooie.* Its slab-sided hull towered above them, and from this lower perspective it looked as big as Mount Tu-Zan. But even as huge as the ship appeared, it still listed in the water, tilting over the skiff and then away.

The tillerman swung parallel to the *Mooie,* close to a large cargo net hanging over the side. He shouted, "One by one, go!"

The Brazilian scrambled to the bow. He crouched, and when the skiff bucked upward, he sprang for the net and held tight. The skiff angled away.

The tension was palpable. If anyone fell, too bad.

The Brazilian scrambled up the net. Next, it was Gary's turn. He inched to the front of the skiff. The tillerman nosed them against the *Mooie*, the bow of the skiff scraping the hull as the ocean heaved them up and down.

Gary pushed aside his fear. As the Brazilian had done, he crouched, hung onto the gunnel, and flexed his muscles. He focused on a spot of the cargo net and timed the rise and fall of the skiff. When he felt the skiff rising, he sprang upward with all his might. His fingers snatched the rope and his body slammed against the hull.

He allowed himself one breath of gratitude, then hauled himself up the net. At the top, a pair of hands grasped his coat and dragged him over the railing, where he landed sprawling on the deck. Without hesitating, he scrambled to his feet and found his balance.

Everything seemed appreciably darker once he was on the ship. The crewmen tending the cargo net were black silhouettes blending into the black mass of the ship. The deck tilted beneath him, but it was nothing like the crazy tossing of the skiff.

The crewmen yanked the Dutchman on board. He tumbled to the deck beside Gary, who helped him to his feet.

Gary took deep breaths. Looking over the railing, he saw the skiff heading back toward land. Formosa was a black smudge across the eastern horizon.

Through the deck plates, Gary felt the rhythm of the *Mooie's* pistons accelerating. Slowly, the ship swung to the west and into the wide expanse of the sea. Gary was humbled by the vastness of the ocean and the sky, and of the unknown that lay ahead. He had already been tested much, and he knew he was about to be tested even more.

PART III

Chapter Twenty-three

December 1941

Gary, along with Piet Drees, the Dutchman, and Oswald Andrade, the Brazilian, were taken below. They traveled in single file through the cramped corridors of the *Mooie*. Gary couldn't see who led them but concluded that he was someone familiar with the ship as he expertly negotiated the many turns and a ladder. Their leader opened a tall, vertical hatch and light spilled out to illuminate his features—that of a wiry older man with a weather-beaten face.

With a nod, the man indicated for Gary and the rest to step through the hatch and into a compartment. Inside, seven men stared moon-faced at them. Some watched from hammocks, that hung sloth-like from overheard hooks. Others sat slumped on thin mattresses covering the deck. Although they appeared to be of many nationalities—with complexions varying from sunburnt pink to ebony—all of them shared the same haggard expression of refugees having escaped a dragnet. Gary noted a few valises and duffle bags lying about, but assumed that, like him, they had all recently escaped Formosa with little more than the clothes on their backs.

The man who had brought them was dressed in well-worn dungarees and a faded blue cap with an anchor on the front. He said, "You speak English? *Français?*"

"English," Gary and Oswald replied.

"Good." The man produced a packet of cigarettes from inside his work coat. "I'm Lucas Nijhoff, the ship's bosun. You answer to me." He shook loose the packet and offered Gary a cigarette, which he refused with a shake of his head, but Piet and Oswald each took one. Lucas flicked a brass trench lighter and the three men lit up.

"I'm famished," Oswald said as he puffed on the cigarette. "Any chance we can get something to eat?"

"At breakfast tomorrow morning," Lucas replied. "Everybody," he panned the compartment with a gnarled finger, "when you report topside for work detail, you'll be fed then."

"Where are we headed?" one of the other men asked.

"Hollandia, Dutch New Guinea," Lucas answered. "It'll take this tub ten days to get there, so enjoy your stay."

"Are we in danger?" the man pressed.

Lucas laughed. "Of course we're in danger. The Japanese have pounced on the French, the British, and the Americans. They've just invaded the Philippines and Singapore."

"What about the Royal Navy?"

He shook his head. "It hasn't gone too well for them, either. They sent a taskforce with their two most powerful battleships, the *Repulse* and the *Prince of Wales*, and the Japs sank them both."

A look of doom darkened everyone's faces.

"It gets worse," Lucas added. "The US declared war on Germany."

"Dear God," someone gasped. "It's another world war."

Lucas continued, "What's working in our favor is that the Germans have occupied Holland, and so this ship, being Dutch, is considered property of a Japanese ally. I don't like that, but if it keeps us from being attacked, then I can live with it."

He pointed to a large wicker basket and said to Gary, Piet, and

Oswald, "Get yourself a hammock and a blanket. We'll see you in the morning."

He left, and with solemn resignation Gary reached into the basket and retrieved the two items. After securing his hammock onto hooks in the ceiling, he removed his shoes and socks and rolled them in his coat to use as a pillow. He took care to keep his money belt hidden under his chambray shirt. Hoisting himself into the hammock, he stretched into it, trying to get comfortable.

The compartment lacked a porthole, and the only fresh air came from a ventilation duct in the ceiling. One man lit a pipe, those with cigarettes passed them around, and soon the compartment was filled with smoke. Gary's consolation was that the overhead vent flowed directly onto him so he could at least breathe clean air.

Someone doused the light. As Gary swayed back and forth, he wondered about his family and his friends in Formosa. And when he arrived in Hollandia, what then?

In the darkness, he heard whispers and the creaking of the ship. One of the men could be heard weeping softly. Gary vacillated between feeling sorry for the guy and wanting to snap at him, considering they were all in the same boat—literally. But he said nothing.

***

The next morning, Lucas returned and rousted everyone out of the compartment. They queued at the head, washed, then filed to the main deck and queued once again at a table arranged between the bridge house and the large central hold. For breakfast everyone received coffee, an apple, a biscuit, and a hard-boiled egg.

Gary stood by himself against the railing. Peeling the egg, he let the shell fall to the water below. After eating the egg and the biscuit, he studied the apple, appreciating the irony that he'd come to the Orient because of apples, and here he was, feasting on one on the deck of a ship bound for yet another strange place.

As he looked out across the ocean, its vastness reminded him of all the time he had with nothing to do but wait and think. Wait and think.

Although he knew there was no point in worrying about those he'd left behind, in both Formosa and America, he couldn't keep his mind from speculating about them. His musing would free-associate, and sometimes he imagined Akito and his father discussing farming techniques as they shoveled at an irrigation canal under a hot Utah sun. Or he saw Kasumi and his mother comparing notes as they scrutinized ledger books. Or Nori Chan and his sister, Chrissy, tending a corner fruit stand in Keelung. Gary smiled. His sister had an adventuresome streak and would have loved to visit Formosa. Maybe after the war.

The war.

Gary's thoughts turned bleak. It wasn't just one war, but two. The Pacific and Europe. How many of his friends back in Utah would be dragged into this bloodbath? Would there be a draft like in the first war? What about Ichiro, his friend back home?

"Would you mind the company?"

The question interrupted Gary's grim fugue. He turned to see Oswald joining him at the railing.

"No, of course not. I'm happy to have someone to talk to," Gary replied.

"Oswald Andrade," the man introduced himself again, offering his hand. "Rio de Janeiro."

They shook hands. "Gary Gatlin. Freetown, Utah."

"We didn't have a chance to speak much on the island," Oswald said. "You were preoccupied with your lady friend."

"We had to say our goodbyes. How about you?"

"My goodbyes to lady friends?" Oswald chuckled. "Many lady friends. Many goodbyes. What brings you to the Pacific?"

"I was studying apples." Gary waved the half-eaten fruit. "My family are farmers. You?"

"A correspondent for *O Globo*. It's a Brazilian national newspaper."

"So, what are you doing here in the Pacific?"

Oswald leaned against the railing. "I was sent out here to report on the possibility of war." He sighed. "Which has happened, unfortunately."

"All right," Lucas the bosun shouted. "Breakfast is over. Time for work."

While the other refugees remained reticent about the work details, Gary volunteered to help repair a crane winch. He didn't know anything about the job but figured the busy work would keep his mind occupied. Oswald must have been thinking the same thing, as he volunteered alongside Gary.

First, they helped the deck crew unwind the heavy steel cable from the winch's drum and lay it across the deck. The drum gear had to be replaced, and all the bolts that needed to be removed were rusted in place. Using out-sized wrenches, Gary and Oswald took on the back-breaking labor of working the bolts free. The drum gear was the size of a car tire and weighed close to two hundred pounds. With the bosun supervising, Gary and Oswald manhandled the new gear into position. Gary's stomach rumbled, and he wondered if they would break for lunch, but they didn't. In the afternoon, a rain squall added to their discomfort.

By late afternoon they had wound the cable back onto the winch.

Pride warmed Gary's spirit as he observed the large crane swivel out over the deck. The work had left Gary's clothing a greasy mess, but he felt a great deal of satisfaction at having gotten the job done. As a reward for their efforts, Lucas gave Gary and Oswald an extra helping at dinner—bread rolls, rice, canned vegetables, and beef. Plus more coffee.

Lucas offered them a nip from a proffered bottle of rum. Oswald took a sip but Gary refused. "I've never been attracted to drinking."

Lucas frowned. "I don't think I can trust a man who doesn't drink."

"All right." Gary took the flask. The bosun grinned, thinking he'd won Gary over. Except that Gary handed the flask to Oswald. "He can have my share and then vouch for me as a character witness."

Oswald downed a hearty swallow. "Some day, Lucas, you must come find me in Rio de Janeiro, and I'll treat you to some very good rum."

After dinner, Gary and Lucas retreated to the head where they scrubbed their clothes with scalding hot water. They hung their wash to dry and climbed into their hammocks. When he lay his head down Gary realized that he was bone tired, and he was asleep in minutes.

***

The next day, he and Oswald were put to work swabbing the decks. That workday ended at mid-afternoon, and as they loitered on deck for dinner, Gary found himself with what he least wanted—too much time alone to think.

He made his way forward to the bow, and as so many mariners had done in the millennia that people have ventured to sea, he stared into the distance and let the wind buffet his face. The *Mooie* rocked gently as it plowed forward. He lost himself in the hypnotic motion of the ship, rocking and pitching on the sea.

After dinner, he remained on the main deck and lounged on a large roll of canvas. Whenever his thoughts spiraled in worry about his friends and family, he'd force himself to think about the future, when the war would be good and over.

Oswald came by and sat beside him. The Brazilian unfolded a *National Geographic* map of the Southern Pacific. "One of the ship's crew let me borrow this." He put one index finger on a spot east of the Philippines. "We steamed from Formosa around midnight two days ago, and since we're sailing at ten knots, I'm guessing we're about three hundred miles east of the Philippine Islands." The spot Oswald indicated was a gray area maybe six by eight inches that ended at Hawaii at the margin of the map, a distance of about five thousand miles.

Gary realized they were in the middle of nowhere--but at least steaming out of harm's way. Surely the Japanese had their hands full with the Americans on the Philippines, and the *Mooie* would be of little concern.

The sun dipped below the horizon, and soon the moon began to rise. Its silver light sparkled across the endless water, and Gary thought to himself that the night seemed quite peaceful. He decided to turn in and see what tomorrow would bring.

***

Gary was slammed awake. The ship shuddered as if it had run into a wall.

In the pitch-black compartment, a chorus of disembodied voices shouted, "What's going on? What was that?"

From out in the corridor, they heard panicked shouts.

"Lights! Turn on the lights!"

"They don't work. We've lost power."

Gary swung out of his hammock, only to land on someone. He rolled over and to his feet. There was a mad scramble for the hatch. When it opened, a flashlight beam shot across the threshold.

"Get out!" a voice hollered. "We've been torpedoed!"

A fresh explosion rocked the ship. Gary's insides knotted in panic. Men cried in terror. The deck heaved to port, and he imagined water gushing into the cargo holds, as if the ocean itself was tearing into the *Mooie*.

An alarm rang, its urgent trill adding to the terror.

Gary realized he was barefoot, but in the darkness he couldn't waste time groping for his shoes or his coat. Wearing only trousers and shirt—the money belt cinched tight around his waist—he bolted for the hatch, arms and legs from every side lashing against him. Reaching the corridor, he dashed for the ladder and climbed to the main deck. When he emerged outside, he stood still, dumbstruck by the disaster he encountered

Sheets of flame billowed from the central cargo hold. Men ran helter-skelter across the deck. Looking up to the bridge house, Gary saw a figure, his pale face shining orange from the fire. Gary was certain this was the skipper, who watched helplessly as his ship was blasted into scrap.

He heard Lucas shout, "Away with the launches!"

Another explosion hammered the ship. A cloud of steam vented from the funnel.

More frantic shouts.

"The boiler's ruptured. Oh God! Oh God!"

The *Mooie* lurched. Men wrestled with the davits of a launch. The launch swung free when another explosion rocked the ship. One end of the launch snapped loose, and it smashed into the hull, disintegrating into kindling.

A stranger seized Gary by the shoulder and screamed like a madman. "The ship is doomed! Get off while you can!"

Gary couldn't decide which side of the ship to jump from, port or starboard. The tilting deck decided the issue. As it heaved to starboard, he ran in that direction and clung to the railing. The conflagration behind him lit the ocean like a bonfire. Orange light glittered the rolling waves and the ocean became ominously black and deep. At the edge of the light, he spotted a slender, shark-like silhouette on a course parallel to the stricken *Mooie,* about five hundred yards distant. He stared at it, not sure what he was seeing.

A fireball rose from the cargo hold, its wave of heat surging across Gary's back. The great leap of flame brightened the sea and highlighted a conning tower with a Rising Sun painted on the side. A Japanese submarine.

Gary wanted to scream, "We're a neutral ship!" when a flash and a boom erupted from the submarine. An explosion tore into the *Mooie's* hull.

"The bastards are using their deck guns to finish us off."

Gary swung his legs over the railing and stood on the edge of the deck. The vista was terrifyingly surreal. Men dropped around him, splashing into the water where they bobbed alongside debris. The *Mooie* groaned like a wounded beast. And in the distance, the submarine pumped another artillery shell at them.

Leaking oil spread across the water, engulfing men who struggled to stay afloat. A tongue of flame from the ship ignited the oil. The men screamed.

Gary knew he couldn't jump clear of the burning oil, but he could try to swim underneath. Taking a deep breath, he catapulted from the deck, pushing as hard as possible and holding his nose, to splash feet-first into the water.

He felt the heat of the fire, then a chill. Opening his eyes, he looked up at the glowing sheet of burning oil on the surface above him. He swam hard away and emerged a good twenty feet from the oily flames that were rising and falling on the undulating surface.

As he treaded water, he tried to take in all the horror. More men dropped from the *Mooie*, bringing to his mind a macabre thought, of ticks abandoning a dead dog.

Another cloud of steam shot from the funnel, and the *Mooie* bellowed as if in great pain. It keeled toward him, the remaining men on deck sliding helplessly, screaming, slamming into poles and stanchions. The ship continued to roll and sink. The gigantic propeller, lifting, rose from the sea, tons of water cascading from its enormous blades.

More belches of steam and bubbles roiled the surface. The *Mooie,* now a huge, helpless hulk, slipped without another sound beneath the waves and disappeared. And just like that, the bedlam fell quiet.

The waves shimmered from the burning oil, the uncertain light outlining shapes on the heaving waves. Men called out, but Gary couldn't distinguish them from the chaos of debris floating around him. Where was Oswald? Lucas?

Looking back to the submarine, he thought it might rescue survivors. Instead, it sank into the water, not a savior but instead like an assassin's knife, hiding and waiting for its next victim.

Gary knew he couldn't tread water for long. After making sure the money belt was cinched around his waist, he slipped out of his trousers, and remembering a boyhood trick, knotted the trousers' legs and whipped them over his head. The trousers trapped air, and by hooking the legs of the trousers under his arms, he was able to use them as a flotation device.

Thankfully it worked, and he floated, limp but steady, head above water. His mind went to other concerns, such as drinking-water and getting rescued, but for now he had to concentrate on staying afloat. To remain on top of the water, he had to repeat the process of trapping air with his pants many times throughout the night. But for the time being, he was alive.

Chapter Twenty-four

December 1941

Gary's mind reeled in astonishment and dismay. He couldn't believe he was in the middle of this nightmare. As he floated on the undulating swells, he looked across the emptiness of water where the *Mooie* had been. Debris littered the scene, and gradually the flames of the burning oil on the surface diminished to nothing, leaving him bathed in weak moonlight.

What was the point of sinking the ship? What was the point of killing all these men? How many? Over a hundred. Surely he couldn't be the only one who survived.

"Oswald!" he hollered. "Piet! Lucas! Anybody!"

He thought he heard an answer. Holding his breath, he kept quiet, but all he caught was the slap of water against his body. He squinted at the shapes around him and thought he recognized what might be another survivor.

He hollered again to draw attention, but was met with nothing. Not another human voice. He tried paddling, but as he moved, his makeshift life preserver started to deflate, so he was forced to keep his movements easy. He felt himself sliding into uncontrolled panic.

Get a grip. Focus on what you can do.

He inventoried what he had. His clothes—shirt, undergarments, his trousers, cloth belt, money belt. No shoes or socks. No hat.

What about his pocketknife? He kneaded where his trousers were bunched under his arms and felt the hard shape of the knife. *Good.* In his haste to make a life preserver out of the trousers he'd forgotten about the knife, but it remained secure. However, he had nothing by way of food or water. And nothing to signal with, such as a shaving mirror.

Every time his thoughts spiraled about the hopelessness of his situation, he coaxed his mind back to positive thoughts. He wasn't injured. The water was cool but not uncomfortably so.

As he rode the swell, up and down, he bumped suddenly against another person floating in the darkness. Excited, Gary grabbed a handful of the stranger's wet clothes and pulled close.

The light of the moon shone across a waxy face, a man's features frozen into a grotesque death mask. Horrified, Gary pushed away. Then he realized that the corpse might have something that could be of use. A trench lighter, shoes, another knife, anything. But when Gary turned back, the body was gone, as if it had never been there.

All this movement caused the trousers—his flotation device—to deflate, and Gary swung them over his head to re-inflate them. This time, the effort took more out of him, and he wondered how long he could keep up it up.

As he floated, he observed in the sheen of water an angular shape in the darkness. Staring at it, he could see that it was a wooden pallet. Kicking his legs, he swam close.

When he grasped it, the firmness of the lumber felt reassuring, and he hauled himself on top. The pallet dipped below the surface and his weight was almost enough to swamp it, but as long as he hung on, he would remain above water. He let the trousers deflate and he lay on the pallet on top of them.

Exhausted, he mouthed a prayer of thanks that he had found the pallet, and put his head down and closed his eyes.

***

The sun's warm rays awoke him. He lifted his head and surveyed the area. The ocean had calmed to a gentle swell, and the tranquility showed no evidence of last night's mayhem. He pushed up for a better view, but the shifting of his weight caused the pallet to tip precariously.

Carefully, he rolled onto his back for the sun to warm his belly. The sky was a high overcast, and for December the temperature seemed unusually mild. But when the clouds parted, he was certain that the sun would soon bake him to a crisp.

His stomach ached from hunger, and when he tried to swallow, his throat hurt from being parched. He rolled back onto his belly and splashed water on his face to cool off.

Something flickered to his right. Looking carefully, he could see it was water cascading off what looked like a dark metal pole, maybe 25 yards away, rising like a specter from the ocean.

He lay on his belly and stared at the pole, not certain what he was seeing. The pole continued to rise to a height of about three feet and remained still, the swells lapping against it. Then the pole rotated, and an oval vertical lens panned toward him like an eye.

A periscope. The lens remained on him. Gary debated whether to wave his arms to signal for help, or to remain still and unnoticed.

If it was the Japanese submarine that had attacked the *Mooie*, then he had no doubt that rescue would not be his fate. But what if it was an American submarine?

The periscope rotated in a circle.

The swells pushed him closer. Fifteen yards. Ten yards. Five yards. Close enough now that he could read the Kanji script embossed in the metal frame around the lens. *Kure Naval Arsenal.* No doubt now. This was a Japanese submarine.

What would happen if he bumped up against the periscope?

Would they surface?

Gary decided to force the issue. First, he dug the knife free of his trousers and slipped the prong from the buckle of his money belt through the knife's metal loop. Next he opened the trouser waist and held it at the ready.

Closer and closer he drifted to the periscope. When the pallet bumped against it, Gary daringly yanked one leg of his trousers over the periscope. He shimmied the leg down until the knot in the leg pressed against the top of the mast, completely covering the lens. He jerked the web belt tight and looped the excess back on itself to secure it.

The periscope retracted underwater, the pants still fastened tight to it. Gary, as perilous as his situation was, had to chuckle, imagining the confusion inside the submarine, which he had blinded at least temporarily.

The periscope popped up again, then sank. It popped up and sank again, in rapid sequence. The crew must be trying to work the trousers loose, not certain what had caused the obstruction.

The swells pulled Gary farther away. Sooner or later the submarine would have to surface to remove the trousers. Maybe if they saw him, they would rescue him. But it was more likely that he'd be shot out of spite.

The drone of aircraft engines drew his attention.

He scanned the skies until he spied a distant shape approaching.

He kept focus as it drew nearer. It appeared to be a large airplane. The disks of four propellers, two on each wing, reflected the sun.

A Japanese plane?

The plane began to circle. Perhaps it was searching for survivors of the *Mooie*.

The aircraft dropped in altitude as it cruised toward him, a gigantic flying machine with broad wings that blotted out the sun. The sleek fuselage tapered to graceful horizontal fins and a similar vertical tail. The cockpit was behind a narrow windshield just back of the glassed-in nose. A bathtub arrangement hung from the belly. The airplane was painted olive drab with light gray underneath. Machine guns protruded from the nose and the teardrop-shaped hatches on the fuselage. The size and shape of the airplane was that of a B17, a bomber he had read about when still back home.

When the plane roared overhead, he recognized the insignia—a large white star in a blue circle—that confirmed that it was indeed an American B17!

He waved frantically and yelled.

The B17 kept circling. Gary was certain they had spotted him. Then he saw the ocean heaving about a hundred yards away. It was The submarine was breaking the surface. Its conning tower breached like an enormous fin, followed by the top of the hull. Sailors emerged on the conning tower and scrambled for the periscope, which was still covered by Gary's trousers.

Flashes erupted from the B17's machine guns, unleashing a torrent of red tracers at the submarine. Bullets splattered across the conning tower and ricocheted into the water.

"Get 'em!" Gary cheered.

The submarine began to slide beneath the water.

The B17 headed away, then banked steeply and returned, its

path lining up with the submarine. Bomb bay doors sprung open in the huge plane's belly.

Gary watched in fascination at the crewman huddled over an aiming sight in the glassed-in nose. Two bombs dropped from the bomb bay, then two more. The bombs arced for the submarine. The first two splashed short and exploded in enormous geysers of white foam. The blasts slapped water and hot air against Gary's face.

The next two bombs landed precisely beside the conning tower. One exploded in a bright fireball, *a direct hit!* The other blew up close in the water, foam and spray clouding the air.

Gary wasn't sure whether the submarine had been damaged, but then its stern angled sharply out of the ocean. The two propeller screws spun in the air, flinging water. The stern tipped vertical and remained in that position for a moment, and then the submarine rolled over, keel pointing upward like the belly of a dying fish. With a great belch of air and bubbles, the submarine swiftly vanished beneath the surface, leaving nothing but flotsam and an oily froth.

The B17 circled again. Gary waved to get the crew's attention. Even though he knew it was pointless, he hollered as loud as he could.

The bomber leveled its wings and climbed, heading away. As Gary watched, it slowly shrank into the distance, and the elation of seeing vengeance meted against the Japanese was replaced by a sinking feeling in his stomach, an all-too-familiar hopelessness. Soon he was again alone, condemned to float on the pallet.

The overcast had cleared, and the sun now beat down upon him with a fierce and unrelenting heat. To try to keep cool, he dunked his trousers in the ocean and draped them over his head. The briny water dripping past his face mocked him, as he couldn't drink any of it.

He remained on the pallet, on his belly, thirsty, hungry—daydreaming about plates of fried chicken and mashed potatoes, glasses of lemonade, laughing and joking with his friends and family. He couldn't tell if a minute had passed or an hour. Time had no meaning.

Then a wave nudged the pallet and a shadow crossed over him. He stuck his head from under the trousers, not certain that he wasn't dreaming.

The shadow extended all around him, an enormous dark shape outlined by sparkling sea.

He turned, and to his amazement saw an expanse of steel. A cargo ship was inching close. He blinked some more, still not sure he wasn't hallucinating.

Looking up, he saw a man at the ship's railing. The man was yelling at him, but Gary couldn't understand what he said. The man tossed a rope with a noose, which landed right on top of Gary. Gratefully he fumbled with the rope and slipped the noose over his head and under his armpits. Rising to his knees on the pallet, he held tight to the rope and shouted, "Okay!"

The rope pulled taut, and Gary was jerked to his feet, then hoisted aloft. He slammed hard against the steel hull. As he was tugged upward, he prayed that this was no hallucination, and that this was a friendly ship.

When he reached the top, hands grasped his arms and hauled him onto the deck. He lay on his back, panting hard, squinting at the men assembled around him.

***

Still not knowing who his rescuers were, Gary, legs shaking visibly from his ordeal, was helped below to the galley, where he was given fresh water which he drank gratefully, followed by cups of hot coffee. Then, draped in a thin blanket, he avidly devoured mouthwatering scrambled eggs, sausage, and bread slathered with butter and jam. Afterwards, finally sated, he washed up, shaved with a borrowed razor, and was given a fresh change of clothes, including a pair of sneakers. He remained at the galley table, clean, dry and full, sipping coffee, and so overcome with gratitude that he had to force back tears.

The crewman who had thrown him the rope was Paul Rimbaud, the ship's quartermaster. Rimbaud didn't look much older than Gary; however, he carried himself with an assuredness the other men obviously deferred to. Gary felt extremely indebted to him, and considered handing over one of his gold coins, but hesitated. Until he better understood the honesty of the crew, it wouldn't be a good idea for the word to get out that he was carrying gold.

"The captain wants to see you," Rimbaud said.

Gary rose to his feet, saying, "Absolutely," and followed Rimbaud out of the galley and up a ladder to the bridge.

Three men occupied the bridge and gazed out the expanse of windscreen facing forward. The man at the left leaned on a table covered by a chart, navigation tools, and logbooks. Another man stood at the helm. Both of these men glanced at Gary, then resumed their duties.

The third man looked the eldest and wore a wide mustache and goatee, both streaked with gray. Epaulet insignia decorated the shoulders of his white shirt, and a dingy white captain's hat sat on his head. Large binoculars hung from a leather strap around his neck.

He offered his hand and said in English, "Andre Nodier, wel-come aboard the *Dame de Marseille*."

"Gary Gatlin, Captain. I can't thank you and your crew enough."

"You are—" Nodier lifted one eyebrow— "American? Your accent."

"That's correct." Gary told him about his time on Formosa and what had happened since, his recollection ending with the torpe-doing of the *Mooie* and the sinking of the Japanese submarine by the B17.

Nodier stroked his beard. "Quite a tale. And one I wish to avoid." He stepped to the chart. "We're sailing toward the Yap Islands un-der a Vichy flag, which I hope protects us from the Japanese."

"Don't count on it," Gary replied soberly. "The *Mooie Zwerver* was neutral Dutch."

"Yes. It's a dangerous time for anyone on the high seas," the captain remarked. "Because of that, our final destination is South America or Mexico, where we'll wait out the war."

"If there's anything I can do to help on this ship," Gary said, "please let me know. I would be more than happy to be of service."

Nodier patted his shoulder. "I shall. You go below and get some rest."

Rimbaud took Gary to a bunk where he stretched out to un-wind. Despite the comfortable surroundings, however, his mind would not allow him to rest, and even when he dozed, he awoke in fits and starts. Gasping and panicking, he sat up, drenched in sweat and fighting back terrifying images of fleeing the sinking ship and again being marooned at sea.

***

Gary lay on his side and stared at the porthole above him. He had watched the sun's rays shine through, shifting as the afternoon progressed into evening, then fading with the onset of twilight.

Rimbaud returned to the compartment. "The captain wants to have a word with you."

They hustled to the bridge, and Gary, aware of the danger in the seas around them, had a gut-wrenching sense of foreboding at this call from the captain. . When they reached the bridge, Nodier was outside on the portside bridge wing, looking aft through his binoculars. Stars were beginning to show across the sky's fading light.

When the captain saw Gary, he gestured with the binoculars. "We're being hailed by a Japanese warship, a destroyer or a light cruiser, I can't tell. But she's signaled us to identify ourselves and prepare to be boarded." He cleared his throat and said in a troubled voice, "If they find you on my ship, I'll be in trouble for harboring a fugitive. In any case, I'd have to surrender you."

Gary's pulse quickened with a disturbing unease. "What are you telling me?"

"If you want to stay out of Japanese hands, Mr. Gatlin, my only choice is to put you over the side. An unpleasant choice, but that's the truth of the matter."

Gary took in the forbidding expanse of the murky ocean. "Can't I hide on board?"

Nodier shook his head. "I can't risk it. But take heart. It may not be as dire as it sounds." He pointed across the water at small mounds in the distance, barely visible in the approaching darkness. "We're sailing through the outlying, uncharted Yap Islands. There, that one," he exclaimed, "see that light?"

On one of the tiny islands, a campfire flickered on the distant beach.

"Who's on that island?"

"I don't know," Nodier answered. "But you will find out soon enough. I'm sorry my friend, but my ship and my men are my first priority. That's the long and short of it."

***

Once more facing peril, Gary was issued a cloth laundry bag filled with tins of food, a canteen of water, and a box of waterproof matches. His pocketknife was secured by a cord around his neck. He fit a life jacket around his chest and tightened the straps. His money belt remained hidden under his trousers. He could hardly believe this was happening again, but tried his best to remain stoic, realizing the captain's plight.

Rimbaud led him to the portside railing.

"Good luck, sailor." Rimbaud shook his hand. "We'll see you when this war is over."

"One more thing," Gary said. Inasmuch as he was leaving the ship, he figured he had nothing to lose by giving Rimbaud a gold coin in thanks for his rescue. "When you get to a safe port, have a good meal on me."

Rimbaud examined the US $10 eagle, weighed the coin in his palm, then flipped it, snatched it midair, and dropped it into a trouser pocket. He gripped Gary by the shoulders. "Until next time, my friend."

Reluctantly and with a heavy heart, Gary climbed over the railing and steadied himself on the edge of the hull. He focused on the campfire, now a tiny spot of light. Thinking that once he was in the water he might not be able to see the fire, Gary noted the position of the stars, now bright in the sky. He'd use them to remain oriented.

Looking down past the toes of his sneakers, he saw the bow wake churning the water as the ship plowed forward. He focused on the campfire again. As instructed, he took a deep breath, both hands gripping his life jacket to prevent his neck being snapped when he hit the water, and slid from the deck. The drop seemed longer than he had anticipated, and then he plunged hard into the water below, then emerged, sputtering.

The *Dame de Marseille* loomed over him. Moment by moment it moved away, shrinking rapidly into the distance, the *chug-chug* of its steam engine echoing in the darkness.

As Gary floated, buoyed by the life jacket, he regarded the blinking light of the Japanese warship as it slowly gained on the cargo ship. He aligned himself with the stars and looked for the campfire. When the swells lifted him, he saw its uncertain light.

He turned in its direction and began to swim.

Chapter Twenty-five

December 1941

Gary swam toward the light on the beach, packet in tow, but the effort proved arduous and frustrating. When the swells lifted him, the campfire was visible, but when he dipped into a trough and came back up, he had to search for the distant flame all over again. His wet clothes and the bag of supplies he hauled with him dragged heavily through the water, and the task of swimming had him near exhaustion.

He stopped to rest and looked for the *Dame de Marseille*. He'd lost it in the darkness, but he did see the menacing silhouette of the Japanese warship trailing after the steamship. He wondered if the lookouts on the Japanese ship had spotted the campfire. In that case, they might launch a landing party. Worriedly, he glanced back toward the island.

The campfire was gone.

He panned the island, panic rising as he searched for the fire. What had happened to it? Did the people tending it see the Japanese ship and put the fire out? Or had Gary drifted to where he could no longer see it?

Something slapped the water, and he glanced apprehensively about. A triangular object, shiny and black as obsidian, cut through the surface. *Shark!*

His breath caught, and his nerves compressed into a paralyzing, tight coil.

Sharks. Of all the dangers he'd contemplated, this one hadn't crossed his mind. Frantically swiveling his head to the left and right, he searched for another glimpse of the menacing fin.

He thought he spotted another one, but in this awful darkness it was hard to tell. What did he know about sharks? Very little, except that they were big, predator fish with a profusion of sharp teeth. Was he better off if he remained still, or if he swam? Was it one shark or was he in the middle of a school of these wolves of the sea? Fear coursed down his spine at the thought. He'd seen what wolves could do to sheep.

Again, Gary steeled himself to face his situation. Whether or not the sharks attacked was something he couldn't control, but he knew he couldn't simply drift out here and do nothing. He reoriented himself with the stars, and cautiously extended his arms and legs and began paddling as quietly as possible toward what he hoped was the island.

On and on he swam, sculling with his arms and legs. No sharks. He breathed a little easier, and when he paused to rest, he could see the ragged outline of what seemed a copse of trees. He must be closing in on the island. He swam a bit more until he heard the welcome murmur of surf crashing on a beach. The familiar sound gave him heart, and he continued to push forward, intensely relieved that the sharks had apparently not been hungry.

A swell carried him, curling into a wave. He tried to keep his head above water but the wave somersaulted him onto a hard, smooth surface, where he landed on his back, his life jacket cushioning the impact, his bundle of provisions tumbling with him.

As another wave surged around him, he staggered to his feet

and wiped water from his eyes. He was on the shelf of a reef, still a hundred yards from the island proper. The beach extended left to right in front of him, the surf lapping on the sand, the colors muted to shades of gray by the darkness.

He walked unsteadily across the reef, amazed that, despite the odds, once again he was about to reach sanctuary. Pools in the reef kept him watching where he stepped, being careful not to fall. Reaching the end of the reef, he hopped down into waist-deep water and waded the last twenty-five yards to shore.

He shambled up the beach to a line of flotsam left by high tide. Stepping a few yards past that, he sank to his knees in dry sand and rolled onto his back. Staring up at the stars, he closed his eyes and prayed. *Thank you, Jesus.*

He took measure of his breath, and despite being thirsty, hungry, and miserable, he discovered he was remarkably in pretty good shape. His plan had been to reach the island intact, and incredibly, here he was. He patted the cloth bag of provisions to assure himself that it was still safely tied to his life jacket. He pulled the canteen from the bag and took a long, sweet drink of water. Then, laying his head back, he gave in to exhaustion and in moments was asleep on the sand.

***

The harsh light of the sun burned through Gary's eyelids. With his hand he shielded his eyes and blinked himself awake.

He was on a wide strip of beach, the surf crashing on the coral reef, itself an irregular patchwork of light-colored shapes just beneath the surface of the water. Beyond the reef, an assortment of small islands dotted the ocean. Close to the beach the water was a brilliant turquoise, farther out, a dark blue.

He pawed at the straps of his life jacket, unbuckling them, and shrugged loose. Sitting up, he dragged the bag of provisions onto his lap and inventoried what he had aside from the canteen. Amazingly, it was all there. He drank again from the canteen and assessed his situation.

The island looked deserted, so for now he was on his own. For long-term survival, he needed to find a source of fresh water. The ocean would provide plenty of fish, but he would have to augment his diet with whatever plants were safe to eat.

What about that mysterious campfire? He saw no sign of it or any other human presence. He'd have to go exploring, but first, a long-overdue hot meal.

After gathering driftwood and clumps of dried grass, he scooped a hole in the sand and lined it with rocks, laying the grass and wood inside. He planned the fire carefully, as he dare not waste a match. With his knife he cut through the paraffin coating on the match-box and removed one of the thick wooden matches, also dipped in paraffin.

Crouching over the hole, he struck the match against a rock and it flared into a bright, hot flame, which he dropped into the dry grass. The grass caught, and he attended to the tiny fire with the care of a surgeon treating a patient, feeding the flame ever-larger slivers of driftwood. Soon he had a crackling fire going and had to move back to escape the uncomfortable heat.

With the can-opener tool of his pocketknife, he opened a can of chicken-vegetable soup and balanced it on a rock at the edge of the fire. He was so engrossed in his labors that when two shadows fell across him, he stiffened with surprise, then alarm, and looked up.

A pair of dark, muscular men stared back. Both had mops of frizzy black hair, broad faces with thick noses, and wore cloth skirts held up by crude leather belts. Sheathed knives hung at their sides. Each man had a leather tie with beads hanging around his neck, and each carried a simple cloth bag of provisions slung across one shoulder. Their feet were wide and well-formed from a lifetime of walking barefoot. The taller of the two had a more wrinkled face and gray mottled his hair. The other man, younger, carried a bamboo pole with the end carved into a barbed fork. Because of their primitive and feral appearance, the two men reminded Gary of the Paiwan back on Formosa.

The older man said something. At first Gary thought the stranger was speaking a native tongue, until he realized the man was speaking either Dutch or German. When Gary didn't respond the man asked in French, *"Faites-vous bien?"* then in English, "You sir, are you doing all right? Do you require assistance?"

"I-I-I-," Gary stammered, taken aback by the stranger's language ability.

Without asking, the two men squatted at the opposite side of the fire. The older man said, "I am Falthin Attao." He pointed to his partner. "My friend, Tano Mafnas."

Tano smiled, then saluted by waving the bamboo pole.

Gary cleared his throat, still fearful and remaining suspicious of their presence. "I am an American. My name is Gary Gatlin.."

"Ah," Falthin replied, "a Yankee. That is why you speak English with such an unusual accent."

The two seemed friendly enough, but Gary kept his guard up, uneasy about their motives. They might try to harm him, or be after his money belt--or worse, they might be working for the Japanese.

Tano tilted his head to read the stenciling on Gary's life jacket, reading aloud, "*Dame de Marseille.*" He mumbled to Falthin, who in turn asked, "Did that ship sink?"

"No. I had to get off the ship before they were boarded by the Japanese. I was swimming toward a campfire on the beach."

Falthin pointed to his left. "That way?"

"Yes, I think it was that way."

Falthin chuckled. "You are a strong man to make such a swim. It was us with the fire. We were roasting crabs. If we had known you'd be coming, we would've saved some for you."

"Thanks for the thought. Crabs would have been great, but I'm just happy to be on land." Deciding it was best to build camaraderie with these two, Gary gestured to the steaming can of soup. "Would you care to join me?"

Falthin reached into his provisions bag and brought out a spoon and a rag. He wrapped the rag around the hot can and lifted it to his mouth. He blew across the soup to cool it, then helped himself to a spoonful before passing the can and the spoon to Tano. After Tano ate a spoonful, he passed the can and spoon to Gary. They studied Gary as he slurped at the hot soup. When done with his spoonful, he offered the can again to Falthin, who raised a hand and shook his head.

"Finish it. You look hungry."

Gary was more than hungry, he was famished. The soup tasted as good as anything he could remember, and he appreciated how it warmed his belly as well. He spooned every morsel and tipped the can over his mouth to catch the last few drops. Falthin motioned for the empty can and the spoon, which he dropped into his provisions bag.

Gary asked, "Are we alone?"

"Yes, just us three," Falthin answered.

"There's no one else on the island?"

"Oh, there are several others."

"I thought you said there was just us."

Yes, here, just us three," Falthin replied. He extended a finger at Gary, "One," then at Tano, "two," and finally to himself. "Three of us here. Isn't that what you were asking?"

Well, no, thought Gary. "Where are the others?" he asked.

Falthin and Tano rose to their feet. Falthin said, "This way. Bring your things."

***

They led Gary from the beach and into the brush, walking lightly through the growth, careful not to leave a trail. They climbed a steep ridge covered in an overlapping canopy of trees draped with vines, and on the opposite side, Gary peered through the leaves and glimpsed more ocean.

The slope flattened into an open area sheltered by trees. Tucked between two of the trees stood a bamboo hut with a thatched roof and walls. A thin cable connected from the hut to a wire array carefully strung between two of the taller trees. A scattering of natives paused from what they were doing to watch the stranger.

From inside the hut appeared a small man, almost gnomish, who, as he stepped into the sunlight, pulled a frayed hat over his balding head. Skin flaked off his mottled, ruddy face. In his tattered shorts and shirt, he had the appearance of a castaway vagabond, except that he moved with purpose.

Falthin explained in English how he and Tano had found Gary. The man introduced himself. "Charles Stirling." He spoke with a British accent. "How on earth did you get here?"

Gary, startled at finding an Englishman in this distant, faraway place, explained briefly how he'd come to land on the island, starting with his arrival on Formosa, surviving the torpedo attack, and ending with his jumping off the *Dame de Marseille*. For now, he kept to himself the details of his part in the sinking of the Japanese submarine.

Stirling crossed his arms and rocked on his sandaled feet. "Well, Yank, the fortunes of war, no?" His bushy copper-colored eyebrows danced as he spoke. He slapped Gary's arm and invited him into the hut. "Let's make the best of it while we can."

A long table stood against one wall, itself covered with several maps and a calendar, the passing days marked with an X. On the table sat a radio and a clock, and a shelf just above the table was packed with ledger books.

On the opposite side of the hut was a cot and a smaller table, this one crowded with cooking utensils. "You can put your things there," Stirling said, giving Gary the impression he was going to be there for a while.

After he placed his life jacket and provisions on the table, Gary turned his attention to the radio and the maps.

"I'm a meteorologist," Stirling explained. "I've been tracking the weather here for two years now."

"Two years out here by yourself? You must really enjoy your work."

Stirling smiled wanly. "Quite."

"Who do you work for?" Gary asked. "I doubt this is a hobby."

"Indeed." Stirling chuckled. "I work for His Majesty's Office of Scientific Inquiry."

Gary had never heard of such a thing, but that didn't mean it didn't exist.

Stirling laid a hand on the radio. "Those wires you saw outside are the antennae. Twice a day I broadcast a weather report. More often if there's a storm."

"To whom?"

"To whomever. I've been told my transmissions reach Melbourne, Hong Kong, Calcutta, San Francisco."

"What about the Japanese?"

Stirling twirled a finger over his head. "The Yap Islands belong to them but they've never ventured here."

"They don't hear your broadcasts?"

"Most probably. Then again, as I also provide a useful service to them, they've left me alone. Temporarily, at least."

As Gary examined the radio, its microphone and telegraph key, he concluded that Stirling was not exactly forthcoming about all he was doing here in this remote, isolated place. He noted a metal placard on the lower corner of the radio which read *Short Wave Tuner, Model 9350, A.T.M. Ltd.* "This is both a receiver and a transmitter. Are you able to listen to the news?"

Stirling inhaled deeply, then exhaled. "Yes, and sadly, I've nothing positive to report. Things in the Pacific are not going well for us Brits or with you Yanks."

Although his first thought was that the radio might be a way to get help, Gary didn't touch it. When he learned more about Stirling and his eccentric business, he'd ask if there was a way to summon a rescue.

"Come on. Let's continue the tour," Stirling said. He showed Gary a thermometer and barometer hanging under an eave of the hut's roof, then a bicycle-powered generator tucked under an adjacent lean-to, a barrel that collected rainwater for drinking, baskets filled with assorted varieties of unknown fruits, and an observation platform built near the top of an especially tall tree. They climbed up, using steps nailed to the branches and lengths of knotted rope.

When they reached the platform Gary smiled and remarked, "This reminds me of a tree fort from when I was a kid."

Stirling arched an eyebrow, indicating he was unfamiliar with "tree forts."

Gary brushed aside the overhanging branches. From this vantage he could see that the island resembled the letter "C" and that they were on the widest part.

"It's the remnants of an ancient volcano," Stirling said, "hence its shape. Just to show you the vastness of the ocean, this island remains uncharted." He pointed in the four cardinal directions. "That's north. East. South. West."

To the north, Gary spied a long strip of bare ground that ran parallel to the central spine of the atoll. Two of the natives used machetes to hack down a tree along one edge of the strip, widening it. "What are they doing?"

Stirling shrugged. "Harvesting some timber. Who knows?"

Gary studied the little village that Stirling had built, and pondered how the Englishman seemed to be on top of everything. "Somehow I think you know exactly what they're doing."

Stirling stared at him.

Gary said, "It looks to me like they're building a landing strip."

Stirling worked his lips, and Gary could tell the Englishman was considering how to answer.

Chapter Twenty-six

March 1942

It was obvious to Gary that he was going to be there for a while. There was nowhere to go and no way to get there. His time on the island unfolded at a leisurely pace even as war raged unseen and unheard around him, and his benefactors were kind. But the quiet and calm around them would soon prove to be an illusion.

The days turned into weeks, the weeks into months. At first, most of his time was spent on housekeeping chores: keeping the thatched hut and its furnishings in good order; accompanying Falthin and the other Polynesian men on their forays across the island to gather plants for their meals; and going on boating expeditions to fish and explore the atoll. Another chore that Stirling insisted on was clearing a wide pathway on the beach between the airstrip and the lagoon, although he never explained why.

Everything seemed tranquil enough until those occasions when Stirling played the news on the radio, which brought war's dark shadow over the little island. In December, Germany had stepped up their submarine campaign against the Americans. Then in January, the Japanese invaded Luzon.

Gary pondered how the war might be affecting his family. He hadn't heard of any attacks on the American mainland, so in that regard, he felt that everyone at home was safe. He imagined the work that wartime would bring to Utah. The military would need rations, which would mean a strong demand for produce and a steady income for the family farm. What about the Mitsuis? Gary was certain that Ichiro would be called to active duty if he hadn't been already.

Gary's greatest concern centered on his friends back on Formosa, now under the Japanese military heel. Considering his violent escape, he was certain the authorities would bring heat on Kasumi and Akito Saito. What worked in their favor was that the Japanese military, like the American, had to feed its army, so the Formosan government needed farmers like the Saitos. For his part, the Paiwan chieftain Wu Fen-jeng knew how to stay out of the law's reach. Nori Chan was wily enough to keep a low profile. Regardless of how Gary considered these matters, much of his time was spent skipping rocks absently across the water, thinking about Kasumi.

In mid-January, Gary's first opportunity to help Stirling with his meteorological duties happened when the Englishman needed someone to operate the bicycle-powered generator. Stirling stood in the open area of the encampment, hands on his hips as he surveyed the surrounding brush. "Bloody hell," he cursed.

Gary had been watching him drag the generator out of its lean-to. "What's the matter?"

Stirling pointed to the generator. "Time for my weather report. Damn Falthin and the rest. The moment they see me getting the generator ready, they disappear."

Gary put his hand on the generator's bicycle seat. "You need someone to ride this thing? I'll do it." He climbed onto the seat and grabbed the handlebars. The device resembled an exercise apparatus from a gymnasium. Should be easy enough. "What do I do?"

"Just start pedaling. There's a little red light where the handlebars connect to the stem. When you hit the correct speed, the light will illuminate. Whenever you're ready."

"Got it." Gary planted his feet on the pedals. Pushing down with his right foot, he expected the crankshaft to begin spinning, but instead it held firm.

"You might need to bear down on it."

"No kidding," Gary replied. He had to stand on the pedal and lever against the handlebars before the crankshaft began to move. When it rotated, he shifted his weight to the left foot, then the right, back to the left. The effort was like cycling through thick mud, but soon he had a steady rhythm going, the generator emitting a low whine.

"Faster," Stirling said.

Even after only a minute, Gary had felt the effort taxing him. He rested on the seat to concentrate on working his legs. The little light began to flicker.

"When it glows steady, you have it," Stirling encouraged.

Staring at the light, Gary increased his speed. Fortunately, the generator was in the shade, for the day was unusually warm. The light at last shone a bright, steady red. Stirling disappeared into the hut. Above his own labored breathing, Gary heard the *tap-tap-tap* of the Englishman transmitting his report using the telegraph key.

Gary thought that upon reaching a constant speed the pedaling would become easier. But that wasn't the case. It was like pedaling uphill against a headwind. Whenever he slacked off, the light would flicker and Stirling would yell, "The voltmeter is dropping. Keep up the speed, Yank!"

Sweat dripped into Gary's eyes and he hurriedly wiped them.

From inside the hut, *tap-tap-tap*.

Christ, Gary thought to himself. What was Stirling doing,

transmitting the entire encyclopedia? His side began to ache, and he appreciated the wisdom of Falthin and his crew making themselves scarce.

Then finally, "You can stop, Gary, we're done for today."

Gary heaved a breath of exhaustion and lifted his feet from the pedals. He watched with satisfaction when the red light flickered and went out as the generator's whine fell silent.

After this initiation into the business of meteorology, Gary asked if there were other tasks he could help with. Stirling showed him how to take measurements with the barometer, thermometer, and wind-direction/speed indicator, and document those observations in the ledger books. The work satisfied a scholarly itch within Gary as it kept his mind occupied on something besides his worries about his faraway family and friends.

But the more time Gary spent with Stirling, the more convinced he became that the Englishman was an odd duck. First of all, he seemed to relish the isolation of the remote island and never opened up about his family, or his past, or what had brought him here. Although Gary was curious about the ledger books and what else was on the shelves, after one quick outburst from Stirling, he learned not to pry about anything related to the radio and the weather reports unless Stirling brought it up.

***

That changed the day Gary returned to the hut from a fishing outing with Falthin. When Gary padded into the hut, Stirling was deep in concentration writing on a message pad while he crosschecked his work with a small book Gary hadn't seen before.

Stirling sat perfectly still. Then he slowly turned on his stool to face Gary, and the two men stared at one another. Gary recognized the awkwardness of the moment and was the first to speak. "I can leave."

The Englishman took his hands from the book and the message pad. "As you might have guessed, I'm more than a meteorologist," he said.

"More as in what?" Gary queried.

"I actually work for the Royal Navy's intelligence service."

"So, you're a spy?"

"Not exactly. I'm an observer." He gestured to the message pad. "I compile what we've recorded in these reports." Next, he held up the book. Its pages were filled with words listed with a series of four-letter groups. "What I can't let happen is for this code book to fall into Japanese hands. Above all other concerns, the book must be destroyed. Burning is the best way. Its pages are especially flammable."

"You have my word," Gary motioned to the radio and maps. "What about those?"

"That's my cover. I'm a meteorologist, remember?"

***

Over the next weeks, Gary fell in step with Stirling's clandestine routine. Some days, Stirling would listen to audio broadcasts. He understood Japanese, though not as well as Gary, and came to appreciate the American's expert linguistic knowledge. The military traffic was almost always in code, but Gary would faithfully note everything he heard.

When Stirling transmitted his weather reports, he seemed not to mind how long they took. But when he transmitted his coded messages, he did so at irregular times and relayed the missives in short bursts.

"We have to keep these transmissions under thirty seconds," he explained. "That keeps the Japanese from triangulating our position using radio locators."

"Won't they figure out that the weather transmissions and these are from the same source?"

The Englishman shook his head. "Completely different frequencies. As far as the Japanese are concerned, our transmissions are completely random."

***

When he wasn't busy helping Stirling, Gary accompanied Falthin and Tano on trips in their outrigger canoe into the atoll's lagoon. Paddling the boat gave his upper body a much- needed workout; his legs got plenty of exercise with the bicycle generator. In the canoe, they would drift slowly through the middle of the lagoon and Gary would peer over the side, into the unimaginable depths of the intensely blue water.

As he gazed downward, he asked Falthin, "Am I looking into a volcano?"

"One of many," Falthin replied, impressed with Gary's observation.

At random times, the war made its appearance. When the drone of an airplane engine disturbed the pastoral quiet, Stirling would sprint into his hut, and he cautioned Gary to stay out of view. Meanwhile, Falthin and his men made it a point to stand in the open and wave. This way, to the Japanese, they had chanced upon a bunch of simple natives going about their simple chores.

Usually the airplanes kept their distance, where they'd cruise serenely through the air, the sun's reflection flashing off their canopies and wings. These aircraft were either small Nakajima floatplane scouts or larger Mitsubishi monoplanes with fixed landing gear shrouded in spats. Once in a while, a plane would zoom low over the island. Gary worried that after one of these low-flying episodes the planes would return to investigate, but thankfully it was always just one quick pass and the Japanese soared away.

Gary realized that their uncharted atoll was but one of dozens in these vast waters, which accounted for the Japanese lack of interest in them. Stirling had taken great pains to make sure the observation platform was hidden in a tree, all but invisible, and that the array of wire antennae had been stretched over ragged grass and brush to break up its outline and shadow. The airfield that Falthin and his men worked on, on a relaxed, intermittent schedule, was but a narrow, uneven strip hacked through the brush.

One evening in March, Stirling called everyone to the airstrip. With a stick he poked holes in the ground along its perimeter. "Falthin, I need you build small fires at these spots, but don't light them until I give you the word. And be ready to extinguish the fires as fast as you got them started."

Gary didn't ask the reason for the task, but he guessed that Stirling was lighting the airstrip for a secret mission. What Gary couldn't fathom was a pilot crazy enough to land on such a tiny strip in the middle of the night.

Sometime around 1 a.m., Stirling dashed from the hut. "Start the fires!"

Gary had been waiting with Falthin, both of them sitting in the darkness. They jumped to their feet. Falthin used a match to ignite a torch made of dried moss wrapped on a stick. When that caught, he lit similar torches carried by Gary, Tano, and another of the Polynesian men. They sprinted around the edges of the airstrip and lit the kindling arranged in the small holes. Gary stepped back from the airstrip, not sure what to expect.

An airplane engine droned in the distance, the sound growing louder, and he could tell it was a multi-engine plane. He craned his neck to search the night sky. The noise grew louder, then louder still, to a deafening crescendo.

And then a humungous shape emerged from the darkness and into the airstrip's glow, the shape as improbably large as a flying locomotive, flanked by two propeller disks like round silver shields. In an instant the airplane flashed over him, displaying British insignia—concentric blue, white, and red circles—under the wings. And then, just as quickly, the plane was gone, the roar of its engines reverberating in his ears. Gary had no idea what had just happened.

Falthin sprinted to the middle of the airstrip, heading toward a box that dangled beneath a descending parachute. The box smacked the ground and the parachute collapsed over it. The box was about the size of two milk crates, and Gary, watching in amazement, wondered what was in it that made its delivery worth the risk to the airplane and its crew.

Stirling shouted, unseen in the murk, "Douse the fires!"

That task completed, Falthin and Tano carried the box to the hut and set it inside. Stirling asked Gary to hold a flashlight for illumination as he cut the straps securing the parachute.

With his knife, Stirling cracked the wooden box open. Packed in excelsior for cushioning were: cans of fruit and soup; a box of note pads; pencils; tins of tea, sugar, salt; and a small, flat package wrapped in paper. Stirling tore the paper, revealing a new code book, the reason for the dangerous airdrop.

***

April 17, 1942

Stirling and Gary huddled around the loudspeaker of Stirling's radio. The evening's news was extraordinarily depressing. Back in February, Singapore had fallen. In March, Java fell. Now, as of this broadcast, the situation for the American army in the Philippines was dire.

The next morning, Stirling gathered Falthin and his men, and in his usual terse way, all the Englishman said was, "We're hosting a visitor. Inspect the airstrip and the beach area that we've been keeping clear."

The hours passed with a heightened sense of anticipation. In the late afternoon, an airplane circled overhead. Stirling joined Gary, and the two men watched through the Englishman's binoculars. It was a flying boat, two engines on a broad wing mounted on a pylon over the gray fuselage. Stirling said it was a Catalina. What most excited Gary was its white star insignia. *An American plane!*

As he watched the Catalina descend toward them, he thought, surely such an airplane is too big for our tiny airstrip. However, the plane circled to the open end of the atoll's lagoon and eased onto the smooth water. It planed gracefully across the surface, water spraying in a V from under its nose. Falthin, Tano, and the others scrambled into a pair of canoes and paddled out to greet the plane.

The throaty roar of the twin engines echoed across the lagoon. The Catalina slowed to an easy cruise, a small wake rippling behind it. A hatch on the nose turret opened and a crewman wearing a headset rose into view, exposed to his shoulders. Falthin and Tano had halted their canoes about fifty yards apart, the men standing in the boats and pointing to the beach they'd been tending. The airplane adjusted its course to taxi between the canoes toward the spot.

The Catalina approached the beach and emerged from the water, rolling on fat tires that had sprouted from under its nose and either side of its fuselage. A crewman in a waist blister position waved from behind his machine gun. Water cascaded from the plane, and Gary expected that at any moment it would shake itself dry like a big dog in from a swim.

Stirling ran in front of the plane and waved his arms. He backtracked up the beach and guided the Catalina past the end of the airstrip, and signaled for it to turn around to face the lagoon. The engines coughed and fell silent, though the drama of the flying boat's arrival still left Gary in awe of what he'd just seen. A crewman in blue dungarees climbed onto the wing between the engines and began a lookout with binoculars.

The blister was opened by one of the crewmen, who was holding a short ladder. He hooked the ladder to the exterior of the fuselage, allowing entry and exit from the aircraft. Two officers in khaki uniforms stepped off the ladder and planted their boots in the sand. Both wore web belts with holstered pistols.

Excited to meet fellow Americans and certain they'd come to rescue him from this island, Gary hustled close. He first shook hands with the man wearing gold oak leaves on his collar and introduced himself. In turn, the man said he was . Lieutenant Commander Gerald Cartwright.

"I'm so glad to see you," Gary exclaimed. "I can't wait to get home."

The two officers glanced at each other with slightly raised eyebrows, then at Gary.

"I'm not sure what you mean," Cartwright replied.

"Isn't that why you're here?" Gary sputtered, confused. "I mean—"

The crewman on the wing interrupted with a shout. "Aircraft approaching!"

Cartwright and his copilot stepped from under the Catalina's shadow and looked upward, shielding their eyes. Gary followed their example.

Moment by moment, as the intruder drew closer, its outline became more apparent.

It was a monoplane with a single radial engine and what appeared to be a pair of bombs under each wing. The airplane banked, as if to display the insignia emblazoned on its wings. Bright red circles outlined in white.

Gary's blood froze the instant he recognized the type.

It was a Nakajima bomber. A Japanese airplane.

CHAPTER TWENTY-SEVEN

April 17, 1942

Gary watched the Nakajima approach. Anxiously, he glanced at Cartwright and his co-pilot to see how they were responding, then assessed the mood of the rest of the Catalina's crew. He thought everyone would run for cover, or ready the flying boat's machine guns to open fire. But the reaction to the Japanese warplane seemed to be of hopeful anticipation to some, while the rest continued with their duties of attending to the Catalina.

"What's going on?" Gary asked. "Aren't you worried that airplane is going to attack?"

"Not hardly," Cartwright replied, distracted.

The Nakajima lowered its landing gear, rocked its wings, and began to orbit the island.

Cartwright ordered, "Chief Donovan, throw a smoke grenade."

The eldest of the crewmen, a squat and truculent-looking individual, jogged from the airstrip to the beach. He carried the grenade—a hand-sized, olive-green cylinder—pulled the pin on top, and pitched the grenade toward an open stretch of sand. The grenade's safety lever flew off with a distinctive *ping*. The grenade rolled on the sand, sputtering at first, then gushed a fountain of yellow smoke. The smoke blossomed into a cloud that drifted over the lagoon.

Stirling joined the group and observed the Nakajima through his binoculars.

"What's with the grenade?" Gary asked him, thoroughly confused.

"The pilot is using the smoke to determine the direction and strength of the wind." Stirling lowered the binoculars. "Fortunately for him, our little airstrip is aligned with the wind."

Gary stared incredulously at the narrow clearing they had hacked from the brush. "He's going to land here?"

"That's the plan."

Gary turned the situation over in his mind. Though the Nakajima was about half the size of the Catalina, it was still a large airplane. Its wings would barely clear the trees on either side of the airstrip, which as a runway appeared much too short. Those thoughts prompted more questions. Why was that plane landing here? And...

"Who's the pilot?" he asked, certain that it had to be Japanese. "A defector?"

"Hell no! One of *them!*" Stirling pointed to Cartwright and the co-pilot, both of whom were focused on the Nakajima.

"The US Navy?" Gary asked, still bewildered. "They stole that Nakajima?"

Cartwright chuckled and quipped, "We'll give it back once the war is over."

The cloud of yellow smoke stretched over the lagoon, undulating and pulling apart like a wad of gossamer cloth until it was little more than a fading stain in the air.

"Nice, steady breeze," Cartwright remarked to his men. "The conditions are as good as they're going to get."

The Nakajima cruised low for a second pass over the lagoon, its vortices twisting through the last of the smoke. The airplane approached on a path parallel to the airstrip, and Gary felt his body tremble from the throaty growl of the plane's radial engine.

The pilot had slid the canopy back a bit, which allowed him a good view of the island below. He sat high in the cockpit and leaned appreciably to one side to scan past the fuselage. Goggles and a cloth helmet masked his features, and Gary couldn't tell his nationality.

In the brief moment when the Nakajima roared past, its image became etched in Gary's memory. The large red roundels on the fuselage and under the wings made it obvious that this was a Japanese airplane. A large finned bomb hung beneath each wing.

The pilot gunned the engine. Smoke belched from the exhaust ports, and the Nakajima accelerated and climbed. It banked to the left in an extended oval track, maneuvering north, and in the distance aligned itself with the airstrip.

"He's going for it," Cartwright said, his tone rising with excitement.

The faraway airplane was but a dot hovering in the air. Occasionally, sunlight flashed off its canopy. Gary scanned the surrounding sky, worried that the arrival of Japanese fighter planes might ruin whatever plans Cartwright and this intrepid pilot had arranged.

Slowly and relentlessly, the Nakajima continued on its gradual descent, the dot sprouting wings, then landing gear, the propeller disk tracing a circle in front of the plane. The Nakajima's flight path remained rock steady.

However good this pilot was, he needed both nerves of steel and split-second timing to execute this landing. The tension was like watching a carnival high-wire act with no safety net. The margin of error was razor-thin. The greatest hazard would be landing short and smashing into the trees at the airstrip's threshold—and the pilot had to consider the foliage on the other side. Or smacking the ground too hard, bouncing out of control, perhaps to cartwheel into the Catalina. Or not being able to stop on the miniscule strip and plow into the trees at the far end. Any wrong move and *disaster!*

For their part, Cartwright and his co-pilot appeared as nervous as Gary. The sailors paused in their duties to watch. Falthin and the rest of the Polynesians emerged from the brush, eager to take in the show.

At a quarter mile out, with its flaps down, the Nakajima had slowed so much that it appeared ready to drop from the sky. The airplane's nose cocked up and to the right, crabbing at an angle so the pilot could peer past the big, round cowling.

Gary clenched his hands so hard that his fingernails dug into his palms. His neck corded with anxiety, and he swallowed to moisten his dry mouth.

Then, in the final dramatic seconds, the slow-motion pace of the approach accelerated into a lightning-fast landing.

At about two hundred yards, the Nakajima yawed in order to center itself with the airstrip but remained in a nose-up attitude. Its landing gear—main and tail wheels—clipped the tops of the trees, scattering branches and leaves. The plane hit the hard-packed ground in a perfect three-point landing, the wheel struts compressing, then pushing the machine up and forward. The pilot bounced in place, like a cowboy riding a bucking bronco, his head bobbing out past the top of the windshield. The Nakajima rolled down the airstrip, dust spraying from under the tires.

A bolt of concern shot through Gary, and he was prepared to run should the airplane careen toward him.

Close to the end of the runway, the Nakajima's main wheels locked, skidding on the ground. The tail swung around and the airplane slid sideways, dust rooster-tailing from the tires.

Then, as though Lady Luck had reached down to prevent catastrophe, the Nakajima halted a hundred and fifty feet from the Catalina, tipping onto its left main wheel for a heart-stopping instant, then rocking in place on all three wheels. The engine coughed once, then fell silent, the three-bladed propeller swinging to a stop. The abrupt calm served as a dramatic counterpoint to all the suspense, and Gary heard a simultaneous exhalation of relief from the assembled bystanders. The muffled sound gave way to a loud cheer.

"Wow," Cartwright whispered as he elbowed his co-pilot.

Gary knew the landing had been quite a stunt, and hearing these officers acknowledge the feat only increased his admiration of the pilot's skills.

Everyone sprinted to mob the Nakajima. Inside the cockpit, the pilot sat still, eyes forward, as if still gathering his wits. Lifting the goggles from his face, he peeled off the cloth helmet and dropped it and the goggles to his side. Grasping the edges of the cockpit, he levered himself up and crawled over the left side of the fuselage to slide onto the wing. Sweat blotted his khaki uniform where the safety harness had been cinched. He stepped along the wing root to the trailing edge, and with an athletic hop, landed on the ground.

Cartwright pushed through the crowd of sailors to congratulate him. The pilot had bright eyes and a toothy grin that beamed with confident vigor. A shock of sandy-brown hair dangled over his forehead. He wore a pair of silver bars on each collar and a gold aviator's badge above his left breast pocket. He reminded Gary of a baseball hero who had just scored a homerun and shrugged off praise in a casual *aw-shucks* manner.

He was lanky and tall, much like Gary. And not much older, maybe in his middle twenties. This observation made Gary consider that perhaps he too might serve in the war as a military pilot.

Gary found a canteen and introduced himself as he offered the pilot a drink. The pilot gulped several swallows and wiped his mouth as he returned the canteen. "Lieutenant Donald Larsen. You look a long way from home. Where are you from Gary?"

"Utah."

Larsen glanced at Gary's civilian attire—faded and tattered dungarees and an equally weather-beaten shirt. "What the heck brings you to the western Pacific?"

"It's a long story." Gary pointed a thumb at the Nakajima. "But not nearly as interesting as yours." He had a lot of questions, such as what was Larsen going to do with the airplane now? He guessed the navy intended to study it, but first they had to get it off this atoll. Or was this the Nakajima's ultimate destination?

Larsen slapped Gary on the shoulder, "Gotta get back to work," and walked off to join Cartwright.

He led Cartwright and a group of curious sailors on a walk-around of the captured airplane. Gary tagged along. One of the sailors brought a folding ladder from the Catalina and set it under the Nakajima's engine cowling. Larsen climbed the ladder and opened the cowling, revealing the complicated mechanics of the radial engine. The Catalina's co-pilot aimed a camera and busily snapped photos.

Continuing the inspection, Larsen highlighted details of the landing gear—the tires remained plump and serviceable, the hydraulic seals still held—then everyone ducked under the fuselage for a closer look at its underbelly.

One of the sailors remarked, "First-rate airplane."

Another added, "No wonder they plastered our fleet at Pearl Harbor."

Gary knew nothing about what made this Nakajima such a good aircraft, but if these sailors were impressed, then this had to be a formidable war machine.

Lastly, Larsen positioned the ladder under the trailing edge of the wing where he, Cartwright, and the co-pilot clambered up for a quick study of the cockpit and its greenhouse canopy. Several of the sailors were eager to take a look as well, and they also crowded onto the wing.

Afterwards, when everyone was back on the ground, Cartwright gazed at the airplane, then at Larsen. "All right, lieutenant, what's your verdict? Is she airworthy?"

"Sir," Larsen replied, "gas her up and let's go."

The chief petty officer clapped his hands and shouted, "All right, all you landlubbers, you heard the man. We gotta push this rice crate to the Catalina!" The six sailors teamed up around the main wheels. The chief glanced at Larsen, Cartwright, and the co-pilot. "We're going to need your muscle, sirs."

To Gary, the nine men didn't seem enough to budge this big airplane. He tugged Stirling's elbow and tilted his chin toward the plane, and they stepped forward to lend a hand. Gary wedged one of the main wheel struts into the crook of his shoulder. Though the Nakajima looked too massive for eleven men to push it tail-first the necessary hundred and fifty feet toward the Catalina, they were going to give it a try.

Without waiting for an invitation, Falthin and his comrades joined the others clustered around the airplane, now bringing the force to fourteen men, arranged four on the horizontal fins and five on each wheel strut.

"Get your backs into it, you bunch of gobs," the chief barked as he grasped one of the tail fins. "Ready...*heave!*"

"Heave!" the sailors replied, half shouting and half grunting. Gary strained with all his might. The Nakajima lurched, then inched backwards.

"Heave!"

Push by push, shout by shout, the men got the momentum going, and the Nakajima slowly rolled toward the Catalina.

The effort provoked unexpected pride within Gary. After the last few months of desperately fleeing and hiding from the Japanese, the act of using his muscles in this simple but vital task with fellow Americans made his spirit swell with self-respect and a sense of accomplishment.

After many grunts and coordinated pushes, they maneuvered the Nakajima to within thirty feet of the Catalina, and when the chief said, "All right, boys, it's in position," everyone let out an exhausted cheer.

Larsen climbed back onto the wing of the Nakajima. The chief and another sailor dragged a thick rubber hose out from one of the Catalina's blisters. Gary looked inside to see that the hose unspooled from a series of drum-like rubber bladders that took up most of the space inside the fuselage. The chief explained that the bladders contained fuel for the Nakajima.

Gary whistled in admiration at the ballsy plan. It wasn't enough to land the Japanese airplane here; Larsen intended to take off and complete the delivery someplace else. When? And where? So far, that was a secret.

He took a turn working the hand pump in the Catalina to transfer fuel from the bladders to the Nakajima. While the open blisters allowed air to circulate, they also let in a lot of sun, so it didn't take long for the fuselage's interior to heat up like an oven.

When both airplanes were attended to, the chief posted a guard—two sailors armed with rifles—and everyone else gathered outside Stirling's hut. He and Cartwright disappeared inside to transmit a message, and a sailor was put to work pedaling the bicycle generator.

Gary started a fire for dinner. Falthin's entourage brought a catch of fish. The chief opened a can of Spam, which the Polynesians relished, much to the amusement of the sailors. As they ate their much-deserved meal and drank coffee, Larsen shared his story of how he'd been detailed to a special team to sneak onto a Japanese airfield on Mindanao and hijack the Nakajima. It made for a great campfire story, and Gary absorbed every harrowing detail of the adventure.

Later, as evening's twilight draped the island with shadow, Gary left the fire to return to the Catalina and the Nakajima, enormous shapes in the darkness, and allowed himself to revel in the satisfaction of having done his part in getting the airplanes ready. But he had other pressing matters on his mind as well. He had to get off this island.

He remembered Cartwright's denial when he had mentioned earlier his assumption that the Catalina had arrived to rescue him. Hopefully, thought Gary, there might be space for him aboard the flying boat.

Cartwright, the co-pilot, Stirling, and Larsen approached from the hut and huddled under one of the Catalina's wings. Stirling laid a map on the ground, they squatted around it, and Cartwright lit a small penlight. Their faces glowed from the reflected illumination.

Gary saw his chance and stepped close. "Commander Cartwright, I need to talk to you about getting off this island."

Cartwright acted startled by Gary's presence. The four men rose to their feet. "I hate to be the bearer of bad news, my friend," he said, "but that's just not possible."

"I don't understand." Gary tried not to sound petulant but he had to make his case. "There's plenty of room on your airplane."

"It's not that," Cartwright replied, "but I've got orders for another mission, and those orders state specifically that I'm not to deviate from the plan for any reason or person. I hope you understand. There's a war on."

Gary couldn't let this opportunity go. He lifted his gaze to the Nakajima. The cockpit accommodated three, and with Larsen at the controls, that meant two empty seats.

"What about the Nakajima?"

"You're kidding, right?" Stirling asked.

"No, sir. Not at all."

Larsen looked from Gary to the Japanese airplane, and back to Gary. "It's doable. But it depends."

Hopes kindled, Gary replied, "How so?"

"I need something to justify the extra weight. In case you haven't noticed, I'll be cutting it close taking off from here. What can you do?"

Gary had no experience piloting an airplane or even navigating from the air. All he could think of was, "I know Japanese and—"

"How much Japanese?" Cartwright interrupted.

Stirling replied, "Speaks it better than the Japs do."

Larsen said, "*Anata wa nani o shitai?*"

The pilot had never let on that he spoke Japanese. For Gary the question was easy enough. He replied, "What do I want? *Watashi wa kono shima o hanareru.* I want to leave this island."

Impressed, Larsen nodded, then reached into a breast pocket and pulled out a folded sheet of paper. He handed it to Gary. "Read this."

Cartwright shined his penlight on the paper.

Gary translated the Kanji script. "It's part of an operational manual. Says, Master switch, On. Battery, On. Main fuel pump, On. I can read it aloud in Japanese if you want." He returned the paper to Larsen.

"You sure about this?" Cartwright asked.

Larsen replied, "Sir, the damn Jap navy is between me and the rendezvous point. I might have to sweet-talk my way in Japanese to slip through."

"Rendezvous?" Gary asked.

"That's the last phase point of this escapade," Larsen explained. "After stealing the Nakajima, I flew it here where these guys—" he pointed at Cartwright and the co-pilot— "were waiting with gas, then I'm to proceed to land this bad boy—" he shifted his finger to the Nakajima— "on the carrier *Lexington* for delivery to the US for inspection by our intelligence folks."

"There's no reason to stick your neck out like this, Gary," Cartwright argued. "It'll be safer for you to remain here. I'll make sure word gets back and that we make arrangements to pick you up."

"Commander Cartwright," Gary said, squaring his shoulders, "I'm long past the point of playing it safe. And it's not just that I want to get home, but considering the present circumstances, we all have to do our part, which I can't do from here. Like you said, there's a war on."

Chapter Twenty-eight

April 18, 1942

Gary stayed up until late at night perusing the Nakajima's aircrew flight manual. Although he was fluent in Japanese, he didn't understand much of the technical jargon and wondered how useful this effort would be. And since he wasn't the one who would be flying the airplane, he decided that getting some rest would be the better option to prepare for tomorrow's mission. Even so, he was unable to sleep. His concern about the mission wasn't the only thing that kept him tossing and turning. He also had those nagging worries about the people he'd left behind, both on Formosa and back in the US. Finally, sometime after midnight, he dozed off.

He was awakened shortly before daybreak by sailors stoking the campfire and heating water for coffee and shaving. After a breakfast of powdered scrambled eggs, biscuits, and Spam, everyone gathered at the airstrip. Gary had swapped his civilian clothes for an extra khaki uniform the crew has stashed in the Catalina. Under the uniform, he wore his money belt with the gold coins. While the co-pilot supervised the preflight checks of the flying boat, Larsen and Cartwright met with Stirling.

"The *Lexington's* task force is operating in radio silence," said Cartwright, tapping the point of his pencil on a chart of the Pacific.

"So we won't get any updates on their position. We'll have to trust that they'll be at the rendezvous point as planned."

Larsen pursed his lips and nodded. "It'll be like finding the proverbial needle in the haystack." He shrugged. "Nothing new for a navy pilot."

Gary scrutinized the chart. It was a rectangle of solid gray that illustrated the remote vastness of the Pacific, the desolation relieved by just a few tiny islands, which only served to underscore just how challenging it would be to find the *Lexington.*

Larsen and Cartwright busied themselves with flight calculations, scribbling with pencils in the margins of the chart. Larsen said, "The rendezvous point is four hundred and fifty nautical miles from here, midway to the Bismarck Sea. With the drag and weight of the two bombs, that will reduce the cruising speed of the Nakajima to 150 knots. That means flight time from here to the rendezvous point is three hours. We're to arrive there at 1330, which means a takeoff time of 1030."

Cartwright read his wristwatch. "It's 0633."

In a little over three hours I'll be on my way home, thought Gary, smiling to himself. *The power of positive thinking.*

He took weather readings and reported them to Cartwright and Larsen. Like the day before, the prevailing southerly wind was right over the airstrip, which he measured at a brisk fifteen knots. "That's great," Larsen said, "because to get that Jap tub in the air we're going to need all the help Mother Nature can provide."

Throughout the early morning the sailors hacked down trees at the southern end of the airstrip. They didn't have time to dig up the stumps, but clearing away the trees and extending the airstrip even a little bit would allow the Nakajima a few more precious seconds to gain airspeed. As Larsen explained it, the biggest risk—aside from flying into the trees—was climbing too soon and stalling. "It won't increase our margin of safety by much," he emphasized, "but on this takeoff the difference between success and failure will be measured in inches."

Cartwright considered this and turned to Larsen. "You're the man with his butt on the line. What's your verdict?"

"Sir, if it doesn't work, it won't be for lack of trying." Larsen looked at Gary. "Still itching to go?"

"My butt's not worth any more than yours."

Cartwright laughed. "Then it's settled."

Gary and Larsen climbed onto the wing of the Nakajima. Larsen slid open sections of the canopy greenhouse to explain the inside of the cockpit to Gary. The interior was a confusion of panels, switches, levers, and struts, all enclosed by the fuselage frame, the frame itself riveted to the inside of the aircraft's skin. All of the metal, save for the instrument panels, was painted a matte light green.

"The front seat is mine, obviously." Larsen indicated the busiest section of the cockpit. "Gary, you'll be in the middle seat, where the observer, or *teisatsu*, sits. Go ahead. Get in."

Gary grabbed the canopy bracing and hitched one leg over the side of the fuselage at the middle section. He sat in the seat and figured out how to adjust it up and down. Thankfully, he had a lot of leg room, a surprise since the airplane was designed for the shorter stature of a typical Japanese crewman.

He opened the flap of a leather box near his feet on the right side. The box contained maps, the maintenance logbook, and the technical manual. Adjacent to it rested a metal box containing a flare gun and spare flares. Above that, at elbow height, protruded a small panel with a few flight instruments and switches for the bomb fuses, and the cockpit lights for nighttime illumination.

A leather flying helmet had been jammed under the seat. Gary put it on and adjusted it, then asked, "How do I look?"

"Like another Charles Lindberg."

"What's this?" Gary put his hand on a long, black, telescope-like device clipped to the wall.

"That's the bomb-aiming telescope. It comes off the wall and fits here." Larsen pointed to small porthole in the floor. "I doubt you'll need to concern yourself with that. However, you need to check this out."

He directed Gary to step, head down, through the narrow gap between the middle seat and the port side of the fuselage and proceed to the aft portion of the cockpit. "This is the gunner's position. He's also the radio operator." The large radio console was right behind the middle seat.

"While in flight," Larsen said, "you'll have to leave your seat and come back here to operate the radio. Right now I need you to familiarize yourself with how to operate it." He handed Gary a slip of paper. On it were code words and frequencies. "When the time comes, you'll need to transmit these back to Stirling."

Gary examined the code words:

Arrived at rendezvous	*go hachi ni washi*	(582 eagle)
Friendly contact	*shichi roku shi neko*	(764 cat)
Enemy contact	*kyuu kyuu ni hitsuji*	(992 sheep)
Returning to atoll	*shi hachi shichi inu*	(487 dog)

He folded the paper into his shirt pocket and gestured to the gunner's seat. "Why don't I just sit back here?"

"You can if you prefer," Larsen replied, "but it's about as comfortable as sitting on a milk crate. For landing and takeoff, you'll prefer the observer's position." Gary planted himself on the seat. It was a flimsy affair mounted on a sideways hinge.

"The gunner didn't sit in it much," Larsen explained, "which is why it folds out of the way. He's usually on his feet manning that—" he pointed to a machine gun strapped to the inside of the fuselage— "and pointing it out the back of the greenhouse. But don't worry about it. There's no ammo on board."

"What if we're attacked?"

"That machine gun is mainly a noisemaker, to make the crew feel like they have a fighting chance. Trust me, our best option for surviving is to keep our eyes open and stay away from enemy fighters."

***

Time for takeoff.

Larsen strapped himself into the pilot seat, and Gary buckled himself into the *teisatsu's* seat. The flight controls had been checked and the engine primed, readied for a cartridge start. Everyone else stood on the ground, waiting anxiously.

Larsen leaned out the cockpit and shouted, "Clear!"

A loud bang erupted from beneath the engine. The propeller started to rotate and gears inside the engine meshed. Acrid smoke rolled from under the wings.

The propeller swung in a circle, the engine whining, coughing, and belching more smoke. The propeller spun faster, faster, and melted into a blur as the engine roared to life, shaking the fuselage convulsively.

The chief disappeared under the wings and emerged, giving a

thumbs up. A pair of sailors positioned themselves past the wing-tips, one on the left, the other on the right.

"You okay back there?" Larsen's voice buzzed through the headset.

"Ready as I'll ever be."

"Brakes off. Here we go."

The Nakajima eased forward, the propeller blast whisking dust behind it. With the two sailors watching for clearance, Larsen jock-eyed the big plane to the airstrip, then, reaching the far end, care-fully pivoted around. Sailors flocked to help rotate it into place.

Gary had locked his seat in the uppermost position to provide a better view, given the airplane's nose-up attitude. Larsen was sit-ting up high, and Gary looked up past Larsen's head and peered over the cowling at the tops of the trees, which didn't seem so dis-tant now. He swallowed hard, concerned that their optimism might have been foolhardy and that Larsen's skill might not be enough to make this takeoff.

"If you're a praying man," Larsen said, "then do your best to ask the Lord to watch over us."

Gary was so nervous that he began with the only prayer that came to mind. *Even though I walk through...*

The engine's noise increased to an ear-splitting scream, and the airplane trembled as though it would tear itself to pieces. Gary's bones rattled, and he forgot all about praying. Clouds of dust bil-lowed behind the plane. But the plane stayed put.

"We're not moving!" Gary exclaimed.

"I know. I was standing on the brakes," Larsen replied. He re-leased the brakes and shouted, "Here we go!"

The Nakajima bolted forward, engine roaring, tires reverber-ating over the ground. The tail abruptly lifted, straightening the airplane, and in one quick blink, the end of the runway popped into view, a jagged line of trees that reminded Gary of the serrated edge of a knife.

The plane accelerated toward the trees, which were in sharp focus while everything to the left and right smeared out of sight. The fuselage bounced and jolted as if its tires had found every divot in the ground.

Gary's insides clenched, and a knot formed in his throat. For an instant he was sure they were going to ram into the trees, when suddenly he felt the aircraft float upward. Still, he imagined the branches snagging the landing gear and dragging them down to their doom. However, Larsen kept the attitude level as the Nakajima skimmed over the treetops, gaining precious airspeed.

They were approaching the spine of the ridge that ran down the center of the atoll. Gary thought Larsen would wheel to the right, toward the lagoon, but instead he threaded the airplane through a gap in the ridge, the Nakajima's wingtips barely clearing the treacherous rocky outcroppings.

And just like that, they were on the other side of the ridge, high above the water, a glorious vista that told Gary they had made it. Larsen lowered his seat. Gary heard him whisper, "Wheels up," followed by a thump as the landing gear locked into position. "Flaps up." The Nakajima continued to gather airspeed and angled upward. They climbed for several hundred feet, then banked toward the atoll to fly past the airstrip.

Below, the sun reflected off the broad wings of the Catalina. Everybody, the Polynesians included, waved frantically. Larsen rocked the Nakajima's wings to acknowledge the sendoff. Gary recognized Falthin and Stirling, wondering if he'd ever see them again.

As they cruised over the lagoon, the aerial perspective made

Gary appreciate the beauty of the isolated atoll. Seen from the air, he could easily discern the little C-shaped island chain that defined the mouth of the long-dormant volcano. He stared into the lagoon and admired how the color of the water changed from turquoise along the shoreline to emerald green and then to a dark blue over the deepest waters. He cast a look back to the tropical paradise that had been his interim home, when circumstances had kept the war at arm's length. It was hard to believe that his four months here had passed so quickly, almost like the blink of an eye.

Gary turned his attention forward, lowered his seat, and settled in for the long flight. The airspeed indicator on his console read 150 knots, their cruising speed.

"That must've been some prayer," Larsen said.

"What do you mean?"

Larsen laughed. "Because for a minute I wasn't sure we were going to make it."

"Truth is," Gary replied, sheepishly, "I was so rattled by the take-off that I didn't finish the prayer."

"What did you pray?"

"Psalm twenty-three, four."

"Yeah, I know that one. Let's recite it together. Keep ourselves in good graces with The Man upstairs."

As they recited the Psalm, Gary was reminded of his childhood in Sunday school back in Utah.

When they finished the prayer, Larsen added, "Slide your canopy closed. It'll cut down on the noise and streamline the airplane." The engine noise was muffled to a steady drone. After another moment passed, he said, "All right, Gary, we're on course. See what you can find on the radio."

Gary unbuckled himself from his seat and made his way to the gunner's position. He powered up the radio and let it warm up. Just as Larsen had told him, the gunner's seat proved to be exceedingly uncomfortable.

At half-hour increments, he tracked the time with the plane's small, illuminated clock as he busied himself working the radio's tuner and locking on Japanese transmissions. Most of the traffic was in Morse code, and even that was encrypted. He concentrated on the word groups, not certain what he was eavesdropping upon. When a transmission faded, he rotated the tuner to find another one.

"We're down to half our fuel," Larsen announced, "and should be close to the rendezvous point. Keep your eyes peeled."

Gary craned his neck to look out the canopy. He saw movement through the wispy overcast below them and stared until he discerned tiny parallel white lines crawling across the ocean's surface.

"What's that, to the right? On the water?"

Larsen banked the airplane. "It's some sort of convoy. Keep your fingers crossed that the good guys are waiting for us."

As the minutes passed, Gary watched them gain on the lines below, which became narrow, V-shaped wakes trailing from a flotilla of ships. As they closed the distance, he could make out decks cluttered with guns.

"I don't see a flattop," Larsen muttered.

"Japs?" Gary asked worriedly.

"Yup. Most definitely," Larsen replied, "and the big ship looks like a Takao-class heavy cruiser."

Gary transmitted: *go hachi ni washi* and added unfortunately, *kyuu kyuu ni hitsuji*

Larsen said in frustration, "Yikes! We're down to half our fuel and there's nobody to meet us but the enemy. Looks like our only option is to return to the atoll."

"Actually," said Gary "we might have another option. Since we're here, there's no point in wasting the trip. Why don't we leave a call-ing card?"

"What, drop our bombs on them?"

"You got it."

"Hells bells! Why not?"

The decision filled Gary with tense excitement. At last, a chance to strike back at the Japs! He scanned the instruments and switches around him. "What do I do?"

"Go back to the observer's position. Unfasten the aiming tele-scope and it should mate with a connector in the port that I showed you earlier."

Gary occupied the *teisatsu's* seat and reached for the telescope, mounted at his right. The telescope was about three feet long. Gary carefully removed it from its stowage mount, maneuvering it to lock into the bracket around the small port between the toes of his shoes. The telescope slanted toward him and he could com-fortably place his right eye against the rubber cup fixed on top of the eyepiece. Looking through the telescope he saw a numbered, graduated scale forming a set of crosshairs, and beyond it a blurry gray haze. His right hand rotated the eyepiece, and the ocean below came into focus.

"Okay," Gary said, "how does this work?"

Larsen talked him through arming the bombs and adjusting the telescope for airspeed—140 knots; altitude—5,000 feet; height above the target—5,000 feet; and drift—zero. He gingerly touched the safety cover over the bomb-release button.

The Nakajima banked to the left in a wide circle. "We're coming back around and I'm going to line up as best I can on the cruiser. It's up to you to fine-tune my approach."

"Why aren't they shooting at us?"

"They've almost certainly identified us as one of their own planes and are probably wondering what the heck we're doing. They'll soon find out."

As they turned, Gary memorized the arrangement of the convoy and noted that two smaller ships, probably destroyers, trailed directly behind the much larger heavy cruiser—their target. The Nakajima rolled to wings level.

Gary took a deep breath to center himself. Larsen didn't have to tell him they needed a healthy dose of good luck to score a hit. Gary cracked his knuckles and then grasped the top of the telescope and placed his face against the eyepiece.

He adjusted the focusing knob to sharpen the images of the ships below, now appearing magnified and in greater detail. He spotted the two ships behind the cruiser. The centerline of the crosshairs was just to the left. "Come right."

The Nakajima barely slid over. "A bit more."

The crosshairs passed over the first ship. "On path. Hold it."

The cruiser slid into the sight picture just as the crosshairs passed over the second ship. Though Gary tried to keep cool, a hard lump formed in his throat.

"Hold her steady."

The crosshairs inched toward the cruiser. He flipped the safety cover from the bomb- release button. The tension within him wanted to drop the bombs the instant the crosshairs touched the cruiser's stern, but he held still.

The crosshairs crawled over the fantail, over the square rear turrets, onto the superstructure, and at the moment they passed between the smoke funnels, he mashed the bomb- release switch. *"Bombs away!"*

The Nakajima lurched upwards and banked sharply. Gary pushed away from the telescope and turned his head toward the convoy.

The two bombs were barely visible as they arced nose-down toward the cruiser. For several long seconds, nothing seemed to happen. Then there were two white flashes amidships, followed by a gigantic fireball. The cruiser shuddered as if struck by a monstrous hammer. Then another explosion tore from the hull, sending streamers of smoke in all directions. One of the forward turrets flipped through the air like a bottle cap, tossed upward by a tower of smoke and fire.

"You hit one of the powder magazines!" Larsen exclaimed. "That ship is toast."

Suddenly, clouds of black smoke erupted close, buffeting the Nakajima, the explosions sounding like slamming doors. Larsen looked down to see the deck guns of the task force ablaze with anti-aircraft fire.

Knowing they were too high to be hit, Larsen quipped, "I think we've overstayed our welcome."

Gary, relying on Larsen's knowledge, realized that despite the anti-aircraft fire, they were not in danger, and some of the tension went out of his body. "Sounds good to me!"

Larsen laughed. He advanced the throttle, the Nakajima's engine growling. "Let's get out of here."

Gary crawled back to the radio and transmitted: *shi hachi shichi inu.*

CHAPTER TWENTY-NINE

April 18, 1942

The Nakajima returned to the atoll. With the airplane low on fuel and without a combat payload, Larsen was able to land on the tiny airstrip without much drama, for which Gary was profoundly thankful.

Larsen taxied the Nakajima close to the Catalina before shutting down the engine. As the propeller slowed, Gary whisked the flight helmet off his head. His section of the canopy was open and he welcomed a refreshing breeze.

The sailors gathered around the airplane to watch Larsen and Gary climb out of the cockpit and hop to the ground. When they had left hours ago, that was the last anyone expected to see of them, and now they were back, absent the bombs. Obviously, there was a story to be told.

After their last transmission, they had maintained radio silence. All that Cartwright and Stirling knew was that Larsen and Gary had reached the rendezvous point, made enemy contact, and were returning.

Cartwright gave the Nakajima the once-over. "After receiving your message I expected to see the Nakajima riddled with bullet holes," he said. Although the commander kept his expression stern,

Gary could detect a smile in his voice. "Your bombs? What happened to them? Did you drop them to ditch the weight?"

Gary didn't know how to answer. Though they'd struck a blow against the Japanese, they had failed to deliver the Nakajima, so in that respect, they were back to square one.

However, if Larsen felt that way, he didn't share it. He slapped Gary on the back and offered a broad smile. "Not hardly. Our farm boy, here, from Utah scored two direct hits on a Takao-class heavy cruiser. We left that ship a sinking, burning hulk."

The sailors crowded around them, cheering, wanting to hear more.

Cartwright ordered them to give Larsen and Gary room. "Once they get officially debriefed then I'm sure they'll have plenty of news left over for your scuttlebutt."

He led Gary and Larsen back to Stirling's hut and held court over a map of the Pacific. While they were served a hot meal and coffee, Larsen recounted what had happened. "Besides the heavy cruiser," he said, referring to notes jotted on his navigation chart, "I saw two smaller cruisers, Kuma-class I think, and five destroyers. All heading on a bearing of 224 degrees. It looked like a scouting force."

Cartwright sipped his coffee. "How about you, Mr. Gatlin?"

On a memo pad, Gary sketched the disposition of the ships as he best remembered it. At the end of the briefing, Cartwright agreed that the good news was that Larsen and Gary had plastered a Japanese capital warship. The bad news: the Japanese knew about the *Lexington's* task force and were now on the hunt for it.

Stirling transmitted a coded summary of the incident to an aircraft serving as a communication link to the *Lexington*, as the *Lexington* continued to maintain radio silence. An hour later,

344

Stirling received a reply, which he deciphered. "New orders." Stirling showed them the message. "New rendezvous coordinates. You're to deliver the Nakajima tomorrow at 1300."

Cartwright leaned over the map and tapped his finger on the location. A point 50 nautical miles west of Tol, in the Faichuk Islands, south of the larger—though not by much—Makur Islands. The distance was a thousand miles, near the very end of the Nakajima's endurance, one-way. Larsen calculated the flight time. They'd be flying clean, which meant a faster cruising speed of 160 knots. Flight time, six hours, fifteen minutes.

"That means a takeoff time of 0645," Larsen said. "What time is sunrise?"

Stirling answered, "Yesterday it was 0632."

"That means you'll be taking off during morning twilight," Cartwright said.

"Unless we get a morning fog, I don't anticipate a problem." Larsen looked at Gary. "What do you say?"

What could he say, other than, "You go, I go."

Cartwright set his coffee cup aside. "All right, gentlemen," he clapped his hands. "Let's get the Nakajima ready for tomorrow morning."

***

The inspection of the Nakajima showed that it needed almost a gallon of oil for the engine, which they topped off with supplies from the Catalina. Since this time Larsen had parked close to the flying boat, there was no need to push the Nakajima as they had done yesterday. The fuel tanks were filled to maximum and everything readied for the 0620 start.

At mess that evening, the sailors pressed Gary for every detail of how he'd managed to slam the Japanese cruiser. To explain the two hits, all he could manage was, "Beginner's luck."

"If you keep that up," the chief joked, "you won't leave any targets for the rest of us."

Stirling called Gary to the hut and handed him a slip of paper with a new set of codes and frequencies for tomorrow. After that, Gary lay in his cot because there wasn't anything left to do now but wait.

And worry, which he tried not to do. While overjoyed that he'd certainly doomed the enemy cruiser, how many men had he killed outright? How many would later drown? And how many more would be crippled and scarred for life? He remembered his part in the sinking of the submarine that had torpedoed the *Mooie*, an episode he'd kept to himself.

He justified to himself that the Japanese showed no such remorse with their sneak attack on Pearl Harbor. How many Americans had died there? And how many more would die on both sides before this war was over?

Gary resigned himself to the conclusion that the best way to end the war was to strike hard and without mercy whenever the enemy presented the opportunity, as he and Larsen had done yesterday. If he had a choice, he would not kill, but he had no choice. The Japs started the war. As they used to say back in Utah, if you poke the bull, then expect the horns.

***

Gary was awake when the chief rounded up the men at 0500. After shaving and washing up, he helped himself to coffee and the usual fried Spam scrambled with powdered eggs.

The camp was on the western side of the atoll, and the ridge with its crest of trees masked the glow of the predawn light. But by looking upward, he could see the dark sky turning to an indigo blue and the stars slowly disappearing one by one. The twilight became bright enough for details to emerge from the murk, showing the men moving like dark silhouettes against the lighter backdrop of sand.

Gary followed Larsen on the final preflight inspection of the Nakajima, done with a penlight. The airplane's fuel tanks had been topped off from the bladder bags in the Catalina. Larsen's biggest worry seemed to be oil leaks from the engine and landing-gear hydraulics, but what seeped out wasn't anything more than normal. A team of sailors walked the Nakajima's propellers to circulate oil throughout the engine's cylinders, and Gary took his turn.

That accomplished, the engine was ready for another cartridge start.

Shortly after 0615, they climbed into the cockpit and strapped in. Larsen completed his checks; all seemed good. Gary made sure he had the note with the new frequencies and codes. As the minutes passed, a band of lighter blue crept across the horizon, and a southerly breeze rustled through the brush and the palm trees.

Gary tracked the time with the instrument clock in the observer's position. At 0635, Larsen shouted, "Clear!"

The cartridge detonated with a bang. A flash erupted from under the fuselage. The engine wheezed and the propeller started to rotate. The engine abruptly coughed, sending flames and jets of smoke out the exhaust stacks on either side of the cowling, then settled into a smooth roar.

Despite the noise and the vibrations, Gary's mood remained fixed in a stoic calm, his mind on the mission ahead. Larsen released the brakes and the Nakajima rolled forward. Larsen taxied the plane back to the airstrip, and as before, the sailors helped turn it around. Gary took stock of the scene, the outline of the trees against the blue sky, the dawn's ambient light reflecting on the Catalina's canopies. As he pondered their situation, Gary realized that this attempt would be the final chance for the Nakajima to find the *Lexington*. With the engine having reached operating temperature, at 0645 Larsen advanced the throttle and the engine shrieked like a banshee, straining to get off the ground. When he released the brakes they shot forward, in a near identical repetition of yesterday's takeoff. The biggest difference was that with no payload, after a remarkably short run, the Nakajima all but leaped into the air. Larsen eased the airplane between the break in the ridgeline and climbed, to then swoop around and cruise over the airstrip, saluting their comrades with a wag of the wings.

When they approached cruising altitude and speed, Gary climbed into the gunner's seat to operate the radio and listen for enemy traffic.

At 1015, Larsen announced, "We're down to half our fuel," and added, "Ever hear the joke about the difference between being involved and being committed?"

"Can't say that I have."

"Let me explain. When a hen supplies eggs she's involved in your breakfast. When a hog supplies bacon, he's committed."

"Your point?" Gary asked.

"Right now, we are committed. We either find the *Lexington* or we've got as much chance as a pig in a butcher shop."

The featureless ocean stretching in all directions amplified Larsen's warning. But so far, everything was unfolding according to plan. Searching for transmissions kept Gary busy and his thoughts on task.

Larsen said, "1200. An hour out from rendezvous point. Keep your eyes peeled."

Then when he remarked, "1230," Gary detected a touch of worry in his voice. So far, no sign of any ship, and no transmission from the *Lexington*.

At 1237, Gary heard a new message over the radio. It was a voice transmission, in the clear, without interference. Gary froze. The voice was speaking Japanese. "We've swept zone nineteen," the voice said.

Where was this zone nineteen?

The reply broke squelch, which Gary couldn't understand because of static.

Then he heard the first voice say, "The area west of Tol is clear. I see the convoy."

Whoever this was had said the area west of Tol was clear, the Nakajima's destination. And the voice's tone upon seeing the convoy wasn't excited, in fact sounded almost relieved, not heavy with alarm as if stumbling upon the enemy.

Gary keyed the intercom. "I think I've got bad news."

"What do you mean?"

"I just heard a Japanese radio operator say that he's west of Tol." Silence.

"Larsen, you okay?"

"Not really, I didn't need to hear that. We're down to less than half an hour of fuel and nowhere else to go."

Gary craned his neck to look out the canopy. Against the sheen of sunlight on the ocean's surface, he saw parallel lines tracing across the water. Ships. A lot of them.

"Convoy to our right," he said, worriedly.

"Yeah, I got 'em," Larsen replied, sounding just as distressed.

He banked slightly to keep the ships off their right wing. The convoy was a flotilla of smaller ships grouped around larger ships, like farm dogs protecting a remuda of horses. Minute by minute they drew closer, and Larsen's continued silence told Gary they were in serious trouble.

Larsen finally spoke. "We found a carrier task force, all right. Only the wrong one. That big flattop is the carrier *Taka*."

Gary stared at the enemy ships. "Can't we try for Tol? Crash-land there?"

"We don't have the fuel. Besides, I have a feeling this entire area is crawling with Japs."

"So, where is the *Lexington?*"

"Not anywhere close, I'm sure. So we have a choice. Either we get as much distance between us and the Japs and then ditch this crate in the ocean…we could be marooned at sea for an unknown time. The thing to consider is that when you land one of these winged sleds on the water, they don't always pancake flat. They tend to cartwheel, which could knock us out, or worse. And once the airplane stops moving, it wouldn't waste any time sinking."

"You said 'either,'" Gary replied. "Meaning we have another choice."

"Not a good one. We land on the carrier and surrender."

"They might be grateful that we're returning their airplane."

Larsen, despite the gravity of the situation, had to laugh. "Yeah, there's that."

"So," Gary said, "I guess we make ourselves guests of the Emperor." He buckled into the observer's seat.

They flew over the flotilla's outlying screen of smaller ships. Gary expected that at any moment they'd be discovered and heralded with a barrage of anti-aircraft fire.

"You think they might be trying to contact us on the radio?" he asked.

"Perhaps. They might also be under radio silence. Or figure our radio is busted."

Larsen slowed and descended toward the aircraft carrier. Seen from this altitude, men scurried ant-like across the long, flat flight deck. "All their planes are gone."

"Is that good?"

"Dunno. But it might mean all their planes are scouting for the *Lexington*. Plus the deck is configured for landing."

"Which explains why they haven't shot at us. They think we're one of their returning airplanes."

A tiny green light flashed from the superstructure on the starboard side of the flight deck.

"They're signaling us," Larsen dropped to an altitude of five hundred feet and zoomed right past a cruiser. Sailors waved their caps, and Larsen wagged the Nakajima's wings.

They flew directly over the carrier. As Gary scanned the deck, his gaze fixed on one man on an upper railing of the superstructure: a sailor in a dark blue Navy officer's uniform. Even at this altitude and speed, there was no mistaking his identity: Admiral Izawa Yoshida, the former governor-general of Formosa.

For an instant, Gary felt as though he'd swallowed poison. *Yoshida of all people.* He imagined the tyrant's gloating face when Gary would be brought to him.

This couldn't be, Gary thought, his mind burning at the injustice. He hadn't been spared so much only to be delivered into the hands of this villain.

The Nakajima began a slow orbit to the left to enter the landing pattern. "Flaps down," Larsen announced grimly. "Wheels down. Hook down."

This can't be, Gary repeated to himself. *There has to a way out of this trap.*

Larsen aligned their flight path with the carrier. They slid open their canopy sections and cranked their seats to maximum height for a better view over the cowling. Gary had seen how huge the *Taka* appeared, especially when compared to the other ships, but at this angle and distance, it was like a cork bobbing on the ocean.

On the port side of the deck, a man in white waved a pair of orange paddles, though appearing miniscule at this range, and it was obvious Larsen was taking his approach cues from him.

As they closed upon the carrier, an ugly thought crossed Gary's mind—that they crash into the carrier. They would both die—quickly, violently—but in the process, damage the carrier.

But he said nothing. They were entering a den of lions, and like Daniel, would survive if they trusted the Lord. But what did the Almighty have in store?

The back of the carrier rushed to meet them. The Nakajima smacked the deck and bounced forward, only to be yanked to a halt when the tail hook snagged a restraining cable.

Gary jolted against his seat harness, and when his insides stopped churning, he expected to see dozens of Japanese swarm around them, guns drawn. Amazingly though, the deck crew gestured with hand signals for them to taxi forward. What was going on?

The truth dawned upon Gary, and with dazzling clarity he realized what had happened. He blurted over the intercom. "Keep your goggles down!"

"What?"

"We're flying a Japanese plane. They think we're Japs like them," Gary yelled. Months under the tropical sun had burnished his complexion to a dark bronze. As long as he kept his helmet on and his goggles over his blue eyes, he could pass for one of the crew. "Let's play this out. We might yet get out of this with our skins intact."

A mechanic scrambled onto the wing, and grasping the canopy bracing, hauled himself close to Gary. He shouted, "Sir, keep your engine running!"

"What's going on?" Gary asked in his best Japanese.

"Our scouts found the American carrier," the mechanic explained excitedly. "You're to be spotted for a hot refuel and armed with a torpedo for an immediate takeoff. The rest of the squadron is on the way back."

With the mechanic riding on the wing, Larsen taxied to the refuel spot and reduced the engine speed to idle. A pair of sailors crawled onto the wing and fitted a thick hose into a fuel port. Just ahead of the Nakajima, a large elevator rose to stop flush with the flight deck, bringing with it a half-dozen torpedoes resting on dollies. Sailors pushed the dollies off the elevator. One team rolled theirs close to the Nakajima and halted. The refueling crew on the wing watched Larsen for a signal that the tanks were full.

"All right," he said to Gary, "we're topped off."

Gary shouted to the mechanic, who in turn shouted to the refueling crew. They uncoupled the hose and hustled off the wing. The armament crew ducked under the wing and guided the torpedo under the fuselage. Then, their work done underneath, they emerged with the empty dolly in tow. Another sailor ran close and handed a folded paper to the mechanic, who then passed it to Gary.

Gary unfolded the paper. His heart lifted with the incredible news, which he couldn't wait to share with Larsen.

The mechanic pointed to a spot beyond the elevator. "Spot your plane right there. As soon as the rest of the squadron arrives, you'll take off in force. For the Emperor." He dismissed himself with a crisp salute and slid off the wing.

Gary tapped Larsen on the shoulder. "This note gives the coordinates for the location of the American task force!" Gary read the coordinates to Larsen.

Larsen consulted his navigation chart. "They're four hundred mile southeast of here, approaching the Coral Sea."

The two men glanced about. Incredibly, no one had yet realized who they were. At the right forward edge of the flight deck, the red-and-white windsock pointed like an omen.

Gary said, "It seems that Providence has just propped a door wide open. Here we sit, all gassed up, armed, and with nothing to stop us."

"Let's do it."

Gary tore a page from the logbook and on it, wrote: *Gary Gatlin sends his regards.*

He beckoned to the mechanic, and when he climbed back on the Nakajima, Gary thrust the note into his hand. "I need you to deliver this to Admiral Yoshida."

The mechanic stared at him incredulously.

"I order you to do it. It is a matter of grave importance."

The mechanic nodded. "*Hai.*" He slid off the wing and dashed toward the bridge.

Larsen taxied forward and gunned the engine. The deck officer frantically waved his arms and pointed. Larsen ignored the commands, and Gary saluted.

The Nakajima shot forward, accelerating, zooming off the deck, the ocean stretching below them. They were airborne.

CHAPTER THIRTY

April 19, 1942

The Nakajima accelerated away from the Japanese carrier *Taka*. The weight and drag of the torpedo fastened beneath the plane caused the plane to dip slightly toward the ocean. As they gained airspeed Larsen gently pulled back on the joystick and the plane eased upward.

Gary looked across the flotilla beneath them. Two destroyers flanked the *Taka*, and another trailed behind. A pair of large cruisers proceeded ahead of the carrier with a dozen smaller ships arrayed in a loose formation, all sailing majestically in one direction. The scene had a surreal, tranquil quality, the sunlight dappling the blue water, the ships knifing the surface, white bow waves cutting through the ocean. He was impressed by how formidable the flotilla appeared. Another thought crossed his mind: that at any moment the antiaircraft guns below would open fire and blast the Nakajima out of the sky.

But incredibly, the guns remained silent, and their luck held out, as if fate itself had propped open this window of opportunity.

"Just so I'm clear about this," Gary queried, "you're going to torpedo the carrier?"

"*Absolutely*," Larsen replied.

Gary considered the *Taka*. "Then I need you to do something for me first. Fly over the carrier again, as low and slow as you can."

"What for?"

"There's someone down there I want to say good riddance to."

Larsen chuckled over the intercom. "Who, for heaven's sake?"

"The guy in charge of every Jap ship in this area. Admiral Izawa Yoshida. I saw him watching us when we landed on the carrier."

"How do you know him?"

"I'll fill you in later. Just before we took off I ordered the mechanic to deliver a note to Yoshida. I sent my regards. You could say that this war has become personal to me."

"Don't let that cloud your judgment," Larsen cautioned. "But in this case, since we've caught the Japs flat-footed, we can give your admiral friend some high-explosive raspberries."

Larsen slipped the Nakajima in a slow, looping turn back toward the carrier, in an arc that took them over several of the escorting warships. Gary remained aware of the sailors watching. "They're wondering what we're up to," he said.

"Once we launch this fish hanging from our belly," Larsen replied, "they'll wise up real fast. After that, it'll get super hot up here."

He piloted the Nakajima toward the *Taka*, losing altitude, making it appear as if he was returning for a landing. The green light on the superstructure flashed on and off, as if chattering an urgent message. He said, "They're probably trying to raise us on the radio."

"Well, since we don't have their frequencies," Gary replied, "they're wasting their time." He lifted his goggles and scanned the bridge superstructure, hoping to spot Yoshida.

Larsen kept the airplane on a steady slope toward the back of the flight deck. Just when it seemed he was going to commit to a landing, he rammed the throttle forward. The radial engine howled and they hurtled over the flight deck.

Gary spotted Yoshida, who was reading something and then looked up at the Nakajima. "Rock the wings!"

Larsen swayed the big airplane, its broad wings tilting in a jaunty salute.

Gary locked eyes with Yoshida, if only for a second, but it was long enough. The admiral's eyes widened in astonishment as he recognized the young American. As the Nakajima roared away, Gary savored the satisfaction that he was to have the last word with the admiral. *You're about to get yours, you bastard.*

Larsen maneuvered to the left and entered a graceful swooping turn. The plane passed close to a destroyer, the crew gazing with amazement at the Nakajima's antics.

"Okay," Larsen announced, his tone hard and determined, "we're going in for the kill. Read the airspeed aloud and keep me apprised of our altitude. For the attack I want to be at 130 knots and fifty feet above the water. I need to focus on delivering our package, and I don't want to fly us into the drink."

Gary read the needle on the airspeed indicator. "OK: 155 knots." "150 knots." "140 knots." He glanced to the left and right, and they were so low that the airplane seemed to be skimming inches off the water. "130 knots. Altitude steady."

He looked past Larsen's head and gauged their progress toward the *Taka*. They were below the level of the flight deck, and from this perspective the aircraft carrier blocked out a huge swath of the horizon.

"Torpedo armed," Larsen said tersely. "I'm not sure what the minimum arming distance is for the fuse, but I'll try four hundred yards."

"Right into Yoshida's kisser," Gary said with grim glee.

As Larsen closed the space between them and the ship, the *Taka* grew larger. And larger. So large that Gary worried that even a solid hit by the torpedo would hardly scratch the colossal ship.

The seconds slowed like chilled molasses. Gary's nerves tightened, compressing, coiling, ready to spring apart on cue.

The *Taka* was close enough to fill the entire windshield. And they still pressed closer.

At last, Larsen announced in a voice steely calm, "Torpedo away."

The Nakajima lifted upward with the jettisoning of its heavy load. Larsen banked sharply to the left, then to the right.

Gary craned his neck and caught sight of the torpedo—a blur in the water at the point of a plume of bubbles—racing toward the carrier. "She's on track!"

Larsen leveled the wings when they soared over the *Taka*. The torpedo was lost to Gary's view and he twisted in his seat to keep tabs on the carrier.

Then a huge geyser erupted toward the back of the ship. Gary started, "Direct hi—" when a gigantic fireball blasted out the stern and rolled over the back of the flight deck.

"Hit a fuel bunker!" Larsen exclaimed.

Smaller explosions lanced smoke through the air. Then another gigantic detonation punched through the flight deck, showering debris in every direction. A shock wave surged across the water. More explosions rippled from under the flight deck and the entire ship was shrouded in billowing smoke.

"She's done for!" Gary shouted.

The Nakajima climbed upward. The destroyers began circling the *Taka*, but the flotilla's guns remained silent. Larsen turned to a heading of 225 degrees. Ahead of them, white puffy clouds graced the skies; behind them, a macabre tower of black smoke corkscrewed into the air, the bottom of the column illuminated by the ragged syncopation of explosions raging along the doomed enemy carrier.

Gary was sure they were now out of range of the flotilla's guns and that there was nothing between the *Nakajima* and the American carrier but time and blue skies. As he scanned the open heavens, he caught sight of a gaggle of airplanes, tiny as flies, coming toward them on a parallel course. His optimism chilled and he cried out a warning, "We've got company!"

"Those are the *Taka's* airplanes returning from their scouting mission," Larsen explained.

Gary imagined their wide-eyed distress at having no place to land. Besides knocking the *Taka* out of action—for good, he hoped—they had also eliminated its complement of aircraft. "Unless there's another carrier close by, these guys are in for a long swim."

Larsen altered course toward a bank of clouds and advanced the throttle. "Let's hope they're so focused on the *Taka* that they don't notice us."

The wave of airplanes cruised several hundred feet above them. Four of the smaller planes peeled off from the group and dove upon the Nakajima.

"Zero fighters," Larsen exclaimed, "and they look angry!"

The Zeros spread out to follow one another in a single file.

"They're gaining on us!" Gary shouted, panic rising in his voice.

"We're going as fast as we can," Larsen shouted back.

Gary swiveled his head from the Zeros to the clouds ahead and back to the Zeros. It was a sprint against time. "One's a couple hundred yards right behind us!" Too bad there was no ammo for the machine gun, otherwise he could at least attempt to shoot them down.

Larsen swerved to the left, then rolled to the right. A volley of tracers shot past, zipping so close that Gary thought sure they were goners.

The lead Zero seemed to hover on their tail, like a hawk riding the wind before it pounced to finish them off. The next barrage of bullets would surely tear the Nakajima to pieces.

Abruptly, they were swaddled in a cloud. The canopy blanked white and the temperature inside the cockpit dropped at least ten degrees. He couldn't even see their propeller, and surely the Zero was just as blind. Gary's breath caught and he hesitated to exhale, not certain if they had cheated death. He worried they would break out of the protective cover of the clouds and then the Zeroes would be right on them again.

Larsen and Gary continued to plunge through the opaque whiteness. The seconds ticked past. Larsen angled the Nakajima to the right and fixed their heading to the coordinates of the American carrier.

Their canopy poked from the clouds, the wispy vapor parting around them. Gary pivoted to spot the Zeroes, but they were gone. Grateful for the reprieve, he let himself relax a bit in his seat. "The coast looks clear."

"Good," Larsen replied, beginning to feel his own tension ease. "We should be flying right for our carrier."

"How long to reach her?"

"About an hour and a half. We've got plenty of fuel, but not enough to fly around forever in case we miss it. The sooner we find her, the better for us."

Gary climbed out of the observer's seat and into the gunner's position. From his pocket he pulled out the note with the codes and frequencies. "I know there's a change in plans, but it wouldn't hurt to let the American task force know we're on the way. He transmitted in code: *Enemy contact. Continuing to rendezvous point.*

The problem with this arrangement was that he could transmit code but had no way to decipher a reply. They had run into the *Taka* at the original rendezvous point, and he hoped the American carrier would figure out that they were en route to the new location.

The clouds thinned, and the Nakajima cruised through an azure sky filled with the blazing light of the sun. The engine continued its relentless, comforting rumble. All the instruments held steady, except for the main fuel gauge, which kept creeping downward.

After an hour, Larsen broke the silence. "Keep your eyes wide open. We run into Americans, they see the meat ball insignia on our wings, they won't hesitate to blast us out of the sky."

"Hopefully they got my message that we're on the way."

Gary continued scanning all around them. From high and to the right appeared a loose formation of four airplanes on an intercept course. He alerted Larsen.

"Got 'em," Larsen said. He slowed their airspeed.

As the airplanes drew closer Gary could make out their straight wings and tubby fuselages, so different from the more graceful Zeroes.

"Wildcats," Larsen explained. "Our guys for sure. Let's hope they don't have itchy trigger fingers. I'm lowering our landing gear to show that we surrender."

"Good move," Gary muttered.

Two fighters remained at altitude high and behind them, ready to attack. The Wildcats were painted in shades of gray and decorated with big white stars on the wings and fuselage. The other two fighters glided closer, like sharks moving in for a taste of blood. The improbability of the situation shook Gary to the core. To have survived all that he had in the last months, only to risk getting shot down at the last minute by his own side.

Larsen wagged the Nakajima's wings. "Open your canopy," he told Gary, "and wave to them."

Gary returned to the observer's seat and cracked open the canopy. One of the Wildcats slid beside them, close enough for Gary to read the pilot's quizzical expression. The pilot raised a gloved hand and made a thrusting motion to the front.

Gary responded with an exaggerated nod. "He's signaling that we keep on this course."

Underneath them appeared faint, parallel white lines, the telltale wakes of ships in a convoy.

"We found them!" Gary shouted.

"Don't pop any champagne corks just yet," Larsen replied.

The Wildcat on their wingtip abruptly opened fire, the blast alarming Gary. Red tracers arced in front of the Nakajima.

"He's warning us to behave," Larsen explained.

"I'm convinced," Gary said, trying to calm himself.

The Wildcat wagged its wings and slowed. Larsen also slowed.

They passed over the task force. "That's our carrier below," Larsen explained, "the prettiest damn sight ever for sore eyes."

The task force's disposition was nearly identical to the *Taka's*: a ring of smaller warships protecting a group of larger ships—cruisers and a battleship—escorting a flattop. Gary gazed at the carrier. Unlike the *Taka*, this ship had a much larger superstructure, with a big, flat exhaust stack extending upward from the right side of the flight deck. "What carrier is that?"

"I can't say for sure," Larsen replied. "But as long as she's flying the Stars and Stripes, we're okay."

The Wildcat pulled ahead of the Nakajima, rocked its wings,

and began a gradual looping descent toward the carrier. The second Wildcat tucked behind them into firing position.

Gary didn't begrudge the pilot. He was only covering his bets. Within a few minutes, Gary knew he would be back among his fellow Americans and soon sailing for home. He yanked the slack out of his seat belt and readied himself for the jarring recovery on the flight deck, remembering Larsen's earlier explanation that every carrier landing was a controlled crash.

The Wildcat circled to the left and entered the landing pattern for the carrier. It zoomed over the flight deck and climbed to join the second pair of Wildcats waiting overhead.

Larsen banked to the left for his approach. Near the end of the flight deck, on the port side, a man waved a set of orange paddles. Larsen aligned his flight path on the flight deck's centerline. "Wheels down. Flaps down. Hook down."

Gary mulled the irony of the situation should they crash on the flight deck, perhaps duplicating the catastrophe they had wrought upon the *Taka*. As an extra measure, to keep them safe, he crossed his fingers and uttered a prayer.

The Nakajima seemed to float toward the flight deck, Larsen making minute adjustments as they descended. Then, everything sped up and the deck rushed up to meet them. The Nakajima slammed on the deck, bouncing once, then again. For a fleeting moment, Gary feared they'd be flung off the side of the ship and into the water.

Then the tail hook caught, and the Nakajima slammed to a halt.

Gary rocked in his seat. He wiped his mouth and tried to swallow. Around him, dozens of sailors in colored jerseys scrambled toward the Nakajima. On the deck near the back of the bridge superstructure, a group of men in bulky silver suits waited beside big red fire extinguishers. Gary appreciated that they were ready to pull him and Larsen out of burning wreckage, but he was more appreciative that their services were not needed.

A man in a yellow jersey waved his arms and gestured to the front. Larsen taxied forward and rolled ahead of the bridge. Yellow Jersey made a cutting motion, and Larsen set the brakes and shut the engine. But the ambiance was anything but quiet. A strong breeze whooshed through the open canopy, and the blare of claxons and the grinding squeal of winches made for a bedlam of noise.

Gary regarded the bridge and noted several men in khaki uniforms staring down at him and Larsen, the bemused expressions on their faces betraying their surprise, as if this Japanese plane had appeared on the carrier deck by magic.

He unbuckled the seat harness and pushed himself upright. No doubt about it, he was here as the result of a string of unbelievable miracles.

Against all odds, he had made it. For all intents and purposes, his feet were on American territory.

Epilogue

April 20, 1942

After a good meal, a night's rest, and a change of clothes, Gary and Larsen met with the skipper of the *Saratoga* in his quarters for an informal briefing. The captain related reports of the sinking of a Japanese aircraft carrier from the intercepted transcripts of numerous Japanese airplanes in distress. Gary and Larsen shared their exploits of the previous two days, confirming the destruction of the carrier *Taka* and explaining their attack on a Japanese heavy cruiser. The sinking of the cruiser was news to the captain, and he forwarded their information to Pacific Fleet Intelligence in Hawaii.

The Nakajima was loaded by crane onto a fast destroyer, where the plane was lashed to the fantail and wrapped in tarps to conceal its identity. Gary followed the Nakajima to the destroyer in a high-line transfer while the *Saratoga's* musical band played "The Daring Young Man on the Flying Trapeze."

Although the destroyer was to sail at top speed to Pearl Harbor, it would still take the ship seven days to travel the 3,600-mile journey. To pass the time, Gary read magazines and books to reintroduce himself to the world, and he reflected on the adventures he'd experienced for the last two and a half years, jotting down those recollections in a notebook.

The destroyer arrived in Hawaii without incident. For all he'd gone through, Gary had managed to hold onto his belt with the gold coins, and he converted several of them into American dollars. These he spent in Honolulu on civilian clothes and a telegram to advise his family that he was safe and homeward bound at last. To be at last surrounded by Americans who never gave him a second glance made it seem like his time on Formosa and his subsequent escape had been a fantastic dream.

But the one item of news that pained him was learning about the internment of Japanese-Americans. He was troubled about the Mitsuis and the fate of his childhood friend, Ichiro.

On his second day in Hawaii, Gary was asked to meet with Admiral William "Bull" Halsey and his staff in the fleet headquarters building. The admiral, who would be leaving almost immediately to lead his task force in the Coral Sea, was eager to hear Gary's story. In short order, Gary learned why the gruff, plain-speaking admiral was known as "Bull" Halsey. Throughout, Gary fought the temptation to add "sir" whenever he spoke with the admiral. He didn't do so, not because he didn't want to be polite, but because he was a civilian and wanted to be sure everyone in the room knew that.

Halsey's pointed questions revealed an intense interest in Gary's activities on the Yap Island atoll and his perceptions regarding the Nakajima and the Japanese in general. Gary learned that the heavy cruiser he'd sunk was named the *Akaishi* and that its loss was a significant blow to Japanese morale. Further in the briefing, Gary commented about his time on Formosa, which prompted one of Halsey's staff officers to lay out a map of the island on the conference table. The officer then quizzed Gary about Japanese commerce and military operations on Formosa. The officer's questions revealed much knowledge about the island, but nothing as comprehensive as what Gary had learned.

When Gary related his part in the sinking of the Japanese submarine that had torpedoed the *Mooie*, eyebrows all around the room arched in surprise and skepticism.

Later that afternoon, Gary was called back to Halsey's office. The admiral commented on Gary's extensive and personal knowledge about the Japanese, his language skills, and his expertise about Formosa. He was especially impressed with Gary's exceptional service as an aircrewman on the Nakajima and his part in sinking both the *Akaishi* and the *Taka*. His tale about the Japanese submarine had been checked, and his recollection dovetailed with the details that had been reported by the crew of the B17. In consideration of these remarkable factors, on the spot he offered Gary a commission as a naval officer. Halsey showed Gary a letter he'd drafted in that regard.

The offer took Gary by complete surprise, and his reaction was one of some dismay. He said to the Admiral, I certainly don't know much about the military. Halsey chuckled and said that the navy would send him to Officer Charm School at Great Lakes, Illinois, a 90-day course. He added that Gary had more than proven himself and that he would be given the rank of lieutenant upon graduation.

Gary answered that he wasn't sure in what capacity he would be best suited to serve.

Halsey said that at the very least, Gary would be extremely useful in the intelligence service where his fluency in Japanese was a much-needed skill. Moreover, if Gary wanted to fly and was physically qualified, Halsey guaranteed him a billet in aviation school.

Gary looked about the room. Judging by their expressions, everyone, Halsey included, expected him to jump at the chance.

But Gary hadn't been home in a very long time, and he felt the tug of obligation to his family and the family farm. Halsey's offer would involve a huge commitment that would take Gary further from his people. But then the thought made him feel selfish. There was a war on and every man should step up to fulfill his duty.

Let me think about it, admiral, he replied. I haven't seen my family in a long while and I'd like to get their advice.

Halsey accepted Gary's reply with a thoughtful nod. He tapped the letter and said, do what you must, young man, and once you decide, please advise the navy accordingly.

I'll do that, Gary said.

The following morning, Gary boarded the China Clipper flying boat for a flight to Long Beach, his first stop on the way back to Utah. While in a rush to get home, he promised himself that he'd first learn what had happened to the Mitsuis. His thoughts also went to Kasumi, and he wondered if he would ever see her again.

***

Seven days later, the Battle of the Coral Sea began. The *Araiski* never got to use her big guns to support the Japanese landings on Port Moresby. However, it was the loss of the *Taka* that turned the battle. The presence of the *Taka* would have tipped the balance heavily in favor of the enemy, and its destruction by Larsen and Gary had crippled the Japanese's offensive operations.

This battle became the first major naval engagement in history during which the majority of the combat was done by carrier-based aircraft. The opposing capital ships never saw each other, and this fight proved once and for all the supremacy of the aircraft carrier.

After five days of furious combat and substantial losses by both sides, the Americans and the Japanese retired from the Coral Sea to lick their wounds. Tactically, the battle was considered a draw.

Strategically, the battle was seen as an American victory, because the Japanese juggernaut was at last halted and their advance toward Australia stymied for good. Plus, the absence of the stricken Japanese carriers would contribute to their later defeats when the might of the American navy pivoted on the offensive.

What then was little known, but is now revealed, was the contribution to America's ultimate victory in the Pacific War by Gary Gatlin, the reluctant hero.

THE END

Made in the USA
San Bernardino, CA
04 November 2018